Gate of Tears

by

James Marinero

Ezeebooks UK

Published by Ezeebooks UK
Ezeebooks UK, 3 Murray Street, Llanelli
Carmarthenshire, SA15 1AQ, UK.
www.ezeebooks.co.uk

Gate of Tears

First Edition 2011

Copyright © James Marinero, 2011

ISBN-13: 978-0-9568426-0-2

The moral right of the author has been asserted.

Printed on paper which accords with
UK: Forest Stewardship Council™ (FSC®) Mixed Credit.
FSC® C084699

Quotations

Excerpt from **The Young British Soldier**, by *Rudyard Kipling
Departmental Ditties and Barrack-Room Ballads (1890)*
(Public Domain)

The quotation from
The Incredible Voyage, by *Tristan Jones*
is with the kind permission of Sheridan House Inc, Dobbs Ferry,
NY 10522, USA

Acronyms

ASIO	Australian Security Intelligence Organisation ("MI5")
ASIS	Australian Secret Intelligence Service ("MI6")
CCP	Chinese Communist Party
CNTF	Combined Naval Task Force – international anti- piracy fleet in the Gulf of Aden and off Somalia
GUOANBU	Chinese Ministry of State Security
ICC-CCS	International Maritime Bureau's Piracy Reporting Centre
MOFCOM	Chinese Ministry of Commerce
MSCHOA	Maritime Security Coordination, Horn of Africa
PLAN	People's Liberation Army (Navy) – China
SBPOK	Serbian Counter-Terrorist Police
VLCC	Very Large Crude Carrier (oil tanker aka supertanker)
Fox Two	NATO brevity code for AIM-132 ASRAAM missile
Fox Three	NATO brevity code for AIM-120 AMRAAM missile

Author's Notes and Acknowledgements

This book is dedicated to my friends and family, past and present. They know who they are, wherever they are.

Much of the technology described in this novel already exists. For example, fault-based cryptographic attacks have been shown to be possible. Where appropriate, I have stretched the facts a little in order to make the plotlines flow better, as this a work of entertainment and not computing, chemistry, biology, oceanography or geophysics.

The ability of organisms to thrive in the deep sea at high temperature and pressure, and to concentrate metals, has been known for many years. The concentration of gold and other metals in seawater is geographically variable, but metallic concentrations are higher near 'smokers'.

For those interested in Chinese Naval Power, Gold in Seawater, cryptographic attacks, and the rich and diverse Red Sea area in general, I have included a list of references at the end of the book, as a starting point.

The politics of the Middle East is changing rapidly. Even as I finish the final chapters in Malta, British Tornadoes and US carrier-based planes are attacking Gadaffi's air defence network. There are major political problems across the region – the Yemen, Egypt and Bahrain to name a few. Demonstrations have just started in Syria and even Gaza – surely a harbinger of several more years of unrest.

In the interests of the story there are some adjustments of timelines and geography – these are, in general, minor, and for those of you who detect them, I hope that they will not detract from your enjoyment. Naturally, all mistakes are my own.

My profound thanks for help and encouragement, readthroughs and sanity checking (including my own), go to Dave King for assiduous proof reading and advice on gold futures trading, Jeremy Hurlbatt, and Tim 'Stigs' Eastaugh for advice on plot refinements, aerial combat and aircraft carrirer protocols. Above all, my gratitude to Rosy Jensen for her help, considerable patience and encouragement.

James Marinero
Malta
March 2011

The Red Sea Region

Map by courtesy of Planiglobe under Creative Commons Licence 2.5

Djibouti and the Gate of Tears (Bab al Mandeb)

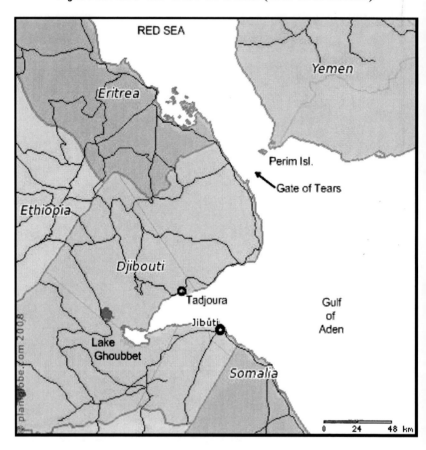

Map by courtesy of Planiglobe under Creative Commons Licence 2.5

Contents

Prologue - Eilat Sunset 1
The Chinese Connection 7
Saunders in Sana'a 13
Andjela's Story – Foundation 27
Djibouti Landfall 41
Tobin Dynasty – Foundation 49
Andjela's Story – Paris 53
Tobin Dynasty – Maturity 64
Djibouti – Overtures 67
Tobin Dynasty – Serious Business 86
Andjela's Story – China 91
Aden Adventure 100
Andjela's Story – Maturity 140
Baldwin – The Formative Years 143
Tobin Dynasty – Academia 145
Djibouti – Interlude 148
Tobin Dynasty – Global Operation 154
Da'ud in Djibouti 157
Farming Gold – Preparing the Field 162
Djibouti Beach Party 168
Thompson's Troubles Start 201
Welsh Gold 208
Djibouti Developments 217
Thompson's Troubles Triple 237
Gold – First Harvest 248
The Coup – Foundation 254
Better Harvests 270
The Coup – Takeoff 275
The Coup – Execution 282
The Coup – Aftermath 294
Platform Problems 298
Baldwin's Bother 310
Trader's Trials 322
Aerial Aggravation 336
Adèle at Last 348
Epilogue 350
References 355

Prologue - Eilat Sunset

"Hello. I'm Maruška, but you can call me Marie – most people can't remember my real name as it's so unusual. Do you mind if I join you?" She giggled deliciously.

She had just walked up to him at the bar and introduced herself, offering her hand, brimming with confidence and a broad smile – good teeth, though not perfect, and he found that appealing, along with a firm, dry handshake, almost manly, in fact. He guessed that she was a few years older than him, but wearing well. Although twenty eight years old, Paul looked older – hair loss did that to most guys, though he had not yet reached the stage where he needed to consider the completely shaven head. He did not consider himself particularly successful with women and Marie was stylish and intriguing, her introduction too good to be true.

"I'd be delighted – er, Marie did you say? Would you like a drink?"

"Yes, I did say Marie, and thank you - a margherita would be good."

He held out his hand and stammered – "I'm P..Paul, by the way."

"Hi Paul, nice to meet you." She smiled that smile again, and he stumbled to reply.

"So, er,..Marie, what brings you to Eilat, and, er.. to me at this bar?"

"A short diving holiday. I learned to dive in the Adriatic when I was a student in Trieste. I thought that you looked like an interesting guy who might enjoy some company. And before you ask, no, I'm not a hooker!"

"Erm… it hadn't occurred to me at all, I mean, er, I didn't think that at all!"

"It's ok Paul, relax, I'm not going to bite you…yet!"

She smiled again and he was hooked. The bite was yet to come.

They were in the bar at the Eilat Sunset, a renowned fish restaurant. Paul had come down from Tel Aviv for a week's break from his research. He was in the final year of a mathematics doctorate, researching large prime numbers and their application to advanced encryption technology. He was currently working on a particularly abstruse area relating to reverse factorisation of prime number products and needed to get away and clear his head.

Since a couple of years after the Six Days War in 1967, his parents had kept an apartment in Eilat and he had holidayed here all his life. He planned to use the family's rigid inflatable boat to do some diving and photography, probably with one of his buddies from the diving school. He also planned to supplement his pocket money, as he did every time a new version of his encryption algorithm was finalised. This would be the final sale now, as he was near to completing his project, and would be heavily engaged in writing his paper for the next year or so. He also felt that what had started out as a bit of fun was now becoming a worry. But, for a research student and extra $20,000 a year was not to be sneered at.

It became clear that Marie was an experienced diver and knowledgeable about reef fish. The best reefs were not accessible from Eilat as they were in Egyptian waters. Marie had dived the Egyptian coast – the reefs of Sharm el Sheikh in particular – which Paul always longed to visit, but travelling and diving there was impossible for an Israeli citizen in the current political climate.

After a few sundowners, they agreed to have dinner together and shared a superb grouper cooked with lime. They rounded off the evening with a couple of brandies and agreed to dive together the following day.

At 10 am the next morning they met at the diving school where Paul arranged to borrow gear for Marie. They loaded the Zodiac RIB and headed out. Although anchorages were restricted in reef areas, Paul knew the area very well and selected a spot which he knew was particularly good for Moray eels. They were one of his favourite photographic subjects, and enjoyed being fed by hand. He had dived here so often now that he knew some of the eels individually and had pet names for them, but Moray eels were short-sighted, they didn't recognised him.

The diving was superb, the lunch better, and they were getting on like a house on fire. They headed back to Eilat and Marie suggested that they go back to his apartment to round the day off in style.

"Shit, I have a meeting arranged" Paul said to Marie, kicking himself silently, "but how about dinner again this evening, and we'll take it from there?"

"I look forward to it – how about 7 o'clock at the Eilat Sunset again?," Marie responded.

"That would be great, I'll see you in the bar," said Paul, still wondering at his good luck.

*

The meeting in the café was brief. Paul handed over the CD case in an envelope, and received an envelope in return. Eli, as he knew him, shook his hand.

Paul had first been approached in the students' union coffee bar in Tel Aviv two years before. At that time he was still working on 'hard' encryption, but using fast Fourier transforms to apply it real-time to speech.

Eli had introduced himself and over a few months a friendship had developed. Eli was reading Philosophy, but finding it did not excite him and he was considering dropping out and going into business. They had shared, beers, holidays and occasionally even girlfriends. One day, Eli said that he had heard that Paul was working on some really interesting maths. Public

2

Key Encryption Technology was not secret – it was after all a mathematical technique based on very large prime numbers. There were practical limitations however. These arose from the sheer amount of computing power required to apply these techniques in real time. The application of the techniques could be sensitive, secret even, but at that time Paul's work was on the borderline. It was however commercially valuable.

*

A couple of months later over a beer, Eli had casually said that he had a friend who might be interested in buying a copy of Paul's encryption algorithm. That was when it had started. Paul now had almost $60,000 in currency squirreled away and had been considering buying his own place in Eilat. However, not knowing what he planned to do after his doctorate finished, he had held back from a property purchase.

*

The friendship had gradually changed into more of a business relationship and now Paul was no longer really sure who Eli was. Over the last few months , he had begun to feel pressured to get his software releases delivered to Eli.

He returned to the apartment, put the money in the safe and then showered, shaved and changed. He got to the restaurant just in time for the sunset. The wind had been slowly building through the day, and the sunset was spectacularly enhanced by sandstorms over the Sinai to the West.

He was really enjoying Marie's company, the conversation was scintillating. She had taken a degree in Modern European languages in Trieste. Europe was largely unknown to Paul except for a couple of visits to see family in London. He sat captivated as she described her memories of Amsterdam, Paris, Prague, Berlin and London.

Marie smiled at him and, standing up, took his hand. "Let's dance!"

Paul shook his head. "The last time I danced was at my brother's *bar mitzvah* eleven or twelve years ago!"

"Come on then, you need practice!"

She was strong, laughing and insistent, and used her body weight effectively to half lift, half drag him out of his seat and between the tables to the dance floor. He was captured, captivated and courted and went willingly with the flow.

He couldn't dance but it didn't matter. They kissed on the dance floor, they held hands as they walked towards his apartment. He was blind to everything, walking on air, laughing, joking, intoxicated with her. They passed a grocery shop and the smell of coffee and spices were overpowering. It was overwhelming, as if he had never used his senses before that moment. They turned a corner, and he turned her, pushed her gently against the wall, pushed his hips against hers, his chest against her yielding breasts, his mouth against hers and she returned the pressure, insistently but gently. Their kissing was urgent, their touching electric. He buried his head in her hair, kissed her neck, grasped her by the waist and pulled her harder against him, grasped her buttocks and pulled her tightly against him. She moved her hand between their thighs and rubbed him, groaning as he kissed her throat. Then, the sound of a car horn on the main street brought him to his senses. This behaviour was not really appropriate for a public place in Israel he told himself, sadly. "We're nearly there" he whispered to her, taking her hand and leading her. They took the lift and as they did so they started again and repeated the street scene. Then, the lift was on its way down again, and stopped on the third floor. A middle aged couple with a poodle stepped in and travelled to the ground floor, whilst Paul and Marie composed themselves, giggling, as the lift started its upward journey again.

"That was Mr and Mrs Landy" Paul said, "Mrs Landy will be telling my mother about us kissing in the lift." Marie laughed.

They didn't make it to the bedroom. He was not very experienced, but improved as the night exhausted them. She was an aggressive, almost violent lover, quite unlike anyone he had ever experienced before.

*

Paul woke first at about 9am, when the sun was well up, and they shared fresh apricots and bread for breakfast. Marie said she had to go back to her hotel to change her clothes. They kissed and she headed off after agreeing to meet later – she was just so very keen to go diving, and he couldn't wait.

They picked up the diving gear at midday at the dive school, collected some chilled white wine and some lunch from the deli, and headed out in the rigid inflatable boat. Marie suggested that they go to a quiet reef anchorage which she had heard about. Paul said that he did not think it was very quiet, but he would head there. Once outside the marina, he opened the RIB up to 30 knots, and they laughed as they felt the wind in their hair and bounced and splashed through the wake of a tourist boat. There was only one other dive boat there when they arrived, a large unmarked black RIB, and the divers were just submerging. They dropped the anchor in 10 metres of depth, as far from the other boat as they could get within the permitted area. Paul inserted a fresh memory chip into his digital camera, checked the batteries and sealed the enclosure. They suited up, and checked each other's gear. Masks on, laughing, and a backward flop over the side of the RIB. Only ten metres deep, close in to the shore, this was a real reef walking area. Paul beckoned and they headed towards a rise in the sea floor and a series of natural steps in the reef as it ascended towards the sandstone cliff of the shore. Marie beckoned to Paul to stop and motioned for him to take a picture of her. She stepped backwards a few paces, and Paul raised the camera.

Both of Paul's arms were harshly grasped from behind and he was hauled, struggling towards Marie and the ascending cliff. He looked around, confused, frightened, uncomprehending. There was a diver on each side of him holding him, pulling him. He panicked, struggled, kicked with his fins, remembered flashbacks to last night with Marie, talking about his work, the CD, his pocket money, Eli. Marie swam to the side and retrieved the slowly falling camera as they reached the stepped edged where the reef began its ascent. One of the divers reached out and started to vent Paul's tanks. He struggled violently, kicked, completed the jigsaw of his time with Marie, tremored, and was then, finally, still. They wedged his right foot securely in a crevice. Finally, they vented his pony tank. The three of them swam gently away in the direction of the black RIB. They found the anchor line and ascended it. There was another RIB entering the anchorage. Marie rolled in over the side after the men, and lay on the bottom of the RIB. One man started the engine whilst the other hauled in the anchor. They waved casually to the new arrivals as they passed and headed south at 40 knots.

*

The starter feedstock was packed in two litre stainless steel thermos flasks, twenty of them, at a temperature of 98 degrees Celsius. These were packed in formed polystyrene holders within a pine box, the lid was nailed down and the box was quickly stencilled in black paint 'WATER MAKER SPARES' along with some spurious part numbers. Easy enough for one man to carry and load into the back of the Vauxhall utility van used by BioPro for local errands.

Dai 'Onions' Davies – the 'onions' soubriquet referring to the champion onions which he grew and with which he won all the local gardening shows - climbed into the van. He threw the envelope of Customs papers onto the passenger seat, started the engine and took a left turn out of the industrial estate on to the A48 road to Milford Haven. This Friday was going to be easy - a run down to Milford Haven and a short wait for customs clearance. Then on down the old Esso terminal to the pier head to drop the crate off at *Universal Trader*.

Passing through the outskirts of Haverfordwest, he took the turn for Milford Haven at Merlin's Bridge, oblivious to the white Ford transit van which was closing up behind. He did however see the flat bed lorry stop ahead of him – he hit the brakes hard, swearing.

Then, a heavy, insistent contact at the back of his small truck, generating a wobble which amplified into a swerve as Dai tried to correct it and then a spinning skid off the road. The lorry accelerated away, followed by the Transit van.

*

It did not enter the traffic policeman's head that this was anything other than an accident, with no apparent witnesses. The small van had demolished the bridge parapet as it shouldered its way through at 55 mph and somersaulted to the copse below. There were wooden crates scattered around the wreckage. The policeman was unaware that one case was missing. Over the next few days, this fact became apparent to two people at BioPro, and would remain unreported, at least as far as the police were concerned. They found Dai at the foot of a tree in the copse. His neck was broken.

*

In a country house on an estate outside Winchester, the matter of the missing case caused consternation. The starter feedstock could be replaced – it would take six weeks to cultivate. A simple calculation indicated that the delay would cost at least fifteen million dollars. Of more concern was the fact that the degree of success of the operation depended on timing.

Of course, the fact that the existence of the case was known to a hostile third party was a matter that would have to be addressed vigorously.

Charles Tobin prepared his e-mail, loaded it onto a memory stick then drove his Bentley into Southampton, parked it and then walked to a Starbucks in St Mary's Street. The e-mail found its way to the server in Chechnya in 3 minutes. It was sent from a one-time e-mail address, to another one-time e-mail address. It was sent at 5 pm UK time, when web traffic was at a peak worldwide.

Copies and trace files eventually found their way in to GCHQ in Cheltenham, Langley in Virginia and into a little known building complex in Nizhny Novgorod, the city formerly known as Gorki on the River Volga. Bots were automatically enabled, tracing their way up the chain from computer server to computer server, following the address trail. In the few minutes they took to locate the source server, all traces had disappeared. The IP addresses of the source PCs would be recoverable from the ISP – standard practice these days, put in place putatively to prevent and track child pornography – but the real reason was national security. The internet had streamlined, automated and facilitated terrorism, money laundering and general high level banking fraud. Governments were fighting back.

*

The Chinese Connection

A week later, the hijacked flasks were in the Key Laboratory of Marine Biogenetic Resources, Third Institute of Oceanography, Xiamen, China, and undergoing analysis.

Four weeks after that, the analysis report was on a senior desk in MOFCOM – the Ministry of Finance and Commerce - in Beijing, alongside the scenario report involving Charles Tobin. The common theme of 'Gold' was glaringly obvious.

*

These reports were accompanied by a third report – 'Gold Supply and Price Changes – A Strategic Threat' which pulled together the information from the other two, and analysed the possibilities in the context of China's economy. It made grim reading for those at the top of MOFCOM, and was further distilled into a brief report for the General Secretary, Chinese Communist Party. The threat level was Grade 3.

In relative terms China did not hold a great deal of gold – only 6% of its reserves in 2011 were in this yellow metal – because it held vast strategic stocks of the US Dollar. However, in production terms it was the world's largest gold producer, reporting 350 tonnes in 2012 and still growing. For well over a decade, China had been buying into mining companies in other countries, not only in gold, but for iron ore, molybdenum and other metals, so as to control its commodity supplies and buying prices. On the supply side, China was the major producer of 'rare earths' – metals which are used to produce very high strength magnets used in high efficiency electric motors, for example. This had almost led to a trade war with Japan when China had stopped exports to Japan in 2010.

The supply of gold is 'inelastic' – that is, production cannot quickly increase to meet an increase in demand. Any threat to gold prices would be serious, and major new production sources would threaten price levels. Not only that, just the idea that as a result of the bio-technology for the extraction of gold from seawater, world gold reserves were, in practical terms, infinite then there would be economic turmoil on a vast scale.

The General Secretary of the Chinese Communist party (CCP) reviewed the report and agreed the recommended actions. The detailed planning commenced that day.

*

The Chinese, as do the Japanese, take a much longer view when they plan than would a country with a European culture. A strategy can span generations; this works well in a country where there is absolute political control and only limited impact from the outside world. Such was Japan in the heyday of its Empire, and as was China during the Dynasties, extending even into the twentieth century under Mao Tse Tung. Despite the relaxations under Den Xiaoping when private enterprise became acceptable, 'for the good of the Party' – i.e. to enable China to keep the lid on the growing social unrest and ensure that the careers and perks of the High Cadres could continue without threat – the 'long term view' was innate to the Chinese character and persisted still into the 21st century. This could even be said about the Soviet Union for a time. However, increasing access to communications and the virtual shrinking of the world led to internal pressure for change in the Soviet Union and China. Japan, of course, was broken by the Second World War, and many of its institutions and traditions continued only superficially thereafter when it became a democratic society under the terms of its surrender.

In contrast, short term reaction takes longer in such societies, because they are not institutionally geared for rapid change.

The need for China to react rapidly to events when the 'Gold Reports' reached General Secretary CCP level was paramount, but planning processes were unwieldy and slow. There was no 'playbook', as the Americans would say, for this set of circumstances.

*

The branch of the Chinese Guoanbu intelligence agency which was responsible for reviewing and tracking cryptography research and development worldwide had monitored the University work of Paul Cahn for some time, and had bought, through third parties, a copy of his encryption algorithm. A team within the Golden Shield program had refined it further and found a novel way to embed a third key in the software, which enabled it to be unlocked whatever the private key was. It was, effectively, a cryptographic 'backdoor'. This software was now being marketed through a US company as a commercial encryption package. US laws prevented export of any high technology deemed to be of use to a potential enemy, and 'strong' encryption software was classified thus. These laws had singularly failed to prevent IBM mainframe computers finding their way to Omsk and Tomsk during the Cold War and being used in the Soviet nuclear weapons program.

Software was much easier to hide than a mainframe the size of a bus, and much easier to copy and ship. Malevolent software – 'malware' was insidious, dangerous and highly effective. This had been illustrated very clearly by the Stuxnet worm developed jointly by Israel and the USA. The worm had circulated freely around the internet and apparently had several authors on several continents – the trail was hard to follow, but clearly bogus. Eventually, in 2010, Stuxnet found its way into the Siemens control programs for the gas centrifuges used in the Iranian uranium enrichment program. Many centrifuges spun uncontrolled and about twenty percent were wrecked, delaying the Iranian quest for a nuclear bomb by several years.

*

While the options for gaining political and economic advantage from the potential gold crisis were being examined in MOFCOM, a junior officer in the Guoanbu special operations department was promoted. Wan Chuntao, a promising female at supervisor grade, was given responsibility for running a new agent as her first assignment in her new position. The agent had been introduced to the agency by an existing operative, a German national (run by an experienced desk officer in the Guoanbu), who had carried out a number of assassinations of dissident overseas Chinese citizens, criminal Chinese businessmen and double agents in Western Europe. The secret war with Taiwanese agents had intensified and there was pressure on the Guoanbu's resources. Although the Guoanbu had an extensive network of Chinese nationals capable of this work, it suited the Guoanbu to keep these particular operations separate from its existing native networks. 'Foreigners' working against Chinese nationals played better in the media should one of these black operations ever come to light. The Guoanbu ran teams from most parts of the world – Europe, the Americas, South Africa, Indonesia, and Russia. In the world of Wikileaks, anything was possible, even in China, and many false trails were laid.

And so, Wan Chuntao took on responsibility for running Maruška Pavkovic. Research and information provided by the German operative had suggested that Pavkovic had a background in Serbia, and was, apparently, one 'Andjela Karanovic' – though this was hard to prove. Wan Chuntao could uncover no hard evidence of this using all the technology and hacking abilities of the Golden Shield teams which she had access to. Even sources within the Serbian counter-terrorism police – the SBPOK - were unable to provide hard evidence – as far as they were concerned, Karanovic was dead.

*

Tobin's e-mail joined the backlog of thirty five other encrypted files that had built up over the last few months in various Government computer directories around the world, as well as in three or four private systems. None of them had been decrypted yet, despite the concerted efforts of the watchers, and despite their disparate hardware, software and analysis techniques. The encryption was very high strength and was causing concern at the highest levels.

Outside of governments, there had been five known users of this software in the world. Four of them were alive, and the fifth, an Israeli research student, had died three months earlier in a mysterious scuba accident whilst photographing fish. Apparently, his leg had got jammed in a rock crevice ten metres down. No trace had been found of his diving buddy, a blonde woman with a central European accent, nor was there any trace of the camera which he always took with him when diving.

*

The UK, US and Russian government investigations were more or less all at the same stage, although there was no acknowledgement at all between them that any investigations were actually under way. Independently, they knew that the there were three geographical foci of the e-mail traffic – one in the south of England, one somewhere in Chechnya, and one somewhere in China. Whilst the work to decode the traffic continued, generally using the sledgehammer approach of teraflops of computing power, each of the countries had its own unique approach to solving the problem.

*

The US Government via the Defence Intelligence Agency, had required that SysWal Inc - a world leading provider of virus protection software - include a piece of code in its software releases. SysWal did not know what the function of this code was, but it went out with their weekly "new virus" file updates.

Kalman Belsky, the 32 year old founder and now billionaire owner of SysWal, had been persuaded to co-operate during a meeting at the SEC in New York. The meeting room had been emptied, and an unidentified, undistinguished and very ordinary-looking, man had entered. Belsky agreed to ask his attorney to leave the room. After a brief discussion, and a considerable increase in his heart rate and blood pressure, Belsky signed a document. A memory stick was then handed to him. When he emerged from the meeting, he did not explain the details of the meeting to his attorney. His limousine took him straight to La Guardia airport from where his Learjet flew him straight back to his headquarters in Denver, Colorado.

*

There was much hostile coverage in the press two weeks later when the US Stock Exchange Commission announced that they had concluded that there was no case to answer in respect of the insider trading of which a certain Kalman Belsky, President of SysWal Inc., had been accused. It was generally concluded to be "another lucky stroke for a clever entrepreneur" as the cover of Forbes magazine recorded.

*

In those two weeks the software patch on the memory stick had ultimately been downloaded and installed in more than seven million PCs worldwide, and in many of the high grade server firewalls which protected commercial websites. The computing world recognized that it was necessary to defend against the dangerous new virus which SysWal had detected and provided protection against. SysWal's competitors took some time to analyse the virus and issue their own protection updates. Belsky's shareholding value increased significantly over the next few months, as the market recognized that SysWal appeared to be able to respond much more quickly to virus threats than could its competition, and SysWal sales increased markedly. Typically, it proved impossible to track down the geographical source of the virus, and the CIA, DIA, Homeland Security and the plethora of competing US government security agencies did not even bother to try, knowing that their resources were better deployed elsewhere.

From now on, every time one of the e-mails with a specific, nominated encryption signature passed from a PC or server with SysWal AV software installed, then a simple encoded e-mail would automatically be despatched and would travel through a server cluster in Washington D.C. It would be switched straight through to a dedicated, automatic tracing system. Simultaneously, this system notified a team of two "researchers," buried away in a basement office in Langley, Virginia of the receipt.

*

In England, GCHQ was pursuing a different track. The focus was on identifying where in the south of England the emails originated (their focus was at that time limited to the UK), and the 'who and why' behind the traffic.

Collection of incoming e-mails took place from random internet cafés, and the e-mail addresses were one-offs.

This suggested the use of asymmetric encryption – that is, there was a list of agreed e-mail addresses, and the one to use for a given day or time was specified in the encrypted message, along with a so-called session key. The session key is the traditional "symmetric" key, used only for a short time and between only two parties, analogous to the one time pads used by generations of intelligence agents. This apparent pattern was causing concern at SIS in Vauxhall in London. It suggested a degree of sophistication typical of a sovereign state, but current intelligence gave no reason to suppose that any sovereign government was currently able to usefully deploy this level of hard technology. The focus in the UK was therefore on high levels of basic intelligence gathering relating to the top five prioritised threats against the country.

*

The supertanker *Universal Trader* left the terminal in Milford Haven shortly before high water on the Sunday evening after Dai 'Onions's' death. Six weeks later, she returned briefly to the terminal for two tides and took on her cargo, along with the new feeder stock. She headed south for the traffic separation scheme to the west of the Scilly Isles, and ultimately southward for the Cape of Good Hope.

*

Saunders in Sana'a

In the capital of Yemen, Sana'a, the British Ambassador had been summoned to the Yemeni Foreign Ministry. His Excellency Stewart Thwaites was shown in through the ornate colonial entrance, upstairs into a large room on the north side, redolent of another era, with high ceilings and fans. French doors opened onto a balcony overlooking a courtyard, with a fountain – a sign of plenty in the Middle East. The fountain, however, was a recent addition, made possible by the dam that the British had helped build in the early '90's, before the kidnappings.

This had been their second meeting in as many days. This time there was none of the Mocha coffee that they made so well, neither was the Ambassador offered a seat.

Abu Bark al-Naji the Yemeni Foreign Minister was incandescent. In the profession of diplomacy, genuine rage was very unusual, it was simply too dangerous. Misuse of words and behaviour inappropriate to a given situation, literally but indirectly, could be fatal. Al-Naji came close. There was a heated exchange of views, and the diplomatic barometer of international tension ratcheted up a couple of millibars.

"Not a bad show" said the Ambassador to his first secretary Bill Samuelson, "he does it well" as they walked to their cars. Security precautions now forced them to travel separately. On the drive back to the British Embassy, Thwaites started to formulate his proposed line to take with London, knowing pretty well what their stance would be. The Yemenis were demanding that the UK should immediately cease bullying the South Yemenis by withdrawing its warships and standing down the 'attacks by its aircraft on Yemeni airspace'. The exaggerated, misused language and invented facts were typical of such a State, he thought, but didn't share that one with Bill.

Thwaites's response had been firm.

"His Majesty's Government considers that the Republic of South Yemen is harbouring pirates, and is in possession of important commercial material stolen from a British Company. We demand that the pirates are handed over to us immediately, and that the commercial property is restored forthwith to its legal owners. Until such events have taken place, then Her Majesty's Government will take whatever actions it considers appropriate to achieving those aims. We have detailed those facts, again, in this note."

The Foreign Minister denied yet again all knowledge of such people and property.

There followed the formal exchange of diplomatic notes between governments. A bit like a ballet, really, Thwaites thought. Choreographed in advance, the music well known, and the performers well rehearsed. But, every live performance is different he thought, and this was no exception.

"Even if there were any basis in fact for your wild and imagined accusations, and my government emphatically rejects any such statements, then there is no extradition treaty between our countries. There is therefore no basis in international law for the return of any such hypothetical persons" the Foreign Minister had said.

"A chink, and not detailed in the note I'll bet. We'll have to amend the script for the next performance," Thwaites reflected to himself.

Back at the Embassy on Haddah Road, Thwaites outlined to Bill what form the cable to London should take, and Bill went to the cipher room to draft it.

*

The interchange with London had not gone quite as Thwaites had earlier anticipated. The Foreign Office had received a note from the People's Republic of China. It requested details of the unannounced exercises which ships and aircraft of HMG appeared to be carrying out in the Gulf of Aden and Arabian Sea. The Chinese were concerned that the Republic of Yemen, which was of course, "an old, trusted and close friend and ally of the People's Republic of China" felt threatened by these actions; and want to clarify any misunderstanding that there might be, in the interests of international peace and harmony. Innocuous on the face of it, but enough to set alarm bells ringing in Whitehall.

As Thwaites settled down at his desk to work through the routine morning diplomatic traffic, the phone rang. It was his second secretary, Kevin Saunders who requested an immediate meeting in the quiet room.

Saunders had just received information, source undisclosed as usual, that the Chinese Shang 093 Class nuclear attack submarine *Cheng Tang 5* had put to sea from the Chinese Naval Base at Aden sometime overnight. The appearance of the submarine in Aden had caused some excitement in NATO defence circles. Their technology was thought to be approaching that of the US *Los Angeles* class, and way below that in terms of performance and acoustic signature of the US *Virginia* Class – in fact still a couple of generations behind the US - so its sudden appearance in Aden was a wake-up call for NATO and SEATO. A *Han Class* submarine, one of the previous generation, had created an international incident in the Yellow Sea off the coast of North Korea in 1994. Reports varied, but it seems that it got through the ASW screen around the US carrier *USS Kitty Hawk*. When finally detected it was tracked by two ASW helicopters, which were then harassed by two Chinese J-8 'Finback' fighters, allowing it to slip away.

After that event the US Navy sharpened up its anti-submarine warfare practices.

Since then, the People's Liberation Army Navy ('PLAN') had advanced rapidly in SSN submarine design, and the latest *Shang* class boats were now capable of indefinite endurance and were armed with land attack cruise missiles. Sensors packages now included towed arrays, and acoustic signatures were patently improving rapidly.

*

Events were now gathering their own momentum Thwaites thought, as he drafted the next cable to London. He smiled wryly to himself - in reality, things had been pear-shaped since the gunfight outside the Embassy in 2002. It had been touch and go as to whether the Embassy would be closed. The then incumbent Ambassador had moved on to greater things. The Foreign Office, in its omniscient wisdom, had thought that in the current state of near-siege, a male Ambassador was more appropriate. "Some attitudes will never change," he reflected.

Two hours later, he was enraged to hear from London that Saunders's information confirmed what London already knew from the Americans. As usual, he was operating with one hand tied behind his back -. "here am I, on the spot" he thought, "and the last to be told!"

*

The phone rang. It was Saunders again, another meeting, quiet room, urgent, but usually useful background. Though Saunders had no specific brief to report to Thwaites or Samuelson (and should actively avoid them), he kept them in the loop when he could.

"It seems that two of the Israeli Sa'ar – that's Tempest - Class Frigates have put to sea from Eilat and are heading down the Red Sea. To cap that, the Chinese have given notice that they are withdrawing the missile destroyer Guangzhou and missile frigate Chaohu from anti-piracy operations with the Combined Naval Task Force in the Gulf of Aden with immediate effect. They are citing 'Joint exercises with Yemeni Forces' as the reason."

"Shit, shit, shit, thanks for that. What's our current knowledge of Israelis on Perim Island?"

For many years there had been rumours on and off that Israel maintained observers on the Yemeni Island of Perim, overlooking Bab el Mandeb - the Gate of Tears, the strategically critical entrance to the Red Sea. The rumours were hard to prove either way.

15

"I have no up to date information, though if there are any, I'm buggered how they can keep them hidden or even in deep cover on such a small island, maybe they're goats," laughed Saunders. "I don't know of any Chinese either, though with the visit to Aden of the sub, then there are probably a few more floating about at present."

"Ok, ok, enough. London will be hot on the wire now. I'll need to start drafting a note. Unannounced exercises are not the done thing you know," said Thwaites.

"I'd never have guessed," Saunders groaned *sotto voce*. For all his bonhomie, HE could be too much at times. "Still," thought Saunders, "some action would be refreshing, and hopefully good for my career. There was always the possibility of a fiasco too, and an early bath as the footballers would say."

By the time Thwaites had got back to his office, there was a secure message awaiting him from the Foreign Office. Our turn to protest he thought. But no, the message was quite bald – basically sit tight and do nothing.

Saunders signed out of the Embassy for lunch. After a few minutes he got into what passed as a cab and headed off past Bab el Yemen towards Suq al-Milh. This area was originally the salt soukh and not really the best place to get carpets or rugs – you'd go to Khartoum St if you wanted that – but it was where Salim had his business, along with a few other small carpet shops. Salim's business was not on the scale of the Al Fardoos Carpet Showroom, but in Saunders's business small meant safe, unobtrusive and manageable. In this part of the world, rugs are a currency and carry stories with them. Sometimes they carry contraband of one form or another, too. Salim carried it all. As always, though, one had to take all his information with a pinch of salt. 'How appropriate' remarked Saunders to himself, and not for the first time, pleased with his wit.

He found Salim in loud negotiation over an apparently fine specimen of a rug which looked too good to be local – probably from across the Gulf thought Saunders. The dye colours were different to those used locally, and the edging betrayed more of the Orient than local designs. A Chinese copy very probably.

Salim's negotiation appeared to be developing into a standoff, then the potential customer turned and left without buying. Salim stepped outside his storefront and spat qat juice into the gutter – this was close to an insult as the whole point of qat was to swallow the juice.

He turned, muttering, to Saunders. "Ah Mr Smith, Salaam Alaikum," he said, Saunders responding "Alaikum Salaam. It's good to see you Salim, how is business?" To Salim, Saunders was Mr Edward Smith, his business card describing him as an Economic Development Consultant.

"Carpet business is bad, but Chinese have been buying. But they only buy samples, take them back to China to copy. I think I need to sell Chinese Persian carpets myself. Not good, not good. What you want today."

In common with most stall holders and shopkeepers in a city, Salim could get by in half a dozen languages, and so his English was passable though painfully grating to Saunders's expensively educated ear.

Saunders's Arabic was excellent, the result of a first class honours degree in Arabic, but he'd kept that to himself. "Let's step inside shall we and see what you've got?" said Saunders walking into the carpet shop ahead of Salim. He picked up a prayer mat and started examining it. "Salim, I wondered what the talk was about the Chinese navy and Yemeni forces." He replaced the prayer mat in the stack and moved along to look at a rug. Salim unrolled the rug on the floor and said "A fine specimen, wool, from Oman, I give you special price."

"How much?" enquired Sanders.

"Five thousand Rial" was the reply.

"I can't possibly afford that. Have you got something similar, but cheaper" said Saunders loudly, moving towards the back of the store. Carpet shops like this were excellent for conversation – the piles of rugs and carpet covered walls absorbed all sound. "What have you got for three thousand rials?"

"Well, sir, I hear that Chinese naval boats in Mayyun harbour, small boats from Chinese ships off island, many soldiers."

"I don't think that this rug is worth three thousand rials, Salim." Saunders knew that HMG would already know that from satellite feeds. "I'd want something of better quality for three thousand."

"My cousin Yousef know someone who works in dockyard in Aden. He say that Chinese submarine was loaded with mines before leaving yesterday."

"OK Salim, I do like this one. Can I wash this in the machine with cold water?"

"Yes, sir, no problem, make sure not hot water."

"What did the mines look like, can you get photos?"

"Photos no, drawing yes, tomorrow. My cousin will have to drive from Aden."

"OK, my final offer is 2,800 Rial" offered Saunders, holding out a wad of notes.

Salim took them and counted the three thousand rials, and his eyes gleamed. "I make no profit on this carpet."

"I need to buy a rug for my sister – I will call around tomorrow morning. Maybe you will make some profit on that."

"Tomorrow morning fine, sir, I may have new rugs to show you."

17

Saunders smiled as Salim tied up the cheap carpet for him and left the shop. $150, and priceless.

Several years before, the Chinese had established a naval base in Aden, Yemen. This had caused some diplomatic difficulties with the US and UK at the time. The Chinese response had been predictable – If Guantanamo and Subic Bay were good enough for the US, then Aden was good enough for China.

It was difficult to put up solid argument against this stance – the Chinese had, after all, been involved with the Combined Naval Task Force for several years.

Nevertheless, the base was rarely used by major ships – mainly by supply vessels and occasional visits by their ships from the CNTF. It was more a symbolic gesture.

Saunders got back to the Embassy and fired off a cable to London. "That should make the Cobra lot sit up," he smiled to himself.

There was a very rapid turnaround and two hours later the response had been basically "we need all you can get."

The next morning he went back to Salim's to pick out a rug for his sister. They haggled as usual and Saunders came away with a rug – more accurately a rag - that cost him another two thousand rials. Salim took care to roll it up carefully.

Back at the Embassy he unrolled the rug and removed the sheet of paper inside. The drawing, if that is what it could be called, was of a box shape with some Arabic writing. His written Arabic was good enough for him to understand that the dimensions of the box were described. The drawing of the box itself was annotated with what looked like Chinese characters. "Arabic yes, Chinese no, he thought." None the wiser, he drafted a covering cable, scanned the drawing into the secure PC, encrypted the package and fired it off.

He heard nothing more. He had not seen Thwaites since the previous day so didn't know what was happening diplomatically – but usually he wouldn't expect to unless he needed to know. He groaned and thought he'd better note down his 'expenditure on various items' into the budget management system. He got a mint tea for himself and settled down to his month end chores. Then, all hell broke loose…

*

Saunders was called to the secure comms suite for a tele-conference with his Senior Officer in London.

'London' wasted no time:

"Saunders, please explain the circumstances under which you obtained the information and drawing. I've got a naval intelligence bod here with me."

18

Saunders took the hint. Without giving anything away about his source, and disguising some of the background information - he'd put chapter and verse in the written report later – he outlined the process.

Then, a voice he didn't recognise who he took to be the Naval representative.

"Seems we're in a bit of a spot here. The Arabic on the drawing refers to the estimated dimensions of the shipping crate. The Chinese stencilling on the box - it's poorly copied – appears to refer to Fengxi Machinery Factory, which is China's naval mine production facility. The drawing also shows a designation of TE-9x. The TE series is the designation for their rocket propelled naval mines. At present we know of the TE series up to TE-6. Nasty beasts. Kill range for shipping of 5 miles radius, 80 meters/second plus for the known weapons – that's 150 knots, which no ship can outmanoeuvre.

We have no idea what TE-9x is capable of. TE-6 we know a bit about - it takes a coded acoustic GPS feed from a surface controller which identifies commercial shipping by the ship's AIS (Automatic Identification System). So, they can pick off individual vessels by name, provided they have AIS switched on, and that's normal in peacetime. TE-6 can be programmed real time with a ship signature – we believe that they can even distinguish between two of our destroyers of the same class. We do have ACM – acoustic countermeasures - now, but these mines are passive weapons and travel so fast that we are still very susceptible. It's analogous to our lads using laser designators to paint a target for missiles or smart bombs. Very similar – it means that they need just one man with a box of tricks within a few miles to cause mayhem. Could be in a fishing boat or on a headland. Potentially it could even be programmed remotely using a plane-dropped sonar buoy.

No need to lay out what that could mean if Bab el Mandeb or the Straits of Hormuz were seeded. They wouldn't even need to use the mines – the threat is enough. We do know that a Chinese replenishment ship - supply ship 887 Weishanhu - visited Aden last week.

The problem we have is that anyone with a bit of imagination and access to the internet could put that drawing together in half an hour. We need to verify it."

"All right Saunders, you will have got the gist that this is pretty bloody important," said his controller, "we'll speak again later today, stay handy."

The conversation ended. Saunders punched the air - some action at last. Things had been fairly low key after the riots and political upheavals which had started in 2011, and continued for a couple of years. The Chinese had taken their opportunity and filled the vacuum, with much needed investment. The US had slowly withdrawn after the attack on *USS Cole* in

Aden, though they had maintained a special forces contingent in-country there for several years afterwards, until final withdrawal

Later that afternoon, Saunders had another secure conversation with his controller. Assets were being deployed into Yemen within 48 hours, and Saunders would be tasked to assist. 48 hours to prepare information, maps, drops and logistics, all to be in place, location to be advised. He knew that diplomatic activity would be grinding into action.

Then, a call to an immediate meeting with Samuelson.

"Saunders, London have decided to up the ante on this Chinese submarine business. HE is off to a meeting with the Foreign Minister in half an hour. In London, the FO has hauled the Yemeni ambassador in to dress him down. Is there anything he should know?" he asked pointedly, to which the reply was "No, Bill, there's nothing he needs to know. Good luck."

*

Saunders needed to get some more background from Salim, but another rug wasn't an option. He called Salim using his 'economic consultant's' iPhone phone, and complained about the rug.

"I washed it in cold water and the red dye started running. I want my money back." he complained.

"Not possible, nothing wrong with rug, you wash it wrong" said Salim. "I give you good price for another rug."

"I don't want another rug."

"Then nothing I can do" and Salim rang off. The meeting was thus arranged.

That evening one hour before sunset just outside Az Zabadan on the road into the mountains at Bayt Nambas, Saunders stopped his Toyota 4x4 at the roadside. He got the jack out and jacked up the near side, and waited. 10 minutes later a Nissan pickup pulled in ahead. Salim climbed out and walked over to Saunders. They exchanged greetings.

"Salim, I need all you can get from your cousin by tomorrow night. Here is a plan of the base from a satellite picture. I want to know what the buildings are, where the guards are posted and when they change the guard, what defences are there facing the sea. There's 80,000 rials for you if you can do it."

"Mr Smith, it will be very difficult, there is not much time and my cousin worry, I worry. It is very dangerous. Just to have such a map is dangerous."

"All right, talk to your cousin tonight. He should be able to add to this plan. There will be 20,000 rials for him."

Salim was a typically slippery soukh negotiator. His eyes gleamed in the setting sun and Saunders knew that Salim's cousin would see a lot less than 20,000 rials.

"Salim, I'll bring that rug back tomorrow evening, the colours are not good."

*

A package had arrived for Saunders in the Diplomatic Baggage that evening. After reviewing the contents, he spent an hour on the secure comms link to London. He left the embassy with a rucksack about 11pm and headed back to his apartment.

He had to install a comms package within half a mile of the Chinese Naval Base in Aden, within 24 hours. No pressure, then, he thought.

Generally, surveillance in Yemen was not too heavy, and not relaxed under the new 'democratic government' – the usual suspects in new clothes. He could not use fieldcraft to lose a tail when there was one – that would be an amateur's giveaway, and was a last resort. In his own case, the tailing seemed to be occasional, and relatively casual, which suggested that his cover was intact. Nevertheless, it was essential to check for such followers.

Internal travel in Yemen was not advisable for UK citizens. Indeed, travel to the Yemen by British citizens was strongly advised against by the British Foreign Office and had been for many years - the FO always erred on the side of caution, even after the Freedom Riots of 2011 which had inflamed North Africa and the Middle East. Al Quaeda in its many guises had been targeting Embassy staff on and off for at least fifteen years. For those who had lived and worked there for some time though, it was not so dangerous – it merely required that basic security procedures were followed. Risk was routine, injuries occasional and deaths mercifully few – in fact only one in the last ten years, and that unfortunate had been a Yemeni female secretary.

Saunders changed clothing and prepared his rucksack, and then left the apartment and the gated complex in which he lived, on foot. Simple unobtrusive checks, no tail. About a mile from his apartment he turned into a side street and then an alley. He then cut through another alley and came back on himself. All clear.

At the lockup, he opened up, stowed his gear and reversed the Toyota LandCruiser out. Once out of the city he headed south on the 160 mile drive through Dhamar to Aden. If he was lucky the drive might take him less than 5 hours. Eight hours on a bus was not an option. He was travelling as a Jordanian engineer, with full papers, including a travel permit, apparently on an emergency call out to service some equipment at the Al Hiswah power station. There were no night flights from Sana'a to Aden and with his electronics bundle, flying was not an option at anytime.

He expected road blocks, he expected goats, and he expected bad roads – he had travelled this way before. His spoken Arabic was good and his build and colouring were Mediterranean, having been the product of a British soldier and a Cypriot mother. His accent would not pass for Jordanian, but that was not unusual for an engineer, and it was unlikely that it would be a problem here in Yemen.

Terrorist activity could be a problem, but he hoped that a prayer mat in the rear of the 4x4 would help – he could, *in extremis*, pass for a Muslim, even being able to recite some of the prayers.

With a detailed map of Aden in the 4x4's TomTom navigator and a few other salient details tucked away in his mobile phone, which itself had TomTom 'plus' functionality, he was fully prepared for the journey. He took a couple of uppers to keep him sharp for the drive through the night. The electronics package, which he believed was a satellite relay package, was hidden beneath one of the rear seats.

He was stopped at one road block on the outskirts of Aden and when he explained the problem at the Al Hiswah power station and showed them a copy of the email purportedly from the Public Electricity Corporation, he was quickly waved through. He drove on to the Lulu Supermarket in the Aden Mall, parked the 4x4 and pushed his prayer mat out of sight. It was still early – about 5.30 am, but incoming fruit and vegetable deliveries were under way. He stopped for a coffee and pastry, at a stall. By the time he had finished his breakfast, the mall was opening up for cleaning. In a toilet cubicle he changed his clothing, dressing down from that of an engineer. His took out an older holdall and put the engineer's holdall inside with its contents.

The mall was modern, the Lulu hypermarket part of a large chain operating across the Middle East. The Government was moving Aden slowly into the twenty first century, yet at its roots it was still a strategic trading centre linking Africa and Asia, with a rich, varied and violent history. Legend held that Cain and Abel were buried here, and therefore if you subscribed to that legend, then the violence could be traced back to the first family.

Outside the mall, he found a taxi and settled down for the 20 mile ride to Ghadir on the Little Aden Peninsula. The early morning temperature was climbing rapidly and the aircon in the old cab was not up to the task – 45 degrees Celsius was not uncommon here in high summer, and riots about electricity failures had been frequent in recent summers.

After a few miles empty sand gave way to camel thorn and palm trees. They bypassed Al Ittihad, the Federal capital, and the Al Hiswah power generation complex, his erstwhile destination. He gave the driver an address in Ghadir and paid off the taxi when they arrived. There were a couple of safe houses retained by HMG – one in Aden proper, on the Rock, and the one he was now walking towards in Ghadir, within half a mile or so of the Chinese base.

After another coffee and discreet but very careful checking that his rear was clear, he walked circuitously but seemingly purposefully to the house. The substantial house was on what had been called Devonshire Rise in the days when this area was inhabited by engineers and managers from the BP Oil Refinery. Ghadir housing was built with stone from the local granite quarry during the period when the refinery itself was built by British Petroleum; much of this housing was now inhabited by wealthier Yemenis whose main interests lay in Aden or Al Ittihad. The two story house had been carefully chosen because its roof was not overlooked, and its front door was obscured by shrubbery. As always, there were compromises. There was no clear view to the east over the approaches to Aden because the 5 million year old volcanic cone (which built Little Aden as it spewed out) guarded the western entrance to Aden proper. The view to the southwest across to the Chinese base, though, was unobstructed, and the outer approaches to Aden could be monitored.

The base had been built several years before after the change of Yemeni government had seen US influence decline and Chinese influence grow. Relations with the West had been reasonable, even following the suicide bombing of USS Cole in October 2000. She had been refuelling when two men in a small powerboat packed with 700 kg of explosive had hit her amidships, killing 17 crew and injuring 39. Following the 9/11 terror attack, the US had inserted special forces into the Yemen, but now even those were no longer in place.

Saunders let himself in and locked the door. A quick check of the windows and rear door satisfied him that there had been no apparent casual illicit entry. He checked the hidden intruder alarm and camera system which confirmed that there had been no professional break in, either.

He climbed the stairs and unlocked the steel roof door, checking the hidden security seals as he did so.

*

The flat roof was edged by a waist high wall, which had been raised further by a few courses of stone, and was now two metres high, though some stones were only loosely fitted. It spoiled the view, but also hid a small dish array and solar panels. Let into the wall there were three cameras which could be tilted, panned and zoomed remotely from somewhere in England – he didn't know where. He knew that through their lenses there was a good view of the Chinese naval base. The solar panels had been installed more than ten years before, when power shortages started becoming frequent during the summer – there was no point in having a surveillance system if you couldn't rely on a power supply. He visited both safe houses from time to time, often in the guise of an Arab businessman.

Most of the roof area was screened by a thin plastic mesh – more plastic than holes, used to provide shade and installed on most houses in the area, but more for privacy purposes here – it wasn't only US satellites that passed over. Besides Russia the list now included India, North Korea, Iran, Israel, China and Japan. The solar panels on the south side of the roof were uncovered and equipped with false piping - from the air they could not be differentiated from water heating panels. Image processing software automatically reviewed all satellite overflight data and any roof with a 'dish' would be flagged up for further examination, Sky and other satellite broadcasters notwithstanding. Radio licensing was no more – he now lived in the age of intrusive satellite surveillance.

He extracted the electronics package from his holdall and placed it next to the other packages in the small instrument cabinet which kept off the rain, and plugged it in to the twenty four volt power line. He connected a feed to the satellite array transmitter. There was a small UHF antenna which he positioned as instructed next to the wall and connected up. He didn't really know what he was doing, he just followed the colour coding, designed to make such tasks easy for non-technical people like him, though God knows one needed a degree to use a mobile phone these days, he thought, and while I'm on that subject…

From his holdall he took his mobile phone, keyed a code sequence of twenty digits and pressed the dial button. A minute later he received a text on his phone which said "Party arrangements confirmed for this evening, look forward to seeing you" so he knew that the satellite data link was operational in both directions, though the inward feed from the base was not yet in place.

It was now mid-morning and after double checking the setup he began the journey back. Finding a cab took some time and after changing at the Lulu supermarket it was late afternoon by the time he got back to Sana'a. There had been some difficulties with a tourist at one of the three roadblocks he encountered – there was a long queue and a delay of over an hour.

By the time he had secured the LandCruiser and the lockup, and worked his way back to his apartment, it was approaching 6 pm and the light was fading. He made a coffee and changed, rolled up the faulty rug and headed for Salim's. His approach through the Soukh was cautious and slow, meandering and checking as he went. As he approached, he could see that there were no rugs on the outside table – the shop was closed. He wandered into a leather goods emporium three shops down and browsed for a few minutes. When he came out he browsed slowly away from the area, taking particular care to check whether he was being followed, front or back.

When he was satisfied that there was no one in tow, Saunders dumped the rug in a side alley, and took a taxi. He planned to walk the last half a mile to the embassy. His face was known in the city, but he had need to be sure that he was not being tailed near Salim's – that would have told him that there might be a problem. He called Salim's mobile number from a café googlephone and after seven rings Salim's voice answered. He rang off immediately and then called again. Salim answered on the fourth ring. The conversation was about a rug and a particular pattern and colour which Saunders wanted. Salim did not have it. That confirmed that there was a problem at Salim's end. He left the café wasting no time.

The signal to London was brief:

"Assignment 'Hillclimb' in South completed. No further information available or expected ref mapping requirement. End"

He was sure that Salim was compromised. What now?

*

The following morning he went back to the lockup and after closing the door, 'went native'. He removed his shirt and put it in his attaché case and then put on an Emirates-style dishadasha all-in-one over his white chinos. With dark glasses, Gucci loafers and a Shemagh headscarf he could easily pass for a visiting businessman. Complete with ostentatious (fake) gold watch and attaché case he set off at a slow pace in search of a taxi into the Salt Market area.

After picking up a copy of the local newspaper, he found a coffee house across from Salim's and settled down with one eye on the still-closed shop and another on Al Jazeera news on the satellite TV wallscreen – the 'unjamming' of satellite TV was one of the few benefits of the Freedom riots. The newspaper was full of the developing situation in the Red Sea. It contained a lengthy, predictable and haughtily worded solidarity statement from the Republic of Yemen's Chinese allies critical of British actions in the Gulf in support of a British multinational mining conglomerate which was raping the Red Sea of its minerals in clear breach of international law.

'Well that's the tripe done, now for the rest of breakfast' Saunders thought. With a large fresh fruit juice he settled down and tuned his ears in to the local chatter in the bar.

There was little being said about Salim, and after finishing his juice he ordered a coffee and sabaya bread to complete his breakfast, with some honey for the bread. In the course of ordering he asked the owner in his best Emirates Arabic about Salim – he'd come especially to arrange some trading of rugs, but Salim's was closed.

Nervous and shifty was Saunders's best judgement of the reaction of the café owner. There was little information other than that Salim had been escorted away late the previous afternoon by two men, who the café owner suspected were police.

After finishing his breakfast, Saunders headed back towards the lockup. Without changing clothes he backed out the LandCruiser and drove across the city to Salim's home, passing by without stopping, and noting the obvious watch car with two men just at the corner of Salim's home avenue. Reflecting his modest business success, Salim's home was a two story villa-type building surrounded by low wall with metre high green-painted railings. As he drove past, Saunders eyes turned and noted that the shades in a particular upstairs room were just short of fully lowered and angled. So, Salim was definitely compromised, but probably still at home. Of course, he might have just given it all away.

*

Andjela's Story – Foundation

In the Chinese global intelligence infrastructure operations, the components of the military and economic/political intelligence gathering by the so-called 'deep water fishes' led to a need for occasional 'dirty work' to be done. Depending on the country involved and the particular operational requirements, the 'dirty work' might be done by Chinese nationals or it might be sub-contracted to one of the wide variety of wide variety of resources who made themselves available. Some are groups of disaffected radicals needing funding or arms, others are mainstream political liberation fronts – they might want funds or arms, but their needs might also involve political support.

Then there are mercenary groupings. These tend to be more efficient, with broader experience; they are simpler to deal with as there is no 'political' side to cloud the issue. It is a commercial transaction – money exchanged for services rendered.

After the breakup of Yugoslavia and the ethnic wars in the Balkans, a number of 'wet teams' set up business. One such team was run by a woman, who worked under the simple moniker of 'Maruška'.

*

Andjela Karanovic's parents had been killed during the war when their village near Novi Pazar had been attacked – the men and boys shot and the women and children raped and then burned in the church. Just another reprisal for a reprisal in the generations-old bloodshed. Andjela and one older brother, Vaclav, had run off and escaped, having hidden in a cellar under a barn, whilst the barn burned down.

She had taken quick revenge by using a pitchfork to spear one of the Muslim attackers whilst he was answering the call of nature. She and Vaclav had dragged the body into the barn and hidden it under hay. Andjela set the hay alight and they retreated into the cellar under the barn. The body lay undiscovered as the barn burned down. That was the first in her long series of personal reprisals. No-one knows where or how she had developed her particular ruthlessness, but an undiagnosed personality disorder left her deficient in her emotional inventory.

Academically, she was gifted and recognised as such in school (until that too was razed). Undoubtedly she would have succeeded at whatever career she had chosen, but fate and another war sent her down a wild and damaged path. Physically, she was a pretty girl with little puppy fat, and with the promise of growing into an attractive woman. Her intellect and her body

27

would together have served her well in any normal professional or vocational pursuit in the absence of any personality problem.

After the savagery at their farm, they spent four days in the heavily wooded hills around the village until they found a band of Serb irregulars, who 'took them in'. At fourteen years of age Vaclav was a strapping lad and full of promise as a recruit. As a twelve year old girl, Andjela was seen as a liability in what was very much a male dominated society, with the irregulars at the extreme.

In her conversation with Srecko Vidovic, the band's leader, she was tough and clearly determined. There was a fire for revenge which came across strongly in her speech and attitude, reinforced by a steely unwavering stare. She told him that she would personally kill one of the enemy for every finger and toe of her dead parents, and that she had just killed the first. She challenged him to let her prove herself; as a child she could easily infiltrate Muslim villages. Her ability to think on her feet was apparent, and her ideas were obviously creative.

Three days later she had her chance. Simple instructions, and no sign of fear, just smouldering determination. She approached a taxi in a Muslim village with the driver still inside. She tapped the window and when it was opened she dropped a grenade in, skipped over a wall and crawled away as the driver died.

Over the next three years she grew rapidly to physical maturity; she trained hard and learned her lessons well. None of the team messed with her. The only one to try – late one night whilst they were in the hills - had a knife stuck in his kidney by her, and bled to death. Vidovic didn't bother trying to save the man. She was special, let the others learn.

*

Towards the end of the 1980's with the rise to power of Milosevic and the start of hostilities over Kosovo, Srecko Vidovic had started to shape his small gang of workless fascist teenage criminals into a militia. At that time, he was little more than a poorly educated peasant himself, with peasant tastes and peasant superstitions. He did, though, have grand ideas and an ability to command respect and a following.

Around a campfire one night, he had watched a spider crawling and picked it up – it had only seven legs, but that did not prevent it walking efficiently and living. He saw this as an omen, and announced to his surprised fellow gang members that from then on their team would be known as the *Sedam Nogu Pauk* - Seven Legged Spider. The SNP emblem was thus created and all recruits wore a tattoo on the upper left arm.

During the hostilities, they grew in strength and ability to inflict terror. He sought, stole and bought the best equipment available for them, and their numbers grew. Vidovic drilled them ceaselessly and they wore the SNP emblem on their uniforms.

The terror groups vied to be the most feared, the title eventually being carried by Arkan's Tigers. Vidovic was less concerned about the SNP reputation for terror – the teenage girl Andjela Karanovic was a driven and creative killer with sound tactical skills and judgement well beyond her age. His men respected her and followed her in action. So, their reputation for terror largely looked after itself. He recognised that the end of the war was inevitable and began shaping other ideas and plans for the end of the war. To him, the Seven Legged Spider mapped the way forward, each leg representing a sphere of operations – extortion, drug trafficking, arms dealing and smuggling, robbery and prostitution.

For a couple of months he pondered about the other two legs and then realised that after the war there would be a massive international reconstruction effort in the country. This did not make him a visionary – his brain leaned more towards native cunning than to intellectual analysis, but the conclusion was nevertheless a sound one. So, construction became the sixth leg. The final, seventh, leg of the spider was to be the creation of a mercenary operation – terror for hire, essentially, making use of the basic skills of the group. During the last couple of years of the war, he started to re-mould the SNP and pick out his future 'capos' for each spider leg. Andjela Karanovic was marked down to run Leg Seven.

When people asked about the missing leg of the spider, he joked that it was the 'rest of the world, and too big to fit into the tattoo'.

*

The SNP terrorised their way through the Muslim villages, and Andjela proved herself time and again. Within a year, she had accounted for the fingers and toes of her parents. By the time she was seventeen, she was leading a raiding party. Her tactical appreciation was of the best, and her cunning – or should it be called 'creative planning under pressure', was exceptional. The team easily deferred to her decisions and commands without question. She was held in awe by her squad and known by them as *Andjela od smrt* – angel of death.

Although not as physically strong as most of her squad, she could outrun them all, and on the weights her power/weight ratio was exceptional. Their muscle bulk was a hindrance accentuated by beer. She pushed herself hard in training and bettered the men in most exercises. She excelled with small arms and a knife, and her hard compact body was used effectively in close quarters combat. What she lacked in sheer strength was compensated by speed and suppleness. She had killed five Muslim irregulars in hand to hand combat, and two had died very slowly and very deliberately at her hand.

Her quirky good looks – no-one would call it beauty in the classical sense - her intelligence, coolness and quick thinking, together with her emerging facility for languages, enabled her to pass through the lines of the UN peacekeepers with ease. She picked up a smattering of French, English and Dutch. The peacekeepers themselves had very little hard evidence in their files about her, though suspicions were starting to crystallize by the time she was twenty and the Bosnian war was moving towards a very uneasy peace and the Dayton Accords - one of Clinton's few worthwhile international achievements. By this time the activities of Vidovic's group were migrating heavily towards the smuggling and distribution of arms and drugs.

As the war drew to a close, the investigations intensified and an International Arrest Warrant was issued for Vidovic who moved to Colombia. Andjela's brother Vaclav went with Vidovic as one of his security team and that was the last she ever saw of Vaclav. He was killed a year later in a firefight with a Colombian gang attempting to assassinate Vidovic. His Colombian enemies had failed to kill him on that and several other occasions, but they eventually stopped his activities by other means - ten years later he was on television, arraigned in the high security dock in the International Court of Justice in The Hague on charges of genocide.

*

After the war ended, Andjela stayed on in Bosnia, running Vidovic's Bosnian operations for him. There was much to organise and manage – the importation of cocaine from Colombia and in return the export of arms. She also identified an opportunity and started to build her own sideline business of stealing and exporting UN heavy construction machinery that was being in used in military and civil engineering projects in the reconstruction of the country.

She was able to skim cash off the various operations she was running, and as long as the returns were in line with Vidovic's expectations, then no questions were asked. He was a realist, and she was too valuable to him. Andjela maintained accounts in several Swiss banks, visiting Zurich and Geneva occasionally.

*

After a year or so she realised that running a commercial enterprise for Vidovic – what was in reality a medium sized international business, albeit an illegal one – was not for her. It lacked the sharp edge of excitement that her earlier terrorist activities with her team had provided. She had got real kicks out of running the 'seventh leg' – the mercenary arm. Then slowly, Vidovic's competitors had nibbled away at the other legs.

Of the 'managers' of the other legs of the spider, three had been killed, one had disappeared and one had defected to the opposition.

The latter, Goran, had pleaded with her, reminding her of their time together in the mountains during the war. It had taken three weeks to track him down, but she had succeeded. She disposed of his bodyguards and shot him through the kneecaps (it was a punishment from the days of the IRA that she had heard about). She had left him crying and tied to a downpipe in a deserted warehouse, with a final belly shot judged to miss the arteries. He would be found by the dogs and feral cats first, then after a tip-off, by one of his team. The warning would be heeded.

The replacements for these 'managers' lacked experience and the degree of low cunning required and she had become increasingly involved in cleaning up and sorting out problems with their individual 'spider legs' when they screwed up. She was becoming increasingly exasperated with their incompetence. Finally, Vidovic had called her to Malta for a meeting, during one of his few, very brief, fraught visits to Europe.

*

At that meeting in the Hotel Kennedy on the Sliema seafront in Malta, Vidovic had appointed Andjela as his deputy. She now had real power and responsibility with day to day operational control of a business turning over more than 200 million dollars a year.

Then, she disappeared. Unable to contact her or her team, the boss of the sixth leg – construction - sent one of his men round to her home. Her guards were found, shot - two inside and one at the gates to her new villa in Vinça, to the southeast of Beograd. The master bedroom was wrecked. Three fingers were found on the bed – they had black nail varnish and had been cut off cleanly. There was a lot of blood.

Vidovic, in Colombia, was panicked. Hostilities between the competing gangs in Serbia intensified for a few weeks with abductions, torture and killing, but Vidovic's people had been unable to find Andjela or discover who was responsible for her disappearance and the murder of three of her team.

*

After accepting the promotion at the end of the meeting in Malta, Andjela had thought long and hard. It was a job that both she and Vidovic knew she could do well – and had been doing for several months now. The problem was that there was no excitement, no visceral feel of the face to face killing she enjoyed so much. Running 'Leg Seven' – the mercenary team – provided that visceral feedback at killing time that flowed through her like the rush of a drug. If she had been a shark, she thought, it would have been almost like a feeding frenzy, but always under control - if indeed such a thing could be possible or even imagined. She enjoyed sex (even occasionally with men), but the pleasure of that did not come close to what she experienced when killing.

It was a new century and she was still stuck in the old one. She was travelling occasionally on assignments overseas and making a few, select links in the mercenary underground.

Andjela had always been one to act quickly – but on good instinctual judgement - as she had that day in the farm when she lost most of her family. Her actions were never impulsive – they were always based on her ability to assess facts and judge situations acutely, but very rapidly. Once she had decided that a future running Vidovic's empire was not for her then she began her planning.

She made her preparations carefully over a period of months, acquiring a range of false identities – simple enough for her with her connections, but requiring a few 'loose ends' to be tied off in the process. Different forgers, different identities. These identities were formal in the sense that they embraced passports, driving licences and ID cards. She even bought herself a new home outside Beograd. On the less formal side, she enjoyed the whole process of slipping into an alternative identity and living that identity, if only for the occasional evening in the demi-monde of lesbian S&M. There were parts of her life that she kept private even from her bodyguards and occasional evenings out on her own were not unusual, after all, she was well able to take care of herself and there were few potential assailants in Beograd that she could not better hand to hand, if necessary.

Her disguises were light, easily donned, and just as easily ditched. They were also effective – hats, heels, wigs (these were very common in her alternative community), simple but powerfully accentuating make-up, coloured contact lenses and facial studs. Most of the clubs she frequented were owned, directly or indirectly, by business competitors of hers. Security cameras and doormen were widespread at the clubs as Serbia was still quite homophobic. So, the disguises, besides providing her with a vicarious thrill, also served a serious personal security purpose for her

Over a period of a couple of months, her disguises simplified and she developed one personality in particular. Andjela became known in the gay bars of Beograd by the name of Senka - which meant Shadow in Serbian.

As Senka, she searched carefully until she found a girl with the right looks and lack of stable background. Finding a suitable girl with similar build and eye colouring was not difficult and after a few failed but enjoyable attempts, she found the right girl – one Maruška Pavkovic.

Money, clothes, drugs, sex – it was easy to bait the trap. The lure of a job was dangled. They shopped along Knez Mihailova and Kralja Alexandara streets with Senka paying for the designer clothing (which she herself chose); and arranged to have Maruška's hair re-styled.

One night, two weeks after they had met, as they made love with Maruška bound to the bed in her one room apartment, Senka introduced her to heroin, injecting her as she reached her climax.

The next day, Senka took Maruška to a tattooist to add a tattoo to the two she already wore. The tattooist recognised the design and was reluctant to apply it, but after a few quiet words from Senka whilst squeezing his testicles he was persuaded that the girl with the grip of steel and eyes of ice was to be obeyed.

Maruška had never been abroad, so Andjela, holding out a shopping trip to Paris as a gift, helped her arrange a legal passport. Five hundred dollars in the right palms helped speed the process.

Senka – Andjela - knew that Vidovic had his informants within her team – he would be a fool not to have – but expected that he would pass this off as just part of her fun. He knew that she was a lesbian as did the whole organisation which she ran for him in Serbia, and now beyond. This knowledge did not sit easily with the people she controlled in Serbia, but they all knew that she was the most capable boss they had worked under – capable in business, capable in combat. They worshipped her and feared her in equal measure and had learned to ignore her sexual preferences – it was no longer discussed. They knew that she was much more clever than they were, and completely without scruples. Some even owed their lives or liberty to her having had her quick wits and sound instincts save them from an ambush by US Rangers. Even in the hardened world of Serbian crime, she was held in awe and competitors joked about her being a *psihopata* – a psychopath.

*

Two days later, one Maruška Pavkovic was installed in Andjela's new house (Andjela stayed away much of this time). It was relatively straightforward – drug dependency was common, well paid jobs were not, and the chance to live in a smart mansion as a PA to a clearly wealthy successful businesswoman was not to be passed up. A bodyguard, Dajbog, was installed with instructions to keep Maruška in the house and under control, and her heroin dosage was slowly increased.

The dental records had proved more difficult, but in the end Andjela had satisfied herself that her own no longer existed, having been destroyed in a fire at the hospital in Novy Pazar during the war. She knew that even if they did exist, matching her records as a child to those of an adult would be difficult in a country where dental care had been poor and record keeping had been paper-based. Incontrovertible DNA matching would merely suggest to the investigators that other records were inaccurate or had been tampered with.

People were still desperate - though the economy was improving much of it was black, from top to bottom. There wasn't much that dollars would not buy. The rest was just a matter of thorough planning and preparation. That final evening, events went smoothly and to plan.

Once the BMW had passed through the gate in the gathering gloom and her driver had stopped the car near the garage as ordered, Andjela stepped smartly out of the car and shot him through side window with the silenced Zastava 'Three Nines' 9mm pistol. The two head shots were accurate and he was clearly dead. She was very well-practiced at killings like these.

She walked the fifty yards quickly, on the recently laid turf at the side of the driveway, back through the light drizzle to the gatehouse. She shot the guard as he sat at the desk inside, torso and head, and switched the light off. Then she strode briskly back to the front of the house. As she climbed the steps to the front door, Maruška's babysitter, Dajbog, opened it and walked across the porch towards her, an inquisitive look on his face.

"Hi Dajbog, how's Maruška?"

"Quiet now, I've just injected her as you ordered."

"No heroin?"

"No, just the drug you gave me to use.."

"And the other job?"

"Yes, all done" he said, adding "*uzivam moJ rad*" – I enjoy my work!

"Working for you is a real pleasure."

"I'm glad you enjoy working for me and followed orders" she said as she raised her right arm from the folds of her coat and shot him in the torso. Dajbog was over six feet tall, and overweight. He staggered backwards and fell against the wall alongside the front door. Then, she stepped forward and fired a second shot into his head as he slipped, blood frothing from his mouth, down the wall. "I enjoy mine too. It was good to have you in the team."

She walked up the stairs, trembling slightly – she could feel herself getting wet and the blood engorging her loins, but she re-focused on the task in hand and pushed ahead, trying to sideline the powerful rush she was feeling. She had never used the master suite - since she had moved in to the house a month before, she had slept in another suite which she kept scrupulously clean. All her fun with Maruška had been at hotels, except that one time she had been to Maruška's one room apartment, as Senka. In the last week, whilst Maruška was at the villa, Andjela had arranged for the apartment to be cleared and cleaned. The landlord had been told by someone who looked very much like her – a sister maybe, he thought - that

Maruška had moved to a new job in Pristina and had asked her to settle the rent. As she walked into the suite, she saw Maruška was tied to the bedframe, naked. She smiled and said *"Zdravo dušo"* – hello darling.

*

Maruška had clearly been beaten as ordered and should have been raped too, though Andjela didn't bother to check. Even a brief examination would bring back memories of nights together, and she kept that door in her mind firmly closed – she'd enjoyed it whilst it had lasted, though 'enjoyed' was a strange word in her lopsided lexicon. Maruška's good looks were barely discernible – her face was misshapen, bruises were welling and one eye was closed. She opened her eye and looked at Andjela.

"Senka, pomozi mi, pomozi mi molimo" – help me, help me Senka please.

"Ja cu, miljenik, a ću vas odvesti u bolnicu" – I will, darling, I will take you to hospital, replied Andjela. "But first there is something more to be done."

Moving to the side of the bed, Andjela took the secateurs from her bag and amputated three fingers from Maruška's right hand, struggling and screaming at first and then passing out, wetting herself. Andjela wrinkled her nose at the strengthening smell from the steaming bed, bagged the secateurs, left the fingers on the bloodstained bed, and left Maruška bleeding.

Collecting her overnight bag from the other room, she went downstairs and picked her way carefully past the spreading pool of Dajbog's blood to the BMW. She took out some tissues and wiped it down carefully, and popped the tissues into her bag, not noticing the one that dropped into the rear footwell as she turned away. She walked quickly around the side of the villa to the garage, then drove the black Range Rover down to the rear door of the villa. Back upstairs in the master suite, she took the ligature used for the heroin injection and used it to stop Maruška's bleeding, then dragged her, half stumbling, moaning and crying all at once downstairs to the Range Rover. She hit her over the back of the head with the pistol as she pushed her in to the rear. She threw a blanket over her.

Andjela knew exactly where her own DNA could be found in her new house – nowhere, unless they planned to analyse house dust, she smiled to herself. She did, though, suspect that her DNA might be on record somewhere from killing scenes where she'd taken some pain herself – but in that case there would be no name linked to it. In any case, she thought, there were so many killings in those days that DNA collection was patchy, if done at all. The Serbian police were still in the Middle Ages then.

35

She tipped the handbag contents onto the dressing table. It contained her identity and life as Andjela Karanovic – two unused mobile phones and half a dozen unused SIM cards, charger, ID card, some cash and some other personal items, all cleaned. With the severed fingers she carefully put some prints on the items. At the dressing table, she found Maruška's new makeup bag and transferred the contents to her own. She did not possess a 'personal mobile' because they were just too easily traced and intercepted, she used only 'throwaways'. All her important communications these days were done using secure emails from her laptop computer which she took with her – it would be expected that anyone with a 'professional' interest in kidnapping her would want to see the contents of her laptop. She had backed up all the important items onto an external drive, and the laptop would be consigned to the Danube.

After removing her long coat and bagging it, she put on a fresh coat, wig, spectacles – the Senka look, she thought - then went down to the Range Rover.

So far, she'd taken about ten minutes. She knew that there were enough clear pointers in her plan to outweigh the weaknesses.

There were just a couple of loose ends left to tie up. She would have to take care of the heroin tracks – she didn't do heroin herself. The heroin should be out of Maruška's system now, and the sodium thiopental administered by Dajbog would confuse the picture and keep her relaxed for the next half hour, if he hadn't overdosed her.

She drove past her BMW, the rear door open, her driver slumped in the front seat, down the driveway and out into a new future.

The drive took about 20 minutes in the dark. She did not expect any difficulties. She found the track to the thin copse and parked the Range Rover, about half way between Zaklopaca and Smederovo. She could see the Danube glinting through the trees about 100 yards away. Maruška was moaning again. She dragged her out onto the stony ground and in the pool of light cast by the interior lamps of the car she gave her a large shot of sodium thiopental – this overdose would kill her soon. More commonly known as 'truth serum' as Dajbog called it, it is in fact a barbiturate – quick acting, short-lived and used as general anaesthetic. In Maruška's case its purpose was to kill and to give investigators the clear impression that death had been under interrogation.

As Maruška slowly relaxed into paralysis en route to death, Andjela took out a knife and levered out her eyes, then shot her through the kneecaps. It should look as if she died whilst being interrogated. This would not be the first body to be found in this area - its seclusion made it one of the favourite drop-off points for inter-gang victims. It also meant that the public stayed away. She wiped the Range Rover carefully, though she had been wearing gloves. Burning the car was not an option – she did not want all the evidence destroyed.

It was a dry night with broken cloud and a half moon on the wane and the light breeze was blowing down the Danube from the northwest carrying a mixture of smells from Beograd upriver, and the farmland around her. She walked carefully through the thin trees to the river's edge and threw the open bag containing soiled clothes and one pair of blue eyes into the Danube. She watched the bag float away downstream in the moonlight. Then, she threw the 'three nines' pistol well out into the river. After changing her shoes, the old ones followed the bag.

And so, after changing clothes and checking the pulse of the now dead body, Andjela Karanovic was well on the way to becoming Maruška Pavkovic.

*

Removing the eyes had been a necessary twist, not typical of Serbian mafia behaviour. Maruška found her way back up the track with a torch as she smiled at the thought of the apparatchiks from the police trying to understand why the eyes were missing – they might even think that they had a sadistical eye collector on the loose – not quite the effect she intended, but then it was all confusion. The fingers and DNA would tie it all together. The tattoo, unless a wolf or bear got there first, would provide the final piece in the jigsaw.

She walked down the road about half a mile and found the old burnt-out farmhouse. It would not be long before a Serb family moved in and started rebuilding, but for now it suited her purpose. Behind the barn, she piled some straw into an oil drum, added some diesel fuel, lit it and dropped her palmtop computer in. Back in the barn she started the non-descript Lada. She backed out of the barn, got out and checked that her palmtop was a pool of plastic and metal in the drum and then drove out of the farm. She was dressed a little too smartly to match the Lada – in keeping with what one would expect of say a dental nurse, with a modest salary and pretensions. Five minutes later, she changed cars in Zaklopaca as planned and slipped deeper into her new identity. Within half an hour she was back in Beograd and heading for a club. She found a partner for the night and enjoyed the sex with a new abandon. Andjela was gone, she was now Maruška, and in six hours time, Senka would cease to be.

*

Maruška (neé Andjela/Senka) caught the train the next morning using her German passport, including visa stamps, and arrived in Trieste late in the evening. She checked into the La Terrazze hotel as Maruška Pavkovic with her new, genuine passport. The hotel was listed as two star and was therefore relatively modest. Conveniently located on the Via Filzi near the sea front and city centre it was family run and busy.

After breakfast the following morning, the concierge arranged a train reservation for her. Strolling along the Via Coroneo she enjoyed an hour buying a change of clothes, some underwear and shoes – a little more stylish this time. At a luggage store, she added a rucksack to her purchases before returning to the hotel.

She spent the rest of the afternoon enquiring about hotels and clinics in Zurich. It was just that time of year between the summer tourists and the winter snow lovers, but nevertheless hotel rooms were hard to find. She would avoid those hotels that she had stayed in previously as Andjela in another life. Late in the afternoon she checked out of the hotel and strolled in the last of the sun. There was a light breeze from the Adriatic, carrying a strong smell of the sea.

She took her reservation on the 19.46 train to Zurich. There were to be changes at Venice and Innsbruck on the nine hour overnight journey and she settled down with a bottle of Pinot Grigio, her laptop and a 'Learn French' CD for entertainment. There were only snacks on this route, but that would be enough for her. She had a private sleeper reserved for the stage from Venice to the 5 am arrival at Innsbruck.

It was just after 10am when she checked into the Hotel Leoneck in Zurich as Marie Dubois - a plain and uninspired French name. Being French would excuse her poor German language ability. It was busy – but that was to be expected in a value for money hotel and suited her purposes. The concierge showed her where to leave her luggage, in a cubicle behind the reception area, until noon when her room would be available. She headed out with her rucksack in search of croissants and coffee.

The weather was overcast and cooling towards winter, threatening snow. It was much colder than in Trieste, which had been basking in some late autumn sun, and occasional snow flurries were whirling down the street - a healthy covering of early snow was visible on the mountain tops glimpsed occasionally between the buildings, to the south of Lake Zurich. Passing a GAP store, she dived in and bought herself a heavier coat and some jeans. Further along Bahnhofstrasse she purchased pair of walking boots and then found a café to catch up on breakfast.

The rest of the day was spent buying more clothes and an attaché case, unpacking and resting – she planned to be in Zurich for a week.

The following day, a Thursday, she took a taxi to a private bank, Clariden Leu, on Bahnhofstrasse. She was met for her appointment by Herr Heinz Grunefeld – one of the senior officers with access to her account details, who led her down to the basement. She confirmed her account number and password and after unlocking her access to the deposit boxes she was shown into a small room with a table and a chair.

She took out 300,000 Swiss Francs and placed them in her attaché case, congratulating herself on having held her deposits in Francs and not in US Dollars – the working currency of Vidovic's business which had weakened significantly against the Franc since she had opened the account three years previously. To the Francs she added a French passport, driving licence, ID card and credit cards. From her rucksack, she took out one of the fresh sets of papers she had brought with her from Beograd – those of Fraulein Gisela Wessel, from Garmisch in the German Alps, and placed them in the open safe deposit box.

She removed the clean Glock G38 pistol from the other safe deposit box, put it in her attaché case and called for the assistant.

Maruška went straight from Clariden Leu to a nearby branch of Credit Suisse and opened an account using her French ID and 250,000 Swiss Francs. Swiss banking was still very secure – the effects of the 9/11 attacks on the US a couple of months before had not yet led to the re-shaping of the rules. For now, she had completed the splitting and segregation of her assets.

On the following Monday, she checked into a private clinic on the Witellikerstrasse in Zurich. Laser removal of tattoos was a relatively quick and painless procedure, but usually, after the procedure, faint traces were still visible. She had elected for surgical excision of the tattoo, because of its size. After local anaesthetic and a few hours in the clinic she had removed the physical 'brand' of the SNP and was eighteen hundred Dollars poorer.

*

Two days after Andjela Karanovic's disappearance, and following a tip off to the police, a woman's decomposing body was found by police alongside a new Range Rover hidden in a copse near the Danube river, close to the town of Smederevo, about 20 miles outside Beograd. Three fingers were missing – they had been cut off cleanly and not chewed off by the animals which had started gnawing the body. The eyes had been removed before death – they hadn't been pecked out by crows. The assailants had beaten the woman badly and she had been dead for some days. There was a spider tattoo on the upper left arm - an indication of the dead woman's criminal affiliations. The fact that the spider had only seven legs pointed to Vidovic's organisation – SNP Sedam Nogu Pauk – the Seven Legged Spider. There were recent drug tracks on the left arm.

Checks revealed that the Range Rover was registered to an import/export company in Beograd.

The SBPOK - the Serbian Counter-Organised Crime Service - took the case over on account of the organised crime association. Enquiries revealed that one of the directors of the company was an Andjela Karanovic. SBPOK visited her house and found the scene of carnage. The three dead men were known to the police, with backgrounds in the SNP paramilitary which Vidovic had led during the war, and criminal backgrounds as young boys before that.

The distorted 9mm bullet extracted from the left knee of the dead woman was a partial match to those removed from Andjela's bodyguards, at least in respect of the hammer marks and a couple of groovings. The other knee had been shot too, but the bullet was not in the smashed bone and flesh, it was found in the stony ground under the body.

The track marks inside the left arm were recent, and there were a few very fresh ones, less than 24 hrs old at time of death, but the marks were not indicative of a long term drug user.

Dental records could not be compared with the woman's body as there did not appear to be any on file for one Andjela Karanovic. DNA tests comparing the body to DNA of the blood in Karanovic's house, and other swabs from clothing and the bathroom were a match.

The autopsy found a high level of sodium thiopental in the body.

The body's identity: confirmed. Andjela Karanovic. Killer or killers – unknown. Cause of death: barbiturate overdose, probably during interrogation.

Gang killings were common, though the methods of torture in this case were not so usual. Vidovic's insiders in the SBPOK could add nothing, but speculation was rife. The case would be put on the back-burner and there would be no further investigation even though there were some unusual aspects to the case which were highlighted in the file, and some unmatched DNA had been found. The overall picture was conclusive – this was a gangland killing and the SBPOK were quite happy that the criminals exterminated each other.

*

Djibouti Landfall

Djibouti was still as good as in the old days, maybe even better, though he had no buddies to share it with. The French presence – both naval at Djibouti and Foreign Legion at the Arta training camp, together with the US Army and Airforce contingents at Camp Lemonnier made for a testosterone-fuelled nightlife in the city. Beer, aggression, bar girls – it was all there to be enjoyed. Although the night hadn't been a rough one in the physical sense nor in the female sense either, Steve Baldwin had woken up with a thundering head reminiscent of the blow-outs the lads had enjoyed back in the Yemen days. Three months in the desert of tracking, locating, killing, disappearing, living on shit – and then, Djibouti for some R&R – and that often included an inter-forces ding dong. Far enough away from the theatre that they could show their faces in public and no worries about compromising their cover.

Only Mick was left now out of that crew, and he was in a bad way. Dave dead in Sierra Leone, and Windy, killed on the M40 riding his Ducati. Mick had tried to cash in on the popularity of so-called survival shows on TV. Mick's stardom stuff was little more than boy scout lore and common sense. As if Hereford would permit a free training course for the world on how it was really done! And now Mick was back on the pop in a big way, blown his TV fees, too pissed to work any profitable follow through. God forbid I end up like that, he thought, glad that it was well behind him now.

Anyway, that's what he'd heard from Mick himself when they had met up in Phuket. Mick was out in Thailand squandering his fees looking for a wife – well someone to cook and wash for him really besides the obvious. That had ended now, and no bad thing. He'd tried to get Mick to join him for a couple of months and get his head straight, but no go. That was before his trip across from Singapore via the Maldives, and his brush with the pirates off Aden.

He felt like shit and probably looked worse. A splash of cold water, and clean teeth, then up on deck, lock up, check the anchor and off to find the strongest coffee in Djibouti, He stood on the dockside and looked back at her. At 36 feet long, "Adèle" was just a bit too short to get the full benefit of her steel build, so she was relatively heavy for her size. The compensations were that she was comfortable at sea, tough and easily repaired. On the other hand, as with all women, time took its inevitable toll. She was now rust-streaked – just cosmetic – but would be in need of some serious repair work soon, with a few recently acquired dings in her hull. He'd got across the Indian Ocean before the monsoon season set in. The plan now was to work up the Red Sea, through the Suez Canal, across the

Mediterranean Sea, and then repairs in Gibraltar – or, maybe Malta. He certainly did not want to be in Djibouti for the summer heat. Gibraltar was about 6 months away.

Adèle had been his home for 4 years now, and he trusted her implicitly. She had been faithful, but occasionally she proved to be a handful and argued with him when the wind and sea conspired. He had wandered, as most men do sooner or later, taking on female crew, but they had been nothing more than transients. Adèle was his constant love.

He found a coffee house, stirred the thick mixture, and considered the last few days. As usual the seven p's had saved him – perfect planning and preparation prevents piss poor performance, but luck had helped. Not that you could really blame the pirates, everybody had to make a living. The trouble was that the commercial shipping was now a harder target – the owners had toughened up security - and the Combined Naval Task Force was active, though it couldn't be everywhere at once. The pirates were turning to smaller, less lucrative targets and moving further offshore, and further afield – even down to the Mozambique Channel in the south and the Seychelles in the east.

*

They came at dusk. As usual he was doing things his own way. No convoys, no ham radio or marine HF nets, no VHF radio traffic. Radar on, set at maximum range. His course was 285 degrees, just north of west, with what wind there was currently from the south west at about 8 knots. The onset of the southwest monsoon was still 4 or 5 months away.

During the night watches over the last few weeks, he had considered the risks and his plans. The chances of a piracy raid were probably 1 in 10 – definitely not negligible. It was unlikely that he would detect them on radar – although he would keep the radar alarm on. The typical pirates came in a rigid boat, simply built, but were becoming more sophisticated. Unusually, this group came in a rigid inflatable boat – a RIB - which did not provide much of a radar target, and if there was any sea running, the echo would be lost in sea clutter. So far though, weather and sea conditions were relatively benign. If the radar did detect them then at 30 knots he would have only five or six minutes to prepare, so his primary plan was based on the assumption that he would have no more than a couple of minutes warning, and perhaps even less if he was asleep. If he was caught napping, then things would be tougher because he would need a minute or two to orientate himself.

Two days before, he had taken his Sig-Sauers out of the waste oil container, wiped them, stripped them, cleaned them, and tested them with a few rounds fired at some garbage thrown over the side. They were both the old P228 model – compact, accurate and with a 13 round magazine. He had worked with them for years. One of them was now taped under the deckhead next to the chart table, and the other with a silencer fitted, was taped under the deckhead in the forepeak. Both easily to hand, yet not visible with a cursory search.

Gun or no gun? This had never been an issue, but it was for many cruising people. Many US cruising boats carried guns, but few, if any, British boats carried them – it was a basic cultural difference between the countries. He was British and definitely an exception - he carried them and knew how to use them. Conventional wisdom was that if one carried a gun then piracy incidents would escalate uncontrollably, even if the user has been trained in use of firearms. Sir Peter Blake had met his end in this very way on the Amazon in 2002, but a long gun in a confined space was not a good idea. For Steve, having lived with guns for more than 20 years, used all kinds in close quarters and long range situations, there was no problem, and no moral decisions to be made about using them. The US crew of the yacht 'Quest' in 2011 had all been murdered, The hassles of getting a gun in and out of countries along the route were trivial. Put simply, for a man practised in a covert way of life, there were no guns declared and no hassles experienced. There were ways and means.

Probably the more fundamental question was why fight? Most piracy attacks on small vessels were over in less than 30 minutes, bloodless, and resulted in loss of cameras, radios, cash and other valuables. With common sense, these losses could be minimised, although it was advisable that the attackers should not go away empty handed. This question was not fundamental to Steve, he hadn't considered it at all. No one was taking anything from him. Latterly though, simple armed theft had escalated to kidnapping.

In 2009, the Chandler couple had been captured by pirates. They were middle aged and had been held for over a year by the pirates. Eventually, in 2010 they were released. Press speculation was that a ransom of $1 million had been paid, but this was never confirmed. There had been other, less well publicised, cases since then.

Steve had no-one who would pay a ransom for him, and even if there were, he would not have wanted it so. He had a couple of thousand dollars in cash aboard, stored in a safe welded to the hull. He split the cash, leaving two hundred dollars in the safe, and putting the rest wrapped in polythene, into the diesel tank. The SSB marine ham radio hadn't worked since Singapore, but he'd left it in place. He had an old hand-held VHF radio, which didn't work – he put that near the chart table and hid the one that worked under one of the settee berths in the saloon.

He had been lucky this time, though he was annoyed that he hadn't prepared earlier – they were now operating further and further from land making the task of the Combined Naval Task Force much more difficult.

He had been on the way up the companionway into the cockpit with a mug of tea, and saw them about a mile away over the port quarter.

He ducked below, headed forward into the forepeak and closed the watertight door. Adèle had been built with watertight compartments, two of them – the forepeak and under the main companionway. In the event of major damage, they could be clamped shut to prevent Adèle flooding completely. He had fitted heavy bolts on the forward side of the forepeak door, which he now secured. He cracked the forehatch open slowly, folded the wings out and rested it on the wings – the gap was about six inches. The RIB was about 100 yards away and closing fast. Peering through the gap between that hatch lid and the deck he counted about 8 heads. Then one of the gang fired a burst into the air from what sounded like an AK47. He made no response.

The RIB closed up alongside to port and two of the men started to climb aboard Adele.

Count again, seven heads. Better. Typically stupid, Steve thought, carrying AK47's in a close quarters situation, even more stupid using a RIB. They moved towards the cockpit shouting in broken English, and calling back to the helmsman in what Steve took to be Somali – it certainly didn't sound like Arabic.

Adèle was rolling slightly in the south-westerly sea, making about 4 knots in about 10 knots of breeze. Timing the roll of the boat, he squeezed off two shots. Of course, the silenced shots were inaudible to the Somalis, with the outboard engine running, and the two wakes slapping between the boats. One of the targets in the RIB fell back onto another and the other target fell across the gunwhale of the RIB as it rolled in the sea. Adèle rolled slightly to starboard and Steve, with his eyes at deck level, lost sight of the RIB. He could hear raised voices and panic, and as Adèle rolled back to port the RIB started to accelerate away and collided with the side of Adèle. At least it would have collided if there had not been a body draped across the side of the RIB. The helmsman's eyes met Steve's just as Steve's third shot caught him in the throat. "Should have been lower, bad timing" he thought.

As the helmsman collapsed, the RIB lurched to port, turning its stern to Steve. The other guys in the RIB were now trying to organise themselves and shouting to the two in Adèle's cockpit one of whom started running forward on deck. Steve picked him off and he tumbled over the lifelines into the sea as Adèle rolled again to port. Steve now threw the forehatch fully open, twisted and squeezed off two shots at the RIB's hull, puncturing the starboard tubes which starting deflating, followed by a third shot which caught another of the crew in the belly. With the rapidly dying helmsman draped across the wheel, the RIB continued its turn to port, at speed, with two of the remaining crew struggling to get it under control, and another trying to bring his gun to bear on Adèle. That was almost impossible given the motion of the RIB and a wild burst went off harmlessly – the tracer made Steve realise that it was now almost dark. The sea was now slopping in to the RIB on the starboard side where the tube had collapsed.

The second boarder was now crouching in the cockpit trying to figure out where Steve was and how to deal with him. 'Six mil steel will barely stop an AK47, just hope he hasn't got any fancy ammo loaded' Steve thought.

"Mister, Mister, no shoot, no shoot" he heard, then the sound of an AK47 in Adèle's saloon and the plating of the bulkhead next to him singing as it was raked with two bullets passing through and hitting the hull next to him. Steve loaded a fresh magazine and hoisted himself through the open hatch onto the deck.

He stood and waited, his gun trained on the open main hatch about twelve feet away. Then, the butt of the AK47 emerged slowly through the hatch, and the voice again "Mister, Mister, no shoot, no shoot," followed by a hand, an arm, a head and then shoulders, facing aft. Steve was moving aft along the starboard side deck.

'Where's the other arm then?' wondered Steve as the man rose through the hatch and started to turn. Steve squeezed two shots off. Not a difficult target even in the dusk. A pathologist would have reported that the first bullet caught the bottom edge of the Somali's left scapula and ricocheted between the ribs down through the heart, lodging in the liver. From Steve's perspective, the guy was hit and fell sternward over the port edge of the cockpit as the second shot caught him in the lower back. Steve stepped aft and put two more bullets in him. He could hear the engine of the RIB spluttering in the gathering darkness and some shouting which faded away as he listened. He didn't expect them to return, and doubted that they would make land or even their mothership of they had one.

He heaved the bodies over the side in the dark, and collected the AK47's. He'd hang on to those for the moment, and dump them as he neared Djibouti waters – about 12 hours at 4 knots, he reckoned, and decided to run without lights all night. Tomorrow he would clean up and knock out the pings in the bulkhead and touch up the paint. Just to be prepared, though, he cleaned and checked his Sigs, re-armed and taped them back in position. Then, a few stiff whiskies.

*

The meeting at MI6 HQ in Vauxhall Cross lasted about half an hour. Anthony Booth of the Africa and Middle East desk represented the sharp end of the business (London i.e. safe end) with David Montgomery, who was at the coalface. There was a third man present. His clothing could be described as 'ill-assembled', he was balding and visibly uncomfortable. Booth introduced him as a 'colleague from Cheltenham', Cheltenham being GCHQ, Government Communications Headquarters. One of the beard and sandals brigade, thought Montgomery, mentally christening him 'Mr Cheltenham'. Booth started the briefing.

"The facts are pretty grim. We believe that we have a problem with our secure comms and the Chinese.

We've run a couple of blind tastings on the humint side which came up all clear, so we're satisfied – for the moment that our tier 1 cables are being read directly. Not all, thank God. Our major embassies are using the latest black boxes and appear to be secure"

Mr Cheltenham was nodding gently as Booth went on:

"Cables to residents in some of our lower tier embassies appear to be leaking. We've run a few more specific intel leakage tests and know that only our outward data from London is compromised – by that, I mean the Chinese are only getting half the story. That's bad enough of course, but could be very useful to us. We need to nail down the facts. Naturally, we don't want them to know that we're on to them so things are proceeding as normal – more or less – and we're using other channels for most critical traffic, but we still need to feed them some juicy bits to keep them on the hook.

Our technical chaps," nodding across to Mr Cheltenham, "think that they must be reading the satellite spot beams near the embassy. We can't make the transmission footprints smaller than about a quarter of a mile across, so apparently they could be monitored outside the embassy. Receiving the signal is one thing, but decoding it quite another. Our best guess – and by that I mean worst – is that they can decode within about 36 hours – we've tested this with some sensitive data. Unfortunately, we may have lost an agent in the process.

Our residents in a number of lower tier countries have been carrying out some pretty basic commercial footwork, literally, and we think we have identified a pattern. You'll know that in almost every town in the western world there are now Chinese bazaars. These are selling the most awful crap made in China. Well, it seems that these bazaars are very often located within the quarter mile radius of one of our embassies. Not only that, but as you know, embassies tend to cluster, so they may well be in a position to access other traffic. It's mind boggling. That's the problem. Now, to finding a solution…"

*

46

Steve Baldwin had sailed into Djibouti two days ago, having dumped the AK47's outside territorial waters and replaced his Sigs in the waste oil container. The approach to Djibouti was uneventful - he had had no more unwelcome visitors. There had been the usual frustrations during his clearing through Immigration, Customs and the local police, but it was good to hear the sound of a European language again. He had taken a 10 day visa for $30, and it was enjoyable to exercise his passable French and Arabic once more.

*

When in harbour, Steve Baldwin enjoyed his ritual of morning coffee and croissants – there were definitely some positive benefits of French colonial rule. Not all French colonies were good though – he cast his mind back to French Guyana and shook his head ruefully.

Devil's Island, the former French penal colony, had left its mark on the country and population. The sailing pilot books were distinctly downbeat about it, but the food was good – the French legacy; nevertheless, one visit was enough. Still, it wasn't quite as bad as Guyana (formerly British Guyana), where it was recommended to have a guard with you when going to the supermarket. Steve hadn't bothered with the guard, but had spent 6 hours in a police station explaining how he'd broken one arm and two ribs of a local man, who had nearly died from a punctured lung.

He found a seat and ordered his coffee. He'd bought a copy of La Nation, the leading local newspaper, and was catching up on piracy news, and regional issues in general, weather forecasts were good too. His French was not brilliant, but good enough to get some value from the paper. The Yemenis were being awkward again in the Bab el Mandeb – he'd be sailing through this strait in the next couple of weeks and didn't want any aggravation. 'The Gate of Tears' was its English translation, and he certainly hoped it would not prove to be a prophetic name for him.

The weather had to be right for his departure – the Red Sea could kick up rough, and strong winds often brought sandstorms which could reduce visibility to zero. Small boat radars were not powerful enough to be effective, and even big ship radar struggled with the densest storms.

Steve knew that there was no ideal time to sail North up the Red Sea. Whichever way – North or South - a sailor could expect contrary winds for 50% of the time, whatever the season. Generally though, late spring was preferred and Steve had planned his passage so far to fit in with that timing. He'd come across the Indian Ocean from the Maldive Islands and was not planning to stop anywhere before the Gulf of Aquaba where he planned to do some diving. He would be carrying plenty of fuel to maintain progress even when the wind was not in his favour. The rhumb line was nearly 1100 miles to the Gulf, and with the high volume of shipping in the Red Sea he would not get much rest. Steve reckoned he could do it in 12 days, but it would not be easy.

So, he would pick his departure date carefully. The sensitivity of the area meant that stops were few and far between, officials were zealous, and Saudi Arabia was out of bounds completely for small boat sailors. Anchoring inshore anywhere was generally illegal unless you had formerly 'cleared in' to a country first, and given the sensitivities of the area and the frustrating bureaucracy involved with 'clearing in', then it was better not to consider anchoring as an option. Patrol boats were common and keen.

He planned to sail alone, as he had done for the last couple of years. He'd taken on casual crew in the past, but you never knew them well enough in advance – when the chips were down he preferred to rely on himself. This would be an arduous passage, and he did not want to have to deal with unknown quantities. Besides which, if there was a problem with a crew member then it would not be easy to put them ashore legitimately.

It came as quite a surprise when the chair opposite was pulled back, and a beaming face with an English voice said:

"Mind if I join you?"

*

Tobin Dynasty – Foundation

Charles Tobin was born in 1970, the fifth generation of a gold mining family which had been moderately successful, and the fifth generation of a convict transported to Australia in 1839. Charles Tobin was therefore born with a golden spoon in his mouth, though the history of the family was not without its share of pain.

John Tobin, the founder of the dynasty, was one of the last convicts to arrive in New South Wales, on the convict ship 'Parkfield' from Sheerness, near London in 1839. After his seven years servitude (for thieving) he earned his certificate of freedom. When John Tobin was freed in 1846, he worked on a sheep farm for a couple of years and then became involved in the Australian Gold Rush.

The first discovery of gold in south east Australia had been in the early 1800's, in the States of New South Wales and Victoria. Several names appear in the records, including those of men of the cloth – such as the Reverend W B Clarke - who were in Australia to minister to the prison population and the government employees overseeing the penal colony.

The first properly verified discovery of gold in the colonies was by Assistant Surveyor, James McBrien, who in 1823 discovered gold in Fish River, about 15 miles east of Bathurst, New South Wales, though there were rumours that convicts cutting a road to Bathurst had discovered gold several years before that. Convicts were closely involved in the gold mining business but convicts discovering or mining gold was not a situation that the authorities were at all happy about, fearing murder and robbery as the lure of the yellow metal further corrupted the already-corrupt. So, licensing was introduced by Governor Charles Fitzroy to impose some sort of control structure and the first official gold mining licence was issued in Victoria, in September 1851 – the year that the Australian Gold Rush started, at Ophir.

In 1872, the world's then largest ever reef gold nugget was discovered by a German prospector, Bernhard Otto Holterman, at Hill End in New South Wales. The massive nugget weighed 286 kg (630 lb), and intensified the gold fever as the prospecting and mining grew exponentially.

John Tobin's son, Zack, was the product of his liaison with a convict called Aileen Keeley, who had been transported from Dublin on the 'Margaret', arriving in Port Jackson (now Sydney) on 17th August 1840.

John Tobin's mining claim, near Bendigo in Victoria, prospered, but the original trigger discovery at Ophir closed after a short time. Gold was being widely discovered across Victoria and New South Wales, and within a short time Australia was mining one third of the world's annual gold production.

At the age of thirty, working on his father's small mining claim, Zack became involved in a fight with another miner and nearly died from infections following wounds inflicted by a shovel, but the other man died of a broken neck. There were several well-paid witnesses who testified that this was self defence and Zack was acquitted of murder. His young wife, Mary, died giving birth to the twins Brayden and Lang Tobin, three months later.

Lang Tobin (Charles Tobin's grandfather), survived the Gallipoli campaign against the Turks amidst the 28,000 Australians killed or wounded; he and his brother had been a part of the Battle of Lone Pine when Australians won seven Victoria Crosses. Brayden, serving alongside his twin brother in the 7th battalion, 1st Division of the Australian Imperial Force, was killed, just three days before the 7th was withdrawn to Egypt in December 1915.

Brayden Lang was the older, by seven minutes, but no one could explain why these two brothers had left the small gold mine that their grandfather John had established, to volunteer for the Army, and Lang never discussed the matter. The family, however, believed that Lang, realising that Brayden, as the oldest, would inherit the business, signed up so that he could go and make his mark in another sphere; following that, Brayden felt that he could not let his younger brother go off to war without him, and signed up the following day. Outsiders, perhaps more rationally, remarked that Zack Tobin was a drunkard, beat his sons (and others) and that the mine was destined to failure with Zack in control.

In March 1916, the 7th Battalion was shipped from Egypt to the Western Front in northern France. Lang was again fortunate to survive that dreadful carnage, but, during the Battle of Pozières in the Somme, he was wounded by shrapnel and lost his left hand. He returned to Australia and struggled to re-learn to write (the brothers had both been left handed). He had a hook fitted in place of his missing hand.

*

When he was twenty five, a year after his return from the Somme, Lang's father Zack died of cyanide poisoning following an accident during his early attempts to use heap-leaching to extract the gold from the ore. Lang assumed control of Tobin Gold, the small mining business outside Bendigo in Victoria. His father's liking for alcohol (which would eventually have killed him, but the cyanide came first) resulted in poor management of the business, frequent fights with the miners he employed, and a parlous financial plight.

Lang set about reviving the fortunes of the mine – his time in France had shown him the power of the internal combustion engine and he could foresee how it might be harnessed to increase the scale and efficiency of mining operations beyond that offered by steam driven traction engines which were relatively immobile and heavy.

During the next 20 years, the mine prospered as a result of his business acumen and enlightened approach to managing his staff – his time in the trenches at Lone Pine in Gallipoli had illustrated starkly, in his eyes, the equality of men, and how comradeship and effective leadership could together be used to produce results in the harshest of conditions. Despite his enlightened attitude there were still disagreements and fights amongst his workforce – hard bitten, hard drinking and hard gambling men. But, amongst these men, Lang's word was law. 'Swinging a hook' was a literal event if Lang had to step in and sort out a problem physically, and that did not happen very often.

In his mid thirties, when the business - now called Tobin Minerals - was expanding successfully, Lang met and married Susan Etheridge. Unlike Lang's antecedents, Susan's lineage came down through the civil service which ran the colony of Australia. They bought land and built a homestead outside Bendigo, and started a family. Anne was born first and died in her infancy from diphtheria, David followed and finally Suzanne, who carried the names both of her mother and deceased sister. The business continued to prosper and grow – Lang was an innovator and constantly striving to improve production efficiency and yields.

In 1940, at the age of eleven, the remaining son David was despatched to Geelong Grammar School one hundred miles south of Bendigo – one of the most illustrious schools in Australia - as would befit the son of a successful businessman. He completed his secondary education there, followed by a degree in Mining at the University of New South Wales in Sydney. Armed with a first class degree and a shrewd brain, he joined the family business in 1961 and set about helping his father develop it further, expanding operations into Western Australia where lower yield land was cheap, and iron ore mining was opening up in the Pilbara area. Though the family's focus was firmly fixed on gold, Lang and David knew that if their business was to grow faster, then branching out into other minerals would have to be considered.

Whilst the gold at Bendigo in Victoria (where the family business had started) was found in quartz reef systems (held within highly deformed mudstones and sandstones or washed away into channels of ancient, long dried up rivers) the shortage of water in Western Australia meant that dry mining techniques were being used and refined there, and the emerging developments were ideal for a bright young miner to earn his spurs. David Tobin was despatched to Coolgardie and set about searching for mine owners willing to sell their holdings.

The company acquired a bankrupt deep mining operation near Kalgoorlie, the first hard rock mining venture for the company. It was an opportunity for David, the first properly qualified mining engineer in the family, to open up another avenue and prove himself.

David married and set up the family home in Perth, about 375 miles west of Kalgoorlie, and in 1970, Charles was born. His mother Judith suffered from pre-eclampsia during the pregnancy, and although Charles was healthy, she was advised to have no more children.

*

Andjela's Story – Paris

In Zürich, Maruška spent the next few days letting the wound on her arm heal and improving her French skills with the CD and phrasebook. On the Thursday, she checked out of the Hotel Leoneck and caught a train to Paris. Travel on trains across Europe was much less conspicuous than on planes – following the 9/11 attacks in New York, that year the level of security at airports was intolerable as the world got to grips with the new terrorist threat, and air travel was not an option anyway with a Glock pistol in one's baggage. Even at railway stations, the heightened security was evident at that time as a consequence of widespread governmental paranoia.

In Paris she found a small, quiet hotel and checked in using her French identity. Her language and accent were certainly not those of a young French woman, but she passed this off with a shrug about being the daughter of an absent French seaman and a Greek mother, and having been brought up in Athens.

Over the next month she sought and rented a four room apartment on the Rue Llomond in Le Quartier Latin. With a large transient student population and busy café lined streets, the area lent itself well to anonymity. She intended to blend in quickly and improved her French language skills rapidly with a couple of French language courses. Her bedtime reading was in French and very focused. She devoured the life of Ilich Ramirez Sanchez – The Jackal. His origins were in Islamist terrorism, and he had been formally trained by Iraqi military staff in Lebanon. Although she had not that formal training, her 'on the job' experience was second to none, though skills in the technical use of explosives would not be easy to acquire. She knew what she liked doing and was missing it, but accepted that this period of consolidation and preparation was essential at this stage.

Had Carlos been motivated originally by religion or socialism? It was not entirely clear from what she had read. Her own original motivation – revenge for the killing of her parents – was no longer a driving force. That shocking experience and its aftermath during the gross inhumanity of the war in the Balkans had dehumanised her and on any scale of psychological assessment, her persona would be clearly psychopathic. Psychiatric professionals would say that there was very probably a neurological component present from birth which predisposed her to psychopathic behaviour. That may, or may not, have been the case with Andjela/ Maruška/ Senka/ Marie/ Gisela, but that she exhibited the symptoms to the extent which went far beyond those of someone with an antisocial personality disorder was beyond doubt. The variety of identities she used was nothing to do with any kind of schizoid behaviour – she was always well grounded in who she was. The plethora of identities was just one facet of her manipulative skills as a psychopath.

She didn't recognise it then, but this variety of identities was a weakness, and would, eventually, almost lead to her undoing.

*

During her time in Paris, Maruška's French improved rapidly and she took breaks in several parts of France. Her life was intense – physical exercise, reading and trying to catch up on a missed education, but it was all directed towards one end. For physical exercise she varied her programme – she liked to run along the Seine on clear mornings and fine summer evenings; she joined a gym - Club Quartier Latin with its renowned Piscine Pontoise - and a martial arts club. As a child she had skied on the family's farm in Serbia - albeit on makeshift skis and thong bindings - so she took a week's skiing in the Alps in the late spring followed up by a couple of weeks in a climbing school.

In the Piscine Pontoise she improved her poor swimming and then flew to Corsica. Over a couple of weeks she learned open water diving at a diving school in Ajaccio and she spent time learning how to handle a small boat at a sailing school based in Port Napoleon near Marseilles.

All this time she was consolidating her French persona and giving herself an all round range of skills for her planned future. As a talented but untrained linguist she was all the time picking up on dialects wherever she visited. She recognised that she was clever, though her incomplete education had meant that her intellect was not trained, but was developing by experience and instinctual analysis. Now she added a self-directed learning component. Maruška would have passed for borderline genius had her IQ been measured, and would have been diagnosed as presenting many symptoms of clinical psychopathy, had she been analysed. She was hungry for life, learning and adrenaline.

In the evenings, there were several lesbian bars she frequented, preferring La Champmeslé on Rue Chabanais above the others. Smart and sophisticated, it was well established. The oldest though, was Chez Moune on rue Jean Baptiste in the Pigalle, having opened in 1936, and this was another regular haunt for her.

She usually – but not exclusively or entirely - took on her Senka persona for those evenings, and never took anyone back to her own apartment. Her sexual behaviour with her female lovers was necessarily more restrained during this period of her life. She kept the affairs brief and kept her violent instincts at bay. Despite the very physical athletic life style she led at this time, and the sexual release of her affairs, she still recognised a need for release which she could only satisfy in one way.

This she found with male S&M partners met at clubs. These were never more than one night stands (or tiedowns) as the partners would never have wanted to repeat the experience. She did not leave them permanently damaged physically, though some might bear mental scars for a considerable time, and some would reassess whether their fetish was really worth further pursuit.

As a reminder of what she believed was her destiny, she kept copies of the various books that detailed what was known about The Jackal; in each room of her apartment there was a constant source of inspiration. For her, though, terrorism was the be-all and end-all – there was simply no higher religious or political calling in her makeup - spiritual and emotional were terms which just did not apply to her psyche.

By the autumn of 2003, she was ready for the next step, and it was from Paris that she initiated contact.

*

It was not a telephone call that Maruška made, nor was it an email. Just a simple note posted to a mail service in Geneva. The note requested that the enclosed envelope be forwarded to Herr Michael Mannesman with a confirmatory reference number.

For a regular mercenary, there are straightforward ways of finding work such as signing up with an agency, signing up with a 'security company' or networking through ex-forces colleagues.

During the last couple of years of her time in Serbia, when, as Andjela, she had been running Vidovic's Seventh Leg – the mercenary leg – she had both worked in, and supplied, teams of mercenaries to such agencies for a variety of operations, some in the public notice, some unrecorded, dead and buried. Fire fights in central African states, insurrections in Central America or being a bodyguard in Afghanistan were bread and butter jobs for most mercenaries and had been profitable for the Seventh Leg. She had had no regular forces training herself, except combat drills and specific weapons training (even including a Stinger missile when the US was using Predator drones against Serbians during Operation Noble Anvil in 1999); neither had she been trained to be a regular mercenary - such work was of no interest to her and that was not the work that she sought for her foreseeable future – and she recognised gaps in her capabilities and knowledge which she wanted to rectify.

Mannesmann's background was in the East German special forces. After the re-unification of Germany he had opted to go freelance – he saw many potentially lucrative opportunities across the world as the old communist orders collapsed and localised power struggles and criminal clashes ensued. The Balkans, for example, was one such area. Andjela had met Michael

Mannesmann in Serbia, when he had been engaged by Vidovic to provide professional weapons training to the SNP, during the time when Vidovic was transforming his gang into a viable paramilitary group.

They formed a mutual professional respect for one another, and it might have gone further if Andjela's sexual proclivities and personality had been more orthodox. Mannesmann marked her out (as indeed had Vidovic) as having great promise for the future, though her enjoyment of killing he saw as a possible problem – mental detachment was important for a professional, emotional perspectives clouded a soldier's judgement. Andjela was still in her mid-teens at the time, and whilst the pleasure of killing was developing in her, uncertainty about her own sexual identity had not resolved. She had felt a strong physical need for Mannesmann, and he enjoyed a brief affair with her during his six week assignment with the SNP. They spent time together during the exercises and he identified her as the most capable to be trained as the future trainer for the group. He also started to teach her some German language basics – her aptitude was clear, and soon her lexicon of German oaths was extensive.

The affair was her first penetrative sexual experience with a man, and Andjela did not enjoy the event. It served only to clarify in her mind that she did not like sharing herself with a man, even though Mannesmann had (atypically for him) been tender and understanding. She found that there was little emotional feeling on her part, but in keeping with her thirst for knowledge, she enjoyed their discussions about weapons and tactics and his stories about his time with the GDR special forces. The affair did make her realise, though, that there could be another side to men, after all the rape and torture she had witnessed with her squad. Her brief time with Mannesmann led to the understanding that for her, sex with men was a tool to be used by her, and nothing more.

*

It was six weeks later that the reply came – a not unusual timescale given the nature of the work Michael Mannesman did. Intervals of as much as six months were not uncommon, and sometimes the replies never came and the men never came home. As Andjela, she called the number given and the meeting was set up.

Some basic preparations were now necessary and she rented another apartment in the name of Maruška Pavkovic. It was off the Rue de Simplon in the 18th Arondissement, where there was a large Serbian community. This would be her working address. She moved some basics in and carefully set up her cover. For the next few months she would close up her other apartment and live here. There were dangers living in the Serbian area, but she was confident that as it was almost two years since she had left

Serbia, she would be unlikely to be recognised now. Those who had known her really did think that Andjela Karanovic was dead anyway, and the tattoo was no more. The Serb community here did not enjoy the best of reputations with the French, and she didn't really want to be a part of it – in no way did she consider herself a patriot, but living here was necessary for business, at least for the next several months.

Two weeks after the email, she took a train from Paris-Nord station to Brussels-Midi and met Michael Mannesmann outside the Hennes and Mauritz department store on the Rue Neuve precisely at 11.20 am on the first Tuesday in December, 2002.

There were snow flurries in the air interspersed with a feeble winter sun as they met. She had to touch him on the arm – he had not recognised her. They embraced, rather formally, he rather awkwardly, with the typical French cheek kiss – '*faire la bise*', outside the department store, and set off in search of a café.

The conversation was banal – trains, planes and journeys, he from Munich, she from Paris – as they sought somewhere suitably secure for their discussion.

Finally, settled in to a warm corner with cappuccinos, and she with a Danish pastry, Michael started, quietly, in German:

"*Schatzi*, I was very surprised – overjoyed actually - when I got your note – I had heard that you were dead - tortured and assassinated in Belgrade. You look so different, wonderful, the change is *unglaublich*."

"Well, as you can see, it is not true that I am dead. I have other plans and needed to move away from my history. I am now Marie, and Michael, if you please, I do not like to be called *Schatzi* – darling. It is really good to see you - I learned a lot from you, for which I thank you, but those days are over. I am now looking for work – occasional, international, and what I am good at. You know what that is, and I thought you probably have connections which could help me."

"Well, Andjela - sorry – Marie, we could always work together you know, we would make a very good team. It's much easier in my business for a man and woman to operate, and more effective. I have been looking for a good partner. There would not have to be anything else than professional respect if you do not want it."

"It is an interesting idea Michael, but I really need to do this myself. You used to talk about professional emotional detachment. I would be detached, but I am not sure you ever could be. You and I have our history, which I think would get in the way of your professionalism. Not good."

Michael smiled and nodded his head slowly. "Yes, you are probably right. I have very good memories of our time together – probably too good - and I hope you do too."

Marie ignored the comment and continued, focused as always "So, Michael, can you help me – is there any interesting work for me?"

"Yes there could be. How do you feel about working for a foreign government?"

"I will work for anyone who pays me what I'm worth and gives me assignments which I enjoy. I have no feelings either way about who it is, except those scum the Bosnian Muslims. I have no government anyway, they are foreign for me. Look at Serbia, how many governments did we have?"

"OK, I understand. I will see what I can do to make an introduction for you."

"Thank you Michael, I couldn't ask for more, except that you don't give away any information that points back to Andjela."

"Marie, they will need to check you out, I must give them something, tell them how I met you, where you can be contacted, and so on."

"It was to be expected, obviously I accept that. Keep your story accurate, but give them the name of Maruška Pavkovic. My address in Paris is off the Rue de Simplon, 18th Arondissement."

"That's useful. I will pass it on to the people I know. They work for Peking, or Beijing, as they now call it."

*

After the meeting in Brussels, Maruška returned to Paris. The suggestion that there might be work for the Chinese had intrigued her, and she spent a couple of weeks researching the country, the people and the national *zeitgeist*. Western companies were queuing up to open manufacturing plants and joint ventures with the local movers and shakers. Political control was still rigid, but the need to unleash local ambition and enterprise had been recognised and was being accelerated. She assumed that Michael's allusion was to the Chinese intelligence services, and she researched that topic, coming across the name 'Guoanbu', though there was little available on the web at that time. At the library, she discovered some political position papers in two obscure journals which were published in Washington D.C. These papers discussed the Chinese 'Golden Shield' strategy.

The 'Triads' came up in her research too, though she discounted them as being the source of Michael's work – like the Mafia, they tended to use their own people for wet work, though not exclusively.

A month after the Brussels meeting, she received an email from Michael which said that things were progressing, but she should be patient as 'our clients take a long term view and proceed with great care and thought'. It would probably take a few more weeks before they could proceed further, if at all. The Chinese connection had intrigued her, and what she had read had certainly conveyed the sense of 'the long view' and patience of the Chinese peoples – or at least, their rulers. Politically, there was impatience from the Chinese people for change – the ordinary workers did not have a long view, they were concerned about their 'here and now'. Their rulers were resistant to change and tried to ease the pressure with gradual reform.

It was now deep January in Paris, and Marie decided to take a break – purely research, of course – and booked a two week tourist visit to Shanghai and Beijing.

As usual when she travelled, she made an effort to acquire some basic language skills in the country. This trip would be no exception, particularly if she was to have an ongoing working relationship with Chinese clients.

She returned to Paris in late February – it was only slightly warmer there than it had been in Beijing. Her trip had given her time to think about the situation with Michael and whether he was, in fact, holding her at bay, seeing her as a threat to his own contract work. She wondered about this, but then concluded that he would not have mentioned the Chinese if that had been his intention. Of course, it might all have been a fiction anyway.

In early March, Michael 'came through'. He said that he had always wanted to see Paris in April, and would meet her there to discuss a project. Marie was impatient, but Michael said that it could not be sooner, and they met in the first week of April.

*

They were seated in a moderately expensive restaurant on the Rue St Honoré. It was 8.30 on a Thursday evening in the first week of April, the clocks had gone forward the previous weekend and the diners were out in force in what was a classic April evening in Paris – the sort of evening that travel writers revel in – a clear sky with a hint of warmth and the promise of better to come, the joy of spring detectable in the evensong of the birds. They sat at a corner table and there was little danger of them being overheard in the regular bustle and the overlaid conversation of a group of four American tourists a couple of tables away. Nor was there any danger of romance, sadly, Michael realised.

"It's quite simple, Marie, and makes good sense," he was saying as they sipped champagne with their oysters. "There is plenty of work for us both. When I started I was doing a couple of jobs a year. Now I am almost full time. The money is good and I could retire tomorrow, but as you can imagine the stress is very considerable, planning and executing each operation. Less time for preparation, more danger of mistakes, not good. I am really glad you will be involved. Maybe it will ease the pressure on me.

They have had to check you out, based on what I told them, and that took time. They are very careful people and they seem to be satisfied. You will need to work directly for them. I cannot know what you are doing and we must have no more contact again. Basic security. You didn't want to work with me anyway."

"That's fine then Michael. How do we go on from here?"

He took a small box out of his attaché case, wrapped in gift wrap with a ribbon around it, and passed it across the table. "This is a secure phone which they gave me for you. They will be in touch. As you probably guess, they have a GPS tag in it, so they know where it is at all times. They might even be listening to us now – I don't know for sure, though it is in a box" he said with a smile. "I don't know the number and don't want to. Now, is there anything else, before we get the next course?"

"Yes there is actually. Something that is a gap in my knowledge. I need to train in the use *plastique*. I never worked with it, and want to learn."

"OK, I will think about what I can do to help, though I shouldn't really. I will make some enquiries and maybe provide a name. Do you remember our first night in the forest outside Pristina? Yes?"

Marie nodded, a dark look on her face.

"Good, then if I arrange the, hmmm, shall we call it, 'educational' opportunity, that you want, then that phrase will be used. Michael repeated it:

Where was the first night?

In the forest outside Pristina.

The question and answer should be exact. If there is any variation either way then there will be no meeting."

Marie nodded. "I don't like your choice of phrase."

"That's what will be used. Now, that's enough business, shall we enjoy our supper?"

They shared a Chateaubriand and followed with ripe Camembert, rounding off with an antique brandy. It was just after 10.30 pm when they left the restaurant, and the Rue St. Honoré was intense with traffic and people.

"Marie, I'm in Paris for a few days more, seeing the sights and I wish you would accompany me."

"We can't do that - you already told me we must have no more contact." She had no intention of spending one moment more than was necessary in his company.

"*Ja,* of course, you are quite correct. It is strange – I have never been here before, but it is good at least to go somewhere where I am not being looked for. Everyone in our profession should keep at least one or two clean countries."

"Yes" said Marie, "but it is becoming difficult to do that as more and more countries cooperate and share their data, so quickly too."

"*Jawohl*, the world is getting smaller and faster. For people like you and me there are new challenges every day, just to stay alive and do our jobs. Anyway, it is a great pity you cannot show me the sights, but I am sure I can easily find a guide in this romantic city," Michael said with a wink. "*Bonsoir et bon chance. Au revoir, ma chère.*" The French, spoken with his coarse German accent, grated on her ear, but she failed to smile and responded in kind, minus the 'darling'. With that, he crossed the road and hailed a cab.

That bastard, choosing that phrase. She would have to wait again to be contacted, but once that had happened then she could cover her trail. It was frustrating, being reliant on other people. Still, she had a gift to open, she thought as she got on to the Metro for Simplon. Progress at last.

*

Three days after she had met Michael Mannesmann in the restaurant and received the parcel, she was in a café reading the second edition of 'Paris Soir' when a text came through on her throwaway mobile phone, autoforwarded from the Chinese phone hidden under a floorboard in her apartment off the Rue de Simplon. She took the metro to Simplon station, and walked the half kilometre to her third floor apartment.

She took the phone out from its cache. Missed call, number withheld. Then it rang again half an hour later. She answered and there was a message spoken with what sounded to be a female, computer generated voice. It merely said, in Serbian "Don't make any arrangements for July."

At the end of April, she received a letter at Rue Simplon, addressed to Maruška Pavkovic. She didn't like seeing the name in writing, but there was little she could do. The envelope contained a slip of paper with a telephone number. Using a pay as you go mobile phone, which she replaced weekly, and always after sensitive calls, she rang the number and a man answered, speaking English with an accent which she didn't recognise (it was actually Irish).

"Hello, my name is .." she started

"No names" he cut across her. She felt like a fool.

"Where was the first night?"

"In the forest outside Pristina."

"Good."

The meeting was arranged. It took place in a café on the Rue Boutebrie off the Boulevard St Germain, a week later. Then in the middle of May, Maruška flew to Palermo in Sicily, and after a few days sightseeing, took a cabin on the weekly ferry to Tunis. She was finding the slow progress and lack of excitement very trying. Always waiting, waiting, too much time to think, not enough doing, not enough excitement. Although Tunis was relatively, a secular country, it was her first contact with an Arab way of life, and the Islamic overtones brought back feelings that she thought she had forgotten about – maybe it was the Serbian fascist streak that was innate in her, implanted in her childhood and nurtured during the war. On the appointed day, she left Tunis in her hired 4x4 and drove south to Dehiba Dahibah, near the Libyan border, where she was met by the Irishman. Again, she was reminded of that first night in the forest outside Pristina, and was asked for the fee – twenty five thousand dollars, which she handed over. As they drove across the border at 2 am the next morning in an old lorry carrying boxes of whisky, she planned a farewell evening with Michael Mannesmann.

She spent the next ten days in a training camp in the Libyan desert with an Irishman who introduced himself as Brendan Keenan "just for the next few days." There were nine other people on the training course – only one other was a woman, whom she thought might have been Egyptian. The men were a mixture of Greek, German, Italian and Turkish, as far as she could tell. There was one Arab who might have been Moroccan or Algerian. They each chose a simple name for themselves, to use during their stay.

The course was surprisingly well organised, with classroom sessions, videos (even of actual car bomb explosions), discussions of explosive types, blast radii, shrapnel and simple bomb construction. They were told that the advanced bomb making course was optional, though there was currently a vacancy for a 'teacher'. Brendan Keenan told them, face deadpan, that "the previous teacher of the advanced course has met with an accident and there are no further courses scheduled at present."

Bombs for killing, the use of explosives for destroying bridges and other infrastructure – the course was certainly comprehensive. They were taught about explosives detection, sniffer dogs and biosensors used at airports, and how to remove explosives traces and confuse sniffers – both technology and dogs. Then, after the first three days, practical sessions started.

Apart from the food, Marie enjoyed her time there. The days when trainees had to hide from satellite overflights were long gone. This was before the democracy riots that had destabilised North Africa and the Middle East. Gadaffi was still in power and the US was on more friendly terms with him. US satellites tasked for the Middle East were fully committed over the Yemen, Afghanistan, Pakistan and Iran. Nevertheless, Libya was tribal and the now elderly and infirm Gadaffi had key supporters still to look after, so the training businesses in the desert (and other illicit, illegitimate and downright illegal enterprises) run by his cronies, continued.

For the trip back to Paris, she took a different route from Tunis, via Malta and Madrid in Spain. She realised that they were at least as careful as she was herself, as she reflected on the complex path she had taken after deciding to leave Belgrade. If she was to be as effective as Ilich Ramirez

Sanchez – the Jackal – had been, then secrecy, disguise and 'no tracks' would have to be the norm. He had eventually been caught, but she did not intend to end up in a prison anywhere. And, she still had some tracks to cover.

*

Tobin Dynasty – Maturity

Within five years of David Tobin's move to Perth with his family, it was clear that the expansion was proving to be a mistake for Tobin Minerals. Servicing the capital investment required to turn the mine around, leveraged on the company's reserves, was almost terminal as gold prices turned down and the value of the reserves fell. Gold mining in Western Australia as a whole was turning down, and would eventually reach its nadir in 1976 (with gold production in the State less than one tenth of the level of that in 1900). Yields were falling as the earlier more lucrative reserves were mined out and poorer quality ores were much less economic to refine with the then current level of chemical and process technology available. New technology was being developed, but the business sentiment had turned against gold.

David, Judith and the young Charles moved back to Bendigo and Tobin Minerals (Western Australia) Pty Ltd put its mining operations into care and maintenance.

At Bendigo, Suzanne had been carving a name for herself as a mining manager, despite not having taken a degree in mining and her parents' desire to raise her genteelly. Her toughness had evolved rapidly in the vacuum left by David's departure to the west, and her desire to achieve and prove herself superior was all consuming. She could drink with the toughest of miners, and was not even averse to using her fists occasionally. They were a practical family with increasing social aspirations, but Suzanne's interests lay solely in proving herself in a man's world – she had no wish to become the typical Australian 'Sheila' or some Australian version of an English rose.

Needless to say, with the return of David and his young family to Bendigo, there were considerable strains in the family and in the business, and the infighting was becoming a distraction. Lang was struggling to maintain harmony between his children and ensure that the focus was on developing the business, but the family rift widened steadily over the years.

Then in 1978, nickel was discovered in Western Australia. This proved to be the saviour of the goldfields, and probably of the family. Once again, David was despatched westward (with the full support of his wife, who was glad to return home from the battlefront at Bendigo) to re-invigorate the Tobin Minerals business there with expansion into nickel production. Activated carbon technology and elution was just being developed for gold ore refining and David Tobin led the company's charge in improving the process as he expanded the company on two fronts.

However, it was not easy on the family side, as Charles, now approaching secondary school age, was a difficult and headstrong boy, and his father was four hundred miles away in Kalgoorlie most of the time. He had attended several primary schools and two high schools, proving to be intelligent but almost impossible to control, and it was the absence of his father that most child psychologists would say was fundamental to the shaping of his character. Though he was not as intellectually gifted as his father, he was a capable rugby player and cricketer but his wilfulness and arrogance did not make him naturally popular with his team mates, even at that formative age.

Finally despatched to Geelong Grammar School, as his father had been before him, he continued to excel at sport but came close to expulsion on two occasions – once for smoking dope (it was rumoured that a classmate had shopped him) and on another occasion for having been caught in a local bar with a girl. He was punished regularly. During his time at Geelong his business abilities developed and flourished. Smoking dope was one thing (the untrustworthy classmate had been identified and beaten by Tobin), but he traded it, very profitably. He was skilled at making a little go a long way – as he would in the future do with gold and other mineral ores.

Whilst in the sixth form he invested his profits from the dope trading on the Sydney Stock Exchange, and on horse racing. The dope trading business itself he franchised out to a schoolchum and took a share of the profits for no risk. When his dealing friend was caught and sent to Borstal (a young offenders institution), Tobin himself was in the clear - he did not take any fall, having seen it as inevitable in a small city. He continued to enjoy success on all fronts, being popular with his sporting contemporaries for prowess – batting at No 2 in the cricket team, and playing as a sterling No 8 in the rugby team, he was invaluable; his largesse with his profits and winnings ensured a regular coterie of hangers-on, both male and female, and although his activities on the turf and the Stock Exchange were probably known to the school authorities, a blind eye seemed to have been turned. After all, gambling was an institution in Australia, and investment on the Stock Exchange was nothing more than developing business acumen. Charles Tobin seemed to be King Midas, but his arrogance and wilfulness grew steadily more pronounced, his drinking parties grew wilder, and he had no really close personal friends.

Before he reached eighteen years of age, his activities with the opposite sex had involved at least one abortion that his parents were aware of. Fortunately – if this event could in any way be deemed fortunate – this had come to light in Perth, and not whilst he was up at Geelong. His arrogant, confident magnetism continued to attract the girls even after this scandal, but he did at least learn from this carelessness on his part.

Given the scope of his extra-curricular and sporting activities, it was no surprise that he failed to achieve university entrance standards at the first attempt. He did eventually get to the University of Sydney where he gained a disappointing second class honours degree in Economics in 1992, rejecting further education in the family mining tradition.

Arrogant, confident, self sufficient, strategically cunning with an ability to do deals and to trade, he was well equipped to become a successful entrepreneur. He also seemed to be one of those lucky people who could fall into the proverbial and come up smelling of roses. Statistically, it is inevitable that there will be a few in every generation, and he certainly seemed to be one of them.

He further rejected the family background when he announced that he was departing for Alaska to make his own fortune. This was an echo, perhaps even a genetic trait, reflecting his grandfather's decision to leave the family when he went to fight in the first world war.

*

Djibouti – Overtures

In Vauxhall Cross, Booth certainly held the attention of his audience. The shocked atmosphere was palpable. These things happened – just look at Enigma in the Second World War. Disadvantage turned to major opportunity.

He continued...

"So, how do we nail down the facts and turn this around? We've been working on it for some time, but recent events in Yemen have presented an opportunity.

Our Embassy in Sana'a is one of the suspect posts, complete with nearby Chinese bazaar. The bazaar appears to have rather too many Chinese coming and going at all hours for a small bazaar, and it also has delivery vans. Satellite recon has shown that the walled roof garden has a couple of dish arrays – don't they all – but this looks like much more than is needed to watch the Hong Kong races. Detailed photo analysis of shadow angles and so on suggests one dish for our satellite, and another for a Chinese comms satellite. So far, so good. The problem is what are they doing with the traffic data? We've set up listening and broad spectrum EMF monitoring from a flat across the road, but we're not getting anything meaningful out of there. Seems that they've got the interior of the bazaar's upper floors well screened.

Then, we put GPS tags on the vans and something really interesting emerged when we looked at the vans' routing. One of the vans rarely moved, but when it did, it was parked for several hours within a hundred yards of our embassy on each occasion. There were no deliveries or collections. The other van would, at the same time be parked up a side street nearby.

Our man on the ground then did the business and arranged an RTA – road traffic accident - with a local lorry driver. Ripped the van open like a sardine can right on cue at a junction, except it wasn't steel – it was plastic. Perfect. We managed to get a video clip and some rather good stills of the inside of the van from across the road. The Chinese were very quick to smooth things over with the truck driver, threw a rug over the inside of the back of the van, a bundle of baksheesh for the policeman too.

We were not sure exactly what we filmed inside, but "we passed the video and stills to analysts, and we now think we know what it was" the Senior officer said.

"We're calling it an EM Pulse Gun. A big one." Mr C continued his nodding, silent agreement.

Very simply, it fires a very narrow, very powerful pulse of electromagnetic radiation, disruptive range maybe a couple of hundred yards. The plastic panelwork on the van was the clincher – steel would have depowered the pulse – and gave our techies the idea. They're a bright lot.

Anyway, we think that the Chinese are using what apparently is known as a power fault based attack on our cryptographic system at the embassy. The pulse gun creates a very brief ripple in our computers' power supplies, and if this is done whilst we are running a decode, then it can enable them to crack our private keys at the embassy end; so, they sit in the van, get the nod from the bazaar that we've incoming traffic and zap, they ripple our system with the EMP gun. Only lasts microseconds, and the computer is only very briefly affected – it seems that it corrects itself – has to - as chips these days are sensitive even to cosmic rays.

They do need very sensitive monitoring equipment to pick up the EM buzz from our equipment when they zap us, hence the other delivery van for recording. Seems there's a bit of risk to our staff too, though we've checked them and no problems found so far.

We have Tempest-standard electromagnetic screening around the comms rooms to prevent this, in theory – even the windows are coated, but the EMP pulse goes through this metal screening, exploiting the imperfections in its manufacture and jointing, which cause it to re-radiate the signal. The lower tier embassies are not screened to the latest standard, hence our vulnerability. Apparently, PCs now use processors so fast that the wavelength they generate gets out through the screening and that's what they monitor. We carefully and innocuously checked a few of our embassies – it seems that there are plants in the gardens which have a very wide mesh of spider-web-thin platinum in their foliage and this is being used to reradiate signals they pick up. Bloody gardeners – you can't trust anyone!

In Sana'a, our embassy has a virile bougainvillea growing around the windows on the east side – that's the side nearest to our computer server room. We found such an aerial spread within the flowers. It is an active multi segment aerial – it seems that some of the apparent wires are solar collectors, so it's self powering. Amazing technology, but of course we don't want to take it apart yet. Needless to say, our top tier embassies are reviewing their gardening arrangements.

And it gets worse. Our PCs use chips manufactured in China and our techies believe that they have a higher predisposition to power ripple faults, deliberately designed in. Damned chips are so small that they could also build transmitters in without us knowing. That's a real worry. We can of course ensure that we buy only US chips, but they are probably doing the same, or farming them out to China themselves.

They need a lot of computing power to do the private key reverse analysis on a useful timescale, and break our codes, so we think that they just pump it out to Beijing using the other dish, where they've got unlimited people and computing power to throw at it.

There's a lot we can do to prevent this, but it could be useful for us as is right now – turn it back on the buggers."

He turned to Mr Cheltenham and said "If you're happy that my technical briefing was accurate, then I shan't detain you any further. I'm sure this situation has given your guys plenty to think about and you'll need to get back." Mr Cheltenham stood up, nodded, they shook hands. An escort arrived to control him out of Vauxhall Cross.

Now, David, for the next step, we've planned a small operation..."

*

"I'm just about to leave actually," said Steve.

The stranger held out his hand, still smiling, and said "I'm Tom, Tom Brown. Yes, I've heard all the jokes before. You are the guy with Adèle, the sloop at the dock? That's a Roberts design isn't it?"

Steve bridled and ignored the offered hand. Interrupting his breakfast was one thing, but suggesting that his boat was a Bruce Roberts design was bordering on insult. Not that he had anything against Roberts designs, they were good boats. But Adèle was a French design through and through.

"No, she bloody well isn't, she was designed by André Mauric. Now, Mister Brown, you can have the table to yourself."

"Ok, ok. Lympstone 1993 wasn't it?" the stranger said, rather quietly.

Steve stopped in his tracks and looked again at Tom Brown. The stance was assured and could have been military, his build was compact, but there was no recognition at all in Steve's mind.

"Ok, maybe I will have another coffee" Steve said, "take a pew."

1993, Steve thought. His training at Lympstone with the Royal Marines had been in 1995. So, how did this 'Tom', make a connection?

Steve introduced himself simply as 'Steve', and they ordered coffees.

"Fact is, Steve, I'm looking to crew a boat up the Red Sea and I heard at the dock that you might be going that way."

"I sail alone," said Steve, "no exceptions, not even pretty girls anymore."

"Fair enough, but I'm prepared to contribute to costs – I know that running a boat like Adèle is not cheap, and you'll probably need a lot of fuel for the trip if the Red Sea is true to form."

"Where's Lympstone?" asked Steve.

"On the Avocet Line," Tom replied smoothly.

"Never heard of it."

"You know where it is. There's a special railway station on the line, not for public use, just for the boys with berets. Yes… it was 1995 then, I saw quite a few pass through" fenced Tom. "I think Windy was in your fire team, wasn't he, it's a shame he ended like that?"

"I don't know any Windy."

"Ok, I'm prepared to pay very well for the trip, I have a lot of backing."

"Who?" asked Steve.

"All in good time, Steve," said Tom standing up, "I'll pick up the tab for the coffees." He put a Djiboutian five hundred Franc note on the table and walked away.

*

The problem with living on a boat was keeping properly fit. Although he did calisthenics and some yoga when at sea, most of the poses - asanas – were difficult to hold on a moving platform, and maintaining stamina levels was almost impossible on a small boat. Once he was ashore after a time at sea, Steve always followed an aggressive and rigorous program to recover full fitness, which seemed to be getting harder as he was now approaching 40 years of age.

This morning was typical. Adèle was anchored off the dock near Dolphin Services, the local yacht and boat maintenance business at the Djibouti waterfront. He rowed ashore in the rubber dinghy. There were some young boys on the dock, as always, and he gave them a Franc to watch his dinghy.

He would have liked to have run on the fabled White Sands Beach, but that was 10 miles north, across the Gulf of Tadjoura. That was a little too far to row his 2 metre rubber dinghy in open water, though he was thinking about getting a ferry across come the weekend.

The morning heat was building, and he was glad it was not summer when temperatures could hit 45 centigrade. There was a dry breeze off the desert to the west, but it was too early in the year for the *Khamsin*, which was the local desert wind and often brought dust storms. So, he headed off west along the coast road on the north side of the peninsular, at a steady jog. There were a few runners out and he noticed a couple of particularly hard looking characters – probably guys from the French warship in the docks, he thought. Then, just as he was leaving the last of the housing blocks, a figure ran out from a side road and fell into step with him.

Tom Brown. Steve accelerated and Tom kept pace wordlessly. After half an hour Steve stopped and took out his water bottle. Tom stopped and turned around. Steve offered him the bottle.

"No thanks, I have my own," he said and took his own out of his backpack. "How's the right ankle these days, Steve?"

Steve was taken aback. No one knew about his ankle except those with access to his medical records. The damage to the ankle in a climbing accident had ended his hopes of joining the SBS. Though he could swim as well as any of them, his running endurance was limited by the slight weakness, but that only made him push himself harder. The water stop was timed to give his ankle a rest.

"OK Tom, cut the crap. What's all this about? You know stuff about me that's supposed to be secret."

"Steve, I know a lot more about you than you would believe. The fact is, HMG need some help with a project right now, and I'm here to ask you to help us. The Hereford and Poole outfits are fully stretched what with the problems in Korea on top of everything else, and we can't recruit and train quickly enough. A lot of the career people were disillusioned with the cuts in the forces in 2010 and left the service, we're still trying to fill the gaps. All at the worst time too, with tactics changing on the Al Quaeda side. Whoever heard of sharing a carrier with the French? Anyway, we've got a very urgent small job here in the Red Sea and you've got just the skills we need."

"Look, Tom, I left all that behind a long time ago, so the answer's no."

"Left it behind? That's not what I heard. The Yank destroyer *O'Kane* in the CNTF found two guys half dead in a shot-up RIB last week, well out to sea off Suqutra Island. Their story was very interesting. Shot at from a white yacht, they didn't see anyone aboard so they said. A ghost yacht they called it, frightened half to death they were, it seems, and you don't usually see that in modern day pirates. Strange how you arrived here a couple of days later too. Fresh paint in places as well – you might say Adèle has some beauty spots. Anyway, the pay is good, it will make the long trip up Suez more interesting."

Steve capped his water bottle and set off at a jog back along the road without a word.

A few minutes later, Tom overtook him and ran ahead and disappeared into the town.

*

The briefing in Vauxhall Cross continued:

"If this works, this operation will be one for the textbooks. We want to put video transmitters in the Chinese Naval Base in Aden. Specifically we want to install them in the cooling grilles of the electric forklift trucks and cargo tugs used for moving stores and weapons around the base. These have their batteries charged up overnight in a parking bay in the open under a tin roof. These machines have access inside all the warehouses and bunkers, and even dockside. The equipment is very compact and is polled nightly from a transmitter in a nearby safe house. This downloads the data every night. We are targeting four machines – two forklifts and two tugs.

What I really like about this is that the electronics and cameras we are using are Chinese. That's really sweet, isn't it?"

The senior officer continued with some sarcasm:

"As you know, we're at full stretch around the globe in this brave new asymmetric world our masters have created and we've been trawling our databases to find out who we can bring in to help. We need someone who's expendable and our SAS or SBS lads would not want to be seen that way, even if they could be spared. We're certainly not putting our own people in line for this. Most of the people who left after the cuts in 2010 have gone private and joined one of the private security firms working in Korea, Iraq, Iran and all the other hotspots the politicos have stoked up.

Our database has come up with a name – a Steve Baldwin. Ex RM, no family. Tough lad, seems he would probably have made special services if he'd been given the opportunity. An experienced Yemen hand too – he's got some heavy history there, cover stayed intact. Anyway, we've run his passport and it was last scanned in Djibouti. Seems he's bang slap in-theatre, or in the wings anyway. That's why you are here David, and why I've given you a full briefing.

You need to go and get him into harness. Tomorrow. Promise him the earth, but remind him about OSA and Reservist status and how we can be awkward if necessary. If he is really anti, we can come up with more pressure if needed. He's only a hop skip and jump from Yemen. Any questions?"

"How is security at the base, what's the entry and exit plan – he's bound to ask?"

"We're working on that, haven't decided yet whether it's a seaborne or land approach. The SBS guys would be ideal for this but they're undermanned as it is, don't even have resources to do an approach survey from seaward. A Chinese sub visited last week, to load rocket propelled mines we believe, so their security will be relaxing now the sub has left."

"This is really urgent now, you need to get out there and work on this Baldwin chap. A Major Don Williams will brief him for the op. Here's an assignment profile, get on to it. I need him on *HMS Ardent* within 48 hours." He handed Montgomery a bright orange one-time memory stick.

Montgomery found a work cubicle and signed into the system. He accessed the CGS option – Cover Generation System, affectionately known as COGS – and plugged the one-time memory stick in. There were three levels of validation and a combined thumbprint check/retinal scan with the webcam. The profile that had been set up was for a freelance journalist researching 'edgy' holiday destinations, with a trip lined up to Djibouti and Eritrea for 'The Tough Holiday Website', a 2 week visit, date of departure

Today+1. Parameters were low-moderate scrutiny expected, country risk 4 (on a scale of 1 to 10), probability of 'hostile contact' 5 (out of maximum 10). Priority 3. That was serious. He clicked the confirm button on screen. The screen returned "Ref: 4673481, ready at 1510 hrs." "Not bad," he thought – relatively low risk so the cover was not too deep and would not have to hang around too long. He clicked the Destroy button, and the memory stick was rendered useless, the internals melted. He unplugged it and threw it in the secure disposables basket.

He went to get some lunch downstairs and then did some reading up on Djibouti at a terminal. Just after 3 o'clock he went down to Resources, keyed in the number at what looked like a payment machine they used to have at car parks. A retinal scan followed, and a chip card spat out. At the reception counter, he handed the chip card to the Resources Officer, collected an attaché case and an overnight bag and they both thumbprinted an electronic receipt pad.

He found a reading cubicle and settled down at the desk. The attaché case contained all the documents and collateral he would be expected to be carrying plus a flight ticket to Paris CDG where he'd pick up an Air France flight. He riffled through the papers and groaned. This system was supposed to generate random cover names. Thomas Brown! The biometric passport was well used – he'd travelled a bit in the Middle East, Europe and South America and this was reflected. It was easier to talk about places you had actually been to. He familiarised himself with the contents and closed the case. There was also a passport for Baldwin in another name, and some backup papers. How they conjured that up in a few hours, he didn't know, but then Booth had probably known about it since the previous day, even longer.

He didn't bother with the overnight bag – that would just contain a couple of changes of clothes for the role, plus a camera, phone and a palmpad computer. He'd add a few personal bits at home before leaving in the morning. This was not deep cover, but nevertheless some stories with his byline would appear in databases and online ezines – they would be thrown up on page 1 of search engine results should anyone be interested. There would be a bio here and there and a few photographs giving him a history. He even had his own website and blog - all very quickly and easily done on the web by the team, and enough to provide a cover capable of surviving moderate security checks.

He scanned and memorised the file summary on Baldwin and fed it through the secure shredder. Then, he left for home to pack.

The next morning, he caught an Air France flight to Paris, for onward connection to Djibouti.

That afternoon, as he was over southern Italy, a 'tour group' comprising a French woman, together with two men – one German, one Czech – were boarding a flight from Berlin to Cairo, also en route for Djibouti.

*

The weather was shaping up nicely for next week thought Steve as he enjoyed his breakfast. The forecast in 'La Nation' was for continuing south easterlies, and the pressure was settled at present. A decent southeasterly up the chuff for a few days would put him well on his way. He'd download a grib file for his laptop later on so that he'd have a five day weather overlay for his electronic charts. He'd also scan the other weather forecasts that were available. He kept the files up to date in case there was a sudden need to put to sea, always assuming one could get a quick clearance from the authorities – that was unlikely in these small countries strangled by bureaucracy.

He was enjoying his time in port, but was now starting to get itchy to move again – when you're at sea you want to be in harbour, and when you're in harbour you want to be at sea. That was the way with sailors.

His fitness was nearly back to peak now, though nowhere near what it had been at its best in the Service. His times for the morning run were levelling out and his swimming times were improving rapidly.

He looked up from the newspaper and noticed a blonde woman across the café – she glanced across and caught his eye. Not bad looking, he thought, and smiled lightly with a slight acknowledging nod of the head. Close cropped blonde hair and face which looked as if it enjoyed the sun. European clothes – trendy fatigue trousers, well worn and faded as far as he could tell, compact figure. He estimated that she was in her early thirties and wondered what she was doing in Djibouti.

Steve had never really had much time for women – his career meant he'd always been on the move, and his upbringing had taught him that families were not all sweetness and light. He'd met Sandy after leaving the forces and they'd lived together for a few months, but then he'd got itchy feet again. They'd kept in touch for a couple of years but that had faded away. The rest of the time it had just been the occasional girl in a bar, never more than a few dates, never wanting to put down roots. He'd had a couple of girls sail with him for a few weeks at a time, but none of them ever worked out. Boats and babies was not an attractive mix to him.

Then, lost in his thoughts, he heard a chair scrape as she pushed her chair back, slung her tote bag over her shoulder, picked up her coffee and strode confidently across to him.

"Do you mind if I join you?" she asked with an accent and a very engaging smile. "Definitely not English," Steve thought.

"Be my guest" he replied, "can I get you another coffee?"

"In a few minutes maybe."

She settled into the chair and smiled.

Steve offered his hand, "I'm Steve."

"Just call me Marie," she said, "that's easier than my real name."

"I've been trying to place your accent, I'm guessing you are from the Balkans."

Marie looked startled and nodded "No, I'm from Prague actually, but spent a lot of time in Paris - maybe the mixed accents sound the same as – the Balkans did you say?"

"I spent some time in the Balkans working on a project several years ago, you sound as you are from there – but then I guess I don't really know what someone from Prague would sound like." Steve cursed to himself, he didn't like talking about himself like that.

"Then what are you, maybe an engineer or were you a soldier?"

Steve nodded. Wounds were still deep after the conflict and he didn't really want to get into a discussion about the real reasons for his time there. He'd done a couple of tours and what he'd seen had left deep scars inside, and a few on the surface besides, and he'd got off lightly.

"An engineer. What are you doing in Djibouti then?" he asked her, moving on.

"I'm here for a little R&R as soldiers say. I've been working on a project for UNICEF in Eritrea for 6 months and I've come down here for a couple of weeks and some fun."

"Well," he said, if you want fun you'll probably want to cross the Strait to the White Beach area."

"That's all tourists, not real people," she giggled.

"OK, then you'll find some French sailors or US airmen on this side," he laughed back.

"Maybe I don't need to go looking" she responded, looking at him over the top of the coffee cup. "Anyway, I'm staying at the "Al Mansour" hotel – maybe we could have a drink one evening?"

"That sounds like a good idea . I know the Al Mansour."

"How about this evening then?"

"OK, I'll call round at about 7pm for you, how does that sound."

"That's a deal, as you say," she said as she slid her chair back, "See you this evening," she smiled and raised her eyebrows, putting a Franc on the table for her coffee and walking away.

That was a bit easy, he thought. The Al Mansour – he remembered a fight in the bar with some French Legionnaires way back in the Yemen days. They'd wrecked the place, not a clever thing to do bring attention to the fire team like that. I hope they've forgotten me.

He paid for his breakfast and strolled back to his dinghy. As he was climbing out of his dinghy onto Adèle, a head appeared in the water. He was startled.

*

His thoughts had been on meeting Marie and the evening ahead when Tom's head appeared in the water next to Adèle. He was trading water lazily. "How about a cuppa then Steve?" Steve reluctantly agreed and Tom swam around to the boarding ladder and climbed aboard. Tom dripped dry in the cockpit while Steve put the kettle on.

They sat in the cockpit with their coffees. Steve had no animosity towards Tom – there was obviously a story there and the guy was clearly 'one of them'. He'd had time to reflect on their earlier meetings and was certainly intrigued.

"Hi Tom, water looks good, what's up?"

"Have you thought any more about what we discussed?

"I don't remember a discussion – it was a just a sales pitch from you."

Tom grinned. "Yeh, well...fact is, things are getting a bit urgent now and we need to move on this."

"Look, Tom, I am open to ideas but I need to know a lot more about the job first."

"Well, it's a quick in and out job in the Yemen, you're ideal."

"The Yemen? I thought you said I would be using Adèle in the Red Sea?"

"The mission profile has changed, that's why I was out of town. There's a lot at stake here."

"Look Tom, that puts it well out of court. I need to be heading up the Red Sea in Adèle in the next couple of weeks."

"Steve, you will be well rewarded, you are still a reservist need I remind you, and there's no 'best time' to sail up the Red Sea. The boatyard here will keep an eye on Adèle for you. Three days max."

"What's the story then?"

*

"You're off your fucking rocker Tom! A solo job like that. Swim into a Chinese naval base, go ashore without cover, tinker with four forklifts or whatever out in the open for an hour, then casually get out of the base and come back – again without cover, leaving without detection. What do you take me for? Is this some kind of joke? I've been on some tough assignments, even in the Yemen. Do I look fucking stupid to you? This should be job for the Poole mob and even they would think twice. On top of that, I'm rusty."

Steve ranted on for a couple of minutes or so, and Tom bided his time. He knew this would be a hard sell, and frankly he didn't rate the chance of mission success very highly, but that wasn't his problem.

"Look Steve, first off, we'll train you up on the equipment; you'll have a good map of the base, night vision gear, the works. We'll have a diversion set up outside. Don't tell me you're rusty – we already know your shooting is up to scratch.

We've got our hands on one of these forklifts and you'll have a chance to practice first – it's being flown in by helicopter onto *Ardent* tomorrow. In case you don't see the news, she's our latest Type 45 Stealth Missile destroyer, third down the line from *Sterling*. Shit hot, better than the Yanks had with *USS Zumwalt*.

The electronics packages are small, they weigh only grams, quick to fit."

"No way, no fucking way, Tom." Tom, though, could see interest starting to light his eye.

"Did you ever hear that story about the Russian fighter in Germany, in the hangar – one of our guys went in and actually sat in the cockpit, in the hangar, in an East German air base, without being discovered?"

"Yes, I did hear about it, and I rate the Chinks as being ten times smarter than the Russians, and they don't drink as much."

"Well, there's no plane in the Aden base, no hangar to break into, they've got no ships alongside right now, just a few warehouses and bunkers ashore, some fuel tanks, so base security should not be heightened.

Tension in the Red Sea is really ramping up, we need the job doing desperately. The Israelis are sending frigates down from Eilat, the Chinese are detaching from the anti-piracy task force. If that's not bad enough, we believe the Chinese loaded a Shang class nuclear attack sub there last week with the latest rocket propelled mines. Our guys are tracking her now, but she's very slippery, at the edges of our capabilities, ultra quiet.

Our special forces guys are already overcommitted. It seems the Yanks are very twitchy and see the chance of their Delta ops people being caught in Yemen as way too risky on the political front, given the current state of the Middle East peace process. The Saudis have got some good people, but we're worried about political control and leakage, though the Yanks are worse than anyone in that respect.

I can't go into details now, but the underlying problem that has caused all this is ours, HMG's, so, whilst we get brotherly help from the US, it's very grudging. We're trying to make it their problem as well, but the diplomatic wheels grind slowly.

And you are right - it should be an SBS job. You were more than good enough for them, but your ankle problem at the wrong time buggered up your chances, and you bought yourself out instead of waiting a bit. So, now is your chance to prove something to them."

"Listen Tom, or whoever you really are, it looks to me as this is bloody high risk bordering on suicidal and you need deniability. Just how could you deny having anything to do with an ex-marine carrying the latest electronics gear into a Chinese naval supply base?"

"Fair point, but we are where we are. Our masters are slippery bastards and they'll find a way. The job needs doing, King and Country and all that. Besides which, I think you could do with a change."

"A change from being alive to being dead is too big a change. I need to sleep on this. I can't see any positives, even the moon is full in a couple of days – it couldn't be worse."

"Fine, but I'll expect you on the road west at sunrise for a run."

*

He called round for Marie at 7 pm and they had a beer in a bar on the waterfront looking out east over the Gulf of Aden, followed by a meal in a local restaurant further along the seawall. Steve angled towards a Djiboutian restaurant because there would be no serious alcohol, and he wanted to be prepared for the next day with a clear head – an evening in a French-style restaurant with good wine and an attractive woman was bound to go in the wrong direction – not good given that he was inclining towards agreeing Tom's proposal.

Djiboutian food is very spicy, and they opted for lamb with onions over local bread. There was light beer on offer, so that was acceptable in the circumstances for Steve. Marie turned out to be very good company – she was well travelled, tough and independent and he found her very enticing. In fact, he was getting a very strong come-on from her and the offer was very tempting. Under normal circumstances she would be very hard to ignore, but the possibilities of the next day and the run with Tom were pre-occupying him.

She probed him a bit on his time in Bosnia Herzogovina and he kept his responses vague on the grounds that what he had seen was not what water engineers expected or were prepared for. He was truthful inasmuch as it had left him with deep scars. Marie was equally vague about her time there as a little girl. She said her father had been a diplomat with the UN and they'd spent much of her time overseas – much of it Paris - when the wars were on. She said she'd studied at the Sorbonne, which didn't really mean a lot to Steve.

After the meal they strolled arm in arm northwestwards along the waterfront back towards the docks. The moon was rising over the gulf and it was all quite romantic – it was a long time since Steve had enjoyed a meal with a pretty woman – six months at least, he thought. Then, the spell was broken. A freight train screeched and hissed past them, slowing for the bend through the railway station and into the docks – Djibouti was the only seaport which Ethiopia had access to, and so the 800 km rail line to Addis Ababa was heavily used. They found a bar which served French brandy. Steve ordered and then they talked a lot about the region in general and her work in Eritrea. She was still interested in his reasons for being in Djibouti, which was easy to explain. Then, Steve paid for the brandy and without thought said "*shokran*" to the barman. He would usually have used French, but he was relaxed and slipped into Arabic without a second thought.

Marie asked him how he'd learned to speak Arabic so well, sounding almost local. He explained that he'd worked on an engineering contract some years before, in the Emirates and had an aptitude for languages. He didn't join Marie in a second brandy, but enjoyed watching her drink it and lick the taste slowly from her lips.

Afterwards, Steve remembered thinking that they had talked a lot with neither of them actually giving very much away, and he'd spent much of his time enjoying looking at her.

They arrived back at the Al Mansour Hotel. This was in the Embassy quarter and just across the road from the main railway station out on the peninsula which jutted into the Gulf of Aden.

"Steve, this sounds clichéd, but would you like to come in for a coffee?" she said, smiling and mimicking a French accent.

"I'm really sorry Marie, I'd love to, but I can't – I have an early start tomorrow."

She looked surprised. "Early start – what's so important? I thought you said you were sailing up the Red Sea next week?"

"I am, but I have a few days work first."

"Work? I thought you just sailed."

"I do, but sometimes I have a chance of work and it's always good to top up the bank balance – I have to replace sails and equipment on my boat regularly. When I'm in port I look around and see what work I can pick up."

"So, what work are you doing?" she probed gently. "It's only one coffee, unless..." she left the invitation hanging and a troubled look clouded her eyes. "Can I see you again?"

Steve had prepared his line but was reluctant to use it, as it was founded on another lie. Sand on sand, he thought.

"I'd love to see you again," he said, "a little engineering job to do for the water company. I've got to go up country for a few days – there's a troublesome pump at a reservoir in the hills."

It was a story that wouldn't bear much examination, but sounded OK in the circumstances. Anyway why was he being so defensive, he wondered?

"I'll be back in few days and I'll call you then, promise. In the meantime, go easy on the French sailors." He kissed her briefly on the lips, resisting the temptation to get drawn in, but feeling uncomfortable with his obvious hardening as she pressed against him.

He squeezed her hand and quickly turned away, heading back towards the pier and his dinghy, thinking about the evening and regretting not taking up the offer of coffee. As he strolled along the dockside he heard an outboard engine start up and looked across the moorings to Adèle. In the moonlight he could see what looked like a small dinghy pulling away from her and heading northeast up, and out of the anchorage. There was nothing he could do at that distance, but he ran back to his dinghy.

He rowed out to Adèle and as he climbed the stern ladder he could see straight away in the moonlight that the hatch was open. It had been forced. There was no one aboard – they'd been and he had seen the culprit or culprits – leave. The saloon and galley were a real mess. They hadn't found his safe and pistols, but everything else had been gone through. He wasn't an expert, but the rummage appeared to be very systematic and thorough - not as if a casual thief had visited – they wouldn't usually check the contents of flour and sugar containers in the galley.

He poured himself a large scotch and set about clearing up, which took him a good couple of hours. There was nothing obvious missing as far as he could tell, which was surprising – on a boat there were always plenty of bits and pieces which could be sold in a bar.

It wasn't the first time he'd been burgled on his boat – it went with the territory – but it was the first time that nothing, apparently, had been stolen.

*

Tom didn't show when he set off just before sunrise. Steve was at his water break, about 4 miles out, ready for the run back, when he saw Tom approaching from the other direction.

"I thought I'd put in 10 miles before sunrise this morning" Tom said with challenge. "You've got a flight to catch this afternoon."

They jogged for a quarter of a mile in silence, then Tom said:

"Any water left Steve?" and stopped. Steve handed him his bottle. Tom wandered off the side of the road, scrambling down a slight incline, until they were out of sight from the road, behind some rocks in the sand. The Gulf of Tadjoura was in front of them, down the slope, about 300 yards away, flat calm in the early morning. The sun was rising red and promising a hot and dusty day once the thermal gradients across the Red Sea sharpened and started to develop wind.

"Steve, we really need you to do this. I shouldn't say it, but I'm authorised to give you pretty much anything you want, within reason, but

I'm guessing you'd do it for basic pay if you thought the job was doable. I think it is, otherwise I wouldn't be asking you. I hope that's enough to persuade you.

Three days that's all – *HMS Ardent* is nearby in the Gulf and we'll get you on to her this evening. Equipment prep – a few things will have changed since your days - orientation, briefing and practice on the forklift tomorrow, then insertion tomorrow night. You'll be back on Adèle in three days time."

"So, how do I get to *Ardent*?" Steve responded.

"I'm working on that, but let's talk about the other details, as far as I know them."

They discussed the plan and Steve mentioned that he had to repair a hatch on the boat before he could leave her overnight, as he'd been burgled the night before. This grabbed Tom's interest and Steve explained the circumstances. He'd been out on a date when the break-in occurred. Tom probed further about the date and asked Steve about Marie.

"Did this Marie seem kosher to you Tom, what do your instincts tell you?"

"She seemed ok to me Tom - a bit unusual to see a girl from the Balkans working out here, but you know how the UN is – all sorts everywhere, or so it seems."

Steve described Marie. "Why are you so interested in her?" he asked.

"It's just that in this game you can't be too careful. I don't trust anyone. The Al Mansour hotel you said - leave that with me. In the meantime keep your eyes and ears open."

They jogged back into town and Steve headed for his dinghy at Dolphin Services. He couldn't help replaying the previous evening in his mind – first the date with Marie (which he had to admit to himself he'd really enjoyed – he was looking forward to seeing her again, despite Tom's caution) and then the break-in.

He made himself some pasta for lunch and sat in the cockpit under the sun awning eating it, washing it down with a beer. He didn't know what the next three days would hold, but a lot of swimming was likely, so he was taking on carbohydrates. The golden rule for sailors and soldiers alike – eat when you can, sleep when you can.

Just as he was finishing his beer, something clicked in his head and he peered down the companionway into the saloon. He swore to himself. There was a slightly faded rectangle on the bulkhead over the chart table where a photo had hung – the only photo he possessed, taken by his father on the day he was awarded his Green Beret and became a Royal Marine. So, they had taken something after all.

*

As Steve was repairing the hatch on Adèle, Tom arrived in Dolphin Services car park, not 200 yards away. He sat in his white Renault hire van for a few minutes and discreetly checked the other cars. One car – a white Peugeot – had a European-looking driver at the wheel, with the engine and air-con running. There was a tin of Coke on the windscreen ledge. He was facing out towards the anchorage. The few other vehicles were empty and seemingly innocuous. Tom settled down to wait. After about half an hour, the driver climbed out of the car and went walking – probably going for a piss, thought Tom.

The man, just over six feet tall and stockily built, walked with an assurance and gait typical of someone with a forces background and still in shape. He wore reflective sun glasses and appeared to be fair haired under his sun hat, as far as Tom could tell from that distance. Tom took a couple of surreptitious shots with his camera phone, then opened a polythene envelope and took out a special plastic polymer glove and slipped it on. As the man disappeared round the side of the building block, he stopped and looked out across the anchorage towards Adèle, then continued out of sight.

Tom hopped out of the van, with a beer bottle. With his gloved hand he grasped the door handle of the car, then slipped the glove off inside out and pocketed it – fresh DNA and fingerprints he hoped. Holding the neck of the beer bottle, he smashed it on the ground behind the back of the van, and taking a couple of large pieces, wedged one under one tyre, guessing that the driver would drive out forward. To be sure, he wedged another piece under another tyre to cover the opposite course.

He was concerned about the way things were shaping up, and that more caution was required. A plan was forming and he drove off to buy a cake and some other essentials.

*

Just after 3 pm, across from the anchorage, parked on some rough ground, Tom watched Steve row ashore, tie his dinghy up and walk in the office at Dolphin Services – the office was closed in the oven-like heat of the afternoon. Steve walked to the 4x4 and climbed in. The white Peugeot started up and followed for a hundred yards or so, then stopped. The driver climbed out and walked around the car. Tom carefully filmed the episode with his phone cam on full zoom. He saw the driver raise his arms and appear to appeal to the heavens, then he made a mobile phone call. Tom threw the empty cans of spray paint to one side on the waste ground, smiling, 'Gotcha' he said to himself.

About a mile away, another man of similar height, build and demeanour, took the call, started his car and headed quickly across town on a course to pick up the N1 west out of the city. He passed within a hundred yards of Steve at a junction, though neither of them knew it.

*

Steve had found some pieces of mahogany planking in the bosun's locker and patched up the damaged hatch. Later that morning, he had gone in to Dolphin Services to arrange guardiennage for his boat. Guardiennage is basically someone to keep an eye on a boat – check her anchor daily in Adèle's case, check the bilges for water and so on, and be available in the event that the weather should turn bad. He explained that he was going "inland for a few days to see some more of Djibouti and fix a machinery problem for a friend" – not that there was much to see and Djibouti was a small country.

After lunch he did his final checks on Adèle, locked her up and rowed ashore. He was carrying a rucksack as would be expected. He'd been a bit puzzled by the apparent subterfuge, but Tom said that it was necessary.

He set off from the parking area in the 4x4 Land Cruiser that he'd hired that morning and headed west out of the city on the N1. As Tom had instructed, he turned back on himself after five minutes and then headed back in to the city and out to the airport. He turned into the airport, just outside the city and into the short term car park. He drove to the northwest corner as Tom had instructed. There was plenty of space in this corner, and Steve sat waiting. After five minutes, a white Renault Traffic panel truck drew up alongside. The van bore the roughly painted legend "Patisserie Marcouf" on its sides. The passenger door was opened. That was the sign that he had not been tailed – Tom had told him that Steve would be checked en route.

The driver wore a baker's cap, white coat and blue and white check trousers. He also wore dark glasses and was mid thirties in age. He nodded, saying nothing, and then Steve realised that it was Tom. He handed a padded envelope to Steve. He saw Steve's questioning look and said "The French are doing us a favour, now that we even share aircraft carriers!

Put this under the seat of the 4x4 and lock it. Then put the keys under the wheel arch." Steve locked the 4x4, put the keys inside the front wheel arch on the suspension arm, and climbed into the van.

He handed Steve a baker's jacket, hat and dark glasses, and they set off, heading back into the city.

"Listen Steve, I'm not happy about that girl Marie. It sounded too easy. Be very careful. I'm trying to find out more – I got some pictures of her this morning coming out of her hotel and I'm digging deeper. Have you got the clothing in the rucksack?" Steve nodded – he'd packed the shoregoing clothing that he wore on his date with Marie. "OK, we'll see if we can get any DNA from it – maybe a hair or something. Also, there's a guy who has been following you – I buggered his plan to follow you out here. He's very probably working with Marie."

"Jesus Tom, what's going on?"

"Just being careful, that's all, Steve. I take it you haven't spoken to anyone about this little trip?"

"Do you think I'm mad?" he replied.

Steve then mentioned the theft of the photograph, and Tom asked for precise details – who else might have been in it, when it was taken.

"It was just me and a few mates the day we Passed Out. We split after that and I went …"

"into 45 Commando in Arbroath" Tom said, finishing the sentence. "You were an outstanding trainee. Your times on the Commando course were better than officer standard. Your time on the endurance course has never been bettered, and your marksmanship score was perfect. You were marked out for better things and they gave you a lot of experience very quickly."

"Yes, well...that was then." Steve was embarrassed and the journey continued in silence for a few minutes.

"This is all just too much of a coincidence Steve, you can see that can't you? Your first date for months and your boat gets rifled. Why do you think we're in a bloody baker's van? It all smells, and not of fresh bread either.

I need you to remember a phone number and a code phrase. If I don't make contact with you on your return, call the number and work the pass phrase. Don't write it down. There's a secure mobile phone in that jiffy bag."

Steve repeated the number several times, and rehearsed the pass phrase with Tom.

"That jiffy bag in the truck has also got some papers, credit cards and some cash. Just in case of emergencies."

Then, as they approached the security gate, Tom said "Here we go, good luck Steve, see you in a few days. They're expecting us."

They were checked through security and into the naval area following another security check. A far as Steve could tell from the French being spoken, they were delivering special pastries to a ship. They stopped alongside the *Surcouf* – what appeared, from her shape and size, to be a stealth frigate flying French colours.

They climbed out and opened the rear doors. They were met by two matelots – French sailors - and asked for ID. Steve handed over the French naval ID card that Tom had given him in the truck.

Then Steve was led aboard carrying a cake in a box. Within 15 minutes he was airborne in the ship's Eurocopter Panther and heading out south east towards the Gulf of Aden, whilst the cake was being eaten by the sailors in the mess.

Gate of Tears

*

Tobin Dynasty – Serious Business

Why Alaska? That was the question that vexed his parents. Alaska was known only for fishing, oil and mining – and snow, of course. Charles Tobin's answer was that he wanted to go somewhere remote, with nothing to his name, and start from scratch. Perverse, wilful and arrogant he certainly was, but until then his parents had never thought him to be stupid.

He obtained his tourist visa, and flew in to Anchorage, Alaska, on 14th April 1993, with $1000 in his pocket and a return ticket to Sydney. On clearing immigration and customs, he tore up his return ticket and started his odyssey. He was never to see his father again, despite the family's entreaties for him to visit Bendigo.

He acquired a Green Card and the next two years saw him spend the first summer in the oilfield up at Prudhoe Bay on Alaska's North Slope. There were almost three thousand workers in the oilfield at that time and there was plenty of demand for support services. Drugs and alcohol were the norm, although Dead Horse, the local town, was technically 'dry', alcohol being banned there. He found his niche there as a bookmaker and poker player. At the end of the summer he left with twenty three thousand dollars clear profit.

His next stop was Seward on the Kenai Peninsula where he persuaded the skipper of a fishing boat to take him on, even though he had no experience. Charles's first winter as a greenhorn deckhand on the boat, fishing for King Crab off the Aleutian Islands, was exciting enough, but convinced him that winter fishing in the Bering Sea was not for him. At that time the crab industry was starting to decline due to over-fishing, the fleets were in competitive disarray and structural reform of the industry was being planned. His brief spell there did, though, re-awaken a love of boats and the sea which had first come to him in Perth, sailing out of the Swan River. This was not a profitable period for him, but he managed to prevent his reserves falling below twenty thousand dollars. He made nothing from the fishing, but funded most of his time ashore playing poker in the bars.

By the spring of 1994, he could put a tick against the oilfields, and against the fishing, both of which he knew nothing about when he started. He had gained in other ways, his body had hardened up and there were few men he feared either physically or intellectually.

At this time he started to shape a plan for his future and found work at the new and expanding Red Bear zinc and lead mine in the Arctic Circle, that summer. It was during this time that he became interested in the actual formation of the lead and zinc deposits – the largest zinc deposit in the world - and how ores in general were formed. Yes, he knew about processing gold ore, but had never thought about the mechanism by which the ores were laid down. While at the mine he first became aware of the term 'black smokers' – a geophysical phenomenon that would be central to his later life and were thought to have been instrumental in the laying down of the zinc and lead ores in that part of Alaska, near the Chukchi Sea, over 300 million years before. He also looked westward towards Russia. Communism had fallen, and there was a vast land of opportunity there.

As the summer turned and the 24 hours of daylight started shrinking towards the equinox, he decided to move on. Next on his list was something he did know about – gold. Although he had not studied mining formally, the process of osmosis within a family which lived for gold mining had instilled in him a level of knowledge which was on a par with that of many mining engineers. Despite his years away at Geelong, he had spent many weekends and occasional holidays up at Bendigo, working with his grandfather and arguing with his aunt, Suzanne. He didn't have the knowledge of hard rock mining that his father in Western Australia possessed, but the actual handling and processing of the various ores, and the other operations of a mine were ingrained in him. Gold mining in Alaska was still very active with both hard rock mining and placer mining deploying the full range of gold mining and ore extraction technologies.

'Placer' gold mining he knew – that was the family business in Bendigo and in the family's declining placer mines in Western Australia. Nevertheless he talked a good story, and with his funds now up over thirty thousand dollars, he got a job at the Jualin mine in the Juneau mining district. This was gold mining on a grand scale, with five inclined shafts and veins which were three to five feet thick, with the ore containing up to one ounce of gold extracted from every three tons of ore.

Although his family business was gold mining, he had never been captivated by the metal, until now.

*

Charles Tobin worked at the Jualin mine for a year, scheming his way up from grunt to the position of tailings manager, all the time gaining knowledge, listening and learning the hard rock mining business. To the management he was obviously knowledgeable about gold in general, and ore processing in particular, and they had marked him out for greater things. His penchant for winning the wages of the other workers at poker was not popular however, and started to cause problems to a level one would not expect even amongst the rough crowd of hard drinking, hard gambling individuals that most miners were. As he worked his way into the management structure of the mine, his arrogant abrasive attitude quickly turned the other junior managers against him. He read the signs and moved on, not because of the internal management problems he was causing, but because his funds at the end of the year were now up to seventy five thousand dollars, and he was ready for his next move.

*

It was relatively easy to become a gold miner in Alaska, and still is. The techniques of mining and recovering gold are manifold, and it was obvious to Charles that he shouldn't waste time trying to find gold. Gold was all over Alaska – and, again, still is. There were plenty of worked out claims with piles of tailings – mining waste – containing gold at low concentrations, which in the past had been uneconomic to recover. He knew that his father had been working with activated carbon way back in 1978 and that it required major capital to build an economic refining plant for the process.

Charles spent a few months looking at a variety of dormant claims and talking to claim owners and working mine owners, then set up a company which he called Tobin Resources Alaska, Inc., based at an old mine in a valley near Money Knob, Livengood, in the Tintina Gold Belt. He bought the mine from the aging and disinterested owner for $1000 down and a 75% share of the profit on gold sold after recovery. The property included a modest heap leaching facility, and a considerable mountain of tailings – the waste left after the original extraction. He then bought 5000 acres of forestry logging rights on the hillsides at the side of the valley.

Of his seventy five thousand dollars funds, he had allocated thirty thousand dollars of capital for equipment and supplies, with another twenty thousand for raw materials stocks. The balance, about five thousand dollars, was allocated for day to day costs and his keep. It was a paper-thin plan. At Annie's bar in Livengood he found an out of luck prospector prepared to work for beer money and a one percent share of the net recovery, and they set to work. Initially they worked through the tailings the hard way, and after three months the cash flow was positive, and with three months left to go before the snows, he move onto phase two, taking on another partner.

With a loader truck and a driver, he bought up tailings from other workings at a dollar a ton and right to return recovered tailings. 1997 was approaching a low point for gold prices, but at the then current spot price of about $320 an ounce they were averaging two hundred dollars a ton net after all costs, and processing anywhere from eight to fifteen truckloads (each of eight tons) a day depending on how far the tailings were hauled. This wasn't a fortune, but enough to prove Tobin's business acumen. Of course, he had paid the previous owner of his mine the 75% of the recovery as agreed from that mine, and the mine was now his, at a total cost of $120,000. The deal hadn't specified tailings from other mines. He still had a mountain of tailings of his own which had been leached with a very weak solution of cyanide, not the regular strength. By Tobin's reckoning, reprocessing that would yield another $200,000. He was pleased with having put one over on the old guy.

By the time the snows came, he had a regular payroll of six men and two trucks. Having taken the precaution of buying sufficient tailings in advance, with options for another two years supply, his raw material costs were fixed (much to the chagrin of his suppliers). And he was returning the exhausted tailings to their source, so dumping was not an issue.

In six months he had acquired a reputation locally as a hard businessman with a golden touch. He 'knew his tailings' and could quickly tell by looking at a mining operation whether the tailings would be worth processing. Bad miners produced worthwhile tailings as they chased the quick bucks from good ore, leaving a small fortune piled up for a smart operator. He bought out his partners and went to the bank with $300,000 cash, and borrowed $700,000 secured on his mine, its processing capability and his own reputation. Gold was usually, but not always, a safe bet in capable hands, and a shrewd bank manager in Dawson saw something in Tobin worth backing. With the banking support lined up, he closed down operations for the winter and moved on to phase two.

He kept his workers on through the snows whilst they constructed a unit to produce activated carbon using the wood from his forestry rights; he subcontracted a local logging company, buying a small shareholding. A basic elution processing plant was constructed with heat from the activated carbon processing to be used in the processing. He expected to be able to improve his recovery yield from the tailings by forty percent, with an increased processing cost of fifteen percent. By the start of the next season, he had run out of funds, having underestimated the time required to complete the work in the cold weather and frozen ground; he had chosen to take on more workers rather than delay the project.

The bank knew though, that given his established (but short) record, the cash flow would be forthcoming. At this time, the former mine owner started a legal suit against him, alleging that he was not complying with the contract of sale. Tobin bought him off cheaply – the owner was in his seventies and the agreement was non-transferable to his heirs or assignees. There had also been mutterings locally about the amount of processing at the Tobin Resources facility, and possible environmental impact – envy was a dangerous enemy. Of course, the other mine owners soon got wise, and his costs started to rise, but as the only viable 'recycler' in the region at that time, he was relatively sure of his cash flow.

With $150,000 further capital from the bank, Tobin managed to keep the Environmental Protection Agency at bay for another season, and although gold prices fell further (and bottomed in late 1998 at about $250 an ounce) the rest was history. Within three years the banks were queuing up to lend to him (he had no borrowings), Tobin Resources Alaska, Inc. was capitalized at $35 million dollars, and Charles Tobin was opening his first hard rock mine.

His operations in Alaska continued to expand, and he opened a Canadian mining and processing operation over the border, repeating the model he successfully operated in the Livengood area, but scaled up. He now had a full time Research and Development division, working on new technology and process improvement. Once his Canadian operation was bedded in, he started up a research project to look at bio oxidation as part of the ore processing.

Charles was by now very well connected in the gold mining business, and he became aware that *The Gold Institute* in Washington, D.C. was maintaining a watching brief on biotechnology.

The farming of bacteria which could be used to clean up pollution – oil and heavy metal digesters was developing rapidly, being seen as a 'clean' way of reprocessing industrial waste, spillages and legacy concentrations (i.e. tips) of pollutants. It was the ability to use biotechnology to concentrate metals that set pulses racing in the mining industry.

This thinking led Tobin on a research quest – strangely for him, as he had never been academic. He spent months ploughing through academic papers, his mind hooked on that term 'black smokers' which he had first heard up in the Red Bear mine. He even commissioned a research project in a German university.

*

Andjela's Story – China

Back in Paris, Maruška spent time re-organising her finances, and took a trip to Switzerland – the Libyan trip had dented her immediate reserves and cross border cash transfers were best done with a suitcase, at least within Europe. After her return from Geneva, she worked hard to raise her fitness further; she gained *yudansha* status in her karate dojo, though the spiritual and inner-self development aspects were beyond her capacity to understand.

Then, in the second week of June – a grey and wet week in Paris that year – further contact was made. The speaker this time was not a computer, but seemed to be a genuine female voice.

"Hello Maruška, you may call me Chuntao. Go this afternoon to the Rue des Alouettes in the 19th Arondissement – the newer of the two Chinatowns in Paris. At number 97, you will find a mailbox shop. Ask for the mail for box number 3865. Take the contents to the currency exchange shop at number 110. Please repeat the instruction back to me."

Maruška repeated the message back to Chuntao.

"That's good. We will speak again soon."

That afternoon, she collected the letter and handed the note over at the currency exchange, as instructed. Following a telephone call a young Chinese girl – probably about thirteen or fourteen years old, Maruška guessed - led her to a Chinese tea house and told her to wait. She ordered jasmine tea, and as she was drinking it an elderly man passed the table and placed a carrier bag by her feet, then walked out of the tea house, without looking at her.

Back at her Rue Simplon apartment, she found that the carrier bag contained a package of twenty thousand US dollars. The next morning she received a further telephone call from Chuntao

"Book a one way Lufthansa flight from Frankfurt to Hong Kong, to arrive on 15th July. You are to travel under the name on your German passport, Gisela Wessel. Take your passport to the Chinese embassy in Paris tomorrow and you will be given a visa."

Maruška was astonished, and bit her tongue. How did they know about that passport?"

Chuntao continued "Do not bring hold luggage. Personal effects only, and your phone. You will be met when you arrive. Are there any questions?"

"No, no questions, that's very clear."

Following this last call from Chuntao she opened a bottle of wine and sat down to think. They knew her German ID, what else did they know?

*

Maruška landed at Hong Kong International on 15th July, late evening. The flight had been re-routed due to bad weather and the tail end of a typhoon. It was dark and the runways were slick with rainwater. The plane had been an Airbus 380 and she queued for immigration control after disembarking amid the hundreds of other tired passengers and restless children. The airport advertisements she saw were promising all visitors an unforgettable experience, and it certainly was. Even in the arrivals hall, the humidity was punishing despite the air conditioning towers around her which were trying and obviously failing to cope. She approached the desk with her passport, which was scanned. The immigration official spoke in clear German and said

"Welcome, please wait one moment."

"Is there a problem?" Maruška asked.

"No problem, *Fraulein*, please wait" was the reply as a plain clothes Chinese man emerged from behind a screen. He nodded to the immigration officer and said

"Good evening, will you please come with me."

Maruška accompanied the man through the immigration gate and into a side office. There was a woman seated in the office who stood up as they entered. She nodded to the man who then left the room.

"Welcome to China, Fraulein Wessel. My name is Chuntao, Wan Chuntao, we have spoken on the telephone."

At last Maruška understood.

*

Only a couple of months earlier, Maruška had been in Shanghai, and now here she was, back again in China, completely unexpectedly. But this was Hong Kong and it was noticeably different to Shanghai. Hong Kong had been China overlaid with a British colonial feel for many years and although it was now formally a part of China, and had been for nearly twenty years, there was still a different atmosphere about the city compared to the other financial megopolis almost eight hundred miles to the north east. Shanghai had seemed to be more bustling, with a sharper edge, a city that knew where it was going and people to whom consumerism was a relatively new experience. Shanghai people were exploring the future, with the peasant legacy of the past still apparent. It had surpassed Hong Kong in economic terms, but was more brash and overstated. Hong Kong was a city that seemed to be living in its past, a city that didn't see a future for itself any more, with a people who seemed to have lost their sense of purpose.

Though she had little time to immerse herself, she felt the difference as the car headed out of Hong Kong towards what had been for many years the frontier between the UK and China, West and East. In one respect both

Shanghai and Hong Kong were very much the same – the air quality was dreadful, despite air conditioning in the car. The temperature and humidity in the car were fine, but it was the taste of the air in her mouth, a cloying, dirty stickiness that recalled her time in Shanghai.

Maruška and Chuntao were seated in the rear of what had appeared to be a Volkswagen copy, one of the larger models.

"We will drive for about two hours and then there will be a short boat trip to your residence. You will stay there for about ten days. I will be there some of the time. Everything will be explained when you arrive."

It was about 3 am when they arrived at a dock near Aotougan, about fifty miles to the north east of Hong Kong city. They were led to a grey launch. The three crew that Maruška saw were not in uniform - they appeared to be dressed western-style, with jeans and tee shirts, and light waterproof smocks. The lines were let go and the launch left the dock as soon as Chuntao and Maruška were aboard. The launch, about forty feet long, was definitely military, and the crew wore sidearms. The tail of the typhoon had left an uncomfortable sea, and there was driving rain as the launched punched over and through the swell, corkscrewing and shuddering.

"The voyage will take about ninety minutes. We will be staying at a training camp on a small island – I will not tell you the name" Chuntao told Maruška. "I was raised on a sampan near here, so I am used to the sea" Chuntao explained, as Maruška vomited into a bucket which a crewman expectantly provided for the western foreigner - *laowai*.

It was after five am when Maruška was shown to a simply-furnished room in what appeared to be a barrack block. Out of the windows she could see only tropical vegetation dripping and glistening in the light from her window. She desperately wanted to clean her teeth and sleep.

"The wash room is at the end of the corridor. There are some clothes in the cupboard. We start today at 8 am," Chuntao said, as she closed the door.

*

Although she had only a couple of hours sleep, Maruška woke refreshed – the remnants of the weather front had cleared away and the morning was sunny but the humidity was already climbing. The facilities were basic but adequate, and after a lukewarm shower she put on the clothing that had been provided a tracksuit over sports underwear. At 8am precisely, Chuntao tapped on the door and led her to breakfast.

"Gisela, what language do you prefer to use?"

"French is probably my strongest – I assume that you do not speak Serbian, and I only have a few words of Chinese, but I am learning."

"We will use French then."

Chuntao led Maruška to an exercise room and basic instruction was given in Tai Chi.

"Whilst you are here, we start every day like this. It helps us develop focus, control and inner strength. It will help clear your mind for the day ahead."

Maruška found this frustrating, as she had when the inner-self aspects of karate had been explained to her in her dojo in Paris. The Tai Chi did at least loosen her up.

Following the Tai Chi, Chuntao led Maruška to breakfast. There were no other people in what was essentially a canteen with benches and tables, with seating for perhaps twenty people, but Maruška and Chuntao appeared to be the only ones there. Chuntao led her over to a serving hatch.

"We will have a traditional Cantonese breakfast of congee – that is rice porridge. It will give you plenty of energy."

Chuntao leaned through the hatch and spoke rapidly in Cantonese to an old lady in the kitchen. There was a staccato reply and Chuntao turned to Maruška.

"Today, the congee comes with thousand year eggs and pork."

When in Shanghai, Maruška had stuck to relatively plain food and had never eaten anything exotic that she couldn't have found in a typical Chinese restaurant in Paris, and although she found the colours a bit off-putting, the taste was quite good.

"The eggs are preserved in lime, which is why the colour of the yolk changes to green. Don't worry, they are not a thousand years old," Chuntao joked, but that was to be the last trace of humour that day.

After breakfast, they settled in a bare room with a blackboard and some tables and chairs.

"You are here for us to train you in the ways we work. We will start the day with Tai Chi and have some basic exercise sessions each afternoon, so that we stay toned. The rest of the time will be instructional.

Undoubtedly you will have questions and we will deal with those as you proceed. First of all though, we will deal with the most basic – why we should make use of a person such as you, and why we would bring you here."

Maruška nodded in agreement.

"The People's Republic of China was created in 1949, but the Chinese peoples have existed for many centuries. You have eaten thousand year eggs for your breakfast this morning – well, the spirit of the Chinese people is like those eggs. It has been preserved and perhaps changes colour, but it endures for the future. Just as someone prepared those eggs to be eaten in the future, then what we do today will provide benefit to our people in many years – perhaps centuries time.

So-called western society, with its focus on consumerism, instant gratification and its elevation of the individual above the state, is incapable of understanding the Chinese culture and mentality. Ways of doing things change, and though we may have ways today of quickly making thousand year eggs in a few weeks, days even, they are still recognisable as thousand year eggs. Our culture will not change. The people who first held the fresh eggs that were later to become the thousand year eggs that you ate, did not know that they were preparing for you or for me. They were preparing them for the future.

When you visited the Special Administration Area of Shanghai a few weeks ago, you saw a new, and very carefully controlled part of China, a part which in itself exists for a specific outward-looking purpose. The West thinks it is a new China. For us, it just 'another colour'. It may change again, as the blossom falls off the cherry tree, then another season will come.

And so it is with everything that I do today, and everything you may do to help me - it will be for the future of China. I do not expect you to understand this – you are not Chinese. Your relationship with China will be only commercial, but my – and China's - relationship with you will be more to us, it will be a brick in the Great Wall that China builds for the future. Beyond this, it will not be necessary for you – or me - to understand why you are given certain assignments.

We will reward you well – in your terms - for work which has to be done. Your own motivations are of no interest to us, unless they affect the way you carry out your work. You know by now that we have vast resources and centuries of time, the capabilities of the People's Republic are infinite. If you should at any time work against the People's Republic, then you will be discovered and punished. You will not be able to hide from us. Is that clear?"

Maruška nodded – she seemed to spend a lot of time nodding these days. She hadn't expected this sort of indoctrination, and didn't buy into the political and cultural crap – she was a firm believer in the here and now. It was sobering to realise that they knew about her visit to Shanghai. She began to respect this slight, wiry Chinese woman of less than forty years of age, a line-free face and with hair held in a tight bun. She was driven by great strength of character and steely purpose from within, and supported by almost two billion people and vast resources from without. It made a formidable combination. Chuntao continued:

"I have worked in the West – in several countries – for many years. I speak several languages, and I play chess at grandmaster level, though you will not find my name in any chess yearbooks. I am not boasting – those are facts. The work unit to which I belong contains comrades who are all equally capable. It is important that you understand that I, and my comrades who will help run you, can outfight and outthink you. There is nothing you will do that none of us has not done already. That experience that we have means that whilst we may be remote from you physically, we will not be remote from you mentally – we will anticipate and understand most difficulties you may be facing on an assignment, and help you make the best decisions.

You are here not only for training, but to understand what lies behind me and my work unit supporting you. I will be your controller."

Maruška thought it was time to set out her own stall, though it was plain where this was going. "Why then are you using me if you are so bloody clever yourselves?"

"It is simple, and you know the answer. The genetic differences between us are obvious. We need people who can move within western society as westerners, to carry out our plans, to put small bricks in the Great Wall. The reverse is also true, and western nations have people of Chinese extraction who carry out assignments within China. The difference is that the west is corrupt at the level of the individual, just as you yourself are, which is why you now sit here. But that does not matter, as long as you carry out your assignments efficiently for the People's Republic."

After breakfast, she was introduced to a doctor who took a DNA sample, fingerprints, retinal and iris scans. Maruška questioned the need for this, but she was committed - they could easily have obtained any of this data without her cooperation anyway. She was beginning to see what it must be like to be a citizen of a state with total control, and she did not like it. There was no way that she could avoid, evade or confuse the system that was now running her.

The rest of the morning was spent on an introduction to communications. The afternoon was physical, with sessions on the mat, and the evenings were devoted to fieldcraft.

The pattern was set that first day, except that thereafter the working day started at 6am, and there was always an indoctrination session.

*

The time in the camp was not about physical development or martial arts – she believed that she was capable already in those areas – but Maruška did find that the afternoon karate sessions with Chuntao were useful. Chuntao was a very able opponent, and extended Maruška's moves and response times. Over the course of a few days, Chuntao invited Maruška to move away from karate and into free style fighting – basically, she invited Maruška to try to damage her, whichever way she chose. After a few sessions of failing to inflict any sort of damage on Chuntao (even with a knife), who seemed able to defend herself using a myriad of techniques drawn from karate, aikido, judo and what was loosely styled kung-fu by the media, Maruška realised that she was being taught practically that Chuntao was in control of her, and that she should have confidence in Chuntao. This was just physical indoctrination to back up the daily speeches. She felt that her body and her mind were being subsumed to China and she already looked forward to leaving and being back in the freedom of Paris or Madrid.

Communications equipment and techniques were taught by a serious man of indeterminate age – Maruška guessed about late 30's. He was introduced only as Ri, and told Maruška that he belonged to Chuntao's work unit. The communications training ranged from one session on the mobile phone she had been given, with an exposé of its technical secrets, to the basic communications protocols and techniques which overlapped into fieldcraft and did not necessarily involve electronics. Her doctored googlephone contained a programmable sim card with preassigned connections to more than eight hundred networks worldwide, plus facilities for local pay-as-you-go sim cards. The phone was also capable of scanning electronic locks – something that she found hard to believe until she saw it demonstrated. Phone chargers were the bane of anyone who travelled a lot, and this phone was capable of using external cells, USB ports and even induction recharging by being placed close to an electric motor such as could be found in a fan heater.

Email protocols, duress checks, one-time websites, encryption software, phone and laptop software patching were all covered – the list seemed to be endless. This segued smoothly into fieldcraft itself with blind drops, meeting protocols and security. Though she was given no practical exercises in tracking a target and coordinating with other trackers, the principles were explained and debated with her, supported by video clips. The corollary – identifying a tail and losing a tail were discussed. Maruška was able to demonstrate her extensive knowledge about the use of disguises and quick 'image' changes as an aid to disappearing.

Another two mornings were spent on assessing her weapons handling capabilities and knowledge, and some regular time on the indoor range was useful – it was a while since she had used a firearm.

*

One evening, three days before she was due to leave, Chuntao said that they would finish early that afternoon, as a special meal was planned for the evening, as a celebration of her progress. Chuntao was joined by Ri and they ate in the canteen, again.

Chuntao placed a white flask with red lettering on the table, and explained. "That is Maotai, the classic Chinese spirit made from fermented sorghum. It has a strength of 53% alcohol and comes from Guizhou province, near here. Everyone in China drinks it. This brand - Beijiu - is the one that Ambassadors of the People's Republic present as diplomatic gifts. We will share it tonight."

The following morning, Maruška was not called until 10 am. She had the hangover of her life and couldn't remember much about the night before. There was pain in her head, neck and shoulders, and she thought she had slept awkwardly – she did not know about the GPS microchip complex which had been implanted in her body overnight, close to her spine between the shoulder blades using microkeyhole surgery. The micro-assemblage was too small to be detected by conventional security scanning and of a density similar to that of bone. The microchip had other capabilities which might or might not be remotely employed in the future by Chuntao's work unit, as circumstances might require. It was programmable, and to that extent it was future-proof.

"Chuntao, I'm never going to drink that Maotai spirit again – it has given me a terrible hangover, everything aches."

"That is not unusual for a westerner. Between the three of us we finished the bottle, but thankfully my head is clear. I think that for the final days of the course we will dispense with the afternoon sessions on the mat.

It is our tradition. Whenever we meet we must share a bottle of Maotai."

The bitch can outthink, outdrink and outfight me, thought Maruška.

The working relationship had been firmly forged, respect developed, and dependency of a kind had been established. Shared bottles of Maotai would feature every few years, but Maruška wouldn't know about the surgical updates.

The final two days of her time on the island were an extended briefing on her future role, and some details of her first assignment. When they had finished the final communications session, Maruška was given a memory stick. "That is the initial software load for your palmpad computer" said Ri.

Four days later, she was back in Paris, having flown via Kuala Lumpur, Sydney and Dallas Fort Worth on a South African passport which Chuntao had provided.

*

On the long flight back from Hong Kong she had time to think. Maruška was not one for thinking a great deal – she was a person of action and rarely reflected on motives and reasons. She kept herself occupied, active and fit. Her childhood had ended when she killed the Muslim murderer on her parents farm, so without an education which developed formal reasoning and analysis, she was usually restless when unoccupied and then driven to action. Her actions though were underpinned by reason, but very rapid reasoning which made her actions (particularly under pressure) seem to herself, and to others, as intuitive and without thought. On the planes though, she was relatively captive with little scope for action. Yes, these old Airbus 380 planes had small gyms to which, as a business class passenger, she had access, and she did spend some time on the running machines. There was plenty of entertainment with 3D films, and even a casino on the Singapore Airlines flights through to Sydney. She did, occasionally, become aware of her own thought processes and cursed. On one such occasion, she realised that she had decided to let Michael Mannesmann live.

This unsettled her. At the second meeting with him in Paris, only a couple of months ago, when she was reminded that the 'first night was in the forest outside Pristina' she had decided that he was a loose end that she would look forward to tying up. Now she no longer had that feeling, and thinking about it was unsettling for two reasons – she didn't like to think, and she had decided to leave a loose end loose. Was she getting soft? No. Was she soft on him? Definitely not. Then why this change of mind, and why think about it?

It was to be several months, and after completing her first assignment for Chuntao, before that she realised it was because 'there was just nothing to be gained by it'. She no longer believed that she would derive pleasure from the planning and act of killing Michael, and there was no personal security issue involved – Chuntao seemed to have infinite resources when it came to discovery – she had known about her German passport, yet she had terminated the supplier in Beograd before leaving the city. Chuntao also knew about the trip to Shanghai, though perhaps that was easier to understand, as the Chinese would have been able to check facial characteristics (and who knew what else) when she entered China, and again later. Nevertheless, it just made her realise the extent of their resources and the capabilities of their technology. Chuntao had also let slip – deliberately Maruška assumed – that they knew about the Libyan training trip. This realisation frightened her – the depth and extent of their knowledge – could she ever be free of them if she chose?

*

99

Aden Adventure

There were two crew in the helicopter, plus a loadmaster. There was little chatter over the comms headset – Steve was obviously not switched in to the crew channel. Just over an hour later they started descending and circling to line up for landing, and he could see a warship that he took to be *HMS Ardent* below. She was the first of a new batch of Type 23 ASW frigates. The sea was liberally peppered with white caps, so he guessed that it might be a bumpy landing. The approach was far from steady – judging by the sea surface, Steve guessed that the wind was a good force 7 - about 30 knots or so, looked like easterly in direction, with buffeting around *Ardent's* angular stealth superstructure. As they came within a couple of feet of the deck the helicopter's quick-securing Harpoon landing system engaged into the deck grid and they were down securely onto the pitching deck.

No time for niceties – the door opened, the loadmaster nodded to Steve – who handed him his helmet. Then Steve was out through the door. The rotary wing didn't spool down and as Steve ducked across the helipad and was guided into the safe area by a rating he heard the helo's twin turbines wind up to full power behind him and the throb harden as the blade pitch steepened. The Harpoon was released from the deck and French 'copter was away. Steve was welcomed aboard by a Navy lieutenant and led down to a briefing room.

Tom had told him that he would be briefed by a civilian and that some equipment familiarisation would be provided by RM people aboard, and that a Royal Marines Major would be running the operation.

The Major shook Steve's hand warmly and introduced himself as Don Williams. "I've heard a lot about you, good to have you back, if only for a few days."

The civilian introduced himself as John, nothing more.

The Major opened the briefing: "We've planned two hours for the installation training on the electronics, two hours for detailed operational briefing and two hours for the practical side – weapons, gear and so on, though we don't expect the use of weapons – that would be mission failure. Then at 23.00 we'll be leaving *Ardent* for insertion. John will take you through the first part."

"Hang on Major – leaving *Ardent* at 23.00? I was told that I'd have 24 hours orientation before insertion, what's going on?"

"The mission has been pulled forward 24 hours. Two Chinese frigates are leaving the Combined Naval Task Force and we don't know where they're going. The pressure is really on now and we've had to advance the timings."

"Hell, Don, that's not what I signed up for – I'm rusty as hell and this is a borderline suicide mission as it is."

"Steve, I know you are fit, capable and smart, the best. We'll get you up to speed on the techie bits by 23.00. Let's not waste any more time. Are you ready John?"

John then showed Steve the camera electronics package and explained that they would have to work with the forklift they had aboard the ship. The forklift model the Chinese used was too heavy to be flown out using the ship's own helicopter, and there were no suitable heavy lift rotary wing machines available in the time frame.

"It's not the same make or model, but they are all pretty much the same. We'll open up the ship's own forklift so you can get the basic picture. We've got our hands on the training videos that the Chinese manufacturers use for training the forklift service engineers and that's being downloaded as we speak."

'First blood to fuck-up' Steve thought. Typical, make do and mend, and no proper orientation time. They went down to the heli bay where the ship's forklift was lashed down. John showed him the four units to be installed and the tool kit.

John pointed out the cooling grille for the electric motors – one for drive and one for lift. He gave Steve a small tool roll. There was a compact electric screwdriver with spare bits. Steve unscrewed the cooling grill and installed the camera package using Velcro straps. John showed him the self adhesive pads which were an alternative. There was manual screwdriver as backup, and a small can of releasing fluid.

Use the fluid first – it will quieten any squeaking of the screws – they may be rusty.

The camera lens was on a small flexible stalk to allow alignment.

"Use the Velcro if you can – the adhesive pads are no good if there's dust."

Then, a cable with two clips clamped to the fork lift's battery leads, piercing the insulation, out of sight of anyone checking the battery itself. There's a short wire aerial, just string it across in a straight line if you can.

Steve practiced a couple of times and pronounced himself satisfied that he could fit and align the camera successfully. Then, John gave him infra red goggles fitted with a small IR lamp, threw a tarpaulin over the forklift and Steve went through the whole process three times, in the dark on *Ardent's* pitching deck.

"Should be easier ashore" Steve said, with little evident enthusiasm.

John packed the four cameras into a small drysack and explained that the cameras had a buffer memory and would transmit their pictures on demand from an external station.

"It's a hell of a scheme you dreamed up" murmured Steve.

"Well, let's hope it works. One more thing" the Major said, holding up a small camera pack. "If you have to deal with a guard or the mission is compromised in any way after you've done the business on the forklifts, then place this somewhere out of the way, but not too cleverly hidden. If you're rumbled, then we hope that they will think this was the reason for the intrusion and we may avoid them doing a full scale search, though a camera in a forklift is way off beam anyway. Different frequency to the others, and no hopping, not as clever. We might just fool them, but let's hope it doesn't come to that." He added the fifth camera pack to the drysack.

"Let's go and see that video."

John was right – there wasn't much difference in the machines. Tom had also mentioned fitting cameras to the cargo tugs. These would be more important as they roamed widely around the base. They had only training film of these, but Steve felt reasonably comfortable now about the tools and the process.

An Admiralty chart was laid out on the table, together with some satellite photos. "The Chinese naval base is on the Little Aden Peninsula, on the south side from the oil terminal and refinery. I understand that you know Aden?"

"Too well," said Steve. "Little Aden is about 5 miles west of Aden itself, across the bay, isn't it?"

"Yes, but the good thing is that the base is close to the flight path to the airport. Whilst satellite photos are great, they don't give the oblique view. We've managed to get some approach shots from a plane flying in. These are from the other side to the mainland side shots we have."

He then ran through the Insertion Plan and the Extraction Plan, with alternative options and fallbacks. Communications was dealt with simply. There would be none, other than an incoming feed to Steve from *Ardent*. Don continued "My communication with them will be limited to my BWT - battlefield wrist terminal - which I will only use if absolutely necessary. It may frequency hop a thousand times a second, but it would still light up any half-decent military scanner, and the Chinese are a right clever bunch. We will have narrow beam comms on the launch but with a 2 degree beam width and the sea that's running, we'll not be able to keep it locked on *Ardent* which will be 20 miles away, or more."

Steve would have a homing beacon for recovery. Insertion and Extraction would be from a distance of 3 miles offshore.

"We'd like to get you in closer, but orders are strict on this. I know it's well within your ability. We'll drop you at midnight, allow one hour for you to get in close using a chariot, two hours to get ashore and fit the equipment, then 1 hour back out. We'll pick you up at 04.00 hours."

"Bloody hell, Don, that's a tough one. Any slack?"

"Half an hour max, we've got to get you back outside territorial waters well before dawn. Tide is slack at 03.25, high water, 2.2 meters. Currents are weak, but may affect you near the island. Moonrise is just before 18.00 hrs and it will be full at about 23.15. It's full tonight – couldn't have been worse."

"Tell me about it" said Steve, shaking his head with light sarcasm.

The briefing continued - "Sunrise at 06.21. Met says the weather will continue at about 25-30 knots from the east tonight, but should start to back into the north east after midnight. Broken cloud all night - that should help a bit."

They then discussed the drop-off and pick up points in detail, examining the chart closely. The new Chinese base had been built at the entrance to Khawr Khadir, a bay to the south of the refinery. There was a sea wall on the north of the peninsula Ra'S Abu Qiyamah, jutting out eastwards for half a mile and another parallel one at the south of the peninsula with a short north-running breakwater. There was easy access to deep water through the east-facing entrance with some shelter from the north east being provided by the small island reef of Jazirat Salil.

With the sea conditions we'll be able to get you within 3 miles using the stealth launch. You will then use the chariot to take you in close to Jazirat Salil and moor it to the sea bed – here on the chart, in about 10 metres of water on the west side of the island. Don't go in closer than a mile from the base with the chariot. Change over from the chariot's air supply to your ccuba. Then you swim about a mile into the base.

"Fishing boats and lobster pots – I expect there will probably be some in this area?" said Steve.

"Yes, you should expect fishing pots round the island, though the area is supposedly an exclusion zone. There may be some on the way in as well and the locals could be out checking their pots. If they are, then you may need to moor in deeper water. There shouldn't be any trawlers though. For night work or murky water the chariot has a deflector autocutter a metre long with a 1 metre spread– it will deal with anything but wire and chain. Deploy it once you are underway. "

All sailors hated lobster pots, especially at night – they had the potential to foul propellers and rudders and create serious damage. This would require a very careful watch. Trawlers would have been an additional hazard, though they made plenty of noise underwater.

"The route and waypoints are already programmed into the inertial navigator, and it will take you right in, and back again. The base would be difficult to get into using a land approach – the peninsula is narrow and the fencing and walls are in the open and bristling with sensors. There should be plenty of noise from the sea breaking against the eastern breakwater, but we don't know if they have any active or passive acoustics covering the entrance, though certainly *Ardent* hasn't picked up anything active, but she's well out to sea anyway."

London had supplied video footage - they reviewed the recordings from the cameras in the house in Ghadir, plus some 'tourist' footage into the base that had actually been taken from the western headland of Currency Bay by Saunders, the previous year.

Don continued "Navigation will be inertial in the chariot as"…

… "GPS doesn't work under water" finished Steve.

"Yes, and it has an autopilot function that will help. Seems they have a patrol launch which is manned 24 hrs, but it spends most of the time tied up. They patrol constantly when they've got a warship in harbour, otherwise patrols are random. We don't expect much movement tonight, but you never know.

We are not sure whether there are any ladders, but there is a small boat landing in the north west corner of the harbour where they keep the patrol boat. That will certainly be floodlit. That will be where you go ashore. So, including the harbour, that's about a mile and a half swim."

"They won't need floodlights with this full moon" said Steve, "I'll be sticking out like a sore thumb, but at least some cloud should help. Not sure about using the boat landing though, if the launch is there and it's manned 24 hrs."

"We were planning to have some more informed layout plans of the base, but they haven't come through. From the aircraft shots and satellite pictures we reckon that the forklifts are parked here in this area in the southwest corner of the base. That's about 400 yards south of where you come ashore. Of course, all may not be what it seems, as they may have false doors and sheds to fool the satellites and cruise missile targeting. Our best guess is that the forklifts and cargo tugs recharged in that southwest corner, under a tin shelter."

"Are you sure there's no way I can come over the south wall from seaward – that would save time and exposure" asked Steve.

"There is an outer sloping 'armour layer' as they call it, on the south wall, big concrete blocks. Easy enough in calm conditions but with the sea that's running you wouldn't stand a chance of getting ashore in one piece. Then there's a razor fence on top of the wall, and from what we can tell, full sensor cover. You could land on the north side of the north wall but the protection's just as strong."

"Given that it is essential that my visit is not discovered, then a half mile stroll through the base does not seem like the cleverest thing to do. For a small base it seems very well protected."

"Yes, I know, nothing is perfect and that's a good question, to which I don't know the answer" said Don."

"What about the southwest corner of the dock – could I climb the wall there?"

"Best guess from all the video footage is that it's flat concrete, probably smooth. You'd need a grappling hook. I'll pack one, though no idea whether there's anything for it to snag. A bit obvious too, on the quay, though it will have a fine wire."

"Well let's look at it as an option. It saves a moonlight walk, minimises exposure, keeps me away from that manned patrol launch. Can we get some pitons that I can use to climb the wall with if it looks do-able?"

"Yes, I'll sort those for you. The dock wall is about 2 metres above high water level, and you'll be there just before high water, so it should be straightforward, except that you can't hammer the pitons in – too much noise. I'll see if we can organise a compressed air pistol – you should only need three or four pitons, plus one below water to hang your gear on when you go strolling."

"Any ships in that corner of the dock that might provide cover and noise?" queried Steve.

They looked at the monitor which had stored infra red images of the last satellite pass an hour earlier.

"Looks like a couple of support vessels – maybe tugs - there that should help give cover. We've had to take what we could get on the satellite feed – we couldn't get the satellite re-tasked for another pass in our timeframe."

In fact, no request had ever got to Fort Belvoir in Fairfax County, Virginia, where surveillance satellites were tasked. No request had left the UK, though Major Don Williams did not know this. The details of this operation were being kept from the US at this time. The worldwide warship tracking system in the US would in any case detect that the *Ardent* was retracing her wake and it would be flagged up, but as a friendly vessel it would attract no interest. In any event the change of course had been covered by a communication to the Combined Naval Task Force that she was investigating some small radar targets and changing her patrol pattern. Not the most original of reasons, but credible enough. There were lots of diversions of this kind in the CNTF.

"Ok" said Steve, "let's make that plan A then. What about guards?"

"Only at the gates as far as we know. We haven't spotted any cameras covering the inside of the base, only the perimeter, on 20 metre pylons."

Don continued "On your way back you'll have to navigate using your wrist compass. 080 degrees magnetic from the entrance should do it. Once you surface though, a mile out, you can use the GPS. We've also got a flasher on the chariot, you'll have a trigger on your wrist compass. One push, one flash. You should be able to see it from maybe 100 metres under water in good conditions. I'm not too worried about a flash or two being seen from above – there will be plenty of wave action and moon glitter on the surface. Then, head due south to the pickup waypoint. When you are surfaced trigger the radio locator beacon. It's got a two mile range, can't be picked up by anyone else. There's an IR flare for the final close recovery. I'll be waiting about 5 minutes out from the pickup point. Right, let's go down to the rear dock and run you through the latest rebreather gear and the chariot you will be using."

*

In the Royal Marines, Steve had qualified as a swimmer/canoeist so the equipment checkout was really an update for him – he had seen most of it before in earlier versions.

The ccuba – closed circuit re-breather – meant that no tell tale bubble trail would be apparent as he swam into the base, and it was considerably lighter than typical scuba gear.

"You'll run at 10 metres depth. I've given you a standard air mix, for this dive and there will be no need for a deco with this dive profile, for a fit man like you" Don winked at him. "This latest rebreather has computer controlled mix monitoring – the gauges are here. So. less than an hour each way on the chariot, and then the swim in and back out at 5 metres, with a gentle stroll ashore in between, so decompression not required. From the moored chariot, you can surface swim until about a quarter of a mile from the entrance – that will help navigation – we don't want you missing the bloody harbour after all this preparation!

Ardent will be to the east and will monitor any traffic in the harbour area. They'll keep us – and you through the headset – updated, though you'll only be able to receive on the surface. They don't have any VLF radio gear aboard and the aerial would be too long for you to work with."

The chariot was similar to a personal water craft – a jet ski – but more compact, electric powered and submersible. They had been around in one form or another for almost 80 years, and used on some notable missions by both British and Italian navies. It was also much slower than a PWC, cruising at 4 knots for three hours submerged. It carried 4 hours of breathing gas. Modern fuel cell and battery technology meant that it was lighter and sleeker than earlier models he had used and the inertial navigation system was new to him, but similar to GPS in presentation and controls. There was a passive sonar display, tool lockers and a payload locker, which the Major ran through with him.

The Major continued: "Sea temperature will be about 25 centigrade – hot for long swims. You can't use a handlebar chariot to tow you in because they might have electromagnetic sensors in the harbour entrance, and we're playing this very carefully. I think a membrane suit would be best for you – we've got a thin skin version - no foam liner, and an extra Kevlar membrane to cut down abrasions. It blocks your IR emissions as well, but the down side is that your body will warm up. Drink plenty of water through your mouth tube and make sure you piss the heat out regularly. That will keep you cooler. We'll give you a neutral buoyancy drypod to tow with the gear – you can wear it like a Bergen out of the water – an extra litre of fresh water, glucose tablets, extra uppers, usual stuff. Your trainers fit into the fins – easy on easy off – are you still wearing size 8 shoes?" Steve nodded in agreement. "And, a swimming helmet with built in radio and night vision goggles, intensity control here, and a normal head torch also." Steve tried it on an adjusted the chin strap.

He raised the issue of sidearms, and Don said that orders stipulated no firearms – their masters wanted no Chinese casualties.

"Jesus Christ, Don, what is this all about – you cannot send me in there without a weapon!"

"Steve, you will have your combat knife, you can do this. Besides, you can take this."

The Major handed Steve what looked like a sidearm.

"Yes, it looks a bit like the standard issue L107A1 – the old SIG 226 – deliberately, with the same weight, balance, trigger pull weight. This, though, is the latest gear – British manufacture I'm proud to say. Mostly plastic. No projectiles – it's an energy pulse weapon. We call it an epigun.

Point and shoot. Lethal, or not, choose as you fire. Aim for torso. A regular trigger pull for stun, a double tap usually kills. The stun pulse disrupts the nervous system of the target for a few minutes, incapacitates them for an hour or so, a bit like a tasar. When hit, a target can't usually remember the pre-hit ten to fifteen minutes once he's recovered, totally disrupted. The double tap sends the heart into deep arrhythmia from which it does not stabilise. Composite Kevlar derivative armour is no protection. Complete recovery from stun in most cases – except memory- but even stun could be fatal if the subject has a heart problem.

Infra red sights with illuminator - here where you'd expect a Maglite torch. Has a high temperature spot target designator– you'll be wearing a headset with night vision goggles even though the moon is up so you can see into the shadows. Charge in the energy cell is good for 30 kill shots, silent, no flash. You'll have one spare cell. Effective range is 20 metres, though we are working on that. Don't lose it – they are like rocking horse shit. By the way, completely waterproof, but underwater range is about an eighth of an inch" he said, smiling. "You may see a slight flicker of light when you hit your target – metal or animal. Oh, and it's good for disrupting most electronics unless they are very heavily shielded."

Steve toted the pistol, and could see that the barrel appeared to be blocked.

Don nodded. "Yes, there's a specially shaped alloy core inside the barrel – room temperature superconductor or so I'm told, together with neodymium rare earth magnetry. It maximises and focuses the pulse energy – like a directional aerial. It's all electronic – no hammer action, decocking lever, dead simple. There is no safety, all done internally, where you'd expect it just like the old 226. The firing rate is electronically controlled to that of the 226 and allows the special capacitors to recharge. There are two, and they alternate. The recoil is artificial and very light, designed just to give you feel. We don't need a firing range for you to test it. Follow me"

They walked out through a watertight door to the port side of the ship. The moon was now well above the horizon, over stern, and the sea was sparkling behind the ship. There was broken cloud occulting the moon every few minutes. In normal circumstances, a beautiful evening, but the tension was now building. Steve aimed the weapon out to port, towards the south, and fired and tested the weapon. He felt a slight recoil with each 'shot'. It certainly was a lot simpler.

"No drop either as there's no bullet for gravity to act on, though it makes bugger all difference at 20 metres" Don continued.

"If you want more recoil then we can adjust that too, but it reduces the load by about 50% if we dial it up to the recoil of the 226. Muzzle energy is 15 kiljoules equivalent – that's the same as a .50 calibre heavy machine gun. Energy cell holds 1 megajoule, only half is usable though."

"Hell Don, I'm a soldier not a scientist. I once went out with a girl called Jools and yeh, she was known as Megajools – 42 double D chest. That's all it means to me. How come *you* know so much about this weapon?"

"I headed the evaluation and operation acceptance testing team, so I should know. It's hot, not even the Yanks have one, that's why I'm here doing the QM's job. War is changing, remote battefields, robot soldiers, intelligent armour, drones. Before long squaddies will need degrees. Let's get you some food and rest, you've got 90 mins before launch."

"One more thing. Put this on." As they walked, he handed Steve a Suunto wrist dive computer/compass. "You've seen one of these?"

Steve nodded "Yes I've used them before," fitting it to his wrist. "I shouldn't need a dive computer with tonight's dive profile, though I wouldn't swim without one."

"It also has a GPS built in – obviously you can only use that on the surface. Look after it carefully. The EP weapon has a phenomenal amount of energy in the cells and *really* is ultra secret. The weapon itself has a pulsed GPS tag too so we know where every one is. It is electronically keyed to this dive computer – within six feet it will keep it coded. The pistol is designed to go into meltdown after 6 hours unless recoded. If it's outside that range for more than 6 hours then the cell's residual energy is used to fry the innards and circuitry become useless and hide our secrets."

"Ok, don't tell me," said Steve, "you can adjust that too."

"Actually, we can't. Six hours and that's it. Meltdown."

*

At this same time, Tom was at a window seat in a café across the street from the Al Mansour hotel. He had been drinking coffee and reading the paper for an hour when she emerged and turned northwest along the road in the direction of the embassy area. His mobile phone was on the table in front of him and he pressed Start. Without raising the phone he moved it slowly on the table as she walked past on the other side of the road, then stopped the recording. It looked as if she was dressed for an evening out. He left some Francs on the table, picked up the bunch of flowers he'd bought earlier and stepped outside. He allowed himself fifteen minutes for the job and crossed the road to the Al Mansour. Earlier in the day, he had called at the hotel. He had mentioned to the clerk that he wanted to send flowers to the blonde lady whom he had seen at the hotel, but didn't know her name. Tom declined the clerk's offer to arrange the flowers, but winked at him and tipped him generously. "No, thank you. I will deliver them myself to Mademoiselle Broussard. That was Marie Broussard you said?" confirming the details.

Now, he crossed the lobby to the front desk, holding up the bunch of flowers and said "It was room 33 for Mademoiselle Broussard wasn't it?"

"*Non Monsieur*, room 34, but you have just missed her."

"Ah, *quelle domage*, I will leave them outside her door. Perhaps you can provide a vase to hold them?"

"D'accord Monsieur."

On the stairway he stopped and snapped on a pair of latex gloves. The corridor was deserted when he got to room 34 and checked the door – no visible tell tales. The electronic lock opened immediately with his programmed keycard. He dropped his keys and checked the carpet below the door - all clear. Closing the door, he started a very quick, careful and thorough search, with no time allowed for a full electronic scan of the apartment. His phone scanner found a large metallic object in the base of a small cabin-case. A Glock 38 pistol, old now but effective enough. It was in a well-made concealment, but would probably not get through an international airport. There were a couple of passports – one was French – in the name Dupont and not Broussard – that would be held by the hotel. The other was Dutch in the name of Willink. They both looked genuine, but he couldn't tell for sure. Neither passport had Eritrean or Ethiopian stamps. He photographed them with his mobile phone and scanned the biometric chips- he could squirt the date through to London. There were two bundles of dollars and a few credit cards. As he replaced the items and closed the hidden compartment – cleverly velcro'ed in place, he slipped a microtag into the lining. It was a simple sub-miniature device, like a security tag on clothing in a shop, or a chip in a pet's neck with a dot of superglue to hold it in place. Unlike the everyday shop tag, this one would not trigger an audible alarm, it would merely generate a database entry in an EU/US shared security database when ever it passed through an airport or seaport security scanner. He took some hairs off the hairbrush on the dressing table and put them in a fold of paper in his pocket.

In the bathroom he opened her toiletries bag and found a dildo. He smiled. No modern girl goes anywhere without her rabbit, he thought. Switched it on, switched it off, ok. He opened the battery compartment and checked it. There was nothing unusual there, so he re-assembled it and put everything back carefully. Switched it on, switched it off, still ok. Don't like the colour, he thought, purple never did anything for me. Ten minutes of careful searching revealed nothing else of significance.

On his way out, he stripped off his sweaty latex gloves, stuffed them in his pocket and picked up the vase of flowers. At the front desk he told the clerk that he had changed his mind and would return later in the evening and deliver the flowers in person, and please to keep it a secret from the lady as he wanted to surprise her, the promise sealed with a few francs. He then made his way across the city to the small guest house – *residence* - where he had been staying for the last few days.

As he had been talking to the desk clerk, the concealed pea-sized webcam transmitter in Marie's room, which had recorded his visit, was finishing uploading the images to a server and sending an instant message to Marie's mobile phone - she was sitting drinking a glass of rather good Chablis in a restaurant with two European men, and examining the menu.

She checked her phone and after ordering, excused herself for a few minutes. In a quiet corner of the bar, she logged on and checked the images on her iLive palmpad computer. Marie emailed a link to a cut-out email address hosted in Serbia and the one-time host account was erased. The email was automatically forwarded three times in a similar way, via Tuvalu in the Pacific, Zanzibar and Sao Paulo in Brazil, finally arriving in Beijing two minutes later. She quickly deleted a couple of the frames which included her cabin-case being searched, then returned to the table. Hans and Petr looked very carefully at the clip - it was the same guy they had tracked on the beach with Baldwin.

"We knew he was coming, now we know what he looks like. How did he get on to us though?" she mused aloud.

They discussed how they might pick up Baldwin's trail again – Hans was tasked with investigating the water company's engineering problem, whilst Petr would check the 4x4 hire to find out when Baldwin was expected to return it. They arranged to meet later the following day on the ferry across the Gulf of Tadjoura to Plage Blanc. After the meal, Marie left early for her hotel whilst Hans and Petr moved on to a bar in search of some fun. Djibouti, having been a French naval base for many years, still catered well for the basic needs of sailors, and with a degree of French style, if you knew where to go...

Within an hour, the facial and physical recognition software in the depths of the Guoanbu information systems complex – a foundation stone in the structure of the Chinese Golden Shield strategy – had five possible matches. Probabilities ranged from 27% to 63% for the matches. The analyst reviewed the output and forwarded the report to Wan Chuntao, Marie's operational senior officer. When she returned to her desk, after taking tea, Chuntao checked her inbox. She reviewed the feed from the analyst and uploaded two image sets to a one-time website and sent a return message to Marie's phone, via another series of cut-out email addresses.

By this time Marie was back in her hotel room in the Al Mansour. Her iLive had signalled a message receipt. She put her finger on the iLive's recognition pad and her private key was confirmed. The quantum computing module in the iLive used her private key to decode the encrypted message and images.

The most probable facial and physical match (63%) was to a man photographed outside SIS Headquarters in Vauxhall Cross in London in 2008. This was coincidental, nothing more, as some particular staff usually used one of two discreet entrances via tunnels with access some way away from the main building itself. The Chinese did not know this. They took their feed from the hidden camera in a railway hut on the approach to Waterloo railway station at face value. Vauxhall Cross was a little like a trophy wife – only for show in public, but the real action took place very discreetly.

There was another match to one Anthony Smithers, who had seemingly worked as a driver at the British Embassy in Beirut for a year in 2007/2008 - the match probability was 52%, with a cross match probability of 40% between the historical pictures. Although the pictures were close to ten years old, Wan Chungtao believed that these three were of the same person, and that the intruder to Marie's hotel room should be treated with extreme caution. There was no more information.

Marie filed the message and images, and smiled to herself – a real challenge at last, the first for a long time - and she savoured the thought. Once more, she played the video clip and studied the man and his actions. He was unremarkable to look at – just short of six feet tall, Mediterranean complexion, slim, fit, mid-thirtyish she guessed. Quite good looking really, she thought. Certainly capable and confident with his search – he had been well trained and knew how to stop and mentally photograph, say the contents of a drawer, search it and re-set it exactly. She could see him search her case, though his back was towards her - he found the pistol and photographed the passports and seemed to fiddle around in the lining a bit. That was a setback – those identities were now compromised, including her backup French ID, and the one she was using now in Djibouti. Her primary French ID though, was secure - she never travelled anywhere on business using her French primary.

Warming a brandy from room service she sat by her dressing table and pondered the situation. She and her team had been re-assigned to track Steve Baldwin as well as 'Smithers'. They had lost him – Hans's car had, strangely, a puncture at the quayside when Baldwin had driven away – that must have been a setup. Petr had failed to pick him up. She only had Baldwin's word that he was away on an engineering job. The photograph stolen from the boat had been analysed in Beijing and none of the faces were on file. There was little more than the fact that he was or had been a Royal Marine, and a unit identification, and that he must have discussed her with this Smithers.

Hans and Petr had eventually found Baldwin's 4x4 in the short term car park in the airport, just before meeting this evening. So far, they had been unable to discover which flight (if any) he had left on. She had requested Beijing to hack the airport camera database, and airline passenger files but they had come up with nothing – the camera database had been corrupted. There was no record of anyone by the name of Baldwin flying out that day.

Her room had been broken into by a British intelligence operative who now knew that she was a player, and had a sample of her DNA. There was surely a link between them – how could he have got on to her otherwise? It must have been through Baldwin - of course, it was obvious! That would fit the facts. The coincidence was otherwise too strong. Hans and Petr had their tasks for the next day. Hers was to home in on the mystery man and maybe retrieve her DNA – maybe even exchange it – that might be amusing. He would surely lead her back to Baldwin at some stage.

Wan Chuntao received the confirmation message from Marie, and the Chinese database recorded another cross linkage as it accumulated knowledge of its opponents.

She fell asleep planning her next move, and how she could turn the tables on her adversaries.

*

After some pasta and plenty of tea, Steve visited the heads to clear his system, As he was seated he felt the motion of the ship change as they made their turn for a run to the east. The ship began surging into the head sea as Steve washed. They would maintain this easterly course for an hour and then turn west again, and Steve would be launched when due south of Little Aden

He checked out the GPS and dive computer – his route was pre-programmed then settled down for a nap. On Adèle as a single handed sailor, he'd learned to be able to manage his sleep and take 15 minutes at a time. It was an effective discipline used by all single handed racing sailors. "Eat when you can, sleep when you can" was the military dictum he was reciting to himself when he nodded off.

He woke up on cue, washed and then the Major knocked and entered. They went down to the suit room. As he suited up the Major passed him some patches.

"Here stick two of these inside each forearm – transdermal uppers – 'amphipads' we call them. If you need a boost just rub one and the micro-capsules will leach an amphetamine and energy-release protein mix into your bloodstream. Only one patch at a time though" he winked.

Steve checked his drypod, took a couple of glucose tablets and drank some water. He and the Major both checked the diving gear and then they went out into *Ardent's* rear dock area.

There was a dark grey low lying shape in the dock with a side hatch open. Steve stared at it – he'd heard about stealth launches, he'd seen stealth frigates and destroyers at sea, but this was new to him. "Blimey!"

The Major looked at him and said "Not many people have seen these. It's a "SWP" - stealth wave piercing design. Ideal on a night like tonight – if the sea was flat we'd use something else as even this beauty's wake would stand out on military radar like a priest's erection. Electric powered – really quiet. 60 knots for 5 hours on a set of fuel cells. Radar cross section of a sparrow. Let's get your rebreather on ready."

He strapped the gear on and climbed into the launch. In the rear cockpit under the solid spraycover he sat down and put his fins on, and checked his gear again, then put his weight belt on. The chariot was strapped next to the gate on the stern platform ready for deployment. The Major sat down opposite. "OK, we're now about 30 miles offshore, 30 minutes due south from your drop, we're heading west, downwind at 15 knots, hold tight". He nodded to the cox'n and the dockmaster gave the thumbs up. The rear dock gate of *Ardent* lowered and the motion of the sea started to increase in the dock. Two seamen took their positions alongside the cox'n.

There was a barely perceptible vibration through Steve's feet and rear and then the launch slid out slowly through the stern gate. As they left the ship, the cox'n accelerated sharply to almost match the ship's speed. *Ardent* pulled away slowly and in 30 seconds they turned to the north and the SWP accelerated smoothly up to 40 knots.

The sea was running at about 3 metres high, across their course, they rolled slowly and easily, but there was a lot of spray coming over them as they pierced the occasional wave. The launch was of twin tunnel formation – sometimes known as a cathedral hull - which was much more stable than a pure monohull and minimised wash – in calmer seas, wash could be identified on the more powerful radars that ships carried.

The launch was running in passive mode. The SWP had a passive array radar receiver built into the structure – this received incoming ships' radar transmissions and displayed them, but their own radar was not transmitting. *Ardent* was acting as their radar eyes and relaying the data to them over a secure data link which gave them a real-time display overlaid on the electronic chart display.

The display was showing two clear lines of ships astern of them – the commercial traffic heading in and out of the Red Sea.

Steve again checked his gear, the Major checked his ccuba as they went through the checklist. Then the cox'n turned and shouted "10 minutes, Sir."

"10 minutes" the Major echoed "and we're not quite so formal in the Marines, you don't need to 'Sir' me all the time."

"Aye aye Sir. Sorry..er Sir." In the glow of the red instrument lights the Major saw the cox'n gulp. I'm picking up the base's radar clearly. Commercial traffic into Aden – AIS says it's a bulk carrier. No traffic in or out of the base, Sir."

Wait five minutes, check again. Then the cox'n reported "1 Minute, Sir. *Ardent* is showing all clear for two miles around us, but two boats off Jazirat Salil island, weak targets – probably fishing boats.

"Hold steady for another 2 minutes cox'n" said the Major.

"2 minutes it is…sir."

"Steve, we'll give you another minute, that's nearly a mile more. Extraction waypoint stays the same."

"Thanks Don."

A minute at 40 knots would save almost seven cables – two thirds of a mile - which would take Steve 10 minutes in the chariot at four knots. Every minute helped.

They felt the cox'n reduce power and the launch slowed and turned east, head to wind, pitching into the swell and stopping. "Stopped, Sir"

"OK, ready the chariot."

One of the seamen dropped the rear gate and then lowered the chariot with the hydraulic arm, which held it steady. He stowed Steve's drypod and towline in a locker on the rear of the chariot. The Major once again checked the ccuba gave Steve the thumbs up as he put his streamlined headset goggles on. There was quite a sea running as Steve went through the gate onto the rear platform and swung himself onto the chariot, and fitted his airline. "See you at 04.00, good luck!" said the Major.

Steve would have grinned in reply but for the breathing mouthpiece, though humour was far from his mind. The tension was palpable in his body, but it was a feeling he had experienced many times and never really got used to.

Thumbs up. "Wait for it" shouted the Major, then as there was a lull in the sea. Steve nodded. "Release!" said the Major and then Steve and the chariot dropped into the water. He was away and running…

*

A shade over two miles to run to the first waypoint - thirty five minutes on the inertial navigator. He was descending now to the planned running depth of ten meters. He switched on the headlight and deployed the autocutter ahead. The sonar was tracking two targets ahead which he thought were the fishing boats. There was no signal from the SWP with the Major, they really were stealthy he thought.

There was a bit of motion at this depth from the swell on the surface, but he was expecting the sea to ease a bit as they came into the lee of Aden itself. He knew that he could safely run a bit deeper for a mile or so – the water was over 25 metres deep here, so he adjusted the navigator running depth which eased the chariot gently deeper. There was a fair bit of light from the moon glitter even at this depth. Then, one sonar target disappeared – he's probably stopped his engines thought Steve.

A magnificent specimen of a sailfish cruised eerily by in the beam of his light – a fish not often seen this close inshore, but they were caught and exported from Yemen, and he'd tasted them in Djibouti years ago.

After about fifteen minutes of steady running, the water was starting to become a little murkier and he saw the bottom gradually rising up to meet him as he closed the coast. He adjusted the depth setting on the navigator and noticed that his heading had changed indicating a strengthening current as he approached the mooring waypoint and the navigator compensated. The tide was setting to the west, which should help his swim towards the dock. The plan allowed that it would have turned by the time he was swimming back.

There was more sand in the water now, and visibility was closing – a combination of the waves breaking on the reef around Jazirat Salil and stirring up the silt, and the current transporting it. Suddenly there was a sharp swerve and the chariot tilted and almost stopped. Steve saw a broken end of line in the water pass him by and another end rising above him through the murk. The autocutter had done its job in deflecting the chariot and cutting what must have been a line to a lobster pot. Steve breathed a

115

sigh of relief as the chariot stabilised and went back onto course under the control of the navigator.

He was at 10 metres now, near the bottom and could feel the accentuated wave action around Jazirat Salil. The navigator blinked the approach warning as he arrived at the waypoint and stopped the motor. There was about half a knot of current so he turned into it and held the chariot steady as he vented the buoyancy tank and the chariot settled onto the sea bottom. He found a small rock and dropped a loop of line around it, temporarily securing the chariot. He switched his airline over to the rebreather on his back and climbed off the chariot. He pulled a sandscrew out of the locker to moor her, and, leaning into the current on his knees, he screwed the sandscrew into the bottom. He double checked the mooring – he wanted to be damned sure that it was not going anywhere until he returned. That would be unfortunate in the extreme.

Then, Steve pulled out his drypod, attached its towline to his belt and ran through his checklist. He checked the time – he was five minutes ahead of schedule - and his dive profile was on plan. "Thank you Don" he said to himself. He checked the sonar one last time – the only signal now was astern of the chariot – due west – and in the direction of the harbour. He pinged the flasher to test it – ok, shut the chariot headlight and master switches off and kicked for the surface. There was a swell of a couple of metres here, refracting round the island, and he clicked the Mark button on his GPS to record the position. He turned and settled in to the swim to the Chinese naval base. He would swim for half an hour on the surface and then descend to 5 metres for the final approach to the harbour.

*

Swimming on the surface on a night like tonight would be safe enough. There would be little chance of him being seen at any distance more than 100 metres, even in daylight, with the sea that was running. His swimsuit and helmet shielded his body heat signature and the rebreather gear on his back was non-reflective to both infrared and radar. He could feel the regular tug of the line from the drypod attached to his belt.

He was swimming on a course just south of west, and there was a danger that with the tide behind him, he could miss the harbour entrance. On the surface he could monitor his GPS until he went to dive depth a quarter of a mile out.

With the sea running and water in his ears, he could barely hear the voice from Ardent in his headset which said 'All clear'.

Then he checked his watch and the GPS and knew it was time to dive to five metres for the final approach and entry to the harbour.

He was just getting down to dive depth so he did not receive the transmission from the *Ardent* which said "Target in harbour entrance, moving out."

*

Steve heard the engines and dived to ten metres, swearing profusely – the difficulty of letting it all out with a mouthpiece in place was obvious - something that many divers found frustrating. The water here in the close approach to the harbour entrance was about twenty metres deep, and what he was hearing was more akin to a launch than a ship, but he dived further to fifteen metres and continued swimming west. The moonlight was very weak here and he was concerned about missing the harbour entrance, navigating by wrist compass.

He heard the engines pass above him, and looking up could see the black moonshadow of a launch pass over him heading south. There was more motion in the sea now.

Then, he saw boulders ahead sloping up from the bottom and felt increased turbulence pulling on him. The boulders presented a sheer obstacle across his course. This must be one of the walls, he thought, he deduced that this was the northward arm of the south wall.

So, he turned north and stayed at fifteen metres depth as he found the end of the wall and entered the harbour. He came up to ten metres – he knew that there were no ships with ten metres draft in the dock, and he wanted to avoid any need to decompress. He turned south around the end of the wall. He planned to work westwards along this south wall until he came to his exit point – still a half mile away in the far corner. He maintained a steady pace and after five minutes he headed up to the wall and came slowly to the surface. He was in the shadow of the arclights on the dockside. There was some surge here from the swell finding its way in through the entrance, and he quickly scanned the harbour, keen to get away from the wall and down below the surface. There was nothing moored on this south wall where he was, but he could see the support vessels in the corner, as the satellite clips had shown.

There was no sign of the patrol boat in the far northwest corner, and he realised that both corners would have some surge – climbing the wall even 2 metres, could be tricky. With the absence of the patrol boat, he could use the boat landing in that corner, but it would still be a risky walk.

Then, through his secure headset link he heard a transmission from *Ardent*

"Chinese frigate on northerly course, appears to be heading for Khawr Khadir base, secondary target left base on interception course. ETA base 90 minutes."

Shit shit shit, Steve thought as he checked his watch. Thanks for the notice guys!

*

Steve shortened the tether on his drypod and dived to five metres. As he moved away from the wall, he concluded that the engines must have been the patrol boat on its way out, taking a pilot to the ship, He decided to stick to plan A.

Twenty minutes later, he was in position and ready to surface. He checked his dive computer and was still ok for surface work without decompression – he hadn't been long enough at fifteen metres for it to have been a problem. Swimming slowly south a few metres towards the moon, he found the wall again, and could see the shadow of a support vessel away to his right.

Kicking gently for the surface he came up on the outside of the boat, near the bow. Looking up, he could see the distinctive pushing pad on the bow of what must be a tug. With his hand on her hull he could feel the vibration of the generator. Then, the surface lit up and he quickly pushed himself down a couple of meters. Steve realised that they would have a tug, or even two, assisting if a ship was coming in, and that they were preparing for her entry – hence the decklights coming on.

He swam aft along the tug and came to the second vessel. That seemed to be all quiet. He surfaced under her stern – there was a gap of about 20 metres to the corner aft of her. There was bit of surge in this corner as he examined the wall – it looked hopeful – the concrete was cheap and porous. Someone saved some money on the cement content, he thought. After submerging again, he pulled out one piton from the patch holder on his suit was able to push the piton into a hole. He took the small plastic-headed hammer and tapped it in gently (the air gun had been rejected as an option). This piton, 3 metres down, was where he would leave his ccuba and fins for the next hour or so. Then, clipping the drypod to the piton, he tried to think about what activity there might be on the dockside – there would probably be half an hour max for him ashore whilst the tug was out, but he would have to assume that there would be line handlers and dock workers around. It was not looking good. He had a carbon fibre grapnel and line in the drypod, but there was no way it could be used now.

At the surface, the heavy throb of the main engine of the tug starting was clear, but the boat next to him – also a tug as far as he could tell - remained silent. He fitted the next piton at water level – there was an uncomfortable and irregular surge of about half a metre, focused into the corner, but the corner remained dark as it was shaded from the floodlights and moon.

Ardent's transmission remained unchanged except that ETA was now 1 hour.

After five minutes work, he had a line of pitons fitted – the engine of the tug was working to his advantage and masking the tapping of his plastic hammer. Back down three metres, he removed his fins, slipped off his ccuba and secured it, unclipped the drypod and fitted it to his front. He hyperventilated, then closed the valve on the ccuba and removed the mouthpiece from his mouth. As he kicked gently to the surface he slipped off his weightbelt and clipped it to the surface piton on a short leash, then switched on his headset camera.

Slowly, piton by piton, sliding the extenders on as he climbed, he emerged, the trash-laded surging harbour water pulling at his body, trying to drag him back down. There was about a metre of weed and slime covered wall – the tide still had a couple of hours rise to go. At each piton he paused and listened. He could hear some talking, and the sound of the seas breaking on the other side of the dock wall. Then there was a deepening throb, some more shouting and looking between the next ship and the wall he could see the dock lines of the tug falling away and being hauled in. Steve waited breathlessly, as a new ETA update from *Argent* came through. 'Why aren't they aborting this?' Steve wondered. He eased himself slowly back down to water level and waited. After five minutes he checked his watch – still on schedule, then climbed slowly back up. No voices. Switching his goggles to infrared, he raised his black helmeted head slowly above the edge of the dock wall, and scanned around in both directions – eastwards along the quay, and northwards along the dock edging the land – the peninsula of Ra'S Abu Qiyamah. He switched briefly to visual and could see a few shipping containers set back along the wall.

'Check again and wait a few minutes, scan carefully in infrared' Steve recited to himself. There was a group of infrared hotspots about 50 yards up the north quay, set back. They were block shaped and did not look human in form – they could very well be the charging forklifts and cargo tugs, more or less where exepcted.

He did not know where the dock workers had gone – probably into a shed for mint tea or coffee whilst awaiting the arrival of the ship – and he could not see any infrared. Slowly, he eased himself onto the quayside, first one leg up and then sliding flat. Now, he was under the floodlights and very visible should anyone be watching. 10 seconds later he was in narrow moonshadow alongside a container on the north quay. He could see his footprints across the quay where the water and concrete had different temperatures. They would dry very quickly. Looking along the south quay, which was about twenty metres wide, he could see a raised wall about three metres high, with a walkway, and beyond that was a metre high wall topped by the security fence. On the other side would be the sea. There at the end of the south wall nearest him, there was a sharp corner where the wall turned north and met the rock face of the peninsula. There were steps in the corner up onto the walkway.

"Don't go in until you know how to get out" ran through his mind and with that he climbed the steps up to the walkway. There was a twenty metre high post atop the corner, with floodlights. On it, he could see security cameras directed east along the south perimeter fence. There was about ten metres of wall from the corner where he stood, to the cliff face, then it continued northward at the cliff face. Was the fence electrified? No warning signs or insulators that he could see. With a pair of wire cutters he cut three sides of a one metre 'hatch' in the bottom of the metal grid fence and left it in place. 'Still alive' he thought. Then, back down the steps.

Slowly, he worked north along the narrow moonshadow and containers, stopping and listening every few metres. The quay here was about 50 metres wide, backed by the cliff face, with heavy steel sliding doors at intervals, marked in Chinese and Arabic.

"30 minutes" came the voice through his headset from *Ardent*. This was getting really tight now. Still no 'Abort'.

*

Aboard the SWP, the Major heard the same message from *Ardent* looked at the data display and cursed. The red symbol marked 'Guangzhou' representing the Chinese frigate had a projected trackline to the naval base, and this now a real problem and risk to the mission. He held full operational control of the mission and took the decision. Though they were in stealth mode, he had with him a specific preprogrammed unit – a small battlefield terminal which looked just like the old Google Android unit – held by a Velcro strap on his left forearm. He switched it on, 'thumbed' (thumbprinted) through security and entered the mission code. A list of options was presented and he selected one. Again a security interlock and he pressed 'Send'.

The terminal frequency hopped a hundred times in less than a tenth of a second, handshaking with *Ardent,* sending the coded message and receiving the acknowledgement.

The Major felt the terminal vibrate on his wrist and saw 'Acknowledged' on the small lcd screen. He signed out and moved across the wheelhouse to study the electronic chart. He would have to figure out where and how to retrieve Baldwin. The *Guangzhou* was not a danger to the recovery – it should be well in harbour by the time of the rendezvous. However, there was always the second frigate to consider – he had no information as yet as to its whereabouts, but it represented an unknown. Unknowns were dangerous. 'Attack risks before they attack you' was a great principle, but there was little he could do about this one except think about possible 'what ifs' and options.

*

Steve could smell them before he saw them. Tobacco smoke. On his knees, he tilted his helmet slowly round the edge of a container. In the gap between two containers, three dockyard workers were having a smoke and chatting quietly. Shit. Not in the plan. He had to cross the gap.

Slowly, he worked back along the container, the way he had come. Forty feet, he knew, the standard length of a shipping container. He eased back around the corner of the container, to the wall. He stretched his arms and jumped, got his hands onto the top of the container and slowly pulled himself up in the corner where the container met the wall at the base of the Qimayah headland's sloping rock face. Atop the container, he could see the top of the concrete wall, surmounted by a mesh screen, probably installed to retain any loose rocks from the cliff, he thought.

To the south, out to sea, he could see the distant steaming lights of the approaching Chinese frigate, but little else in the way of heat signature. The launch was clearly visible some way off, waiting to put the pilot aboard. Her lights and the plume from her exhausts was clearly visible in his IR goggles. At that moment, an updated ETA of 25 minutes came through his headset from *Ardent*.

He crawled carefully along the container, in bright moonlight now, unobserved. At the edge, he peered gently over and could see the three workers clearly, their cigarettes flaring brightly in infrared. Some small clouds crossed the moon, but there were no shadows in the infrared that Steve was viewing.

He rolled himself onto the top of the wall, and he started easing himself along on hands and knees. The moon was now west of south and the clouds were casting narrow intermittent shadows onto the wall and container as he eased along – the top of the wall was half a metre wide with the mesh screen set on the back edge. As he was about to edge along the wall above the gap between the containers, he heard the workers laugh. He lay flat and their voices slowly faded. Peering over the edge of the wall he could see the dying embers of their cigarettes on the floor. With a sigh of relief he continued along the wall until he came to the end of the containers. The fifty or so yards from the corner where he had climbed out of the dock seemed like fifty miles and fifty hours.

*

The hair samples from Marie's hairbrush were in an envelope ready to be sent, together with Target Two's gloved sample from the Peugot's door handle. Tom would take them round to the airport's DHL office the next morning. Sending by commercial DHL courier to a drop address in London – from Djibouti was quicker than the diplomatic mail route which would have to be via the Embassy in Addis Abbaba. It would probably be three days before any DNA results came back. The video clip outside the café and the passport photos Tom had taken with his mobile phone were squirted directly to the assignment database in London, where they would be flagged for analysis, high priority. He keyed a brief status report, including the essential tag words for the analysis.

After the search of Marie's room and the comms with London, he had gone to a bar for a glass of wine and supper, and to give himself time to think. How did Marie latch on to Baldwin? Baldwin himself was an 'innocent' until a few days ago. What was the connection?

Then, back at his *residence,* he barely slept, his brain struggling with the facts and possibilities. He himself was the obvious link to Steve Baldwin. He wondered how Baldwin was getting on...

*

In fact, at that moment, Steve Baldwin was just lowering himself down from the last shipping container. He could see a concrete abutment and heavy doors set into the cliff face, and next to that was the covered area where the forklifts and cargo tugs were recharged. Just 20 yards more. No sign of the dock workers. He eased himself along the wall – the moonshadow was widening a bit. Then, at last he was in amidst the forklifts. 'Twenty minutes' came the update from *Ardent.* There were three forklifts and three cargo tugs. He removed his gloves and set to work, spraying all of the grille screws with the releasing fluid first. The screws came away easily and the innards were pretty much in line with what he expected. He fitted the first camera and saw the small green LED indicate that it was active once he had connected the power leads. He aligned the camera and refitted the grille. Then the second forklift, just as straightforward. 'Fifteen minutes' from *Ardent.* 'Plenty of time' he said to himself.

Next the cargo tugs. He was still out of sight of the north arm of the quay, but open to the south. The charging units were humming as they recharged the batteries. Then suddenly he heard voices close by. He paused and made sure his drypod backpack was out of sight. Six dockyard workers walked past the cargo tugs as Steve squeezed himself in between them. They were heading for the south quay. He got the grille off the first tug and fitted the camera – the internals were not arranged exactly as in the manual he had seen, but close enough. 'Ten minutes' from *Ardent*. Then 'Mandrel, Mandrel, Mandrel. Abort abort abort' came through his headset. 'Fucking typical' Steve thought, 'it's a bit late now you tossers.' Mandrel was Steve's operational ID.

Check the activation – ok, grille back on ok. Now the last tug, three grille screws OK, fourth grill screw not moving. Screwdriver battery flat. Shit! Manual screwdriver, off with grille, in with camera, connect power leads. Activation none. Damn Damn Damn. Check power leads. No activation. Tap camera unit. No activation. Damn. No time for anything else. Refit grille. Drop a screw, rolled under forklift. Manually tighten remaining three screws. 'Five minutes' from *Ardent*. Tools into drypod, arms into straps. Mental checklist – shit – gloves, where are they? Off with drypod, find gloves, on with drypod on with gloves. Pause, slow, think, breathe slowly. 'Now get out of here' he said to himself.

Peering around the end of the cargo tugs he could see the group of dockyard men walking along the south quay, past the second naval tug where he had emerged from the water. At the other side he could see nothing to the north but there was a rumbling – he could now see a pool of light enlarging on the quay as one of the large sliding doors into the rock face was rolling aside, just 20 yards away. A worker in a boilersuit emerged in the pool of light through the opened sliding door and walked towards the forklifts. At the harbour entrance he could see the shape and lights of the Chinese frigate entering slowly, with the tug fussing alongside. 'The buggers are early' he thought.

Steve crouched behind the cargo tugs just feet away from the forklifts and withdrew the EP gun from its holster. The man in the boilersuit approached the forklifts, went to the charging box and unplugged a forklift. He hung up the charging cables – through his IR goggles Steve could see the heavy, warm cables glowing on the hook by the charging box. The workman climbed into the seat of the forklift and turned the power switch on. Then he put the headlights on and Steve, between the cargo tugs was clearly illuminated in the beams. In the infrared spectrum, Steve could not see the look of horror and surprise on the man's face, but he could see his bright red laser target designator spot on the man's chest, and then the single tap stun pulse from the EP gun hit him. The rippling flicker of power over man and forklift was clearly visible to Steve as the man slumped forward in the seat of the forklift. Steve holstered the EP pistol and stepped to the side of the forklift, reached across and scrabbled for the switch to turn off the headlights. He confirmed that the Arab forklift driver still had a pulse in his neck, though it was weak and irregular. He'll live to forget, I hope, thought Steve.

Moving smoothly to the side of the nearest container, Steve hoisted himself up onto the top. He could see that the frigate was now well in to the centre of the harbour and beginning to turn – she would moor starboard side-to on the south wall.

Stooped, he took out the fifth camera pack and clipped it to the base of the fence atop the rock-catcher mesh screen on the back wall. The two inch high package with its small solar panel on the top should be barely visible. He slid back down off the shipping container, moved into the forklift parking area and checked up and down the quay. There were headlights a few hundred yards away driving down the quay in his direction. He guessed it was a truck – a big heat signature was clearly visible. He could also see some figures at the boat landing in the north west corner. The forklift driver was still unconscious. Steve lowered himself to the ground and slithered his way the 20 yards across the quay to the edge. The truck was now about a hundred yards away as he swung over the edge, hung by his hands with feet just above the water, and dropped smoothly into the harbour water. He slowly worked himself along the wall and back into the corner where he had emerged forty five minutes earlier. Sixty yards and it seemed to take an age -the trainers he wore were not much good for swimming and his hands were bleeding.

It took him another fifteen minutes to remove the pitons, then refit his weights, fins and ccuba.

*

At four am Tom's laptop jingled its secure message tune. He worked through the intricate log-on process and finger print check. The email informed him that for Target One – the female - the facial/head recognition was a low match – 35% to a face on file in a routine surveillance picture taken at British UN contingent roadblock in Serbia in 1997. The UN IFOR files said that she was a suspected associate of the Serbian SNP paramilitaries. A cross-check with Serbian police turned up the name Andjela Pavkovic, who had apparently been murdered in Beograd, Serbia in 2001. The SBPOK in Serbia had no photographs – except of a severely beaten body. They also had a DNA profile.

London had checked the passport details with French security and it appeared to be genuine. Dutch security had reported that the Dutch passport was also genuine, but belonged to a woman believed missing from a cross channel ferry from Ostend to Dover two years previously. All European passports were biometric now and a retinal scan would easily confirm this. Tell me something new, Tom laughed to himself – how fucking easy would that be to arrange? Had she come across land or by air? Leakage across the borders from Eritrea, Ethiopia or Somalia was hard to control. What passport was the hotel holding for her? Given her apparent confidence, he would have to assume that her overt documents would bear scrutiny.

Certainly, when he had arrived by air, the entry check had been professional and his passport had been machine read and compared with his retinal scan, but how could she have got on a plane with that pistol? She probably didn't he thought. Easy enough to get here, or she had help in-country.

Tom replied that DNA samples would be couriered to the designated London drop address for this assignment, together with Target Two's prints from the car door handle. This was highest priority.

Both his pictures of the man in the car at the dock (which were taken through a dusty windscreen), and the video clip (which was taken much too far away), could not be used by the recognition software, even when enlarged. At least Tom knew what Target Two looked like having seen him fairly close up in the car park, even through a dusty windscreen.

He added nothing to the email about the matter at the forefront of his mind. Was he himself compromised, or was the missing link further up the chain? 'Amy' the real-time assignment analysis software would be scanning and analysing the assignment events database in London and should in any case flag this as a *non-sequitur*. Amy took on the task of cross checking with all the other DNA, fingerprint and official document databases across Europe and the US, and provided status updates to the Senior Officer. Unless there was a problem with the database…

*

Steve checked his watch. He was still on schedule, just an hour to get back to the chariot. He submerged and swam under the port side of the hull of the moored tug. He could hear the engine of the other tug getting louder and surfaced slowly at the bow of the tug to recce. Off to the north, about fifty yards away, he could see the active tug turning to come in and moor ahead of where he was treading water, where it had been moored just forty minutes earlier. He ducked below the water and waited. Then about 30 seconds later a tremendous wash of current hit him and drove him hard into the hull of the tug. He groaned as his helmeted head banged into the steel hull and the two tons of thrust from the directional propeller of the turning tug pushed him aft along the hull and rolled him along. Stunned, he grabbed out and held onto the rudder of the second tug. Then the wash stopped. He waited and gathered his wits and orientation. He could see a bright patch ahead where the deck lights of the newly-moored tug were shining into the water.

Kicking hard for the bottom of the harbour, he got down to ten metres and swam east, heading well out from the wall to keep well clear of the frigate.

There was more silt in the water now after the thrusting of the tug and the frigate's engines, and he settled into a fast rhythm, wanting to get out of the harbour. After five minutes he came up to eight metres depth and then once he had cleared the harbour entrance he came up to five metres. He was beginning to feel a bit breathless and muzzy and checked his ccuba gauges. It seemed Ok, but he knew there was a problem. Maybe there had been some damage when he was pushed against the tug's hull. He checked his dive computer – all ok, so he ripped his mouthpiece out and kicked quickly for the surface as he started to black out.

*

The call to prayer from the *muezzin* woke him at about 6.15 am. Tom had eventually managed to sleep for a couple of hours, and felt refreshed. He checked his palmpad – one new secure email.

"Do not courier samples. Deliver personally to US base, Camp Lemonnier, Djibouti marked for attention of Master Sergeant George C Nielsen, hand over person to person. Code phrase Blue Bayou. Urgent. Acknowledge."

After sending his acknowledgement, Tom logged on to the London assignment management system – the cross checking was slow, with several challenge questions which changed daily, and his thumbprint (there was a 'duress' test built in to both the questions and the thumbprint). Then he did a general database search for details of 'Marie Broussard'. No matches. He tried Maria Broussard. No matches. Then, Female Broussard. One hundred and twenty seven matches – Broussard was a very common French name. He refined his search and put a time frame of last 12 months – nothing. Last 5 years – 2 matches. He reviewed what little information there was. The record of the name was cross linked (link strength LOW) to the death of an Israeli cryptographic researcher, Paul Cahn, in Eilat more than five years ago. The name Marie Broussard was one of the 780 names of guests in local hotels at the time of the diving accident.

Tom flagged this as a possible connection for deeper search (which Amy would automatically do) and logged out.

'No run today' he thought as left the *residence*, 'I've got to do this the hard way'. He took his hire car and drove out to Camp Lemonnier, the only US military base in Africa. It was a short drive and although early, the roads were busy with open vegetable trucks and container lorries which had hauled down from Addis Abbaba overnight.

He was cautious with his driving and although he didn't notice that he was being followed by a Nissan 4x4 ahead, and a white Peugot to the rear, his precautions - short notice unindicated turns, late light starts and retraces - were successful in losing them.

At the base he enquired after Master Sergeant Nielsen, and quoted Blue Bayou. After a fifteen minute wait in the guardhouse, George Neilsen appeared. He wore the uniform of a master sergeant, though Steve doubted he was mainline army and guessed probably CIA or Homeland Security. He was a bear of a man, well over six feet tall and over 120 kilos in weight, with all the evidence of too many hamburgers. He had the blue eyes and fair hair of a Scandinavian. Tom guessed he was from the Great Plains region, and his accent certainly bore out the origins of his name. There was little more than a gruff exchange as Tom handed over the padded envelope. He then headed back to his *residence* and parked his car just around the corner. As came into his street, he walked up behind and past a white Peugot. The driver was reading a newspaper, with a tin of Coca Cola perched on the dashboard. Shit shit shit, how did they find me? He cursed to himself and he continued straight ahead and into the *residence*.

He packed his bag immediately, settled his bill and left by the rear entrance to pick up his car, to head for a fallback *residence* which he had previously scouted and which satisfied his demanding security and communications basics checklist.

*

The sun was now well up in a clear blue sky, and day was already hot – it was just after 10am – as Tom headed towards the café outside the Al Mansour hotel. To a casual observer, he was enjoying a morning stroll, but inside he was tense and focused and observing his fieldcraft to a 'T'. It was now Friday morning and although it was technically the day of rest in Islam, there were still many shops which were preparing for the morning's business, and he could smell fresh bread and coffee mixed with the smell of the desert and the smells of the city – the garbage, the drains and the bougainvillea – wafting along the Boulevard de la Repubique on the light south westerly breeze at his back.

He bought a copy of the La Nation and settled down to breakfast and waiting in the café. The problems in the Red Sea between the UK and the Yemen were the lead story. These days, with palmpad readers and 24 hour news feeds, Tom had forgotten about the simple pleasure of reading a real newspaper – few were available now, except in backwaters such as Djibouti.

Tom was here more in hope than in expectation – the trip to the airbase had been unscheduled and had set his plan back. Then, just before 11 am, she emerged from the hotel. Marie was dressed in jeans and trainers, with a tight sporty short sleeved top and a small rucksack on her back. Not *too* Western to offend the orthodox, he thought, nice arse too. She appeared to be quite relaxed as she set off to the west, with the rising sun at her back. There was some traffic in the street, and a few pedestrians, so Tom could not follow too closely. He pulled a baseball cap and dark glasses out of his rucksack, and set off in leisurely pursuit, after checking that she herself did not have Target Two in tow – he had inferred, correctly that there was a linkage between them, yet to be absolutely confirmed, but highly probable.

By 11.30, it was clear that she was out for pleasure and he had had to pull back further to obviate any risk of being spotted as she window shopped. It could be genuine, he thought, or it could be that she is checking for a tail. She stopped at a café for a coffee and it was impossible for Tom to loiter. He went into a shop across the street from the café, and groaned as he realised it was a high-end bathroom shop. He studied a selection of bathroom taps as he watched her through the window, wondering how long he could sensibly stay. She made a phone call, and Tom brushed off an offer of help from one of the sales staff as he feigned interest in a shower fitting. He made his excuses as he saw her rise and leave her money on the table.

As he left the shop, he saw Marie turn into a narrow alley. He walked on directly ahead and glanced across and down the alley. Too risky, he thought, I'll have to re-think this. Turning right around to head back towards his hotel, he did not see Target Two appear behind him, using a mobile phone, and follow him. Tom took his usual, careful precautions, but did not pick up the third Target ahead of him, as he wondered about the success (or not) of Baldwin's mission and how soon he would be back in Djibouti. Clearly, there was a dangerous situation developing, which would only get worse with Baldwin's return – and how soon would that be?

At his new *residence*, he checked his palmpad – no messages - and fell onto the bed and into a fitful sleep, not knowing that he was now severely compromised.

Meanwhile, outside, Hans had called Petr who had parked his hire car in the shade and settled down for a long wait in a hot car, with no convenient café or bar at hand with a line of sight to the *residence*. The omnipresent can of coca cola was out of the sun on the central console.

*

The jingle from his palmpad woke Tom just before 2pm. A secure message from his senior officer. The text of the message was apparently innocuous:

"Grandmother seriously ill. Please contact her."

Tom grimaced. This particular message was rarely, if ever used. It meant that all primary current comms channels – secure email and encrypted mobile phone, for God's sake, were compromised. He shut his laptop down and went downstairs to speak to the *maitresse* of the *residence*. She had an old laptop PC which he could use in the back office.

Tom quickly found the very dubious adult website which was a 'front' - really the back door into the fallback assignment communications bulletin board. After a downloaded scanner checked the working laptop, the interminable security process followed. Given that there was no 'hard' security such as thumbprinting available, security involved being online with the webcam and answering 5 challenge questions with answers out of sync prove that there was no gun pointing at him. The webcam images were watched by a case officer in London. You needed privacy for this. A body signal was necessary and once Tom had touched his right thumbtip to the tip of his right little finger, in camera, the case officer permitted access. After fifteen minutes, he got through to the message board.

Again, more security – self erasing messages with a three second timeframe to read each and a downloaded virus to remove any traces afterward.

Following the instructions in the message, he connected his mobile phone to a USB port on the laptop and the website downloaded a new cryptographic patch to his phone after scanning and reformatting its memory. The message said that this phone was now the only secure comms channel until further notice. The website shut down and was wiped within thirty seconds.

The protocol now was that he should establish contact with his senior officer within 2 hours of the phone refresh. He headed up to his room to make the call.

Meanwhile, outside his *residence*, Hans had driven off in response to a call from Marie. They met up with Petr at a car park on the coast a couple of miles south east of the docks, near the flight path into Ambouli airport.

"So, what have you managed to find out?" Marie asked Petr.

"I called the Water Company – the silly bastards only spoke French and Arabic, but eventually I found out that they did not seem to have a problem with pumps, they have had no breakdowns this month. They had not heard of my friend, Baldwin either. I asked if maybe the problem was further in the mountains, maybe over the border in Ethiopia, but they said that they did not get any water from Ethiopia."

"So, it looks as if that was a lie he told me then, as I thought. What about you Hans?"

"Well since we picked him up when he arrived at the airport, he's stayed in the same *residence*, and I'm getting tired of sitting in that fucking car." Petr grunted in agreement. "We've got the bastard nailed, he doesn't know about us, we don't need this level of surveillance. One of them is sure to come to the 4x4 at the airport, and Baldwin will certainly go back to his yacht at some time. We could put a tracker on the 4x4 too."

"OK, let's do that. We'll put a tracker on the 4x4 and stop the full time surveillance on the *residence*. We'll park Petr's panel truck in the airport car park and put a tag on the 4x4.

"Good, that makes sense" said Hans.

"I've got a spare GPS mobile we can use as a tag. Petr, you've got the tracking set, yes?" said Marie.

"Yes, it's in the van."

"Good, let's get started then."

It was now late on Friday afternoon as they headed back into Djibouti. The sun was a deep red behind them and the smell of the desert was in the air, somehow more intense than usual, maybe presaging a storm.

*

About 200 yards away, when he bobbed on the top of the swell, Steve could see the red and green entrance lights of the harbour. He spluttered and spat water and tried to clear his head. His watch said 03.05 am. Slowly, the details came back to him – he couldn't have been blacked out for more than a few seconds otherwise he would have drowned. He rubbed one of the amphipads through his suit and as he set off at a fast crawl into the swell he could feel the surge of energy released by his body as the amphetamine cocktail flowed into his brain. The wind had backed a bit into the northeast, off the land here, as forecast, but it would be along time before the swell went down. It was slow going – his drypod and ccuba was dragging and the swell made it difficult to swim quickly with an efficient stroke pattern. After ten minutes or so, he paused and unclipped his snorkel from the recess in the side of the drypod, and fitted it to the side of his helmet. This was a big improvement and his rate of progress improved.

He counted his strokes and every five hundred he paused to check the time and his GPS. The swell and spray made it difficult to keep clear sight of the few stars that were visible in the strong full moonlight, but navigation was relatively easy as the moon was now well over his right shoulder and starting its slow descent to the west. At about the halfway mark he paused for a brief rest and opened the drypack as he bobbed in the swell. He found his water bottle and took a couple of small sips and a glucose tablet, then ditched the open drypod which would sink to the bottom and probably turn up in a fishing boat's catch in the next few weeks. The ccuba though would be too much of a give-away and he had to take that back with him. Finally, as he approached the GPS waypoint above the chariot he checked his position more regularly. When he was just about at the waypoint he stopped and rested whilst he hyperventilated.

Ardent was now reporting all clear in the vicinity of the base, but there was a ship moving north, apparent heading Aden at 20 miles range, believed to be the second Chinese frigate *Guangzhou* which had left the Combined Naval Task Force, and with an ETA 1 hour. Shit, that's all I need now, thought Steve, a fucking Chinese frigate between me and extraction – where will that leave the Major?

Then, with a final check of the GPS, he kicked and dived, and then pinged the chariot. There was no visible flash in an easterly direction. He surfaced to breathe again, descended and pinged, looking south. Nothing. Then, at the third attempt he saw a flash in a westerly direction. Bugger, he'd over swum – or more probably the tide had turned. Something wasn't right.

*

Steve surfaced and swam a little to the west, rested and hyperventilated, then dived again, at last finding the chariot easily after another ping. He scrabbled for the chariot's air line once hooked up he checked it over. The chariot was not anchored. There was no sign of the sand screw and the anchor line was a frayed end. The chariot was held to the bottom by a taut hawser stretched across it at an angle. A line of bloody lobster pots Steve thought. They shouldn't have been laying them here, and especially whilst that Chinese frigate was approaching! Bastards.

Taking out his ceramic knife from its sheath on his lower right leg, he sawed through the hawser and the chariot started bobbing in the slight current flowing over the uneven sea bed.

Mounting the chariot, he turned the master switch and checked the inertial navigator and timing. All ok, but he was now twenty minutes behind schedule. He started to move forward slowly and the autopilot turned the chariot on to the heading for the extraction waypoint.

He increased speed and the chariot began to vibrate. He slowed to a stop, guessing what the problem might be. A quick check confirmed his suspicion that one of the propeller blades was damaged – probably by the hawser. The carbon fibre at one tip was frayed and split. That meant slow speed only at best, or the blade would break up completely and he would be left with another swim – probably to nowhere, he thought. Fuck fuck fuck, what else can go wrong? Two knots was the best he could manage and that was with frequent checks on the propeller. As the chariot moved along, slowly descending and following the sloping bottom out into deeper water away from Jazirat Salil island, Steve started thinking. He was going to be late for extraction, maybe twenty minutes or more over the extra half hour that the Major had allowed. There was a Chinese frigate approaching, and his recovery beacon had a range of 2 miles. His pickup launch was stealthy, yes, but even so would not want to be anywhere near the Chinese frigate.

Steve set a new waypoint on the navigator and headed southeast, out of the path of the approaching frigate. Just before the planned extraction time of 04:00, he came up to five metres depth and tethered himself to the chariot on a free line. He surfaced and set off his recovery beacon, counted five seconds, then turned it off. Back on the chariot, he descended and went back on to course. After ten minutes, he repeated the procedure. This time, as he set off again, the chariot's passive sonar display was showing an active sonar on his starboard side. So, he thought, that's where the frigate is. Underwater he wasn't receiving updates from *Ardent*, but at least he now knew where the enemy queen was on the board. Question was, did they know where he, the pawn was? Depends how good the stealth is on this chariot he thought. There would certainly be some noise from the damaged propeller, but that was probably, hopefully, pray to God whoever he or she was, below the detection threshold of the Chinese at this range.

Though he doubted that their radar could pick him out when he surfaced – there was still a big swell running out here further away from the land, and a choppy sea on top of that - he was only going to risk one more surfacing. He just hoped that the Major would get the message...

*

At 03:50 hours on the SWP, the Major was carefully tracking the Chinese frigate on the displayed data feed from *Ardent*. The planned extraction point and the closest point of approach by the frigate were less than a mile in distance and only 5 minutes in time. The SWP was two miles south of the latitude of the waypoint but the Major had stood off 2 miles to the east as well as a precaution. *Ardent* was well to the south and heading east prior to her turn to run west for the rendezvous, and was well away from the Chinese frigate, which the display screen now labelled as 'Chaohu'.

It was unlikely that the SWP would be seen in this sea and the moonlight, but it was just possible that the Chinese radar would pick them up at that close range, even if they were stealthy. There were a lot of variables... radar power, software, operator quality, tiredness, threat level. Some positives too, as the Chinese were now inside friendly territorial waters and looking forward to going in to port. Nevertheless it was still marginal in the Major's judgement.

At 04:00, there was no signal from Steve's recovery beacon on the receiver in the SWP. The Major was not surprised – it would have been too much to expect 04:00 on the dot. Then, the data link from *Ardent* showed a triangulated position with a blue colour denoting a transmission labelled 'Mandrel' now inactive. Bugger, what's going on? thought the Major. *Ardent*, though 20 miles away by now would have a much greater aerial height and a more powerful receiver. Why aren't we receiving him?

The signals tech on the SWP checked the beacon receiver settings and all seemed well, but there was still no reception.

At 04:10, another blue 'Mandrel' position appeared on the data display, this one to the south east of the first one. OK, thought the Major, we can work with this. Baldwin seems to be heading southeast at about two knots. That's towards us at least. Slow. We can't go in close especially with the frigate so near to us, and it will be close to dawn before we can pick him up.

04:15, and the remote data display is now showing red target designators coming our of Aden.

"What the fuck!" swore the Major out loud.

"Probably the local fishing fleet coming out for a day's fishing, Sir" said the cox'n.

"I bloody well hope so, I just bloody well hope so."

*

04:20 hrs on the SWP. The red target designators had changed to orange a few minutes ago, meaning that they were not believed to be hostile, and the tension in the wheelhouse notched down a click, but it was now climbing again after the brief respite and the minutes ticked by. The crew were tired after several hours of rolling and pitching motion in the SWP and then the SWP beacon receiver bleeped and startled them all. The LCD panel legend showed 'transmission Mandrel bearing 320 deg relative'. A few seconds later, this was reflected on the data feed display from *Ardent*, then the 'inactive' label appeared.

"Well at least we know that the bloody receiver works – sometimes!" said the Major ruefully, continuing, to no-one in particular, "Baldwin is being a canny bastard – he obviously knows about the frigate and he's just letting us know what he's up to. Let's see where we'll meet him."

The Major now had a clear trackline for the chariot, and there was a distinct release of tension as the Major checked the position and confirmed Steve's course and speed from the three recorded transmissions. He plotted an interception course and ETA – a few minutes at most at 40 knots, without going too far in beyond their orders limit of three miles closest approach.

His calculations with the electronic chart suggested that Baldwin would reach the three mile closest approach limit at about 05:10. At that time the false dawn would be approaching, but the frigate should be well abed by then. And we should be back on *Ardent*, he thought. The cox'n reported that the energy cells were down to 50%. He prepared a message on his terminal and squirted a request for a half hour slippage to *Ardent*. 'Acknowledged, waiting' came back, then 30 seconds later '20 minutes max, wpt P + 10nm West 05:20'. He squirted back his acceptance, the original Pickup waypoint moved 10 miles west and 20 minutes later. This was going to be tight, very tight, and by then, possibly, probably, very light.

The supposed fishing boats, were now showing as a cluster of orange symbols with westerly heading vectors headed across the course of the Chinese frigate. The *'Chaohu'* was now past the original extraction waypoint, and the danger was decreasing, but nevertheless the Major was still concerned about their radar visibility so close to the frigate. And those fishing boats – I bet they have to stop for the frigate even though they technically have right of way. *Ardent* reported a target leaving the base and it duly appeared on the data display. Just the pilot on his way out, guessed the Major, probably a tug to follow shortly. However, ten metres below him, and a couple of miles to the north, a problem was developing.

*

Aboard the chariot, Steve felt the vibrations increasing and he slowed to a stop. Using his head torch, he examined the propeller and saw that the damaged blade had split further and was seriously fractured. He checked his watch – 04:40 hrs and still more than a mile to go. The chariot was close to being unusable. Then, an idea came to him. He opened the tool locker and found that magic solution – duct tape. He cursed for not having thought of it earlier. This was no ordinary duck tape though – it was an active epoxy microcapsule tape which worked underwater – but it looked like duct tape to Steve. "Got to be worth a try" he thought as he wrapped it around the damaged blade – he could probably swim the last mile, but abandoning the chariot was not an option he thought wise, at least yet. He could anchor it the bottom for now, if need be – and if he had an anchor…bugger, bugger, bugger!

The chariot moved forward slowly, there was less vibration and Steve checked it every couple of minutes. After about twenty minutes though, the vibration suddenly flared and this time it was terminal. The damaged third blade had gone completely, shredded to the boss of the prop.

After checking the inertial navigator, Steve long-leashed himself to the chariot, unhitched his airline and kicked for the surface. He waited 30 secs or so whilst his GPS reacquired its satellites and then checked position. All ok, the inertial navigator was accurate within a few tenths of a cable. The swell was still running under him, but the choppy sea was easier as the wind had backed a little more towards the North and he was therefore in the lee of Aden itself, but quite close to the shipping lane. After hyperventilating, he dived, pulling himself back to the chariot by the leash, and gratefully sucked on the airline. He checked the chariot's air supply gauge – plenty in the tank, and his dive computer was happy with the profile so far. Just the small problem of the chariot propeller – can't see an easy solution to that, he thought.

Well, it's 05:00, and I'm about half a mile short of a pickup - I'll chance my arm. They may well have gone back to *Ardent*, but I doubt it, he thought, knowing that the ethos was not to leave anyone behind. Steve vented the chariot and she rose gently to the surface, and wallowed in the uncomfortable swell with the cross sea from the north east. He squawked his beacon twice, then after a minute, twice again. And again.

*

Aboard the SWP the crew jumped, startled into to action as the locator receiver beeped and reported, and the data display from *Ardent* refreshed.

"Shit, he's a half mile short – there must be a problem" cursed the Major. "Cox'n, we're going in, full power, set the waypoint for his last transmission. 60 knots, 20 seconds only, we don't want to run him down." The crew fastened themselves into their bucket seats and braced.

The SWP surged with the power as she came up to speed, giving an uncomfortable ride as they head north east, with the swell on the beam and small chop from the wind. She was piercing the waves with a vengeance now – one, two, three heavy surges and then

"Twenty seconds Sir, closing down power to dead slow."

Two hundred yards ahead – one cable – one tenth of a nautical mile - Steve was slowly treading water in the swell. It might just as well have been five miles. There was no chance that he would be able to see them in these conditions, and it would be difficult for them too – stealth and stealth attempting a rendezvous in semi darkness and a rough sea. He squawked his beacon again three times hoping that their directional receiver was accurate and wondering what he else he could do.

He was still tethered to the chariot, but had been keeping away from it as it surged in the decreasing but still awkward swell from the east. He cursed as he half-hauled and half-swam back along the leash to it. Too much new stuff to take in at one go, he said to himself as he located the item which he'd totally forgotten about. With difficulty he managed to unclip it, close the tool locker and swim away from the chariot, though still leashed. He clipped the cord to his belt and pulled the tab on the small plastic case. There was whooshing sound as the small transparent balloon inflated and rose to 5 metres above him, the electronics package switching on as it did so.

Aboard the SWP they aligned their course with the last received transmission direction and moved ahead at dead slow. The wheelhouse screen had cleared of water but seeing anything was difficult if not impossible in the semi-darkness. Then a shout…

"Sir, the thermal imager is picking up a point source just off to starboard, about 100 yards away. Spectrum analyser confirms that it's one of our narrow band IR flares."

"At Last! Cox'n, home in on it dead slow and let's prepare to recover him."

Once Steve was hauled aboard, the seamen deployed the inflatable stern fender and using the leash and hydraulic arm retrieved the chariot, though not without a lot of banging and swearing in the awkward sea and half-light without any deck lights to work with. The Major checked Steve's dive computer – the possibility of confusion by a tired returning diver was always there, and there was a one-man decompression chamber up forrard, just in case, but not needed this time as Steve's dive computer profile was showing healthy.

It was now 05:16 and they had twelve miles to run in four minutes to make the rendezvous. Only 180 knots, thought the Major. They went to full power and headed off at 60 knots to the south west. They were rapidly overtaking the swell and piercing through it with a porpoising motion. Strapped in and helmeted, it was still very uncomfortable and all of them tapped a couple of their transdermal antiseasickness patches.

After squirting a signal to *Ardent*, 'recovery confirmed, we'll catch you up P +40 minutes' the Major began his debrief of Steve, and twenty minutes later, in the brightening pre-dawn, they were steering into *Ardent's* rear dock at 20 knots, with just enough propulsion energy left to do so. The Major pressed 'Send' and the assignment database in London noted the event 'Mandrel successful, qualified'.

He would send a full report later.

*

Back in his room in the *residence*, Tom used his phone to recheck the room for listening devices or other electronics. Scan clear. He switched the bedside radio on and checked for transmissions. Christ, are they still playing Charles Aznavour these days? Scan clear. He put his earpiece in and dialled the number allocated for the call.

His senior officer answered and Tom listened whilst a brief summary of events 120 miles away in Aden were relayed:

"Mandrel was substantially successful, we're getting a useful data feed. Expect return of asset reverse route ETA 1800 AST your end. I'm advising extreme caution given the compromise of our secure comms. It's hell here – there's a major panic on and we're locked down and I've got two people watching me make this call. Target One is a big concern to us. The US airbase has DNA testing facilities – an autolab was installed years ago for the special rendition program; so, we have the DNA analysis through. We are now pretty sure that it is Andjela Pavkovic, though the DNA doesn't match the supposed DNA of the dead Pavkovic from Serbia. We're working with SBPOK in Serbia to find out more – it seems that there were some odd aspects to her supposed death. The DNA does match that found on a used tissue in the back of a car involved in the killing. They obviously did a good job at that crime scene – after all, British police trained the buggers! They are *very* interested – they don't usually pay much attention to gangland killings.

We also have a possible ID of target Two from the same location as Target One in Eilat, so the joint probability is high by association. This Pavkovic lady is a seriously dangerous operator – I cannot stress that highly enough. The partial prints on the sticky glove were usable. The Bundesnachrichtendienst - BND - in Germany have told us that the primary match is to a Hans Grüber – German national, mercenary, with a background we believe in the KSK – German special forces – though the BND wouldn't confirm that, strangely. Some of them served in Serbia. Not a good picture. Have you got any update?"

Tom outlined his day's problems – compromised, but now moved bases; laying low and waiting for Baldwin's return. The current problem was that the opposition know Baldwin will return to his boat. They briefly discussed how Baldwin had been uncovered by the opposition. London's view was that it could be related to the comms problem they had – the other possibility – betrayal at the London end - was too ghastly to contemplate.

"OK, we'll update Baldwin on *Ardent* (he's still recovering), that his 'Marie' is extremely hostile and that returning to his boat is not a good idea yet" said London.

"Fine," Tom replied, "I'll change the return route and move him to my place. Can we fly him in to the US Base?"

"I'll arrange to use *Ardent's* helo if it's available and fly him to Camp Lemonnier then – I hope our cousins will agree. In the meantime I hope that we can sort the secure comms problem," said the senior officer. They discussed some further operational arrangements and closed the call after ten minutes.

Tom sighed and laid back on his bed, to wait and think.

*

Saturday morning and back at the Embassy in Sana'a, all hell was let loose, again. Saunders had received the message 'Grandmother seriously ill, get in touch' and followed the lockdown communications protocol. He updated his phone from a one-time website and then called in.

The senior officer in London was clearly very stressed.

"We're locked down here in London. Four eyes and four ears on every communication. The Chinese are reading our diplomatic traffic to Sana'a, among other places, and an operation across Bab el Mandeb from you is going tits up and we don't know how it has been penetrated. We're stretched with the trouble over Tobin Resources and Yemen. Cobra has got strategy papers coming out of its ears, but can't make a decision. What have you got for me?"

"Re my last cable, my Aden network is compromised. My own cover could be compromised."

"What about your other networks?"

"All quiet, I believe they are ok, it's just the Aden link that stinks."

"That's a bugger. The work you did recently was top rate. We've effectively got a film crew roaming around inside the base. That at least is something to cheer about, Let's hope your man holds it together.

Get out of there on the next plane to Cairo and wait – you'll get your instructions there. I will need you to move on quickly from Cairo. We'll not be putting much on the assignment system for you until we've cleaned up the leak. Hand to hand, mouth to mouth. When you get there get in touch and we'll set up a meet."

Saunders closed the call and quickly prepared to leave.

*

Across Sana'a, Salim, the carpet seller, had finally been persuaded to talk, and a mystery English tourist called Smith was being sought. The Interior Ministry had contacted the Chinese Embassy to advise that an Englishman had obtained information about the base. The interior police in Aden had arrested Salim's cousin and family and that led to Salim. They were being interrogated, with a high degree of prejudice.

The base commander had initiated a search and the guards' night log had shown that a Yemeni forklift driver had been checked by the doctor after having apparently fainted. The local was now being interviewed by the head of base security, with the local interior police in attendance, but it did seem to be entirely innocent. Drinking alcohol was a popular pastime amongst the workers – but surprisingly when tested he had shown no trace of alcohol in his blood.

A search team had checked the perimeter and found a partial cutout in the base fencing. They had also uncovered a small camera package, sloppily hidden further along, on the retaining wall at the base of the cliff. The search was continuing.

*

In London, the analysts monitoring the feeds from the Chinese naval base via the safe house transponder in Little Aden were being taken on a guided tour of the base, from unloading food in the canteen, to moving machinery and stores. The munitions were stored in reinforced tunnels deep under the headland, and the first transmissions had astounded them. What were apparently, in NATO parlance 'CSS5 Mod4 anti-ship ballistic missiles' - rather more picturesquely known to the Chinese as the Dong Feng 21D, complete with three truck mounted launchers and mobile control room, were parked in the bunkers. This was causing near panic in the UK and US naval circles. NATO had been proven prone to leakage, and this information was being kept away from NATO headquarters in Europe.

Back in 2010, these missiles were a world first for the Chinese. Using satellite based synthetic aperture radar, and GPS guidance accurate to less then 40 metres, these solid fuel ballistic missiles had a range of 3,000 km and could hit a moving aircraft carrier. This range was not enough to reach the Red Sea from Western China (where they had previously been deployed), but now, from the Yemen, area denial of the whole Middle East, the Suez Canal and the Eastern Mediterranean was a real possibility. Defending against them was difficult without land based ABM systems, although high power lasers – again land based, were now close to being deployed, but certainly not in a configuration that could defend capital ships at sea in the Middle East.

This development rendered the visible US and UK projection of power impotent – there were still the submarines, but visibility was important. The power of the subs was in their stealth.

*

Andjela's Story – Maturity

Two months after her return from Hong Kong, Maruška was reaching a peak of frustration. There had been little contact of substance from Chuntao, merely a few conversations to tell her that the circumstances for her first assignment were not yet optimal, and that she should be patient. Apart from timing, the details of the assignment had not changed. Then, in mid October, the 'go' was given for the mission, and she flew to London on her German passport. After a couple of days in London, she caught a British Airways flight to Johannesburg, travelling on her South African passport.

The assignment was straightforward – torture and murder Ruud Vermaak. He was the chairman of the South African gold mining conglomerate SA-Rand Metals. The murder was to appear to be the work of native South Africans. It took her a month in Johannesburg to plan in detail and prepare, and she enjoyed the clear air of the veldt.

The task was completed when the chairman was out riding alone on his farm, as he did on weekends - 'clearing his thoughts and planning the week ahead' was what his wife of twenty three years explained to the police team. A machete was used and the information Maruška obtained about the company's true level of gold reserves (considerably overstated) was provided to Chuntao.

The local police received an anonymous tip-off, and quickly found the machete – still with traces of blood – concealed in the home of one of Ruud's farm workers, who was 'shot by an officer whilst trying to escape', as the police report stated simply.

A month later, following 'information provided in confidence', the South African financial regulators began an investigation into the company. The share price tumbled and the shares were suspended on the Johannesburg Stock Exchange. A year later, following the regulators final report, the shares were relisted and the company was taken over by a Chinese mining corporation.

*

Back in Paris after her South African trip, Maruška received a congratulatory call from Chuntao, and her course was set. Over the next dozen or so years Maruška carried out two or three assignments each year, across North and South America, Africa, Israel, Australia and Russia, even Alaska. Most of the assignments involved men who worked in or ran mining, minerals and ore refining companies and one involved a surveying company engaged on surveying an old gold mine in Wales. Only once was a woman a target, and few of the assignments involved torture. Most were arranged accidents which aroused no suspicion.

The complexities of her assignments and the desire to mislead the authorities meant that occasionally she had to work with others – equally accomplished – and introduced by Wan Chuntao. Maruška always insisted that she should lead the team – she could manage these men very well, though establishing her authority sometimes required a practical (and for them, painful) demonstration of her abilities.

She and Wan Chuntao met again a few times over the years, always in China, but never twice in the same city. And, as Chuntao had vowed, they always shared a bottle of Maotai. For Maruška, though, the hangovers never improved, and the details of those evenings were almost completely absent from her memory. Her mobile phone and other technology were updated more frequently, usually in Paris.

Although she lived a comfortable life, the time in between assignments was difficult to fill. She made best use of it to extend her abilities and skills, returning to South Africa to gain a private pilot's licence; she took up parachuting, becoming an accomplished sky diver; she extended her scuba diving skills and worked up to instructor level, diving in Australia, Cuba and even during one particularly enjoyable assignment in the Red Sea, at Eilat.

Her personal life involved visits to Berlin, Hamburg, the Philippines, Amsterdam, Moscow and other cities which offered the type of nocturnal diversions and deviations that she enjoyed. She usually took one of these trips to reward herself after a successful assignment. Partners were transient – she rarely saw them more than once and there were no further deaths in her private pursuits.

One evening, during a private break in Moscow, Maruška was out in the Izmaylovskiy district. It was a run-down area between the inner and outer ring roads, to the north east of the city centre. Famous for its flea market – anything from fine art to battle tanks, shiploads of diesel oil to Kalashnikovs - could be obtained if you knew the right people. Even if the clubs were unproductive, then she could usually expect to be attacked on the street and enjoy some carnage as she taught the local street punks that she was not what she seemed.

One evening when she was at a Goth club looking for some diversion for the evening, a scene developed between an apparently hetero couple. Although Maruška didn't know it at the time, it turned out that the girl had been having difficulties with a man trying to turn her into an addict and become her pimp; she was not a working girl and had no intention of becoming one. Maruška intervened and resolved the dispute by beating up the man, much to the enjoyment of the clientele of the club. She and the girl, who introduced herself as Natalya, then took him to the *Ismaylovskiy*

Lesopark nearby. They spent an enjoyable few hours in the park teaching Andrei a few basics about bondage and sex with objects. He would never be a problem again to women, straight or otherwise. That evening, on an adrenaline high, Maruška and Natalya had become lovers. After a few weeks wondering whether there could be a future with Natalya, Maruška reluctantly realised that there was no way forward for them – her life was incompatible with having a steady partner. She never again returned to Moscow for pleasure.

Ilich Ramirez Sanchez gradually faded from her focus over time, and she rarely referred to her books for inspiration. The Jackal was famous, and in prison. She had sought to emulate his notoriety, but her life was lived in secrecy - except for Wan Chuntao and her team, no-one knew how successful Maruška was at her job. Did she want notoriety? She wasn't really sure, though she did know that something wasn't quire right in her life.

Baldwin – The Formative Years

Steven Baldwin had been born and brought up an only child in Portsmouth. The family home was a council flat near Fratton, a mile or so from the naval and commercial docks. His father was a fisherman, running the 'Jenny C', a 38' trawler out of the Camber – the dock in Old Portsmouth right at the entrance to Portsmouth Harbour.

His father made a living at it, just, but when the catch was poor then he would come home after a skinful at The Bridge – a well-known pub on East Street hard by the Camber - and give Steve's mother a beating.

When the catch was good, then Mike – Steve's father would celebrate with a skinful, then come home and give his mother a beating. Steve started fighting at school on a regular basis (and out of school too for that matter) and this was coming to the attention of the educational psychologists.

By the time he was 13, Steve had started stepping in-between his parents during their nightly battles and getting a hiding for his trouble, but as he matured and grew he started giving almost as good as he got, and his father was more wary. Nevertheless, within a couple of years his parents had split up. Steve still saw his father occasionally – his father had taught him beach fishing at 6 years of age, and by the time he was 10 was helping out regularly on the trawler at weekends. Now, he lived with his mother and worked weekends with his father – their relationship was pretty good now that his mother was safe; his father had shacked up with another woman down in Southsea, but Steve knew nothing else about that side of his father's life.

He was far from a star pupil at the Priory Comprehensive school, but he'd stabilised since his parents had split up, and was able enough, though not academic. The fighting was in the past – he'd won his reputation. He still missed a day from school occasionally and took his gear down to the beach at Southsea to do some fishing. He watched the ships – tankers, warships, cruiseliners and more – entering and leaving the Solent, and his horizons widened as he matured.

He'd started thinking about joining the forces. The Royal Navy appealed, but after a discussion at the recruiting office in the city he wondered if there would be enough action. Yes there was travel, yes there was the sea, but he was unsure. He'd talked to his father about it, but his father was keen for him to go into partnership with him on the trawler. Then one evening over a beer in The Bridge, after a good day with the nets, his father suggested he think about the Royal Marines.

"Steve, get it out of your system," he said, "do a few years, sow your wild oats, and come back to the trawler. We'll buy a new boat when you return and you can take over."

By the end of the week, Steve had taken the first step and committed to the entrance assessment. A visit to the Royal Marines museum across the road from the beach at Southsea had cemented his resolve. Physical sports had never really been his thing, and he had to work himself hard to get up to the fitness levels required to pass his entrance and aptitude testing. Running on the shingle beach in Southsea for an hour twice a day worked his stamina up, and he joined a Portsmouth boxing club to gain access to the gym and a trainer, though the weekend work on the trawler had built him a half-decent upper body.

He passed his entrance with flying colours, and then worked his way through the batch of tests and trails and completed the 32 week training course as an outstanding candidate. He passed all the timed physical tests at better than the standard required of an officer candidate, which itself was significantly higher than that of a trooper.

A year later, when he returned from a winter survival exercise in Norway, Steve heard that his father had been lost overboard one bad night whilst trawling off the Nab Tower, east of the Solent. His crew had been picked up but the 'Jenny C' had been lost. His body had been recovered the next day by the Bembridge lifeboat. The trawl had snagged on foul ground and the inquest returned a verdict of accidental death.

Then, six months later, on a visit to see his mother, his mother had told him that she had terminal ovarian cancer, with only a few months at most left to her.

The insurance money from the 'Jenny C' and a fishermen's benevolent fund had gone into the bank. Steve arranged for his mother to go into a local hospice and was with her when she died eight weeks later.

"That's it," he thought as the grave was closed, "the RM are my family now."

*

Tobin Dynasty – Academia

What could live at 200 degrees Celsius and in a chemical mix that would strip paint? Admittedly, it was a less harsh environment than the primordial soup out of which we had all crawled, or was it?

The original discovery had been made in 1949. A deep water survey found anomalously hot brines in the central portion of the Red Sea. Later work in the 1960s confirmed the presence of hot, 60°C, saline brines and associated mud with high concentrations of metal compounds. The hot solutions were belching from the Red Sea Rift. This is a seafloor spreading axis between the African landmass and the Arabian peninsula. The Rift runs the length of the Red Sea, stretching from the southern end of the Dead Sea at Jordan and Israel to a triple junction with the Aden Ridge and the East African Rift in the Afar Depression of eastern Africa.

The rift zone includes the island of Jabal al-Tair, formed by the basaltic stratovolcano of the same name, located northwest of the Gate of Tears (Bab el Mandeb) straits at the mouth of the Red Sea, about half way between Yemen and Eritrea. The volcano last erupted on 30th September 2007, after being dormant for 124 years.

The Red Sea has at several occasions in the geological past been joined to the Mediterranean Sea, but is currently joined only by some bridges and the lock gates of the Suez Canal, a man made channel which links the perforations of the salty lakes and acts as one of the world's great shipping routes.

Research continued by a variety of research teams and undersea fumaroles or chimneys, which became known as 'smokers', were discovered. They emitted what looked like smoke, but which was in fact gas and high concentrations of dissolved minerals at high temperature ejected from magma – that is, the earth's mantle, and occur where there is sea floor spreading.

Sea water at the ocean floor is usually very stable in temperature (around 4 degrees centigrade) but near fumaroles, sea water temperatures varied, and could be as high as 300 degrees centigrade. The 'smoke' varied in colour – black or white - and the chimneys became known as white smokers or black smokers. The colour of the smoke was dependent on the content of the ejecta from the chimney.

What was really surprising was that life was found to exist in these extremely hostile conditions, ranging from bacteria to clams, limpets, shrimp and giant tube worms. Over 300 new species had been discovered.

Microscopic organisms known as *Extremophiles,* had in 1991, been shown to be able to extract metals from seawater. It was believed that some sulfur-oxidizing bacteria of the genera Beggiatoa, Thiothrix or Thiovulum played an active role in this precipitation.

These chemosynthetic bacteria derive energy from the oxidation of sulphide compounds directly from the scorching hot hydrothermal liquids. Basically, they feed on chemical soup from the earth's crust.

Evidence suggests that these bacteria can efficiently remove gold, silver, copper, and other metals and minerals from dilute aqueous solutions. One theory involves the increase in pH in the micro-environment of the microbial mats that line these vent chimneys. These metals are less soluble in this chemical soup and are then stored within the cell walls of the bacteria.

Projects were underway to recover rock from the sea bottom using chain buckets, and some success was reported. The 1960's and '70s saw a great deal of expenditure in the recovery of manganese nodules with varying degrees of success. Mining of manganese nodules served as a cover story for the elaborate attempt by the CIA to raise the sunken Soviet submarine K-129, using the Glomar Explorer, a ship built specifically for the task by Howard Hughes - Project Jennifer - and the cover story of seafloor mining of manganese nodules may have served as the impetus to propel other companies to make the attempt.

Projects of the scale of Jennifer were so expensive that only major corporations and governments could afford them. They also needed a degree of vision which was very rare. How many people would have had the vision, commitment, drive and resource to deliver projects such as a satellite broadcasting system such Rupert Murdoch had done with News Corporation? Or the tenacity and sheer criminality with which Robert Maxwell had built his publishing empire? These individuals were rare, and Charles Tobin was one of them.

Gerhard Wechsler's research paper was, at last, completed and published. His doctoral thesis at the University of Regensburg had been a study of bacteria near fumaroles in the Red Sea.

Charles Tobin had funded the work at Regensburg University some time before, and commissioned a series of oceanographic research projects and monitoring surveys in the Red Sea, and in the Kebrit Deep in particular in the northern Red Sea. He had, via one of his subsidiary companies, provided funding for this particular project. The project was closed down and the staff dispersed.

Over the next few years, Tobin began to shape the project into a hard edged set of objectives. Unquestionably, the best and chemically 'richest' fumaroles were to be found on the Mid Atlantic Ridge, and on other mid oceanic ridges where sea floor spreading was most active. The problem was that extraction in open sea conditions was just too risky, impossible even as a commercial venture – wave heights were bigger and there was no protection from the wind for hundreds, even thousands of miles. The Red Sea however, was only a couple of hundred miles wide and winds were very variable which meant wave heights were not extreme, and the climate was benign.

The main problem was the politics and economic zones. Countries now claimed rights over the sea bed out to 200 miles, but in law this was restricted to continental shelf areas. The United Nations Law of the Sea Convention governs these issues, and this was brought into the spotlight in 2007 when Russia planted a flag on the seabed under the Arctic Ocean. Lurid headlines such as "Russia Sparks Arctic Goldrush" were typical. Under Article 76 of the convention, a state can claim a 200 nautical mile exclusive zone and beyond that up to 150 nautical miles of rights on the seabed. The baseline from which these distances are measured depends on where the continental shelf ends.

So, whilst the middle of the Red Sea was within 200 miles of the countries on each side of it, the sea bottom near the centre was not technically, either legally or geologically, on a continental shelf. His legal team had been discussing this issue in greatest secrecy with the UK Government. It was a moot point. There were other conventions about exploitation of the sea bed, but these were more to do with 'tidying up the mess' and protocols for mineral extraction.

Wechsler's findings had been utilised in another of the discrete projects which Tobin had set up. Each project was 'standalone', an orchestral section, yet Tobin was orchestrating them following a master score. The next project, headed by a geneticist named John Appleton had refined the bacteria and optimised it for gold extraction.

Based in a state-of-the-art laboratory tucked out of the way in West Wales in the UK, Appleton had genetically cross-bred and tested the *Beggiatoa, Thiothrix and Thiovulum* with another bacterium, *Cupriavidus metallidurans*. This latter bacterium plays a vital role in the formation of gold nuggets, by precipitating metallic gold from chemical solutions in rocks. The resulting bacteria were hardened and tested, and the most productive strain was selected for production.

The optimised bacteria had been informally named *Thiovulum Aureus* by Tobin. It had taken almost ten million generations of the bacterium to achieve the minimum desired level of gold concentration and environmental hardening. It had also taken $30 million dollars of investment to get to this point.

*

Djibouti – Interlude

On the morning of his return from Little Aden,, Steve had eaten breakfast and been debriefed by the Major by 8.00 am. His helmet camera contained much of the mission details and the Major settled down to review it whilst Steve crashed out for six hours. It was far from being enough sleep, but the Major had a long list of questions arising from the infrared video recording, with supplementaries from London, where the video and debrief had been observed. When he was woken, Steve was given another shot by the ship's doctor to reduce the after effects of the amphipad, but the respite would be only temporary. He was longing to get back to Adèle and crash out again for however long it took, then maybe catch up with Marie – he still found it hard to believe that rubbish that Tom had come up with about her.

At 17:15, the debrief follow-up was closing, with London online. The feeds from the three camera packs were working, and they had a real time view of the loading of the Chinese frigates in the couple of hours of daylight before they departed. The *Guangzhou* had left the base within 3 hours of arriving, and the *Chaohou* followed two hours later. The material was still being analysed. The feed from the decoy camera had also proved very useful, but due to the darkness the removal of the supposedly 'fainted' Arab dock worker had not been recorded. The Major's view was that the epigun had just stunned the forklift driver, and certainly there was no increased dockside security activity on the cameras to suggest otherwise.

Ardent was now at the western end of her patrol run and about sixty miles from Djibouti. Steve and Don shook hands warmly and without any further delay *Ardent's* Merlin helicopter took off for Camp Lemonnier.

*

Meanwhile, back in Djibouti, Tom showered and prepared to go and collect Steve. He spoke to the *maitresse* and arranged another room for a visiting friend, arriving that evening. He left the *residence* by the rear entrance and picked his way through the plentiful garbage in the alley, finding his way out on to the cross street, crossed the road and walked out to his car. He walked past it and onwards around the block, turned and approached from the other direction. There were no obvious watchers. He strolled on and found a taxi. He asked the driver to turn right, heading past his hotel. All clear, he saw, with relief. After a mile or so, he changed taxis a second time and headed back. He stopped a few hundred yards short of his *residence* and walked into a grocery shop, browsed, checked out the window, bought a newspaper and left. The third taxi he found took him out to the airport. He a paid off the cab and walked into Arrivals and out through Departures towards the short term car park. After walking past the barrier he headed towards Steve's 4x4 hire truck in the north west corner.

There were a few cars parked in the area, all dusty and with foil sunshades inside their windscreens, baking in the early evening as the sun set. It was a deep red ball low in the western sky, the red colour a sure sign of a lot of dust in the air and a sandstorm on the way. There was a small grey panel truck, also dusty, parked a few spaces away from the 4x4. He was just a few yards away when the rear doors of the panel truck opened beside him and two men hopped out, balanced, capable, moving apart, silenced pistols levelled at him. One man he recognised as Target Two. The other looked equally hard-bitten and capable.

"If you are going to act, then do it immediately" the instructor at the training school near Stokes Bay had taught him.

They were 3 yards away, 3 yards apart and widening. No chance, Tom thought. He raised his hands and stopped. If they wanted me dead, I'd be dead. Get them closer.

"Don't shoot please, what's going on" pleaded Tom in Arabic. "I think you've got the wrong man here. I've got some dollars if that's what you're after."

The one to Tom's right front stepped forward, gun still raised and unwavering and in a heavily accented voice, said

"Shut up. We know who you are. Turn around. Hands behind your back."

Mid European accent thought Tom, responding in Arabic "I don't understand what you are saying. Dollars?"

Tom stood his ground and Target Three continued towards him, now within striking range as Tom moved his weight onto his left foot and pushed sharply forward off it and to the right, landing on the other foot, striking down and outwards with his left arm and rolling his trunk to the left, and following through with the firmly rolled up newspaper, still in his right hand, into the throat of Target Three. Target Two, to Tom's, left was swinging his pistol to bear in the single second it took. Tom's crunching blow was off centre of the throat, but good enough to stop Three. Tom continued moving to his right and heard a snapping sound as Target Three started to collapse backwards under the force of the crushing blow to his throat, with a barely any sound coming out of his mouth.

"Hans, hold fire. Stop *now* Mr Brown, or I will kill you *now*" said the female voice sharply, further off to Tom's left. The words deflated him - just words, but Tom knew from her stance and assurance that she surely would. Shit, Target One, she must have been in a car nearby, he thought. "Yes, we know a lot about you Mr Brown, or should I call you Smithers or maybe something else? I thought that one of you would come back here eventually" she continued, smiling, seeing the poorly masked look of surprise on his face. "Let's find out what you know about us, shall we? Hans, get the cable ties on him and search him. Then put Petr in the truck – you seem to have shot him. Imbecile!"

Tom was searched thoroughly, but all they recovered was his mobile phone and some money. There was little chance of them being able to access any of the phone's secrets – it was tamper-proofed and would burn out its own chips if opened. The phone was clean – Tom had erased the passport photos after squirting them to London.

Hans put heavy duty cable ties around Tom's wrists, then dragged and pushed the dying Petr into back of the panel truck. Petr appeared to be bleeding from a wound in his back, and there was a dribble of blood from the side of his mouth as he coughed and spluttered. Tom's plan had worked only that far. One down, two more to go. Pigs may fly, he thought.

"Mr Smithers, get into the back of the van. If I suspect that you intend to resist in any way, I will shoot you. I am a very good shot, and will disable you, painfully. That will be only the start."

Once in the van, Tom was lashed with more cable ties to the frame of the van and his feet were likewise bound to the inner frame of one of the rear doors.

"You know where to meet me Hans, you have the map coordinates. I will see you there later tonight. Leave him in the van when you get there."

The journey began smoothly in the evening twilight, and Tom once heard the blast of a train's whistle, so he guessed that they were fairly near to the Addis Ababa line. After an hour or so, the roads became very uneven and much slower. Petr had stopped making any kind of sound soon after they started, and Tom could feel his cooling body fluids on the floor of the van seeping through his own trousers. There was little traffic, just the occasional beam of headlights lighting up the interior of the back of the van as vehicles passed in the opposite direction. There was no traffic at all going in their direction. Tom tried to use the time to plan a way out, but his wrists and ankles were bleeding from the cables ties as he lolled on the floor as the truck bumped along, and it was difficult to maintain his focus. He judged that they were heading in a southerly direction, climbing slowly into the hills bordering Somalia. It was getting quite cold in the truck.

Eventually, after about two hours by Tom's estimation, the road became even worse for a mile or so and then they stopped. They would wait for Marie…

*

It was eight weeks before Tom's body was discovered by a goatherd. It was one of two found by the young lad in a ravine near Holhol in the Ali Sabieh region, 30 miles south of the city of Djibouti. Beyond the damage inflicted during his torture, and the predation by the local wildlife, what remained had been desiccated in the dry hill air. The British Government, via the French Embassy which represented British interests in Djibouti, had been enquiring for several weeks about a missing English journalist. Eventually the journalist's DNA was matched to one of the bodies. The cause of his death could not be determined. By then of course, other events in the Red Sea had overtaken the significance and priority of Tom Brown's disappearance. The second body remained unclaimed and unidentified.

It had been a long and brutal night, and Marie enjoyed her work. Hans merely observed – as an ex-soldier this sort of behaviour was not to his taste, but he had to admit that it was effective, up to a point. At the outset, she had given Tom a simple choice. His first option was to answer her questions truthfully and completely, and then be shot quickly. The second option was to resist interrogation, and die slowly and painfully, having given up the truth anyway. Tom took the first option (though this verbal dancing was moot) – his time in the van had enabled him to embroider his cover story in preparation – but how it would be decided if he was telling the truth was unclear. Torture was by its nature unreliable as a technique - most victims would eventually say anything to please their captors and relieve their suffering.

Using a rope, Hans dragged Tom from the van by his feet – he was by now stinking of Petr's drainings – and lashed him to a very old, very thick and solid cactus in a ravine. He was bound, on his knees, one foot each side of the cactus, with a rope from his feet to his wrists and around his neck. Hans then went off to dispose of Petr whilst Marie got into her stride.

"My professional name is Maruška" she said to Tom. "The only people who know that Maruška is me are dead. You will be the next."

Yes, he had heard of Maruška. Not yet a legend, but a dedicated terrorist and assassin with a reputation for detailed planning and ruthless execution of both plans and people. No way was he going to give her the satisfaction of admitting it.

"Maruška who?" he said in Arabic.

"You might as well speak English, Smithers, don't waste your time."

Working by the light of a small battery lantern, she opened her palmpad and showed Tom the video clip of his search of her room.

"I don't like men who search through my underwear when I'm not wearing it" she said, with a chilling smile. She relished telling him that she had sent mercenaries into Afghanistan and had even paid a brief visit herself. She related how their stories about the fate of captured Russians years before at the hands of tribesmen had intrigued her, and she had always wanted to try some of the ideas out. Then she showed him a short clip of the aftermath of a session in Afghanistan which one of her mercenaries had videoed when their fire team discovered bodies in a cave.

Tom determined to stick to his story, but Maruška would not be cheated of her fun. He focused inwardly and tried to think back to those training courses about resisting interrogation, but all that was in his mind was the last verse from that Kipling poem:

When you're wounded and left on Afghanistan's plains,
And the women come out to cut up what remains,
Jest roll to your rifle and blow out your brains
An' go to your Gawd like a soldier.
Go, go, go like a soldier,
Go, go, go like a soldier,
Go, go, go like a soldier,
So-oldier of the Queen!

Though the sentiment was dreadful, at least it gave him something to focus on and recite to himself. He wished he'd had a gun and been able to follow the advice. He tried to fall forward and strangle himself against the rope around his neck – passing out would give him some respite - but Hans always pulled him back. Marie was a capable interrogator, in both her physical and psychological approaches, and relentless in her pursuit of the details. She had been in contact with her Chinese case officer and some more background had been uncovered about Smithers/Brown - she had enough knowledge about him to destroy his cover story and ensure an enjoyable fencing match about the extra details. Her first question had been about his reasons for the search, and his answer, as he struggled to grope for a cogent reason in the face of the damning evidence, inevitably disappointed her. It was downhill from there. His back was scratched raw, and his knees were on fire, his lower legs dead. Tom knew that the outcome was certain to be slow and agonising. He struggled to use his training to resist, managing to stick to his story that was close to the truth, but inaccurate in the key details.

By 2 am, the wind was getting up and there was a lot of dust and sand in the air, which was making further progress slow. The lantern battery was failing and Marie told Tom that she had enjoyed the session; with a frisson of excitement she said to Hans that they had to leave and return to Djibouti to 'get the other one' whilst 'this one died slowly'. Then, something clicked in Tom's brain penetrating the fog and fear, and he realised he'd seen Hans before, one morning when he and Steve had been running on the road along the beach. One of the other runners. Too late, he thought, too late.

Though Tom didn't know it, 3 am came and went. He was terminally injured and through black, swollen and barely open eyes he was looking at his intestines, steaming in the cold night air, still connected and working as the sand blew around them. Maruška had never discovered who he really was, and he barely remembered himself. He had at least protected the current operation. That was some small comfort at least, but what a God-awful way to die.

The sandstorm was just getting well into its swirling, stinging stride as Maruška drove away in her car, and Hans started the engine of the van. Then, thinking again, he left the engine running and climbed out. Tom Brown had passed into unconsciousness for the last time, and as Hans walked towards him, he drew his pistol. I am not an animal, a brave man deserves respect and a soldier's death, he thought, as he delivered the *coup de grace.*

Food was scarce, and fought over with the intensity that survival dictates. The gathering wild dogs and desert warthogs which would normally shelter from the coming sandstorm, had smelled the blood and bodies and fear, and prepared to feed in the last few hours of the night, whilst the sandstorm blew around them.

*

Tobin Dynasty – Global Operation

Tobin's operations in Alaska and Canada continued to expand. By this time, 2004, his businesses were worth over six hundred million dollars, and his patented recovery processes, including, by now, a strain of bacteria for bio-oxidation during gold extraction, were being licensed to other mining conglomerates.

That year he bought a major stake in a gold mining operation in Nevada in the United States. Gold mining was a major industry in the state, and Nevada is still one of the largest sources of gold in the world.

Technology transfer was the buzzword of the day, and Tobin used his golden touch to invest in mining companies in Indonesia and Brazil. His modus operandi was now established: buy a small stake in a mining company in return for licensing them his patented refining technology, for two years. The yields and share price would then increase dramatically, and then Tobin would refuse to renew the license on pain of a larger shareholding. It didn't work in all cases, and he caught a cold to the tune of over $27 million dollars on one investment in South Africa when reserves had been overstated. All this time he kept out of Australian gold operations.

Tobin Resources International, as it was now called, was growing relentlessly, and Tobin moved his headquarters to London. London was the most important gold market, and it was in London that the world price of gold was fixed twice daily by the members of The London Gold Market Fixing Ltd. London was where his great great grandfather had come from on the convict ship 'Parkfield' from Sheerness in 1839, and whilst Tobin was not an emotional man in the conventional sense, he felt a strong sense of destiny when he moved to England in 2008 and bought an estate outside Winchester.

In 2009, he achieved his ambition, when he bought out the family business. Relations with his father had been getting worse for years – Charles's desire to 'do it his way' had led to a final break between them. For the 6 years up to his death in 2008, David had not spoken to his son at all and had disowned him. His aunt Suzanne, who jointly owned the business with Charles's father, was unmarried and childless and had become increasingly difficult in her old age. There were no heirs other than Charles (disowned) and no new family blood to re-invigorate the business. With falling ore yields, the business was becoming even more capital intensive – the gold recovery had to be run on a large scale to derive the economic benefits, and with the growth of the environmental movement and health and safety lobbies, the business was consuming capital at an unsustainable rate.

The gold reserves of the business were holding steady as the ability to extract efficiently from lower grade ores improved with new technologies. Tobin had not been approached to license his bio-oxidation to the family firm, his aunt was too stubborn to do so, but their Australian competitors were reaping the benefits. However the revaluation of the reserves was not in itself enough to keep the bankers happy, and with the new wave of technology about to break and production costs which were nowhere near the industry benchmark, it was quietly made known that the business was for sale.

And so, Charles Tobin came to own a business that he could by right have inherited. In fact, the money did come back to him as Suzanne relented in her dotage – there were after all no other heirs and even in her addled state she would not let it go to the Government.

In 2010, he gained British citizenship. He was forty years of age, and his business was now worth over three billion dollars. He owned an estate in England, flew in his own corporate jet, and his motor yacht *Auric Adventurer* was well known on the French Riviera. He had no family and few friends, and his vision was unbounded.

*

When he opened his first operation in Livengood, Alaska, gold had bottomed at $250 and ounce. In late 2010 it was approaching $1400 an ounce. Where would the climb stop? The gold price graph had been climbing at $125 per ounce per annum between 2002 and 2010 – in fact tripling in price in 8 years. Tobin did not think that this price was sustainable, but he had plenty of gold reserves, new technology in the making that would revolutionise the industry. He also had a penchant for gambling, playing poker now at clubs at a standard that would have taken him to the world championships in Las Vegas, had he been inclined.

The question that was exercising his mind was how he might back gold both ways. During his poker playing evenings, he had met a successful 'futures and options' trader who did in fact occasionally play in the world poker championships.

Gold, unlike pork bellies or wheat, was more resilient to price fluctuations – it was not subject to bad harvests, feed cost changes, floods or political whim such as OPEC exhibited from time to time. Demand for gold was continuously growing – India was still the biggest 'retail' market - and supply changed only slowly. Prices did change though, in response to that nebulous entity known as business confidence. Worldwide currency problems, oil supply problems, the credit crunch – in fact any loss of confidence across business as a whole – usually led to investors 'fleeing to gold'. Gold prices and its availability were also subject, above all, to wars.

Tobin had not been involved in 'futures and options' trading in the widest sense. Yes, he had bought options on mine tailings, and his company had been involved in acquiring other companies. This was a normal part of business, but as for speculation in its own right, never. Yes, at Geelong he had speculated on shares, but always in the expectation that the price of an undervalued share would rise, and he had been good at picking them. The idea of making money when prices were falling had been completely novel to him.

He took informal advice from his poker playing friend, and invited a man by the name of Richard Thompson to dinner at his estate in Winchester. For important meetings, you did not take guests to The Ivy or other public institutions, not when you were a planning a coup that would reshape the world gold market. Private clubs such as Whites were discreet, but public in their own way. Just being seen with someone could start tongues wagging.

*

Da'ud in Djibouti

Saunders left the Embassy in Sana'a with a holdall and headed for the nearest supermarket. He was concerned that the Embassy might be under surveillance and it took him an hour, two taxis and a couple of innocuous errands before he felt certain that he was in the clear, without any overtly suspicious behaviour on his part. In the supermarket toilets he changed into his Emirates businessman persona, and gave his outer holdall with the western clothes in it to a beggar scavenging the dumpsters outside. He reflected that he had been spending a lot of time in supermarket toilets recently, and hoped that this would be the last for a while, or the Religious Police would be getting suspicious. His high-end leather overnight bag, in keeping with his well-off Arab businessman demeanour, contained all he needed for his flight to Cairo. He found a taxi in front of the supermarket and headed for the airport where his professional eye noticed an increased presence of anonymous looking men who appeared to be waiting around and doing very little, and to whom most travellers would have been oblivious. At the Gulf Air ticket desk he bought a business class ticket to Cairo for cash, leaving within the hour.

Within three hours, he had landed, and once cleared through the immigration and customs, he headed in to the city and took a room in the Shepheard Hotel on Corniche el Nil St.

It was now late Saturday afternoon, spring in Cairo, and much cooler than in Sana'a, almost a thousand miles to the south east. Politically, it was still unstable in Egypt following Mubarak's departure in 2011, with the Army still lurking in the background and providing 'guidance and support' to the fledgling democracy.

He strolled for a couple of hours, enjoying the fresher climate and a shower of rain, taking a couple of coffees and searching for a suitable location. Finally, he found a café, with booths, inconspicuous with a clear approach and a rear exit. There were a couple of dozen patrons there, watching an African Nations Cup football match on the wallscreen – apparently Egypt were playing Sudan that very evening in Cairo, and judging by the raucous cheering, Egypt were winning. He bought a fruit juice, and picked up a card from the counter. At his seat in a booth he took out his mobile phone and pressed the key combination for Send Location. The encrypted GPS coordinates were picked up in London and queued out (together with a location map) to the courier who was already on a plane flying over Greek airspace at that moment, en route to Cairo.

Back at his hotel, he called London – he was relieved that another phone patch download was not necessary. They acknowledged the meeting location and a time and meeting protocol was agreed for the Sunday morning. They're obviously keeping Cairo Station out of the picture, thought Saunders.

*

The Sunday morning was grey, with showers blowing over from the west, a refreshing change from the dry dust and oven heat of Sana'a, and Saunders put on a shirt and chinos under his dishadasha. He arrived early at the café having first walked the street outside and wandered in through the rear entrance. He enjoyed a leisurely breakfast. Al Jazeera was the news channel of the morning. The Gate of Tears Crisis, as it was being called (the name was a great one for the media), was not the lead item. A half-hearted pitch riot following Egypt's late surprise defeat in the football was the lead story. What had once been an edgy news channel, making its name through Osama bin Laden's patronage in the early 2000's was now shaping its news agenda to suit the tastes of the man in the street. A sad reflection, thought Saunders as he watched, with all that was going on.

The news reported that two Chinese frigates had left the Combined Naval Task Force and joined up with a Chinese carrier group. The carrier, Pennant Number 083 Shi Ling, the first in the Chinese fleet, had been bought from the Ukraine in 1998 for $20 million (including blueprints) and converted and updated over many years – the Chinese had little background in carrier operations and Brazil had been assisting them to develop the skills and support infrastructure. China had identified carrier operations as central to it future strategic requirements under Den Xioaping – the US doctrine of using carriers to project power was still widely subscribed to – though less so in the US itself these days. The Chinese carrier was believed to be carrying the latest version of the J20 'Annhilator' stealth multi role fighter bomber and Chinese copies of the Russian Sukhoi SU-33.

The China News Agency had announced that China was sending naval and air forces in response to a request from its Yemeni friends in the face of foreign aggression.

There was speculation as to why the US was not rattling its sabres, and opinion was divided as to whether the UK was acting as the US policeman, using US technology, or whether the Middle East was less strategically important now that the Iranian nuclear problem had been neutralized by Israel and the vast US appetite for oil was being fed by the vast reserves discovered in the Arctic off Alaska, the latter issue moving US focus to territorial disputes with Russia.

Al Jazeera said that there were unconfirmed reports that the latest British Queen Elizabeth class aircraft carrier, 65,000 tons, carrying the J35 fighter, was en route from a goodwill visit to South Africa (following exercises near the Falkland Islands oilfield) to the Red Sea. The British Government, in response to questions, had said that "The United Kingdom Government does not comment on the operational deployment of its armed forces. It seeks only to ensure the free movement of shipping in international waters and observance of international conventions on the peaceful and environmentally safe exploitation of seabed resources." Bollocks, thought Saunders. They only say that when they are up to something. We're only there for the gold. That Aussie bastard Tobin has got everyone by the balls.

To Saunders's surprise, Al Jazeera then went on to report that elements of Australia's naval forces had put to sea. The Australian Government declined to comment.

That makes sense, thought Saunders. The Aussies have been selling iron ore and nickel in vast quantities to the Chinese for decades, but they've always been wary about Chinese ambitions in their own backyard. They had fought in Japan, Korea, Vietnam, and lost people in Bali, Indonesia; they were even nervous about India now – the concept of 'lebensraum', so disastrously espoused by Hitler, was still relevant for nations with rapid;y expanding populations. The Australians were very, very nervous about other countries eyeing up all their empty land and natural resources. They'll want to make a point.

The meeting had been set for 11 am, and at 10.50am the courier entered on time, as Saunders expected, but not in the personage *as* expected (if he had any expectation at all). Yes, a copy of the Al Ahram newspaper (previous day) in the left hand, and a black attaché case in the right hand. He rose from his seat, surprised to see a woman in orthodox Islamic burka stand in front of him and say

"Doctor, it is good to see you again."

"And it is good to see you again, Professor."

"Would you like a fruit juice?"

"I would prefer a mint tea thank you."

"Please have a seat, whilst I fetch your drink."

If she were a strict Muslim, then she shouldn't be meeting a single man in a café, Saunders reflected as he walked over to the counter and ordered a mint tea, but a lot had changed in Egypt and the Middle East in the last few years. The meet protocol having been followed to the letter, they entered into the prearranged cover - an innocuous academic discussion in Arabic about the Rubaiat collection of Omar Khayyam poetry, and whether so-called 'mystical metaphor' was essential to understanding it. Saunders was able to converse in some detail, the subject having been an essay topic during his Arabic degree, and it was clear that the 'Professor' also knew her Khayyam. Over the course of the next 10 minutes, the newspapers were exchanged and Saunders was passed the envelope. No agreement was reached on 'mystical metaphor'. The professor thanked him for the tea and made her excuses to leave for a seminar. Saunders dropped the newspaper into his leather case and left by the rear door, smiling – it was a rare event to enjoy a meet so much. Brief as it was, he had almost forgotten its ultimate purpose.

*

Back at his hotel, Saunders opened the envelope and found a new Emirates passport with visa for Djibouti, a debit card and some other typical 'wallet contents' – even a condom – ready to go. They think of everything, he smiled to himself. There was also a memory stick. He plugged the stick into his palmpad and it auto-started. He plugged in his earphones, and after the exhaustive security process, he was presented with a comprehensive briefing, complete with photographs and video clips – Marie, Hans, Baldwin, Tom – they were all there. He connected his iPhone to the palmpad and the pictures and salient excerpts of the briefing were automatically transferred to a secure drive area on the iPhone. He memorised the number for Baldwin's phone and securely scrubbed the memory stick permanently.

On the web he discovered that most flights to Djibouti from Cairo were routed via Sana'a and he definitely did not want to go back there, definitely not he thought; however, Ethiopian Airways did have a flight via Addis Ababa, leaving the next morning. He had been briefed to base himself in Plage Blanc, so after checking Googlemaps he booked himself a hire car at Ambouli airport. His current briefcase contents would continue to be used for his cover as a Carpet and Rug importer. He had learned quite a lot about the rug trade during his dealings with Salim – where was he now, he wondered? In fact, Salim's immediate family had been released under heavy threat of severe penalty, but Salim and his cousin were imprisoned awaiting trial on espionage charges. Theirs would not be a public beheading as rapists and murderers suffered, just a bullet in the back of the head following a trial held in secret.

Early the next morning he called London. When he eventually got the callback from Booth, the senior officer, the mood was different:

"The lockdown here has been relaxed, I'm glad to say. The security of the operation is now tight again. I can't say more."

There was no update on the situation in Djibouti, and the call was very brief.

In fact, the situation in London was far from relaxed. A pinhead laser transmitter, believed to be of Chinese origin, had been discovered, and one of the support staff on the Africa and Middle East desk had committed suicide in a shower cubicle. Vauxhall Cross was supposedly transmission proof, and it was not yet known how, or where to, the data was being relayed. It had not been detected by the regular sweeps and was being taken apart so that suitable detectors could be built. In fact, the laser transmitter was able, even at low power, to interact with sunlight and generate encoded 'interference fringes', within a supposedly secure quadruple-glazed window panel on the south face of the building. It was reading emissions from nearby laptops and relaying the data to the heart of the Guoanbu intelligence service in Beijing. Of course, it didn't work at night or when London was grey and miserable, but what was obtained was better than nothing.

It would be two years before a Network Rail project in London required the removal of the railway switchgear hut on the line out of Waterloo. A camera, laser and electronic relay equipment would be discovered by some workmen. They would not recognise it, nor would they know what a laser interferometer was used for and that it had been idle for two years. It would end up in a commercial waste recycling plant in south London with all the other scrap from the switchgear hut.

*

Farming Gold – Preparing the Field

The *Universal Trader* made her way up the East Coast of Africa, well out into the Indian Ocean. For the first 2000 miles from the Cape of Good Hope, the *Trader* had kept well away from the coast, passing outside of Madagascar, but now her course was adjusted slowly to start converging with the coast.

The weather and seas off the Aghulas Bank south east of the Cape of Good Hope had been moderate, and they had made good time. That area was very dangerous in the wrong conditions, when a quickly moving depression could hit the Aghulas current flowing south west down the east coast of South Africa, and generate freak waves. Since the development of satellite radar technology for ocean wave monitoring, research over the Aghulas Bank had turned conventional wave theory on its head. Previous models about the frequency of freak waves had been demolished. Now, oceanographers finally believed what mariners had been saying for centuries – freak waves were much more common than previous theories predicted.

The *Trader* was now 400 miles off the coast, which was normally enough to minimise the risk of piracy by Somalis. The failed state of Somalia had been a problem for years, ruled by a variety of warlords whom even the Americans had failed to tame, having retreated after the 'Black Hawk Down' fiasco in Mogadishu, the capital.

Now, the international anti-piracy task force known as the Combined Naval Task Force, was aware of the *Trader's* position and progress; they did not really expect any trouble on this leg as they were not carrying oil. Tankers laden with crude made especially attractive piracy targets. 200,000 tons of crude oil at 7.3 barrels to the ton and, over a hundred dollars a barrel, was a lot of money. Such sums vastly increased bargaining leverage. Nevertheless, even empty tankers and their crews were worth a fortune – a VLCC cost $120 million dollars to build. A ship plus cargo was valued at over a quarter of a billion dollars. This made insurers very pliable – in secret, of course.

With Madagascar now falling well astern, the *Trader's* course was adjusted slowly to start converging with the coast as she approached the Horn of Africa and her turn into the Gulf of Aden.

*

The *Universal Trader* was a VLCC – Very Large Crude Carrier – of 290,000 deadweight tons, originally capable of carrying two million barrels of crude oil. She had been built in 2011 by the Guangzhou International Shipyard in Guangzhou, China, but was not the largest they had built – they were building them close to 400,000 tons by this time. The Chinese engine weighed 2,000 tons and delivered 52,000 hp, using 270 tons of oil a day to drive her at her service speed of 16 knots. From the generators to the cutlery, the radar to the liferafts, she was Chinese through and through. The ship was too large to have taken the shorter route through the Suez canal. Scaling was important in this project, and a so-called *Suezmax* tanker would not have been large enough - Charles Tobin never did anything by halves. Time also worked in favour of the cargo, as the extra voyage duration around the Cape was beneficial to the *extremophile* breeding density at this initial stage. Eventually, the breeding cycle at the production platform would be self perpetuating, but for now, onboard enrichment during the outward voyages was essential.

*

Tobin had commissioned a survey of the Kebrit deep in the Red Sea, to locate the optimum site for seeding. The research team had been tasked with finding a geothermal vent – known as a chimney – which was in a depression in the sea bottom. The chimney would provide the rich chemical soup, and the depression in the sea bottom would minimise the effect of currents. Currents had to be avoided because they would wash away the feedstock *extremophiles* and with them the gold.

Tides are small in the Red Sea, only 2-3 feet in range which is enough to generate strong currents in shallow, constricted areas such as around reefs or narrow channel; however tides in the central part of the Red Sea are almost non-existent. In landlocked bodies of water in tropical and near tropical areas, there is also non-tidal current flow, driven by seasonal winds; these though are surface currents.

Tobin's scientific team had concluded that sea bottom currents would be minimal. Some movement was required though, to ensure that the bacterial concentration was kept properly supplied with the golden food they were designed to thrive on.

The planned process was to pump down the initial 2 million barrels of feedstock from the *Universal Trader*, into the sea bottom depression close by a chimney and let it incubate for three to four weeks (which was the estimated time required for the gold concentration to reach the required level for this stage of the process). The average concentration of gold in seawater is about 13 parts per trillion. Tobin's research projects had established that near some chimneys, the concentration could be as high as 200 parts per trillion. This was 10 times higher than previous research had indicated. In gold ores on land, the Canadian company *Genprobe* had been experimenting with bacteria to refine low-yield pyrites ores. With the specially engineered extremophile bacteria that John Appleton had produced, Tobin hoped that he would be harvesting at a concentration of 1 part per million, which would start to make very profitable economic sense. A tanker load – 200,000 tons – could yield as much as a quarter of a ton of gold by Tobin's calculations.

*

Since the so-called Credit Crunch of 2008, the world economy had been in turmoil, with currency wars and trade protection endemic. The International Monetary Fund had failed miserably and international banking had danced with returning to the gold standard in 2011. Countries were now fighting to underpin their currencies. Gold prices were climbing steadily and had tripled in ten years to over $3000 per troy ounce - equivalent to $100 million a ton. So, gold was now a strategic mineral again, but still not officially a Standard.

*

The process had been modelled, and pilot trials had been undertaken, but the harvesting on this large scale was critical. The effect of any sea-bottom currents and the local thermal circulation caused by the chimneys could wipe out the 'harvest'. A network of sensors had been deployed on the sea bed. These would monitor current and temperature, relaying the data back in real time to a survey vessel in the area, carrying out a bona fide oceanographic research project, under the auspices of an obscure marine conservation trust funded, once again, by Charles Tobin.

When the first harvesting cycle was completed, the *Universal Trader* would transport it back to the Tobin Resources refinery in Pembrokeshire. By that time, the second ship, *Universal Enterprise*, would be ready to seed the marine goldfield with her cargo of feedstock.

The final stage was the refinement of the harvest in Pembrokeshire, when the *extremophile* cargo would be unloaded into storage tanks and the gold would be extracted.

*

Aboard ship, the daily routine was steady and boring for the seamen, but the Ship's Master kept them occupied. There were reviews of the ship's anti-piracy plans and procedures, rehearsals and equipment testing even though the threat risk was assessed as low; this was all in addition to the usual tedium of maintenance which seemed to be endless. Entanglement lines had been rigged, firehoses checked and rolled out ready, the ship's safe area had been replenished, flare guns made ready – a whole panoply of precautions.

In the years since the Combined Naval Task Force had started operations, piracy had moved away from the Gulf of Aden towards the Seychelles, the Maldives and the so-called Mozambique Funnel. Pirates were now using larger motherships with small groups of attack boats.

The Master was regularly online to the Maritime Security Centre Horn of Africa (mschoa.org) and the International Maritime Bureau's Piracy Reporting Centre (icc-ccs.org) with updates on progress and to get the latest news. The MSCHOA was located in Djibouti and coordinated the Combined Naval Task Force of the Horn of Africa.

*

The nature of the cargo had introduced additional requirements and brought scientific crew aboard. Though the ship's tanks were fitted with bio-sensors, the sensors were very basic and much more detailed analysis was essential to keep the cargo evolving. It was still necessary to take samples each day and analyse them in the ship's laboratory, which had been specially built for that purpose.

*

John Appleton was the principal scientific officer responsible for the lab, reporting daily to Charles Tobin. Appleton was the most important man aboard, ranking in Tobin's eyes well above David Wallis, the Ship's Master. The whole project depended on the genetic feedstock in the holds being at its maximum potency when they arrived at the seeding area in the Red Sea.

Appleton's background was in genetic engineering – he had been recruited from AllGenTech, a fast growing genetic engineering company based on a business park in Cherry Hinton in Cambridge – the birthplace of so many hi-tech fortunes in genetics and computing. He had been an outstanding Natural Sciences graduate from Cambridge and it had cost Tobin a small fortune plus some heavy personal threats to bring Appleton into the project in a suitably malleable frame of mind. The share options in AllGenTech which Appleton had been forced to sacrifice were in themselves worth several million dollars. Nevertheless he was fully committed to the project by now, with a serious financial stake in its success.

The challenge was to multiply and maintain the feedstock at a temperature and pressure suitable for the continued multiplication of the genetically engineered *extremophiles*. The initial feedstock loaded at the refinery was to be bred to maximum density by the time the *Trader* reached the 'seedbed' in the Red Sea, by which time the *extremophiles* had to be living at a temperature and pressure in a chemical soup close to that they would experience at 2000m depth in the seeding area.

The particular bacteria to be deployed had been 'hardened' during breeding, and could tolerate lower temperatures and pressures than their genetic ancestors. The original bacteria had been brought from the Red Sea four years previously, and genetically engineered by Appleton in one of Tobin's myriad of discrete projects. The current generation was millions of generations removed from the original research batches recovered from the Red Sea several years before. Natural selection had been managed in the laboratory for the 'hardening process', and the current operational generation was capable of surviving below the boiling point of water, and at twice standard atmospheric pressure. Most importantly, at the other end of the scale, it was also able to survive at 180 degrees centigrade and 300 atmospheres pressure, where it would do its gold extraction work.

There were still areas of uncertainty – thermal shock would have to be controlled by limiting the rate at which the feedstock could be pumped down to the sea bottom, so that the bacteria acclimatised during the one hour it would take them to be pumped the 2,000 metres through the feedpipes from the ship to the fumarole area. This would be done by mixing them with bottom water. Barytropic shock – the reverse to the 'bends' that divers suffer from too-rapid a decompression - would be no problem given that the bacteria had originally evolved at high pressures. This had been proven in the pilot processing projects.

During the initial voyage from the refinery, the bacteria needed nutrients to survive, and these were sulphur based. This was straightforward to provide as a ship's bunker oil is sulphur rich. Tobin had installed a combined biological/mechanical sulphur dioxide scrubber to remove sulphur dioxide from ships' exhausts. This was a very profitable commercial project in its own right, as ship pollution is a major source of atmospheric pollution – in 2007, the world's 15 biggest ships emitted as much sulphur dioxide as all cars combined, and a major international effort was underway to address this. These exhaust scrubbers would shortly be mandatory worldwide on large ships.

The *Universal Trader* had been installed with what was in essence a small chemical plant, together with pressure vessels to grow and nurture the feedstock in the right conditions during the outward voyage. Appleton was responsible for this in-ship factory and its product and making sure it was in optimal condition at the right time, ready for pumping down 2,000 metres to the sea bottom.

So, with fuel being burned to power the ship, and bunkers (fuel tanks) full of sulphur rich oil, the feeding of *Thiovulum Aureus* was neatly accomplished.

*

Djibouti Beach Party

Just after 18:00 on that fateful Friday of his return from the expedition to the Chinese naval base in Little Aden, Steve Baldwin had landed at Camp Lemonnier and disembarked from *Ardent's* Merlin helicopter. He was led to the mess to await Tom's arrival, and allocated PFC Walsh as a babysitter. After two hours wait, which included a really good steak, he asked Walsh if he could use a telephone, and was shown to a Skypephone booth that the lower order base personnel used.

Recalling the number and test phrases that Tom had given him, he dialled and after what sounded like a couple of re-connections, a female voice answered:

"Switchboard, how can I help?"

"I'd like the number for Mandrel Brown please, Flat 3, 127 Fulham Palace Road, London."

"We have no-one of that name at Flat 3. There is an M Brown at Flat 3 117 Fulham Palace Road."

"OK, please connect me."

"The line is busy Sir. I cannot see your number on my console. Let me have your number and I will put a callback on for you."

Steve recited the second number that Tom had given him and rung off. London's NEAT net tracing software verified the number that he had called from, and a minute later the Skypephone rang. There was another password challenge and then he was connected.

"Mention no names or places, your location?"

"As delivered."

"Has your contact shown?"

"No, two hours overdue, they are getting a bit shirty here about me hanging around - they've given me a babysitter who's obviously pissed off at the task."

"Listen carefully, these are your instructions."

Steve listened carefully for a minute or so"

"Any questions?"

"I have a boat here. There's no way I'm doing that. Besides, my papers are on the boat."

"Mandrel, we believe that your contact is missing. We have identified the woman you met. She is the very worst kind of terrorist. We're certain that she's taken your contact down, and he was the best. She has at least one other in her team. Security is compromised. Follow the instructions. Don't worry about your papers."

"OK, I'll take it a step at a time."

The call was closed. Steve felt sick. All that work, and now I'm in even deeper, he thought. Walsh, his babysitter was waiting nearby and called for a taxi. He escorted Steve to the gate of the camp and signed him out. The cab arrived, but Steve ignored it, choosing to walk in the dark around the airport perimeter to the public terminal and to the 4 x 4 in the car park. There was an old one-legged Welsh sailor, Tristan Jones, who had written some great yarns about sailing. Steve had read them all, and couldn't help thinking of Jones's maxim about foreign ports:

'If in danger, or in doubt,
Hoist the sail and fuck off out'

That sounded like good advice. Bugger London, Steve thought, I'll play along, but in my own way. My papers might not be important to them, but they are to me. It was now nearly 9 pm and Steve was deep in thought and didn't see the sticky pool of Petr's drying blood next to the 4x4 as he walked into it. He cursed when he felt his deck shoes sticking and saw the mess on them, not knowing its significance. He scrabbled about to retrieve the truck keys from the wheel arch and took out the envelope from under the seat. It contained a British passport with Djibouti visa in the name of Stephen John Baldry – at least the first two names are Ok, he thought - drivers licence, two thousand dollars cash and some other receipts and bills for collateral – the sort of items you would find in anyone's wallet. There was also an open one way flight ticket to Cairo and an apparently basic iPhone. He used some of the cash to pay at the exit as he drove out of the car park.

London had told him that he should check in at a holiday village near Plage Les Sables Blancs – a chalet reservation had been made in the name of Baldry. Les Sables Blancs was 10 miles across the Gulf of Tadjoura from Djibouti city by boat, and over 80 miles by road. The holiday complex at Hotel Du Golfe Bleu was much less conspicuous than international hotels, probably safer, and out of the way. Before he drove there, though, he had a few things to sort out.

*

Steve parked the 4 x 4 in a car park well away from the docks. It was 11 pm now and the wind was getting up. He walked purposefully, but cautiously down towards the dock along the Avenue Admiral Bernard, and at the roundabout next to the sea he turned left. On his left hand side was a marsh, the road being built on a boulder causeway. He went down into the boulders and stripped down to his basics, but keeping his deck shoes on. The wind was getting up, and the waning moon had risen, though it was an eerie, unnatural reddish colour through the dust in the atmosphere, and didn't offer much light.

There was no traffic as Steve crossed the road, picked his way through the boulders down to the dirty waterside – it couldn't be called a beach by any stretch of the imagination – and into the sea. The swim to Adèle was about three hundred yards and took Steve about 10 minutes, not rushing it. Once aboard Adèle, he retrieved his keys from the cubby hole in the gas bottle locker and opened up. Working without a light he packed a small drysack with his passport, ship's papers and customs declaration in their folder, a change of clothes, pair of trainers, razor and washgear. Then, he dug out one of the Sigs from the waste oil container, and a couple of spare clips of ammunition. Cursing his cleverness in choosing such a filthy hiding place for his Sigs, he cleaned his hands – still, that was the right idea he knew - and added a torch, fighting knife and a portable GPS. In the galley he found some packets of nuts and biscuits, and a carton of orange juice to go with him. Then, finally, he stuffed a towel and a small rucksack on top of everything else in the drysack, and sealed it. He paused and ran through his mental checklist. Satisfied, he locked up, slipped back into the water, and pushing the drysack ahead of him, used his legs to propel him back to the shore and his clothes. The wind was getting up and blowing against him, with sand devils blowing out from the shore, but it was an easy swim against a small surface popple.

It was almost 4.30am by the time he arrived at the holiday village – it was a painfully slow drive on a bad road - he was seriously tired and it had been difficult staying awake as he drove through the billowing sand, getting slower as the sandstorm intensified and trying to keep sight of the road and stay on it. For the last hour and a half he saw no other traffic and almost missed the turnoff to the holiday site in the billowing sand. Any partying had been ended by the storm and there was no-one about. The security guard was asleep in his hut and not too pleased to be woken to open the gates. Steve found a corner of the car park, nibbled some biscuits and settled down to wait until breakfast time and check-in. He slept fitfully with his Sig at the side of the seat as the 4 x 4 rocked in the wind.

Just before 6.30 am the sun woke him and he roused himself for a barefoot run on the fabled white sand beach, which he had intended to visit anyway - though hardly under these circumstances. The sandstorm had petered out and the air was dry and cool with a light northwesterly breeze. The palm-frond sun shades were scattered across the beach, and a few tables had been overturned by the storm front. After his run, he found a shower on the beach and then by 8am a café on the site was opening.

*

Events in London had moved quickly. The Cobra committee was meeting daily, and the disappearance of Tom Brown in conjunction with the apparent security breach was hampering the Department's ability to deal with the crisis and deploy more human assets into Djibouti. Yemen had stopped issuing visas to British nationals and movement of diplomatic personnel was limited to Sana'a.

That Friday night, the senior officer on the Africa and South East Asia desk had a team working on Tom Brown's communications and mobile phone. The GPS tag in the phone had left a position data trail out to the Ali Sabieh region south of Djibouti. The maps showed the area to be mountainous and sparsely populated (Djibouti was in any case one of the most sparsely populated countries in Africa). The phone had been in position for about four hours and had then moved back to Djibouti where the battery had been removed. The non-standard, higher power backup battery would enable the GPS tag to transmit every hour for three days. The latest position had shown it to be in the Al Mansour hotel, Djibouti, room 34.

*

After breakfast and checking in, Steve collapsed on his bed in the holiday chalet and fell asleep again for a couple of hours. It was near midday when he woke and after a shave he settled down to sort himself out. First the phone. He called 'the switchboard' as he had the night before.

Following the security rigmarole, he also was told to log on to a website, follow the instructions and update his phone and call back. This proved to be a real fag, as he had to go to the camp office and use one of their laptops. Steve then called back and the senior officer told him there was no update from his contact, and that they believed the situation now to be very serious, with Tom's phone being in the possession of the female terrorist. Steve was told to sit tight and do nothing. Call again in 24 hours.

No fucking way am I doing that, he thought, not if that bitch has shafted Tom. After lunch, he packed his rucksack and left his chalet. He didn't bother signing out, just in case he needed to return – he hadn't yet planned beyond the next twenty four hours. In the nearby small town of Tadjoura he found a men's clothing shop and bought himself a *tobe* robe and a *taquiyah* for his head. The choice was not great – most of the city men now wore western style clothing, and he explained to the clothes shop owner that he wanted it as a souvenir. The drive back to Djibouti was much quicker in the daylight with no sandstorm and in just over two hours he was on the outskirts of Djibouti, having stopped briefly en route to change into his new tribal clothing. He parked the 4 x 4 in a shopping mall and caught a bus into the city. It was a ten minute walk to the café across the road from the Al

Mansour hotel, where he settled down with a coffee and newspaper, to watch, wait and plan. After ninety minutes or so he was becoming restless and wondering what to do. Then his phone signalled a text. "Call grandmother." I'm no good at this spook stuff, he thought. I might as well head back to Plage Blanc. He walked back to the 4x4 and decided to change it for another car - a basic precaution he thought.

He drove to the hire company – it was late Saturday afternoon by now but it was still open. He handed back the keys of the 4x4, explaining that his girlfriend didn't like it and changed it for a Nissan Patrol 4x4. The clerk was a bit confused to see him dressed in a *tobe* and *taquiyah*, but smiled when he explained that he found it more comfortable in the climate. The address he gave remained the same, care of Dolphin Services.

As he drove away, the Chinese bot in the hire company's computer notified Wan Chuntao in the Guanobu complex in Beijing that the original 4x4 Land Cruiser had been returned and exchanged for another vehicle. Chuntao was asleep, and would not pick up the email until the next day, but the database was updated and a priority text sent to Marie.

*

They were sat in Marie's car in the short-term car park at the airport, alongside Petr's blood, where the 4x4 had been parked. She was ranting at Hans. "What do you mean you didn't put the tracker on the 4x4?"

Hans shouted back at her: "I thought you had done it. We'd just got here when Smithers turned up, we had no time, and then I headed off into the mountains. You were there too, it just got overlooked. Why didn't you do it? Shit happens. Anyway, we know that Baldwin will come back to his yacht sooner or later."

It was unfortunate for Tom that they had arrived just before him and caught him, but he had given them very little of use. They planned to get more out of Baldwin.

"OK, we mount a 24 hour watch on that yacht, no excuses."

"That will be very difficult now we do not have Petr with us" Hans responded.

"It has to be done. You will be there tonight, I will relieve you at 8 am. Do it."

Hans grumbled, but accepted that it had to be done.

As they drove back from the airport into Djibouti, her iPhone jingled. She dropped Hans off at his hotel to get his car, and headed back to her room at the Al Mansour Hotel.

*

After leaving the car hire depot, Steve drove down to Dolphin Services, feeling safer, almost invisible, dressed in his *tobe* and with a new vehicle. He stopped in the car park and standing at the edge of the landing he could just make out Adèle at anchor in the fading twilight. Everything seemed fine with her – he'd been worried that her anchor might have dragged during the sandstorm, but she appeared to be lying in the same position, unmoved. He turned, and climbed back into the Nissan as a white Peugeot drew up in the car park and a man climbed out, picked out in Steve's headlights. Shit, he recognised the guy, but where from?

He drove off slowly and two hours hour later was back in his hut in the holiday village at Plage des Sables Blanc on the other side of the Gulf, still niggled by the sighting of the unknown man.

At Dolphin Services, Hans was sat in his car, listening to Marie on the phone telling him about the vehicle switch.

"Fuck, I've just seen the Nissan truck" he said, "here, at the dock. I couldn't see the driver though, but it must have been him. Half an hour ago."

Marie continued "We will not find him then after half an hour. I went straight round to the car hire company and spoke to the clerk as he was locking up, looking for my friend Mr Baldwin. He said his customer was dressed as a local, and wanted to change the truck because his girlfriend didn't like it – was that me, he asked. Very original. And we still don't know where he's staying – he gave his address as that boat dock. Go back to your hotel and get some rest. He knows about us and you will be wasting your time waiting there."

*

It was late evening when Steve got back to Plage Blanc after stopping en route to change out of *mufti* and back into his regular gear. He was concerned that Adèle was being watched and that he was now up against that Marie bitch and also a guy; he just wanted out, to be away from Djibouti and up the Red Sea, though even that did not look like a good option now with all the naval shenanigans that were developing. He walked down to the restaurant for dinner. The visitors in the restaurant were oblivious to the trouble in the Gulf. When he got back to his chalet, there was a missed call on his phone, no number. He turned the TV on to catch the news at midnight. Britain had issued a statement strongly advising the Chinese not to send their naval forces into the Red Sea – that would be seen as a provocation. This is unreal, Steve thought, either that Prime Minister has got very big balls or he is an idiot, though he actually could not remember who the PM was. Britain against China. Must be mad, ours not to question why…

*

Sunday morning, and Steve was up with the sun for a run and a swim. There was quite a lot of activity, even at 7 am, as some whale sharks had been spotted in the Gulf, and trips to swim with them were being organised for the visitors. Though he'd seen some himself over the years, he'd never had the inclination to swim with them - although they were very big, they were also harmless and gentle plankton-eaters. Another time, maybe.

He called in the café for breakfast and as he got back to his chalet his mobile phone rang – the secure call icon was showing. He answered, and an English voice said:

"Mandrel, can you talk freely?"

"Yes on both counts."

"I'm your new friend en route to meet you at your location. You can call me Da'ud. Stay where you are, do nothing, I should be with you about 5 pm this afternoon."

"OK. I'll be calling my grandmother later to discuss family news."

"Fine, I will see you later."

Steve called London – the security process this time was much more straightforward, he noticed. He updated his controller about the previous evening's events, and cursed when it was suggested that changing the truck might not have been a great idea. They confirmed that Marie had at least one accomplice, and that he was thought to be a German with a special forces background, Hans Grüber. Fucking great, thought Steve, that's really all I need. London also told him to expect some local support – Steve mentioned he'd been contacted already – and that the next steps were being planned.

In fact, things had been moving quickly. London had been in touch with the DGSE in France – the equivalent of MI6 - as Marie was travelling on a French passport in Djibouti – still with strong French connections. DGSE were very interested – they thought they might be able to tie this in with the killing several years before of a German mercenary in Paris. Though London didn't know it, a proposed operation had gone to the French Prime minister for sanction (the French were a lot more careful since the days of the Rainbow Warrior sinking). There had been a delay on the French side as the DCRI (Internal Security) tried to wrest control of the operation from DGSE and failed, as Djibouti was now a sovereign country, not a French territory. That Sunday morning, as Steve was speaking to London, the final preparations were being made by a team on the French frigate *Surcouf* in the harbour at Djibouti.

*

Just before lunch, Steve called Dolphin Services on the off chance that there might be someone in the office. There was, and André was happy to tell him that he had personally checked Adèle that morning and everything was fine. Satisfied, Steve went off in search of Sunday lunch in the air conditioned restaurant at the site – not his normal style, but it was Sunday, and he thought he'd earned it.

*

Marie was in her room with Hans watching the lunchtime news when her palmpad jingled. A message via Wan Chuntao. A mobile telephone call enquiring about the yacht Adèle had been made to Dolphin Services within the hour. The message included the mobile phone number used. Her Chinese technicians had gained access to the Djibouti Télécom system and were attempting to triangulate the location of the call. It looked like the call was made from the Plage des Sables Blanc area, but because there were not many mobile phone masts in the area, a precise location could not be determined. They were hacking the hotels' reservation systems to try and locate a list of arrivals within the last 24 hours, and further details would follow. There were no international hotels in the area, just small local hotels and beach resort clubs, so the search would take longer.

"Come on Hans, let's go and find that 4x4." She checked the map on the dressing table. "We've got an hour's drive to get round there." She opened her carryall, and dropped the tourist map in. She found a tourist guide book in one of the desk drawers, which she added. She took out her pistol and checked it. Hans checked his and replaced it in his waistband holster at the small of his back under his shirt worn outside his jeans.

"We'll get over there and once I have the guest register details through, we'll narrow the search down and check the car parks for that Nissan. If we take both cars then we can search more quickly."

They went down the two floors in the lift and out into the blistering midday sun. There were few people about as Marie stepped onto the pavement to cross the street to her car – Han's was fifty yards down the street on the same side.

"Stop, raise your hands" came the shout in French.

The French guys in black overalls and balaclavas had stepped out from two people carriers, one each side of the entrance.

Hans stopped in surprise and looked round in puzzlement – his French was very poor. He saw the guns aimed at him and started to raise his hands.

Marie put her carryall down slowly as she assessed her options.

'Bad tactics', she thought as in one fluid moment she stepped behind Hans, lifted his shirt and pulled out his gun with her right hand, and pulling his belt with her left hand stepped back, dragging him, now off balance, with her. The split team of French commandos, facing each other and having been surprised by Marie and Hans coming out of the hotel, were in a crossfire lineup and held fire, just giving her enough time to back up and release Hans as their angle improved and they opened fire.

Hans took the fusillade as he fell. She got back in through the door, ran across the lobby shooting the concierge in passing and hitting the lift button on the open lift. She ducked back behind the concierge's desk as the commandos stormed in, across the lobby towards the lift door. The capitaine sent two men up the stairs and two towards the back entrance. Marie grasped her pistol two-handed, counted one-two-three, stood up and shot the two remaining guys, head shots, first time from less than ten feet. Coming out from behind the desk, she crossed the lobby and walked out of the door. There were two commandos in position on the pavement, startled to see her, having heard the shots, one now holding her carryall and the other stooped, searching Hans's body, looking up. 'Still bad tactics', she thought as she fired twice. They fell backwards together, one hit in his body armour. The stooped commando took the bullet down through the top of his head. The fallen first commando tried to swivel and bring his Steyr TMP to bear, with a raking burst across the pavement as he swung the weapon. She took more time placing the head shot accurately as she stepped across Hans's body. They hadn't bothered with helmets – macho French, and mucho dead, she thought.

People were now coming out on to their balconies, and then rapidly retreating when they saw the scene. She picked up her holdall next to one of the dead commandos. "I think that's mine guys. That was very sloppy work. You shouldn't underestimate a woman" she said aloud in French, then crossed the road to her car.

She climbed in and accelerated away, hearing a burst of shots, two of which spanged the rear of her car. After two blocks she got out, opened the boot and took out a Heckler and Koch MP7 from under the carpet. With its stock folded it fitted neatly into her carryall, along with two magazines. She left the car, walked around the corner and put a black headscarf on. After another two blocks she hailed a passing taxicab.

"*Plage des Sables Blanc, s'il vous plait*" she told the driver.

*

Steve got back from lunch. He was still strung out after the exhausting mission in Little Aden and the to-ing and fro-ing since. He turned on the television with the intention of listening to the news channel and dozing off in the chair, as most normal people did after a Sunday lunch, at least in England. Sleep didn't come though, as he heard an excited reporter talking about a shootout in Djibouti – a woman and some men in black uniforms, believed to be French commandos. He sat up with a start, wide awake. There were at least five dead – one of them a male terrorist, believed to be German, plus a hotel concierge. Four French commandos had been killed. A woman terrorist, believed to be French, had escaped. Neighbours had witnessed the woman apparently executing two commandos outside the hotel.

Djibouti police and armed forces had sealed off the area and it was believed that four French nationals were being questioned. The Djibouti Interior Minister was pontificating about 'unauthorised foreign operations on sovereign Djibouti territory.'

Steve picked up his phone. He hoped grandmother was not at lunch. She was, there was a desk officer standing in. "There's a big mess here – do you guys really know what the fuck is going on?"

No, they hadn't heard any news from Djibouti.

"French commandos have taken it up the arse, big time. Tell grandmother to call me back," he said with easy sarcasm, cutting the call. It was now after 2 pm, and he had to sit tight. No way, not with that mad cow on the loose.

*

The taxi driver had not been happy about the destination – it was a four hour round trip for him, but three hundred dollars had persuaded him. They were heading north on the N9, passing Lake Ghoubbet, with a local French music station on, when the 1 pm news bulletin came on. Marie heard the lead story and saw the taxi driver's eyes look at her in the rear view mirror. She took the gun out of her carryall, and put it to the driver's head.

"I want to see the lake. I hear it is one of the best dive sites in the world."

"Jesus, Madame please, I have a wife and family, I will say nothing, not charge you fare. Take taxi and go. Please don't kill me, please. I will do as you say."

"*D'accord*" she said, just take me to the lake and I'll leave you there."

They pulled up in a picnic spot at the side of the road on the hills overlooking the lake – an almost land-locked bay - and got out of the taxi. The sun was glittering on the lake, ruffled by the light breeze. There were no picnickers in this heat, though she could see a tourist schooner on the horizon, sailing into the almost land-locked bay from the Gulf of Tadjoura through the Ghoubbet Pass. On the north side, Marie could see a couple of dive boats – it was a pity that she wouldn't be able to dive here on this visit – uniquely clear water, two hundred species of coral, manta rays, whale shark, barracuda, sailfish, and a place really not to be missed by a diver. It was quite beautiful. She sighed. Another time, she thought.

"The Devil's Cauldron. It is a beautiful sight" she said to the taxi driver, and as he turned to look at the lake, she raised her arm and shot him in the head. A flock of startled birds rose noisily from the surface of the water as the echo of her shot reverberated around the Cauldron. She dragged his body into the nearby brush, then, back in the car, she checked the clip in her pistol, and put it next to her seat, between her thigh and the door. She adjusted her headscarf and put her sunglasses on, then headed north again.

As she drove, Marie took stock of her situation. She had one good passport in the lining of her carryall - the others were blown and in her room anyway. In her carryall she had an iPhone, a palmpad computer, Hans's pistol with seven rounds left, a couple of spare magazines for her own Glock 38, an MP7 with spare magazine, a knife, a few hundred dollars and a credit card, and a stolen taxi which would soon be missed. Plus, one change of clothes, which I really should get in to, she realised. She was still about thirty miles from Tadjoura when the 2 pm news came on the radio – there was a description of her being broadcast. She pulled off the road behind some scrub, and changed into her tight red top and skimpy shorts – 'to keep their eyes off my face' she thought. She added a white bandana.

Just then, her palmpad jingled. She ignored it and drove to the outskirts of Tadjoura, and parked the taxi up a stony track behind some cactuses alongside a dried up watercourse' hidden from the road. She wiped it down and left it – she might have an hour, she might have a day - she didn't know, and set off on foot for Tadjoura.

There were no people about at this time on a Sunday, and after ten minutes walking in the punishing heat she found a bar and a corner table. There were a few locals in for a Sunday afternoon beer, watching an Italian football match on the wallscreen. She knew she was attractive enough to look at and a few of them were diverted from the football, but not for long. At least they are not watching the news she thought, and I look like a holiday visitor. She arranged her carryall on the floor next to her, with the zip half way open. She ordered a St George beer and some local injera bread with beef sauce then logged on. The palmpad message had a list of reservations for that weekend in Djibouti.

Unfortunately, it was a weekend and changeover time for many visitors – there were more than four hundred new reservations. Wan Chungtao's team had sifted them to eliminate couples. Singles attached to tour groups were listed separately, and the final list contained nine single men with no obvious attachments, three of whom were English. One was registered at the Kempinski Palace, and one at the Sheraton – both in Djibouti City. There was only one new registration in Tadjoura in the last twenty four hours, at the Hotel du Golfe Bleu, Chalet 12, in the name of Baldry. Another single Arab man was expected at the Golfe Bleu that day. Of course, Baldwin might not be registered on an English passport anyway.

Still it was a good place to start. She googled the hotel on the web – there was a little information – location, phone numbers, email address, and clicked the link. It was a small hotel with a 'five star restaurant', ten luxury suites and twenty beach club chalets (all with wifi) with a swimming pool and beach café. Unfortunately there was no site layout plan, though the half dozen photographs were useful. She checked her tourist map and marked the location. The web link here was slow – area wifi but via the mobile phone network, suffering because of football on Sunday afternoon. She cursed – even here in the back of nowhere people watching online were choking the bandwidth.

*

Saunders cleared quickly through the officialdom at Ambouli airport - he had only a carry-on holdall with him. He changed in the toilets into chinos and a shirt. The *galabaya* would have been more comfortable, he thought – it was normal in Cairo but too conspicuous down here in Djibouti, and not easy to run in if it comes to that. He strolled across the concourse to the kiosk, to buy a local newspaper, and then to the bar where he bought an imported beer. While he was seated, a man slid into the seat opposite him.

"What's the beer like?" he said in Arabic.

"I prefer a lighter taste" Saunders replied.

"I think I'll get one for myself then" the man said. He got up and walked away towards the bar. Saunders sipped his beer, reading the lead story in the newspaper. It was Saturday's edition – he assumed they didn't publish on a Sunday. Tension in the Red Sea was ramping up. Two Chinese frigates had joined a carrier group in the Gulf of Aden – the Chinese aircraft carrier, Shi Lang, was on station, with a flight wing of the Chinese copy of the Russian SU-33 Flanker-D – a high performance fighter with vectored thrust engines. There was an in-depth analysis inside the paper which he scanned quickly.

Acquiring a blue-water carrier capability had been one of China's strategic goals since the 1980's. They had four carriers under construction, two of them nuclear powered, but the Shi Ling was the only operational platform at present, as the construction programme had been subject to delays. It was the old Russian carrier '*Varyag*', an uncompleted *Kuznetsov* class carrier which they had bought from the Ukraine, stripped down and rebuilt. It took the US six years to build each new supercarrier, and they had been doing it for ninety years. The Chinese first had to 'build the capability to build', and that took a lot of time and money. The Russians were no longer in the carrier game, though France and Spain had both tried to sell them carriers. It was amazing how the access to information on the web had actually improved the reporting in the few traditional newspapers that were still published. He looked forward to finishing the article later as he checked his watch – ten minutes in the bar, and time well spent. He finished his beer, not having obviously rushed it, got up and picked up both bags by the table and walked out.

He collected his 4x4 from the car hire office and was glad of the air conditioning in the afternoon heat. He checked the map, and headed for Plage des Sables Blancs. When he turned the radio on he was astonished to hear the non-stop babble on all the stations about the shoot-out outside a hotel off the Place Menelik. He pulled in at the roadside and called Baldwin.

"I've just heard the news – I'm guessing one of our targets is involved, what do you know?"

Steve outlined what little he knew and that he was getting restless.

"I'll be there in an hour. I'm in a blue long wheelbase Korean 4x4 – I can't pronounce the bloody make. Kissin' something I think. Stay put whatever you do. Do you have any protection?"

"Yes, I can look after myself. I've got some tools."

"OK, remember, this woman is at the top of the heap, seriously capable."

"Yes, I know, I've kissed her."

*

Once he had got out of the city and on to the N1 route, he found a spot to pull off the road. There were no other cars about as he got out and retrieved the other holdall from the rear of the 4x4. It was an Adidas sports bag, and he checked the contents as he sat in the front seat. The man he'd met in the bar at the airport had come round from the US base and provided a bag of tools for him, at London's request. Obviously Booth was keeping his distance from the French after the fiasco outside Pavkovic's hotel. Still, tools were tools, and very welcome. He hoped he wouldn't need to use them, but thought that unlikely.

In the sportsbag he found a GPS, a palmpad computer and chargers, a compact easy-carry Glock 26 with threaded barrel and silencer, along with 5 clips of 9mm ammunition, a belt holster, and a knife. At the bottom, wrapped in cloth, was a Heckler & Koch MP-7A1 and four magazines. A bit OTT for my taste, Saunders thought, but you never know. He checked the weapons. There was also a road map, a bottle of water and a couple of Hershey bars. The guy obviously had a sense of humour!

He pulled his shirt tail out of his trousers and fitted the holster behind his back, then after putting his sportsgear back in the rear of the truck under a suncover, he opened a Hershey bar and drove off, munching.

*

Marie was browsing the map of the area and marking out the route to the Hotel du Golfe Bleu, and the getaway options. It was about a mile and a half to the hotel, not a pleasant walk in this heat. She would be on foot, and that could be a disadvantage if Baldwin was on his guard, and necessitated an inconspicuous approach. It would have to be done at night. Her palmpad jingled and the football fans in the bar turned to look – she looked back at them and shrugged in the way that the French do best.

It was just a message that the mobile phone had been used again, and that the location was now confirmed as the Hotel du Golfe Bleu. Maybe she should call him and flush him out? She had no car, and if he got past her then she would lose him again, unless…yes that was the way she would do it.

She finished her beer, bought a couple of small bottles of water and a chocolate bar, and left the bar. A taxi had pulled up outside, and there was no sign of the driver. She went back into the bar.

"Taxi?" she enquired.

One of the football spectators turned and, with food in his mouth, said

"*Ce n'est pas possible – le déjeuner et le football. Attendez une heur.*"

She shook her head and turned. Another reason I hate men – beer, food and football first, if there's no sex on offer. Covering her head completely with her scarf, and sipping her water, she set off for the hotel.

*

Something that London had said was nagging him – 'not a good idea to have changed the car'. He put his SIG in the back of his waistband and locked the door of the chalet. It may be out of the way he thought, but if anybody wanted to kill me, it would only take a shotgun through the chalet wall – little more than thin plywood, cheap and cheerful. A shotgun shack as the Americans would call it. He strolled over to the Nissan, wondering what the plan would be when his new 'friend' Da'ud arrived. He started the engine and drove around the site, looking for somewhere less obvious to park. He found a spot around behind the dumpsters by the back entrance to the restaurant kitchen. The area was stinking and buzzing with flies, with three healthy-looking cats stretched out in the shade nearby.

He locked the truck and started walking back to his chalet.

*

The entrance road to the hotel was well marked with a large blue (and fading) plywood sign. She had been walking for more than half an hour and it was impossible to hurry in the heat. Across the main road, behind some scrub she sat on a rock to rest – there was no shade anywhere – and think through her plan once more. Out of sight of the road, though there was no traffic about, she checked her weapons again, leaving the bag unzipped. Marie stood up, adjusted her headscarf and sunglasses and crossed the road to the turn-off for the Hotel/Beach Club complex.

The access road was stony and unmade, but relatively smooth. She could see the beach down the slope to her right, about 200 yards away, as the road turned and angled down to the hotel complex and chalets. There had been some attempts to 'prettify' the approach road, with palm trees, but even these were looking somewhat sad in the arid soil. There was a barrier and turning area at the bottom of the hill, with the hotel car park beyond that.

There was a noise behind her, and she moved to the side as a 4x4 came slowly down the road. She kept her eyes ahead as the vehicle approached her, aware that the driver was looking at her as the blue truck passed. It continued on down the hill, and stopped at the barrier. The driver spoke to the security guard and continued into the car park once the barrier was raised. She could see the driver park the truck in the car park and take his bag, walking towards the doorway with a sign marked Hotel and Beach Club Reception over it. She nodded to the security guard as she walked through past the barrier – she was obviously a client or visitor, certainly not a local peddlar or hustler, and was not challenged.

She paused by a fig tree and took out her mobile phone, making to take pictures of the site for a holiday album or more likely a Facebook page. She scanned the car park as she did so, and moved position to get a better perspective for her pictures. There was no Nissan 4x4 in the car park that she could see, at least not one with the colour and number that Wan Chuntao had provided from the hacked car hire database. Walking on, she put her phone in the pocket of her shorts and headed toward the beach huts, with her carryall in her left hand.

The chalets were strung out in a long line along the edge of the beach, with an access path in front of them; some ground cover plants and sea grass had been half heartedly planted with the opposite effect to that intended. There was a service track to the rear, and the gap between the chalets was about three yards. The beach wasn't that clean, nor was it really that white, but in the heat the sea looked inviting. There was a slight swell which was breaking lazily with a gentle murmur as the tide was coming in. She followed the access track at the rear of the chalets. Half way along – she could see '10' on the chalet door - there was a large area with maybe fifty yards between chalets 10 and 11. In this paved area was an open air bar, some tables and a few people reading, talking and enjoying a beer alongside a swimming pool, with some 'chillout' music playing quietly on the sound system. The pool was somewhat incongruous given the sea less than fifty yards away, but it looked well maintained, and was being used by a few children and an obese blonde woman who appeared to be speaking in German to the children. Marie continued her survey along the rear service track, passing chalet number 12. At number 13, she stopped, took out her mobile phone and appeared to read a text as she turned and checked the rear and side of No.12.

She could hear what sounded like a TV news channel, and continued on her way to the end of the line of chalets, where she rounded the last chalet. The beach appeared to end here at a rocky outcrop which ran down almost to the sea, though there was a rough path continuing up and over the rocks. She climbed the path and at the top, stopped and turned, appearing to take a photograph of the chalets with her mobile phone.

*

Da'ud Al Haidar signed the register and provided his passport to the young Djiboutian woman behind the counter. She was attractive as the pure Afar people were – not typically African as might be seen down towards Kenya, and not really Arabic as in Egypt, although the Afar (or Danakil) claimed descent from the Arabs. She was tall, and slender with a well defined facial bone structure and sparkling dark eyes, well dressed and clearly very capable at her work, with a welcoming attitude, despite the somewhat jaded ambience of the hotel complex. She introduced herself as Ashkaro and took some keys from a cupboard and said in Arabic that she would show him to his chalet, number 14. As she led him out through the door he admired her hips and couldn't help but wonder if this beautiful young woman had been subject to the brutal female circumcision tribal rite of the Afar. Should we judge others by our own cultural standards? This had been an essay topic during his Arabic culture module at university and he had never really come to a final decision. Any other day and he wouldn't have minded doing some in depth research.

As they walked, she chatted about the restaurant, and the excellent fish, fresh daily from the dock down the road at Tadjoura, then talked about the beach bar and the pool, pointing out a fresh water shower – a real luxury to her as an Afar, to whom fresh water was the most precious of resources. They walked across the paving around the pool, and as they walked on Saunders noticed a woman at the far end of the path – yes, in shorts with a white headscarf, the one he had seen walking in on the access road.

She was taking a photograph and now climbing off the rock outcrop at the end of the beach and strolling back along the path towards them. They passed Hut 12 and just as Saunders and Ashkaro reached Chalet 14, the woman passed them. Saunders glanced at her and nodded with a half-smile, but she ignored him, apparently lost in thought. He ran through the mental checklist of the description he had been given and the picture he had on his mobile phone. There was nothing that ruled her out, and several things did fit. His mind was racing, though such a coincidence was unlikely. He took the keys off Ashkaro, smiling and saying that he'd see himself in, and no further help was necessary, *shokran*, and he would call her if he needed anything else. Oh yes, one more thing, that lady that just passed us, was she a guest here? No? I guess she's just a visitor then.

*

Maruška walked past the man and woman. She noticed a logo on the woman's blouse, it looked like the logo on the sign at the entrance, Hotel du Golfe Bleu, staff then. The man must be the other Arab they have a reservation for. She walked into the reception office and waited, examining some 'What's On' brochures – diving, fishing, barbeque, minibus trip into the Day Forest National Park – all the usual stuff and more. What was it like to have a normal family life, she wondered? Boring for sure. Then, Ashkaro came back into the office.

"Do you have a spare suite for a few days?" she asked in French.

"Yes, we do, there are several to choose from, would you like to see them?"

"That would be great, thanks." Ashkaro showed Marie two of the three available suites and while she was looking at the second one, which was at the far corner of the building and had a view down over the chalets, she noticed the front of a blue Nissan 4x4 parked at the back of the hotel. "I think that this will be ideal, thanks."

"One more thing, I'm meeting an old friend here, a Mr Baldry. Where is he staying?"

"That will be chalet number 12."

"Thank you. If you see him, please don't mention that I'm here. I want to surprise him."

"*Certainement Madame, je comprends.*"

*

Steve's phone rang.

"Da'ud here. I've checked in, I'm in number 14. I'm going to come and see you – ok?"

"Sure, come over."

"I'll be there in a couple of minutes. Don't answer the door to anyone else."

"I'll leave the door unlocked, come straight in."

Saunders grabbed his Adidas sports bag and went to number 12.

"Baldry, it's Da'ud".

184

He turned the handle and went in. It was very hot in there – there was no aircon and little draught. The wallscreen TV was on, tuned to the Al Jazeera news channel and Steve was standing in the corner with his SIG cocked and aimed. Saunders nodded and closed the door behind him. He placed the sportsbag gently on the floor in front of him and raised his arms.

"I'm Da'ud. The phone is in my pocket, I'm going to take it out slowly."

He held the phone in his hands and dialled a number from memory. Steve's phone rang and Saunders pressed Cancel as Steve lowered his gun.

"Ok, we know who we are at least. Have you been out since I called?"

"No, not even for a beer."

"Tell me about the other guests you've seen here."

Steve ran through descriptions of the others he'd seen, though he hadn't been paying too much attention.

Saunders described the woman with the white headscarf he'd seen, and no, Steve hadn't seen her - "A bit conspicuous isn't she – that's unlikely to be her, but size sounds right, fit looking too?"

With a nod, Saunders continued "Well, Marie – let's call her Pavkovic - her description is all over the radio. She's going to try and look different isn't she? One of our guys here has disappeared – you met him didn't you?"

"Yes, knew him as Tom, I know he's missing, she had his phone it seems."

"Well, it looks like she took him out. It seems she's hooked up with the Chinese."

"I guessed they'd fit into the picture. I've been doing some work on that."

"Ok, well, I don't need to know about that. Safer that way. We don't know what she wants with you. We've had a security leak, which is how they got on to you in the first place, but that's been plugged and we are secure now."

"I know what I want from her, and it's not between her legs. She offered me that on a plate already. Bitch."

"OK, what are we going to do next?"

*

Back in her suite, Marie looked out of the window and with her mobile phone camera zoomed in on the front of the Nissan. She squirted the picture to her palmpad and zoomed it. The plate was at an angle, but with a bit of twisting and adjustment, she could see that the registration appeared to be the one she was looking for. She walked down to the lobby and strolled around to the back of the hotel. A chef was dumping some kitchen garbage into the dumpster, throwing some bones to the cats, and he smiled at her as she took out her phone and snapped the cats, with the Nissan in the background, confirming that the Nissan Patrol was Baldwin's; it convinced the chef, finally, that all women tourists were crazy. He walked back in to the kitchen shaking his head in amazement.

Back in her room there were no new messages from Wan Chuntao – she had time for a sleep and a shower before the night's proceedings.

*

Saunders walked over to Reception and chatted to Ashkaro about the Day Forest National Park, glancing at a brochure and asking if it really was true that he could see velvet monkeys there. He mentioned the woman they'd passed earlier, and that he would like to meet her if Ashkaro saw her again at the hotel. Ashkaro smiled and volunteered that the lady was now a guest. Saunders didn't push it, but managed to establish that she was in a suite and not a chalet, and that her name was Fräulein Wessel. Ashkaro was happy to agree not to mention his interest to Fräulein Wessel, so that she would not be embarrassed.

Back in his chalet, Saunders contacted London. It seemed to him that Booth was struggling with interdepartmental politics, even more intense than usual, following the security fiasco - a re-organisation was being touted. The view was unequivocal (Booth having consulted widely in the current poisoned atmosphere), that if Fräulein Wessel were proven to be Maruška Karanovic/Andjela Pavkovic then she should be terminated. The French had screwed up an apprehension, the Djiboutians were in the French pockets and, frankly, Booth said, "she's taken down one of ours and we need some kind of trophy right now. You have Baldwin there as bait – she seems to be following him round like a dog."

"Well," said Saunders, "I can tell you that Baldwin wants to terminate her with very serious prejudice – she's taken down his controller, and made a fool out of him in a big way. Oh yes, they broke into his boat too. That's worse than raping his wife."

Saunders then asked about involving the US and getting help out of the base at Camp Lemmonier, and Booth had 'gone to consult' colleagues. Saunders was tasked to try and be certain that Wessel was who they thought – that meant more DNA or other irrefutable proof, if a termination was to be sanctioned.

"Unless it's self defence, or an accident" he thought, "either could be arranged."

In London, the internal security review was underway and the obvious question being asked was why only some operations were compromised. The data feed from the fork lift trucks in the Chinese base in Little Aden was still operational, and the review concluded that the breaking of the Little Aden network that Saunders ran was due to routine surveillance of

Salim's cousin. No link could be proven to the problems in Vauxhall Cross, though clearly the Chinese had got on to Baldwin.

Back at Chalet 14, Steve was waiting, having left his non-essential gear in number 12, with the flatscreen TV switched on. He'd checked, cleaned and re-checked their weapons, and boredom was setting in. Most of a soldier's life was about waiting, and coping with it was important. He'd once spent five days with Mick in a hide - a hole in the ground - in the Yemen, waiting for a target, with scorpions and snakes as regular visitors. Five days, for just one shot, but he'd taken it, a three second flight time for the bullet, and a kill, and then they got away cleanly. This was different. He was the target.

On his way back from Reception, Saunders has picked up a couple of cold beers from the beach bar, but as they opened the bottles, Al Jazeera interrupted a sports report to broadcast a breaking news item.

"The United States and the United Kingdom have jointly requested an emergency meeting of the UN Security Council. Notwithstanding that, and in view of the threat to free passage of shipping and other maritime developments in the Red Sea the two countries, with NATO support, were considering ways in which they might cooperate to provide additional security in the region.

"Fucking hell" Steve said, beating Saunders to the expletive.

Al Jazeera said that the Chinese Government had not yet responded. The political analyst commented that it was certain that high level secret representations must have been going on in the background without success, before such a statement would be issued publicly.

Saunders's iPhone rang. It was London, and Booth was fired up.

"Where's Baldwin?"

"Right beside me"

"Have you seen the news?"

"Yes, just caught Al Jazeera"

"Well, we're running behind the politicos on this and need to move ahead. Two days, that's all it's taken and the world is going mad. Baldwin's piece of work the other night given us serious cause for concern – you've probably guessed that. Forget the Pavkovic woman, you and Baldwin are to get out of there now and across to Camp Lemmonier. We're battening down the hatches, there's another operation in planning. Your contact at Lemmonier is Blue Bayou. It's madness here. The Chinese are denying that they have missiles there. I've seen the evidence with my own eyes. Fucking madness. Get out now. Call me when you're at Lemmonier."

Saunders was startled – he'd never heard Booth swear like that before.

"Ok, we're moving now" Saunders said and closed the call.

Steve looked up in surprise, only having heard half the conversation.

"Don't even think it, Steve, we're getting out now."

He stuffed five hundred dollars into an envelope, with a brief note about settling the bill for Chalets 12 and 14, as they had changed their plans. He wrote Ashkaro's name on the outside, and explained the plan to Steve.

"We do nothing about Pavkovic – we're heading straight for Lemonnier. Just wait here, on your guard, do nothing. I'll bring my truck up the track to the rear."

They checked their pistols, Steve closed the holdalls, and Saunders left. Steve waited by the rear door to the beach hut.

*

Marie, or Fraulein Wessel as she was today, came out of the shower. She didn't have the TV on and as she dried herself she looked out of the window – the sun was setting and this side of the hotel was in long shadow, but Baldwin's 4x4 was just visible still parked at the rear. She dried herself and thought she'd order room service food. If Baldwin was about she didn't want to be seen, yet. Choose your battleground and time - basic Sun Tzu strategy. The Chinese had figured it all out centuries ago.

She was brushing her hair by the window when she saw a 4x4 driving up the rear service track of the chalets. Yes, it was that blue 4x4 which she'd seen earlier, with that guy from hut 14. The truck stopped outside the rear of hut 14 and turned around, taking a few chews at it as the track was narrow, with rocks, cacti and brush on the other side of the track from the hut. Then she saw a man – yes Baldwin – come out of the chalet and get in to the truck. Shit shit shit! They are together! As she reached for her pistol, she ran through her options, whilst the 4x4 was bouncing slowly along the track towards the hotel and the exit. No, she had no clothes on – that wouldn't have stopped her, but she couldn't get downstairs and out in time to catch them. It would take minutes at least to grab transport, and that wasn't certain. She was pushing open the window and taking aim – the 4x4 was about 20 yards away to the left, and she took aim.

*

"Incoming, Go Go Go" Steve shouted and Saunders reacted.

The truck lurched over a bump and the first bullet passed through the windscreen and smashed into Saunders's left forearm. He floored the accelerator as Pavkovic fired smoothly and carefully. The second bullet caught the front left pillar of the windscreen as Steve was punching out the windscreen glass and drawing his pistol. The third shot came through the side window and into the headrest next to Saunders's ear. Marie was leaning out of the window and firing again, but the truck was lurching and she hit the doorpost. Steve got a shot off through the open windscreen as another shot came through the rear side window and the next hit the rear tire. His shot caught the window frame next to her head and he saw her head snap back as the truck got past the end wall of the hotel and neither had a line of fire.

"Stop stop stop" Steve shouted at Saunders, whose right arm was spraying blood over the centre console. "There – my truck is there – let's go. I'm driving." Steve grabbed the bags and ran across to his truck, followed by Saunders, who was limping, with blood spurting over his trouser from his wound. He scrabbled for his keys and they accelerated away from the rear of the kitchen. Steve hit the security barrier at fifty miles and hour and woke up the gateman with a start.

Saunders was putting pressure on his wound as Steve accelerated on to the main road, heading for Tadjoura, less than two miles away. Glancing across, Steve could see that Saunders was looking pale – he'd probably lost a pint of blood already. Pulling off the road, he tore the arm off Saunders's shirt, tied a tourniquet above the elbow, and got going again, all within less than two minutes. As he pulled back onto the road, a police 4x4, lights flashing, passed them, undoubtedly heading for the Hotel du Golfe Bleu. The last rays of the sun were fading away into the brief tropical twilight as they approached Tadjoura dock.

"We've got a choice, Da'ud, we either drive round to Lemmonier in this, or nick a boat. If we could find a RIB then we'd do it in fifteen minutes –*if* we could find a rib, and then start it. It's nearly dark, and I'd feel safer at sea, but we'd have a problem at the other end – we can't take a taxi with you like that. Marie – Pavkovic – will probably know what we're driving, though she may be out of action – I think my shot caught her. We're going to drive, OK?"

"That seems to be the best option" grunted Saunders "but we'll need to adjust this, on my arm, the..the… tourniquet." Steve could see him grimacing as he spoke – the adrenaline was wearing off and shock was setting in. It would take them at least a couple of hours to get to Lemmonier.

*

Marie was swearing as she ran into the bathroom. Finding a towel, she dabbed at the left side of her head, where her damaged ear was bleeding. The ear does not have a large blood supply, so the rate of blood loss was not life threatening, but it was a mess. She looked in the mirror and swore - she could see that the ear had been lacerated and a large piece was hanging off, with a couple of wood splinters in her cheek near the joint of her jaw. She pulled them out. Baldwin's shot had caught the window frame maybe a splinter had caught her. No time for cleanup, move move move, she urged herself. With a towel wrapped round her head, she changed the clip on her pistol, grabbed her holdall, threw her iphone and palmpad in and moved to the door. With a start she realised that she had no clothes on. Cursing, she stopped to pull on her shorts and tee shirt, and threw her headscarf into her bag. Trainers on, and away, another minute lost. Shit, there were her knickers on the floor, She threw them into her bag.

*

It had been an unusually busy afternoon at the police station in Tadjoura. Not even weekdays were like this. They had been investigating a taxi which had been found, apparently abandoned, just outside the town. It had come from Djibouti and the driver was missing. Now, a call had come from the Hotel du Golfe Bleu reporting shots. There were only two on duty there, they locked the door and headed for the Hotel.

*

Nearly five minutes now since she had missed that bastard Baldwin. Out of the door - no-one in the corridor, Marie heard a distant police siren over the almost deathly quiet overlaid by the faint sound of chillout music from the bar down by the chalets. Down the stairs, into Reception, that native Receptionist looks at her, startled, uncomprehending, frightened, yes a pretty girl, would have been nice... her mind is racing, coldly calmly assessing, calculating, cover your tracks she thinks, and now she's aiming, one shot and a small spurt of crimson blood from the face followed by a grotesque abstract pattern splashed on the wall behind Ashkaro's head, spreading, running down the wall as the receptionist drops without a sound, the envelope with five hundred dollars in the pocket of her shorts.

Move move move, Marie urges herself - around the back of the reception desk, find the little steel box they used for passports, yes, shit box is locked, where's the fucking key, yes, there, hanging on a hook, fumble with key, box, yes there's her passport, not in the safe yet, then the gateman is coming in through the door and he looks at her, realising, turning too late as she steps from behind the desk and moves towards him, his mouth opening to shout as she pulls the trigger and he's knocked back over some chairs against the wall. OK, out through the entrance door and there's a police 4x4 coming through the broken barrier, past the car park, towards reception. She lowers her right arm to her side, puts her holdall down, stops and waits as the police SUV pulls up and two of them get out, drawing their pistols.

"La bas, un homme a tué deux personnes," she said, pointing into Reception, trying to look and sound terrified about the double killing inside.

190

"*Attendez ici*" shouts the first policeman looking at her towel headdress and the blood on her shoulder as he runs past her, and she raises her arm and shoots the approaching second policeman, then turning shoots the first in the back as he is going through the door and trying to turn round at the same time.

I'm not waiting here for anyone, she thinks, as she climbs into the police 4x4 and accelerates up the entrance road, cursing at her poor shooting and Baldwin's escape with that other man. Who the fuck was he?

*

As they were leaving Tadjoura, Steve kept up a constant chat to Saunders while he was looking for a suitable place to pull off the road.

About twenty minutes after they left the hotel, well on the other side of Tadjoura town, Steve found a track and turned off the road. Battlefield triage had been drilled into him during training, but despite all his operational experience, he'd never had to use it in anger and he struggled to remember the drill. He spent ten minutes cleaning the wound as best he could, putting a pressure pad on and easing the tourniquet. There was only slight bleeding now, but he didn't feel he could remove the tourniquet completely, yet. He found the galabaya in Saunders's case and wrapped it around him to try and keep him warm. He was pale and in a lot of pain.

"Stay with me, it'll be ok Da'ud, only a scratch, not life threatening. We'll get it sorted soon. Got any pain killers?"

"Washbag" Saunders grunted in response.

The washbag contained the hangover mixture - paracetamol and ibuprofen, and he dosed Saunders with a couple of each with a little water. He needed treatment soon if his arm was to be saved. The bullet appeared to have clipped the bone and artery, and exited messily and was probably on the floor of the other 4x4.

"My leg" grunted Saunders "What about my leg?"

Steve cursed – he hadn't checked the casualty properly. The bullet had exited the arm and gone into his thigh. There was so much blood on Saunders's trousers that Steve had assumed came from the arm. He ripped the trousers open and saw it was not a serious wound, just messy. The distorted bullet had lost most of its energy and torn the flesh raggedly, but had not gone as far as an artery.

He patched it with a pressure pad made from one of Saunders's shirts, then took out his phone and called London.

Booth was not there, but a desk officer took the call.

"We've got a bad situation here after a shootout with Pavkovic, we are running in a 4 x4. Da'ud is injured, needs attention urgently. I've done what

I can. He's lost a lot of blood. Can you get a medic from Lemmonier to meet us?"

"Is it life threatening?"

"Is it fucking life threatening? Not right now, but unless you get your arse in gear it will be. Why do you think I'm calling – because he's got toothache?"

"Ok Ok, I can see your location on my screen. I'll need to clear this with the senior officer, but let's aim for the junction of the N1 and N9 roads. I'll get back to you once I've got something in place."

"OK, but get a move on."

He put the phone on the ledge above the windscreen

Steve was realistic about the chances of an international link up at short notice as he turned back on to the main road. The switchback sections of the road would slow them down, and he was not optimistic. Saunders was groaning and Steve was trying to keep him conscious, talking about his time in the Yemen, but he could see that he was starting to drift into unconsciousness.

*

As she got to the main road, Marie wondered which way they had turned – it would have to be back to Djibouti city she guessed. There were only small towns and harbours the other way as far as she remembered. She took the left hand turn heading for Tadjoura and on to Djibouti.

She guessed that she would have half an hour at most before the police 4x4 would be looked for. There might be other police in the station at Tadjoura, though it was only a small town, but she recalled seeing a ship in the harbour when passing earlier that day. With cargo ships docking there, then there was bound to be a significant police presence. She found the switch for the blue lights and turned them off as she cruised slowly through the town and picked up speed on the other side. Her ear was throbbing and she knew she would need to attend to it soon and the towel would have to go.

There was little choice - she had to get another car, soon. After that she didn't know what she would do. It would not be a good idea to go back into the city, though they would probably not expect it. She had only what she was carrying – her fallbacks were exhausted – and she stood out. It was a barren, simple country and the only ways out were, as ever, air, land and sea. Her half hour was up and she pulled in to the side of the road. There was no traffic – she hadn't seen a vehicle since Tadjoura - as she turned the 4x4 across the centre of the road and stopped.

The tropical twilight had quickly faded into full darkness. She checked her gun and waited. Some lights came into view and she heard a truck changing gear as it came up the hill. She backed off the road with lights off and let it pass – it seemed to be carrying cattle – and then pulled back into position. No more than a minute or two later she saw the beam of some headlights appear and seem to turn on to the main road. They were now approaching her from the Tadjoura direction. This didn't sound like a truck hauling cattle, but the engine was working hard. When she judged them to be about two hundred yards away, she put the blue flashers on and climbed out, crouching out of sight alongside the 4x4.

*

"Jesus, there's a fucking roadblock" he swore as he started to slow. To try and turn would be pointless and only result in a chase and this police crew would soon have others in full cry after him. "Get down Da'ud." No reply – he was unconscious. Steve slowed, judging the gap each side of the police 4x4 and picked his spot. He could see no police personnel in the headlights. Maybe there was a vehicle off the road. He was about twenty yards away when a figure stepped round from behind the police vehicle, with a pistol raised. It was someone in a pair of shorts, red tee shirt maybe, with a towel on his – or was it her head? Not a policeman, but shit, it's Pavkovic...how in hell?

*

The vehicle approached and as it slowed she stepped out holding her pistol steady and aimed. She was illuminated full-on in the headlights. Then, when it was almost at a stop less than ten yards away, she heard the engine accelerate as the vehicle changed direction slightly and came straight at her. Totally surprised, she had no time for a shot, it was only yards away and she had to jump for her life as it swerved around the rear of the police SUV. It was dark in colour, a 4x4, and she glimpsed the driver in the reflected light and then saw the illuminated registration plate. "Baldwin!" she shouted, getting up off the road, running round the rear to try and get a shot, but his lights were off. She thought she heard one hit from the three shots she squeezed off as her blue flashers intermittently lit up the fast disappearing Nissan.

*

Steve accelerated hard as Pavkovic jumped for her life, got round the back of the police truck and scrabbled to switch off his lights. He thought he heard a few shots and maybe one hit the rear of his Nissan. Driving for maybe a minute - not more - he nearly came off the road twice. He had to slow down - it was impossible to drive without lights on this road, he realised. Unless… yes – just after a turn which he nearly missed, he pulled up alongside some scrub, got out and ran round to the rear, and with the butt of his pistol prepared to smash the rear lights. No time. He could see the loom of the headlights of the police vehicle as she came after him, blue lights still flashing. "My turn now you bitch." She came screaming around the bend at about fifty miles an hour as he got down on his knees, hands braced ready for steady accurate shooting. Her lights had not yet swung into line with him. After a breath, he squeezed six shots off, steadily. Pavkovic's vehicle lost one of its lights, and he didn't know what else as the police car failed to complete the turn and went off the other side of the road into the brush, starting to roll as it went down the incline on the outside of the bend.

Had she survived? He hoped not, but had no time to lose – Da'ud was his first priority. He scrambled back in checked Da'ud – he was looking a bit grey and clammy. They had been driving for another ten minutes when his phone rang. He pulled in.

"You're not making very good time, is there are problem?"

"Too fucking right there's a problem, Pavkovic ambushed us using a police car. She's off the road now, but I'm not writing her off yet. Da'ud is unconscious. I reckon I've still got another forty minutes to the intercept."

"Ok. I can see where your last stop was – a couple of minutes at the most according to my monitor. We'll make sure that the local police have that location. There's a US helicopter on the way to you, they can home in on the GPS tag in your phone – I've given them your tag details. Find a flat landing spot off the road and clear of trees – well, you know the score, I'm sure you've done this before. They'll find you. I think you'll need to go on another two or three miles till the ground levels out."

"Ok, I'll check the map."

"That's good, I'm on my way now."

It took about twenty minutes for Steve to find the right spot and by that time he could hear the helicopter approaching. He parked the Nissan about fifty yards from where he judged the best spot to be and left the headlights on, illuminating his shirt - laid out with some stones on it as a rather poor marker, with his phone in the centre.

Ten minutes later they were airborne, and Saunders was being treated by the medics.

As they were approaching Camp Lemmonier, Steve didn't see the lights of a Eurocopter with a squad of French marines aboard as it passed them. It was two miles away to the north on a mission to capture a terrorist. The marines were pumped up, with a reputation to recover and the deaths of four comrades to avenge.

*

Marie groaned as she recovered her senses. The police truck was on its left hand side. The pain in her left arm was excruciating – it was trapped under her against the door and her left ear was throbbing and hurting like hell. She struggled to work herself vertical, until she was on her knees amid the glass fragments. The arm didn't seem to be broken – maybe just twisted and jarred, though the pain extended from her elbow to her shoulder, and there was a massive graze where her tattoo has once been. The side window had broken, but it seemed that the window and top of the door had not dragged along the ground as the truck slid on its side. Her left thigh was also giving her pain. After scrabbling around she found her pistol, and used the butt to clear the shattered windscreen and clamber out through it, cutting her legs in the process. The truck had come off the road, tumbled onto its side and slithered to a stop after about a hundred yards. She was lucky it hadn't rolled, as she hadn't had a seatbelt on.

That bastard Baldwin, she thought, still trying to clear her head. Move move move, came the instinctual commands in her head, feeling her way round to the back of the truck, smashing the rear screen - a steel box inside – locked. Retrieve the truck keys and her carryall, open the box – yes, a large flashlight, a Mossberg short barrelled shotgun, ammunition, some other gear. Take the flashlight, leave the shotgun, stagger up the slope to the main road.

Move away into cover. I can't move far at night like this. I need to wait, but how long, she wondered, how long do I have? She started to plan. Lights were approaching from the Tadjoura direction – she could hear an engine – it sounded like a truck working up the incline. She walked out into the road and lay down off centre, leaving just enough room for the truck to swerve round her if the driver was not in a frame of mind to stop. The flashlight was switched on with its beam across the road, her arms were spread, her pistol was under her.

She watched the truck approach, heard the power come off as the driver spotted her and then, she heard the air brakes come on and the groaning as the truck slowed, shuddered and stopped, with a hiss of air from the brake reservoir. Lying in the full headlight beams, she heard the cab door open and saw the driver, in a tee shirt, shorts and boots, walking through the beam towards her. As he bent, speaking in Arabic, she rolled way, came up onto her knees, lifting her pistol. The driver was astonished – he almost jumped - and stood open mouthed.

"*Levez les mains*" she ordered.

He raised his arms slowly, either guessing her command or understanding French.

"*Vous parlez Francais*" she said, a statement, not a question.

"*Un peu*" he murmured.

"*Bon.*" She staggered to her feet, her pistol not wavering as he raised his hands. "You drive as I tell you and I will not shoot you." He nodded, swallowing hard, fear in his eyes, starting to speak and thinking better of it.

She motioned with her gun and he moved back to the truck. He climbed in and as she held the door open said "Stop the engine. Pass me the keys." She slammed the driver's door and once she was seated in the passenger seat, she passed him the keys.

*

"Is there a first aid kit?" she asked the truck driver. Her ear had started bleeding again when she crashed the police truck and knocked her head on the side window. It was throbbing strongly and she could feel a warm trickle of blood on her neck.

"No."

The towel was sodden with blood and she took it off, grimacing as she pulled away the caked blood, and opening the wound more. Her ear hurt like hell, though her left arm was less painful, but stiffening – she must have jarred the shoulder joint. She found some sanitary towels in her carryall, and pressed one against her ear.

"I'm going to put my gun down for thirty seconds. If you try anything at all, I will shoot you, put my knife into you, take your eyes out. Whichever way, I will kill you. I have nothing to lose. Maybe you have a family, *oui*?

"*Oui.*"

"Then think about them."

In the glow of the instrument lights, she could see him lick his lips and swallow.

She put the gun down next to her, and tore a strip off the hotel towel, then use it to tie the sanitary towel in place.

Forty minutes later, in the lumbering milk truck, they were passing the N1/N9 road junction. There was a police roadblock on the other side with a few vehicles heading out of the city, queued up.

Though Maruška didn't know it, the French marines' commander at the base had decide that the third option – the Addis Ababa road was the most likely, and so the helicopter had headed back towards Tadjoura, to follow the N10 road which looped through the *Mile Serdo* wildlife reserve and connected on to Addis Ababa.

The plan was clear in her mind. She knew where she was going to hide, and how she was going to get Baldwin, finally.

*

At that same moment the French Eurocopter was hovering over the police SUV. After a scan of the area with a thermal imager, the marines abseiled down to the scene and checked out the site. They talked to their mission commander at the base and widened the thermal scan. The road had cooled quickly in the dark but there was a warm patch showing on the road – a large vehicle had obviously stopped there very recently and for a few minutes, just enough to warm that area by a quarter of a degree or so. Which way had it gone though? The helicopter climbed to 5000 feet and the crew checked the road for lights – there were several sets in both directions. Would the terrorist have gone back towards the hotel, or back towards Djibouti where she had been earlier in the day? Or maybe the third option, back to the junction with the Addis Ababa road which would take her away from both her killing grounds.

*

At the same time, Saunders was in the base hospital, undergoing surgery on his arm and having his leg wound stitched, with a blood transfusion underway.

In the mess hall, Steve had caught up on some food and watched CNN as he ate. The emergency meeting of the UN Security Council had been held and adjourned amid rancour.

The Chinese had put out a statement saying that the US and UK were using the situation in the Red Sea as a way of attacking China for her success, by undermining the economic foundations of China's Middle Eastern and African allies.

A joint statement was expected from the US and UK governments the following day.

The atmosphere in the mess hall was one of subdued excitement – the guys were obviously expecting some action soon. That's the last thing I need thought Steve, I just want to get away to sea. But where – the trouble in the Red Sea could go on awhile yet?

After his meal, Steve settled into a secure comms cubicle, to talk to Booth in London, though neither of them had any illusions that their conversation was secure from US ears when inside a US base. Booth was not at all happy to have been called in late on a Sunday evening.

"Let's be clear Baldwin – you only shot at that Pavkovic woman – no other casualties down to you at the hotel?"

"That's right. I didn't even know that there were any."

"Well, she killed a receptionist, a security man and two of the local police. Plus what she did to the French at her hotel in Djibouti. The French are frantic – they found the police car after you put her off the road, but she had gone. In a truck they think. Of course the French know we're involved

197

somehow – after all we pointed them at the police SUV - but if they can't find her then they will start slinging mud at us. The Djibouti government is really worked up – not that we're too worried about that, we're clean so far and need to keep it that way. By the way, there was blood in the police car – she's definitely injured. The French said the car had been hit at least six times."

"That's good then, that's all my shots accounted for" said Steve, with little satisfaction in his voice. Ashkaro dead, what a pointless waste, he thought, with anger rising inside and a bad taste in his mouth.

"We're flying Saunders – Da'ud – back tomorrow. You are there on your own, holding the fort for us ashore. The situation in the Red Sea has the potential to create a confrontation like we haven't seen for a generation."

"Yes, it looks that way - I caught some of it on CNN earlier. I just want to get out of here, the sooner the better."

"Look Baldwin – Steve – we, that is the British government needs you there now. There's a lot at stake – even your own freedom to navigate in he area."

"Well, I'm going to head back to my boat tomorrow and get ready to leave."

"Very well, but give it some thought, we really do need you there."

Steve closed the call. The procedure for leaving the country officially, on a boat, required clearance by the Police, Port Control, Customs and Immigration. These procedures could be exhausting and time consuming. Just one hiccup could easily prevent his departure indefinitely. He had no illusions about people like Booth, and he had his 'ships papers' with him.

*

"What is your name?" Maruška asked the truck driver.

"Albert."

"Albert? That is not a local name is it?"

"I was named after my father, who was a Legionnaire."

"Ah, I see. You said you have a family?" He looked at her as he changed gear on the truck and nodded. They were grinding along on the N1 towards Djibouti.

"Tell me about them then."

He was scared and not keen to speak, but he gradually told her about his wife and children. They lived in an estate on the outskirts of Djibouti. He had a full load of milk on the truck, and was delivering it to the processing plant and then going home to his family.

"Well let me tell you this, Albert. As we drive into Djibouti, you are going to drive the truck to a store, and then I will give you some money. I need a first aid kit and some other items. You will go into the store and get

198

them for me. If you do as I ask, then all will be fine. If not, then I will find your family and kill them, but you will live and see them die, then you will live with the memory of how you helped them die. I have killed many people – men, women and children. Even today I have killed. I have nothing to lose. Do you understand?"

Maruška watched with satisfaction as the terror developed, and saw the sweat break out on his face – he was clearly having difficulty focusing on the driving.

"You know a store that is open at this time of night?"

She could see the whites of his eyes lit by the instrument lights against his dark face, as he looked sideways at her and nodded.

*

The store was only a basic shop, but good enough. When Albert returned from the store, she checked and packed the items into her bag.

"Good, you have done well. I want you to follow this road along the coast, towards the docks and then turn west on the N3, OK?"

Albert nodded.

Once they were on the N3 – a road which was decaying into a track - they progressed ever more slowly. They drove to the end where it petered away down to a beach.

He stopped the truck once they had almost reached the end, in a stony parking area, desolate, just before midnight, and turned to look at her.

"Turn around and head back towards Djibouti" she ordered. He looked at her in puzzlement and shrugged, then turned the truck around and worked through the gears. She had chosen the spot on the way out, and as they approached, told him to stop the truck again. As he pulled up the parking brake, she swung her right arm and hit him as hard as she could in the face with the butt of her pistol. He hadn't seen it coming and after the crunching, squelching wet noise of the impact there was no sound from him as he bounced back against the rear of his seat and fell forward across the steering wheel, bleeding heavily from his face, his laboured breathing whistling and burbling through his smashed nose and mouth. She wiped her gun carefully and checked it, and wiped the blood off her arms.

*

She estimated that it was about two miles to the boat dock as she trudged along the stony road. She had patched up her ear and taken some painkillers. The moon, now a few days past full, was rising over her left shoulder, and the sea was glittering. She could hear insects in the sparse grass along the shore, and there was a cloud of mosquitoes trying to track her, but the lotion Albert had bought was effective. Behind her there was a light breeze from the west, carrying a crackling, spitting noise, and the pungent smell of the burning truck, which was now well alight down in a dip in the track.

Less than an hour later she was carefully approaching the marina dock at Dolphin Services. She expected a night watchman, and after waiting about twenty minutes behind a wall at the end of the car park, she saw a man appear from the side of the building and light a cigarette. She watched as he turned around and appeared to sniff the air – she could still smell the fumes of burnt tyres, oil, and flesh from the now cooling truck still drifting on the breeze. He was probably wondering where the smell was coming from.

The watchman made a perfunctory inspection of the boats, walking up and down the quayside on what was obviously his regular patrol pattern, and then disappeared around the side of the building.

After a few minutes, she slipped in to the water and started swimming, pushing her bag, wrapped in a plastic bin liner, ahead of her, unaware that this was almost a repeat performance of Steve's swim the night before. He had left the stern ladder down, and she climbed aboard. The newly repaired hatch gave way (with some noise) to a large screwdriver she had found in the truck. She climbed down below, closing the hatch as best she could – it would at least pass a quick inspection from a dinghy.

"Right you bastard, I'm ready for you now" she thought. She would be safe enough here whilst she figured out her next moves and waited for Baldwin.

*

Thompson's Troubles Start

The preparations for the meeting had been meticulous. *Auric Adventurer* (the second of vessel of that name) had been built by Cantieri Liguri of Riva Trigosa in northern Italy in 2014. She was amongst the largest private yachts in the world, at 70 metres length overall, sumptuously appointed to accommodate 22 guests, with a range of 4000 miles.

Her triple Deutz engines were driving her cruising speed of 18 knots. Her stabilizers, although engaged, were relatively inactive as the mid morning sea resembled a shimmering mirror with the horizon in a haze induced soft-focus.

She had been regularly swept, with the latest full sweep by two security managers after leaving her mooring at Antibes, and one was currently on the bridge monitoring the radar. They were now three hours out from Antibes. The main radar was set at the maximum of 48 miles, Bill Johnson, her captain, altered course continually to ensure that there were no closer approaches to other vessels than 20 miles - a difficult achievement in this stretch of water at this time of year, but the changes of course were less frequent now as they moved well away from the coast and the flesh-pot hoppers decreased.

He was well used to operating under high levels of security that Charles Tobin demanded. In 1996, following the change of Israeli government and renewed tension on the West Bank, Tobin had provided the first *Auric Adventurer* as a base for secret negotiations to resolve the situation and put the peace process back on course. It was much easier to protect a party of diplomats on a ship at sea, than on land, and with her helicopter deck, access to *Auric Adventurer* was straightforward.

Ships were becoming the preferred locations for out of sight meeting and negotiation as security was relatively straightforward – the only worries were submarines, planes and high speed assault craft. Those were easier to protect against than land based locations open to attack by terrorist teams and very public protest by anti-globalisation demonstrators.

Auric Adventurer was fitted with a state of the art communication suite directly uplinking to the Inmarsat geostationary satellite network.

For these sea conditions and her normal cruising speed, the ambient sound in the passenger areas would usually be a barely detectable murmur. The recently fitted phase shift sound inverters however, removed all noise of the engines in the day saloon, and ensured that any laser microphones trained on the saloon superstructure would be completely unexcited by any sounds from inside. The 6,600 horsepower that was propelling *Auric*

Adventurer was therefore not at all apparent to those seated in their leather covered chairs.

In this artificially hushed saloon, those present were totally focused on the speaker as Charles Tobin continued his presentation:

"The basic, conservative business model is that initially there will be 8 tanker loads in year one, capable of providing almost 2 tonnes of gold in total. Gold prices are climbing steadily and were expected to be at an average of $3,500 per troy ounce for the next two years after production starts. In the 25 years from 1975 to 2010 the price of gold increased by a factor of ten, from $150 an ounce to almost $1500 an ounce and its climb has continued steadily since then. The production platform can handle double the volume, though there is some uncertainty as to whether the fumaroles can sustain this level of extraction without increasing the number of 'recycles' of the feedstock.

World demand for gold is increasing steadily, with China having the largest demand now after overtaking India. China is also the largest producer. Gold is used extensively in electronic circuits and connectors, and demand is increasing exponentially as the *nouveau riche* buy in heavily.

In due course, I plan to bring other production platforms on line, and I am now in the process of developing plans for mid ocean recovery. In such areas the political problems are fewer, though so are the areas where weather and sea state will allow present generation production platforms to operate.

And so, gentlemen, in summary, the ultimate potential derives from 400 million cubic miles of sea water. Of course, we have to be realistic, recognising that we can only currently extract within the Red Sea area until the yield becomes uneconomic. By then, we should be able to replicate the process in the wider oceans, so to speak. As we develop the technology further, we will be able to operate at greater depths and in more hostile environments, such as the Atlantic and Pacific Oceans. The potential of extraction from the Red Sea is therefore limited, at least in our terms. We see it as workable for about three to five years.

The whole operation introduces compound political complexities. Strategic metals are by definition, politically sensitive.

I am confident that, given the scale of opportunity here, Her Majesty's Government will be wholeheartedly behind this. Indeed, their generous assistance so far with grants has meant that we have been able to accelerate our research, and I am now delighted to announce that we have achieved economic production scaling of the technology. We plan to start production in twelve weeks time.

As you know, we chose our research and production facilities carefully. The need for large scale refining facilities with deep water access led us to looking at oil refinery installations world wide. We identified suitable installations in Japan, Venezuela, Nigeria and the UK. "

"Again, HMG was most helpful – thank you, Richard - and we have now concluded the purchase of the former Murco Oil Refinery in Wales. It has deepwater access and handling facilities for vessels of up to 300,000 tons. We have two suitable tankers – the *Universal Enterprise* and the *Universal Trader*, each of more than 250,000 tons capacity, undergoing modifications. We expect *Universal Trader* to complete her sea trials and handover next week and then commence her trip from Japan to the UK."

"The round trip to the Red Sea and back will take about 9-10 weeks in total, via the Cape of Good Hope. For the first trip, *Universal Trader* will be seeded at the refinery terminal in Milford Haven. She will be carrying 200,000 tons of hot seawater from our refinery, and breeding our *extremophiles* – I have christened them '*thiovulum aureus*' - on route. Once she reaches the Kebrit Deep in the Red Sea – our initial mining pool - her cargo will be pumped down to the bottom to seed the breeding and concentration of the metal in the saline pool surrounding the fumaroles. It will take, we estimate, about six weeks to reach harvestable concentrations – that is to initiate the cycle. Once the cycle is established, then the outward cargo will be replaced with bottom water from the Kebrit Deep. This will be shipped back to the UK where it will be further concentrated and extraction completed in our refinery.

The next seeding cargo will be derived from our high concentrate at the refinery. Thus we have a virtuous circle, with increasingly concentrated cargoes and falling unit production costs. After a few cycles, we will no longer need to 're-seed'. However, as I said earlier, there is a limit to what we can extract. It would take probably five years to replenish the Kebrit Deep from the volcanic flows after we have harvested it, but we aim ultimately for sustainability – a regular predictable gold flow. There are other suitable saline pools at the bottom of the Red Sea, but in total, as I said, we think there are at least three to five of years economic production to be derived from Kebrit, worst case. Then, we would have to let it be fallow, just as farmers do, to recover. By that time we should be operational in the Shaban Deep and the Atlantis II Deep in the Red Sea."

Richard Thompson, Secretary of the Board of Trade attempted to force a smile. This only resulted in a pinched, almost painful expression, as the content and contemptuous tone of Tobin's words sank in. Thompson shifted in his seat, and adjusted the now unfashionably crumpled white cotton trousers. Unconsciously, he felt a trickle of sweat run down his lower back and tickle him as it navigated under the force of gravity. Consciously, he was breathless, both with the scale of the operation and its risks.

Tobin sipped his whisky and soda, and let the implications sink in.

He then drew the presentation to a conclusion:

"You all know that this project is being undertaken in great secrecy. We do not want the Red Sea littoral states involved in this. So, thank you, Richard, I am sure that we can rely on your total discretion. I realise that you have to get back to your holiday in Tuscany. My helicopter is ready."

Following handshakes and smiles, Thompson left the meeting. A brief call to Tobin on the intercom confirmed that the helicopter had left the ship – it was completely inaudible in the saloon.

"Now," said Tobin, "let's go through the business plan. World production is closely controlled by agreement between the main producers, as with OPEC and oil. Introducing a new source of supply equivalent initially to a few percent of annual world consumption will not rock the markets. I estimate that our cost of production will be around 27% of that of the traditional mining producers. The cost of running the tankers and the production platform are significant, though the refinery will break even as it will be used for commercial refining of crude oil - though not matching the most modern refineries in terms of efficiency.

Our strategy will therefore be to force closure of deep mine production by driving the market price down over the next four to five years. Our Red Sea gold production will be masked by other metals and other activities which I have planned. This will be done in such a way as to avoid raising any suspicion about our sources. Then gentlemen, I – or rather we - will have the gold market by the balls."

There were a few detailed questions from the two remaining guests about timing and politics; there was some concern about a politician being involved.

"Gentlemen, be assured that Mr Thompson is completely under my control. In fact, he will be retiring from politics shortly, though I haven't told him yet," Tobin said with a laugh. "No, not retiring in the sense that you gentlemen might use - he will live on and will be joining one of my companies. He has a good brain and knows commodity markets very well. I know he will work well for us."

The meeting ending with a celebratory glass of champagne.

The other two investors were then collected by their launches and headed off to their own vessels which had now approached to within a couple of miles. They would be back in Sardinia and Sicily respectively later that day, using their own helicopters.

*

Thompson's rapid rise through Government ranks had been based on talent alone. However, he had three years earlier reached stall point, as had the likes of Keith Joseph and John Redwood in generations before him, when his intellect and rigid analytical ability obstructed the need to compromise, to become party to political accommodations and above all, to adopt an ambiguous style of speech. Politicians who gave straight answers rarely made it to the very top. Also, there were some skeletons in his cupboard, skeletons which Tobin had engineered. However, Thompson did have charisma, something which those predecessors lacked. This combination meant that he had been marked out as a potential party leader, and led to a year of re-education and transition while he changed his communication style and introduced more grey into the black and white of his espoused political views. This phase had been highly successful and led to rapid elevation through junior ministry into his current position.

Richard Thompson's background was modest, his father a foreman in a Corby shoe factory, and his mother a primary school teacher. There had been no more than current generation financial substance in the family. At the age of fourteen, he had been strongly affected by his father's redundancy as a direct result, apparently, of cheap Korean shoe imports. His continued asking of the question "Why?" developed an interest in economics and the realities of the British disease of business short- termism and under-investment in industry. It also answered to his satisfaction the reason for his father's death, in a Ford Cortina parked in woodland and assisted by eight feet of hosepipe and a bottle of whisky. Although he did not recognise it, it also became a driving force in his life.

At the local comprehensive, his penetrative questioning of teachers in mathematics and the sciences, together with a strongly analytical approach and unusually wide lateral thinking ability had tagged him for greater things. Coupled with strong debating skills founded on his analytical approach, his ability to generate hypotheses and knock them down led naturally to a successful university career and across the bridge to politics in the Cambridge Union.

After taking a First in Mathematics with little effort and much energy dissipated in other directions, he joined Lehmann Brothers as an investment analyst. His interest in economic modelling developed further, as he worked on software which would identify potential company failures based on published accounts and macro-economic indicators. This arena, relatively little-known to the general public, enabled analysts to "get an edge" in providing advice to investment managers on their investment portfolios.

This was a lucrative area of work, and several academics had already retired comfortably on the proceeds of their proprietary formulae for predicting company failure. Two years of inventing new and refined combinations of economic indicators and balance sheet items which marginally improved the confidence levels of predictions began to bore him, but this period enabled him to save enough to fund a twelve months break from paid employment, during which he worked apparently full time as agent for his local Conservative candidate in the run up to the 1997

General Election. His political reputation was strengthening, and his network extending all the time.

His late evenings and early mornings were spent, not in a Trattoria with a lovely young blonde county-set conservative, but at home in front of a PC hooked up to a Reuter news feed and a Bloomberg market feed. A very tight employment contract at Lehmanns had meant that he could not "invent" his software during the twelve months after leaving the firm's employment. On a wet and dismal December afternoon, eight months after joining Lehmann, he had, during one of his lateral thinking sessions at his desk looking out towards St Paul's cathedral, asked himself the golden question:

"Why do all these predictive models use published company accounts?"

The answer was that published accounts were all that *the analysts believed* were available in an easy to process, automated form. There was, of course, other data, arising from private briefings of analysts and market research, and from the media. The difficulty was that these were subjective statements and therefore not easy to factor in to equations, as interpretive work would need to be done, and this was difficult to deal with statistically.

If anybody asked (and nobody did) why Thompson was paid to sit with his hands behind his head, his feet on his desk, staring out of the window, or tapping a keyboard in the small hours, the answer would be that this was the way in which he generated shareholder value for his employer. His latest refinement had predicted the fall of an automobile manufacturer, and a killing for a select few of Lehmann's clients. He had received several offers to move to other firms, but the proprietary nature of his knowledge would have meant a very long period of contractually-bound gardening leave. His main reason for not moving was that a career in politics beckoned, and he had first to build a fighting fund. Whilst the now insubstantial golden hello of £500,000 from another firm might have helped, he was not prepared to write off a year at this stage of his career. In the interim he had also asked himself that golden question, and realised that the answer begged another question. The next firm would be his own.

The received wisdom was that an asset price (e.g the share price of a company) always reflected the complete public knowledge about that company – that is, the news was always priced in. The corollary was that insider information was valuable, and that was why it was illegal – it tipped the scales in favour of those who had that knowledge and could profit from it. Thompson had dreamed up a way of using lexical – word pattern – analysis to automate the scanning and weighting of real time financial news feeds and predict market movements of individual companies where the 'pricing in' of news was, on the basis of similar past events, incomplete.

At this time there was still plenty of excitement in the equities markets and fortunes could be made quickly, if not overnight. However, Thompson had recently been re-reading the legendary tale of how George Soros had bet against sterling and essentially caused the UK government to fall. This led his interest to move from equities into commodities – after all, money was just another commodity.

It was at this time that he first met Charles Tobin, who was interested in commissioning a research project into gold price movements, and this was an ideal opportunity to test his forecasting concept. The project led ultimately into Thompson developing a gold pricing model for Tobin. This proved lucrative for both parties, but as always in these matters, word leached out and one or two other major investors caught on to the techniques.

The following year Thompson was adopted as a Conservative Party candidate and cut his by-election election teeth fighting a safe Labour seat in the North West. Following the break up of the Coalition Government in 2012, he was imposed on a local party in a safe Tory seat in Cheshire and won the seat at the General Election. The Tories were returned with a small majority, and the Liberal Democrat Party was consigned to history. In fact, their presence in the Government had work well in dynamically shaping policy – both Cameron and Clegg were able political realists, but the core Liberal Democrat vote collapsed. Better follow principle than take power – an own goal almost akin to the failure of Michael Foot to win an election with the Labour Party's notorious election manifesto that was, in Gerald Kaufman's unforgettable words "the longest suicide note in history."

*

Welsh Gold

Welsh gold was and still is highly prized because of its origin and scarcity. It occurs naturally in two well defined areas of Wales. One area is in the North in a band stretching from the small seaside resort of Barmouth, past Dolgellau and its slate quarries and up towards the mountains of Snowdonia. In South Wales, it is found in a small area in the valley of the River Cothi at Dolaucothi in Carmarthenshire where it is known to have been mined by the Romans. In the last century, the gold was used to make the wedding ring of Queen Elizabeth II.

The mine was 'owned' by CADW, the Welsh equivalent of the National Trust. It was a Scheduled Ancient Monument and a valuable example of Roman gold-mining technology. However, in the stressed post-Crunch years of the twenty-teens, after the sell-off of the Forestry Commission had been narrowly avoided, and public expenditure was being cut left, right and centre, a proposal for a long lease on the mining area was accepted by CADW. The proposal was to open new access shafts which would not disturb the Roman mining infrastructure, and be unobstrusive to visitors. A long lease was necessary as the investment would be considerable and payback time at least twenty years. The industry was sceptical, but the successful lessee had been convinced that new bio-technology could work with very low yields, and a licensing deal (plus some capital investment) had been secretly agreed with Charles Tobin.

There had been numerous attempts to make a profit from the low yield mines, but the best of the seams had been cleaned out by the Romans. Nevertheless, gold exerts a powerful force on many men and there had been several recent prospecting and surveying expeditions with a view to profitable mining before CADW took over. All failed, but the most recent by the small, FTSE listed exploration company D'or Mining Plc led to the successful bid for a twenty five year lease, with strict environmental and archaeological constraints.

*

The geological survey team, led by Alan Hill, had spent one month on library research, and had four weeks in the field at the mine which D'or Mining had bought. They were under contract to D'or Mining - Hill himself was an experienced field geologist, having surveyed prospective goldfields in several continents, both successfully and unsuccessfully. Working with him he had two recent geology graduates, Bryan Allinson and Peter Duerr, to carry the equipment and do the donkey work.

The team had been able to obtain internal reports from the previous mine owners (before CADW) and the investors behind D'or Mining believed that with improved extraction processes providing improved yields, they could run a profitable mine. Gold is subject to the same market forces as oil or wheat or any other commodity, and profitability in low yield conditions and a weak market was always doubtful.

One evening into their second week of fieldwork, in a local pub far up in the valley of the River Towy, Alan Hill had got into conversation with a couple of hikers.

He introduced himself as Franz Müller, and his girlfriend as Gisela. He was on a break from manoeuvres nearby with a German tank regiment and his girlfriend was over visiting. His English, which he spoke with only a trace what Hill thought was a trace of a South African accent, was good.

"I guess you are from South Africa," said Hill, "I've worked with a few during my career – even spent some time there in the gold fields."

"You are mistaken," replied Franz, "I am German absolutely and so is Gisela, maybe you worked with many different nationalities and get them confused!" Hill shrugged and the conversation moved on.

Müller was about 6 feet tall, medium build with a hard edge to his features and typically Germanic blue eyes and blond hair. His handshake was firm and his hand had the leathery feeling of someone used to hard physical labour. They were dressed for hiking, with Rohan trousers and jacket. His boots – Timberland – leaned more towards fashion than serious hiking though, Hill noticed absently and thought no more about it.

The chat was general about the area, and strangers' impressions of West Wales and the Welsh. The mine was 'up above' – that is, north of the Landsker Line. This notional line across South West Wales divides Welsh language speaking Wales from "Little England Beyond Wales." It can be unnerving to newcomers when they enter a pub 'above the line' where all the locals are chatting in English and switch immediately into Welsh when the strangers appear. The locals resumed chatting in English having got to know Hill's team over the previous week or so, and Hill's colleagues headed back to their rented farmhouse. Hill, though, stayed on in conversation and the locally made Welsh whisky began to flow.

Hill was interested in Franz's knowledge of the area, but Franz said they were just hiking for a few days whilst Gisela was visiting. He was based for the summer at the tank range at Castlemartin. After the whisky bottle was empty, Hill headed out to his Land Cruiser and as he put the key in the doorlock, he was pushed hard against his truck, his left arm pinioned against his side, and his right arm twisted up behind his back. A voice which he recognised as Franz's said:

"It was good to meet you tonight Alan. I'm putting an envelope in your pocket. If you know what's good for you, your survey report for D'or

Mining will be VERY negative about the potential yield levels from the mine. We'll be watching you, and we'll be talking to you again soon, as we want a copy of your final report. We like to work on a positive basis, and we hope that the envelope will be an encouragement. We don't really want to go to your mother's home in Carshalton and speak to her now, do we? So, we'll just say goodnight for now."

He felt his arms released, but by the time he had summoned the nerve to turn around there was no one there. It seemed like something out of a bad novel.

Hill was shaking by now and it took him ten minutes to get into his 4x4 and steady himself. He drove slowly back to the farmhouse. The other two of his team were drinking coffee. Bryan asked why he was looking so pale.

"It's that damned Welsh whisky" was all he could say as he climbed the stairs and collapsed, trembling, on his bed.

*

Hill awoke the next morning to the smell of bacon and eggs and what he thought was the memory of a nightmare. Then, as he turned to get out of bed, he felt the soreness in his right arm and realised he was still fully dressed. As the memories came trickling back into focus, adding more pain to his hangover, he checked his pockets and found the envelope. So, no dream, and the envelope contained a thick bundle of used fifty pound notes.

*

At breakfast, he announced to Bryan and Peter that he had been disappointed with the results of the survey so far and had been considering a change in the methodology they were using for the survey; costs were mounting and results were not promising. Discussion became a bit heated, but given Hill's considerable experience and the fact that the others were no more that recent geology graduates they had little option but to follow his line.

After breakfast, Hill tried to call his mother, but there was no signal out here for mobile phones; the survey budget had not extended to the satellite phone which would be the norm in most survey teams. Given the international nature of his work, and his extensive travelling, Alan Hill, at 35 years of age, had not got around to marrying; his father had died a few years before in a car accident, and his mother was his only relative. He still lived at the family home when he was in England. When he was in the field he called her a couple of times a week, and he had kept this up even when prospecting in the mountains of Borneo. Now, here he was, 200 miles from home, and he couldn't call her!

Bryan and Peter set off for the mine in their Land Rover; Hill followed behind stopping en route at a phone box in the village to call his mother.

"Hello Alan, I'm so very glad you called, I've been so frightened. I had some strange telephone calls last night. Not heavy breathing exactly, just no sound and then the caller rang off. Three calls I had and I'm ex-directory. I couldn't sleep after that."

"Look Mum, it's probably just someone getting a wrong number – maybe a drunk trying to call a taxi, don't worry about it."

"But Alan, THREE calls!"

"Well Mum, if it happens again we'll contact the phone company, don't worry, these things happen."

Hill was ashen-faced when he got back to the Land Cruiser and his colour hadn't improved by the time he met the others, who were assembling their gear for the day's survey schedule.

"What's up Alan, you like a ghost?"

"Damned Welsh whisky, that's what's up, leave me alone!"

*

Hill was in Sainsbury's, in the wine aisle.

It was the day after his return from the survey in West Wales, and he was looking for some decent wine to go with his mother's cooking. The late night telephone calls hadn't been repeated and it did all seem like a bad dream. He had started work on his report, and the brown envelope was in his briefcase.

He picked up a bottle of Bordeaux and held it up to read the label.

"Don't turn around" a voice behind him said very firmly, a voice he recognised. He started to turn and this time he felt a hand grasp his arm tightly.

"Don't turn around I said. I wouldn't recommend that bottle – not a good year and the wrong side of the river. By the way, I'm looking forward to reading your survey report before you hand it over to D'or Mining – I do hope that it will be suitably negative about prospects. I trust that your verbal reports to the Board have not been encouraging either."

Hill was by now trembling, and a hand took the bottle of wine out of his hand.

"We don't want you dropping that now do we, and causing a scene. Just be here one week today, same aisle, same wine, with a copy of your report."

Hill stammered "But it's not due for presentation until the Friday."

"Well, that'll give us just enough time for a little tweaking, then, won't it. Same place, same time, next Monday. Don't look round now, just study the wine – that Bordeaux is crap, find a better one."

That night there were three more phone calls. Hill took them all and told his mother that it was definitely a crossed line with a taxi service. This time though, there had been a voice on the third call. The message was brief:
"The wine is better from the other side of the river."

*

Hill drove into the car park and found a space. It was dusk and he could see the drizzle starting to blow across under the neon car park floodlights. He got out of his car, holding the carrier bag in his left hand as he clicked the button on the key to lock the car. The alarm squeaked and the hazard lights flashed once. There was a gentle push in his back and a voice he knew said
"Let's make this quick - I assume the shopping bag is for me?"
Hill swallowed and nodded.
"Good, don't hand your report in until you hear from me, understand?"
Hill nodded again.
"Try the Rhone next time."
Hill got back into his car and sat in the drizzling gloom whilst he recovered himself. There was no doubt that the initial survey results, before he had started doctoring the instrument readings and rock samples, were positive, and held the prospect of a fair chance of profit for D'or Mining. His report however, was written in quite the opposite sense. He banged his head against the steering wheel, getting a very strange look from the mother who was now strapping her child into the babyseat in the next car.
One night later, there were three more telephone calls. The message on the first one was:
"We want some changes."
The second one was:
"Log into email tomorrow at noon, name *rhoneisbetter@hotmail.com*, user ID is veryhilly and password the same."
The final one was:
"*rhoneisbetter@hotmail.com* , veryhilly, got that?"
Hill said yes.
"Check that email tomorrow noon, and read the message saved under drafts but not sent, I hope your mother is well" and then the dialtone.

*

A week later and it was all over. The Board presentation had been a grim affair. Although they had been warned in advance about the conclusions of the Assay Report, the Directors were still incredulous. Of course, it was nothing new in the world of prospecting, where a shell company floats on a tide of gold fever and then sinks without trace.

Hill was severely grilled, but he managed to hold himself together. There was some discussion about the fees involved and whether a second opinion should be sought. However, a poor survey result on a mine that had repeatedly failed in the past should have been no surprise to anyone, and there was little appetite amongst the directors for another shot. They were hung with a worthless goldmine and a twenty five year lease. On top of that there was a two year commitment at £500,000 a year to license Charles Tobin's bio-oxidation process.

The meeting broke up early, and Stuart McCrombie the managing director left for an urgent meeting with the firm's merchant bankers at which the terminal Stock Exchange Announcement would be prepared ready for issue at 7am in the morning.

*

Having been brought up in a gold mining family, Charles Tobin learned about gold whether he liked it or not. He knew about what was supposedly the world's oldest goldmine in India (though a mine near Tbilisi in Georgia was also in contention) and that the Romans were the first to introduce mining machinery to the business of goldmining. During his research to locate a suitable industrial site for purifying his gold extract, he had learned about the Roman goldmine in West Wales. That was when the 'romantic' idea of owning a Roman goldmine told hold with him. The barren Welsh goldmine dovetailed neatly into his planning and although some substantial investment would be required, the outrageous bluff would bolster his hand in other ways.

*

The story made front page news in the *Carshalton Advertiser* as it was a quiet week for news:

Local Geologist Killed in Train Tragedy

Alan Hill, 35, a Carshalton geologist, was killed instantly on Tuesday morning when he fell under the 8.35 Carshalton to Waterloo train as it entered Carshalton Station. Inspector Thomas Ashurst of Surrey Police said in a statement that it appeared to be a tragic accident but their investigations were continuing. Mr Hill was single and lived in Sussex Gardens at his mother's home. An Inquest has not yet been arranged.

213

*

The dawn raid was thoroughly planned and superbly executed, and by noon the takeover was complete. Working from *Auric Adventurer*, Tobin had orchestrated his bankers and advisers. D'or Mining Plc, the small listed prospecting company, with no assets other than a barren goldmine in West Wales, was easy prey, and it was all over by lunchtime.

D'or Mining Plc was delisted and merged into Tobin Resources International by the end of June 2014.

Investment in the mine's infrastructure started.

The Press Release was unambiguous:

Nov 21 2014
London:
Tobin Resources International ("TRI") announce the discovery of significant gold reserves in its Welsh goldmine in West Wales. At current and forecast gold price levels, the low-grade ore reserves would be considered to be uneconomic to mine and refine using current methods. However, using its newly-developed two-stage bacterial refining processes based at its new facilities at the former Murco Refinery in Milford Haven, Tobin Resources forecasts extraction of several metric tonnes per annum from the low-grade ore.

End

There was considerable press excitement and speculation about the announcement, revolving around Tobin Resources's capacity to refine low grade ore in sufficient quantities to yield 'several tonnes' of gold per annum. The Government, in the form of the Welsh Assembly, was quick to start claiming credit, having "assisted Tobin Resources to acquire the former Murco Refinery site and invest in the Welsh economy."

In the industry itself, there was a high level of scepticism – most qualified observers believed that there was no gold left at all – too many had tried and failed to make the mine work, and the detailed geology did not support anything beyond trace levels.

*

Tobin had not planned for the death of the geologist – the people he had engaged to 'apply influence' had gone much further than expected. In the rough and tumble of the mining world, the use of muscle was not unusual. For 'heavy' work, Tobin usually used trusted people he knew and had employed in the past, though on this occasion Matt Hardacre, his Head of Security, had subcontracted the project without his knowledge.

"The fact is," crowed Tobin, "the mine is worth bugger all really. Yes, we'll mine some ore and refine it using our bacterial process, but we're only talking a few ounces a year, if that. It's just window dressing really. The main production will come from the Red Sea fumarole harvest. Still, we need to build this pipeline from the mine to the refinery."

Thompson was aghast. "But Charles, it's an 80 mile pipeline across West Wales, the Welsh Assembly and the Nationalists will not tolerate it."

"Look Richard, Wales is already criss-crossed with oil and gas pipelines, one more won't make any difference. You just make sure that you bring them into line. I'm sure that they will see economic sense. Anyway, have you thought any more about my offer?"

"Yes, Charles, I have and my answer is still the same. As attractive as it would be to get back into the commodities business, I still have things I want to achieve in Government; your offer is extremely generous and very tempting, but no thanks, not right now. Commodities are in my past."

"I would strongly advise you to reconsider, Richard. It's better to go out positively near the top, than to be shot down in flames with the wrong kind of news headlines that you or your family would never recover from. Consider it again – I'll give you until the end of the month. Here, take this and think about it some more. Don't open it now. Thanks for dropping by," laughed Tobin as he handed Thompson a white A5 envelope.

Thompson put it in his attaché case and left.

*

Back at his riverside London flat in Southwark, Thompson opened the envelope to find a DVD, which he loaded up on his 72" wallscreen. The video file was well produced and edited, obviously taken during a recent few days on Tobin's yacht. A bisexual Russian actress for God's sake, what had got into him! Vala, she'd got into him – or more accurately the other way around. He was shaking and stopped the DVD immediately he realised the drapes were still open. Jesus, he thought, his life was falling apart. "Get a grip, get a grip" he told himself.

*

The first call was put through the switchboard at Downing Street, with very little delay.

"Hello George, Charles here."

"Hi Charles," the Prime Minister replied, "how are things going with the Welsh goldmine – though everything you do seems to be a goldmine?"

"Things are coming along nicely. The mine's now in pre-production, and that pipeline that you and Richard Thompson helped us with is just being tested. I'm glad to say that our original production projections look very solid, even conservative!"

"Droll, Charles, droll, but good news. Listen Charles I've got to go into Cabinet now, how can I help you?"

"I'd like to have 30 minutes with you sometime in the next few weeks. I know you're going to Davos, and I'll be there, but it's all a bit public for my taste. I hear you are taking a week's break in Cornwall next month. How about a meeting aboard my yacht Auric Adventurer? Just a short heli ride across the Bristol Channel, a quick visit to the refinery in Pembrokeshire, and lunch on Auric Adventurer at the dock. Helicopter back, can't guarantee the weather, mind."

"That sounds like a big do Charles, rather unseemly for a Prime Minister. I avoid yachts after that show with Mandelson on Deripaska's yacht in Corfu in 2008. That was long time ago, but the hacks never forget, nor will Multibrand on the Opposition benches."

"George, I need a one to one meeting with you, very soon, very secure."

"Sorry Charles, I can't do that in the next few weeks. What with Davos coming up, and a country to run, my diary is very tight. Besides which, you've already had your fair share of help with that pipeline. Have your people call my diary secretary and we'll see what we can do."

"Prime Minister, we need to have that meeting, in both our interests. Maybe you should ask Richard Thompson if it's worthwhile" Tobin replied with steely impatience in his voice.

"Now look here Charles," the PM began, but Tobin had put the phone down.

*

Djibouti Developments

Monday morning, and Steve awoke in Camp Lemonnier, stiff and aching, and shaking his head as the bad memories of the previous day and night came back to him. He no longer had a baby sitter to watch him, and had relative freedom of movement on the base. 'Blue Bayou' – the master sergeant George Neilsen - had given him some fatigues to wear. After a shower he went in search of breakfast. As he walked in to the mess hall, the was a sign on the wall which said "CURRENT DEFCON 3." It had notched up overnight from 4 to 3. Lower numbers meant higher alert status, with DEFCON 1 meaning war imminent. In the mess hall, CNN was on the wallscreen and he watched the analysis of the Gate of Tears political and naval situation by CNN's resident Middle East correspondent, speaking from Cairo. They've probably got a news team already on the way to Djibouti, Steve thought.

There had been developments overnight. The Red Sea states of Sudan, Eritrea and the Yemen (but excluding Egypt and Saudi Arabia), had issued an ultimatum, to Tobin Resources to remove all its production facilities and ships from their offshore economic zone, within seven days, or be subject to forcible removal. The littoral states had asked their ally, China, to assist with diplomatic and military support. The UK was highly defensive of TRI's legal rights and the freedom to exploit the resources in that region, under International Law and the various conventions. The Saudi Arabian government, was urging caution, and trying to find middle ground. The CNN political analyst commented that this was a strange stance, as the TRI production platform was as much in the Saudi economic zone as in that of the Sudan, and Egypt also had a claim.

There was a brief news item about a widespread hunt in Djibouti by the nation's armed forces with the assistance of French forces. Several French marines, local policemen and civilians had been killed, by a female terrorist, it was believed. One terrorist had been shot dead.

After breakfast Steve sought out 'Blue Bayou'. Neilsen had been rather more approachable the previous evening – he knew more about Steve's actions the previous day, and obviously Steve was in credit with him.

"Did you get a good breakfast?" Neilsen asked.

"Yes, great thanks George, I feel a lot better. How's my pal Da'ud?"

"He's good, should make a full recovery, we're flying him out this morning to England – Brize Norton I think."

"That would be it" said Steve.

"Don't know if you noticed, but we're now at DEFCON 3."

"Yes, I did notice, in the mess hall. It's ramping up."

"Depending how today goes at the UN and the President's address later, we could go to 2."

"Did you get the news – I see your operation made it on to CNN?"

"Yes I saw it, but it wasn't an operation, just wrong place, wrong time."

"Yeh, I guess twice in one day is a coincidence" said George, half laughing, "maybe she's got the hots for you."

"Not funny George. She's got a fucking lot to answer for. I'll settle the score next time, for sure" said Steve.

"Yeh, well you give her one from me, okay, soldier."

*

Once below, Maruška had risked torchlight and checked her ear. She stitched it together – mostly cartilage and not heavy with nerve endings, so it hadn't been too painful, but some plastic surgery would be required – another place and time she thought, ruefully. She treated the graze on her arm which was stinging from the seawater, and the few she had on her knees and thighs after diving out of the way of Baldwin's truck. She lay back on the settee berth in Adèle's saloon. Her ear was throbbing as she thought about the day's events. How many kills? The looks of surprise, horror and death were all there in her vivd memory. The centre of the throbbing was now focused elsewhere as she replayed her memories. Then, she found her special, secret, soft, hot spot and her fingers moved. Finally, after a few minutes she drifted into sleep. Then, when a few minutes had become a few hours, the sun came up and she awoke and started to search the boat. There was a very good first aid kit, even with antibiotics – obvious really, she realised - for a guy sailing long distance on his own. She re-checked what was left of her ear and applied some antibiotic ointment and put on a proper dressing.

She had, though, underestimated the problems she would face. The morning sun was warming up the steel boat, and even though the hull was insulated, it was still over 35 degrees inside, and humid, with plenty of busy insects. Unable to show herself on deck, she had to keep the main hatch closed so as not to tip Baldwin off if he returned, though she did chance opening a couple of deck hatches slightly. There was plenty of canned food and water in the galley, though the gas didn't work and she couldn't find a shut-off – must be outside.

With no real experience of boats other than diving RIBS, she spent a half hour trying to figure out how the sea-toilet worked, and failed. Her ear and head was throbbing – the wound was not looking good it was very inflamed.

There were a few books and she scanned the ship's log – boring stuff – days and days of hourly entries about wind strength and direction, clouds, speed and position, ships. What a life! Still, what was hers? Years of hiding and killing – and yes she enjoyed the excitement and the kicks as thoughts of the previous day came flooding back. She dragged herself back to the present. What was she going to do when Baldwin returned. Kill him yes, but what then? Steal his boat? She knew next to nothing about boats – couldn't even have a shit properly on this boat. She could dive, and had used RIBs and larger dive boats – maybe she could take one of those. But go where? Ultimately back to Paris – she still had money and papers, but getting out of Djibouti would not be easy – realistically her only way was by air – maybe going to Addis Ababa was a possibility. A visa would be needed at the airport there. Her phone didn't have much charge left and somewhere along the way – maybe at the Al Mansour – she'd left her charger behind. She had enough for a couple of calls or texts, and sent an update to Chuntao, while she thought about what she would need from her controller.

It was mid morning and her ear was throbbing, and the pain was reaching down into her jaw and around the back of her head. She took some more of Baldwin's antibiotic tablets and some pain killers with water. She checked her gun and feeling unsteady on her feet she sat down to rest.

*

Chuntao was far from happy. The news feeds had told their own story, even before the text had come in. Maruška's operation was going badly wrong. These were supposed to be discreet operations, but they were becoming very public. Fortunately, the other news in the Red Sea was making the headlines, so the 'mad woman terrorist' headlines were local to Djibouti only. Maruška had been a good operator for nearly fifteen years now since the Guoanbu had started employing her, but perhaps it was time to move on? She still had the nanochip assemblage in her body. Chuntao would discuss it with the supervisor of her work unit later in the day.

*

The statement was issued simultaneously in Washington and London. It was 6 pm local time in Djibouti.

Press Release
Dateline: March 22, 2017
Washington

"The United States and the United Kingdom are disappointed about the adjournment of the UN Security Council emergency meeting. This is a time when a concerted international effort is required to persuade The People's Republic of China to reduce its aggressive stance in the Red Sea region.

Our governments have agreed to form a joint naval task force, with the support of NATO and some other countries in the region, including Saudi Arabia. The work of this task force will be known as Operation Free Seas.

The aircraft carrier *USS Gerald R Ford* and the British aircraft carrier *HMS Queen Elizabeth*, will form the core of this Task Force, and will be accompanied by a full complement of supporting vessels as appropriate for such a serious international situation.

We have incontrovertible evidence that the People's Republic of China has deployed powerful and accurate ballistic missiles in The Republic of Yemen. This deployment is a threat to the right of free passage, to maritime trade, and to the region in general. Both Governments, and NATO, are in communication with the Government of the People's Republic of China and the Republic of Yemen.

We urge the People's Republic of China to withdraw its ballistic missiles from the republic of Yemen. Further, if the Peoples Republic of China does not agree to withdraw its ballistic missiles within fourteen days, then the US and UK reserves the right use the task force to impose a naval blockade on the Republic of Yemen in both the Red Sea and Gulf of Aden.

In the meantime, we await the re-convening of the UN Security Council emergency meeting as a matter of critical urgency.

The President of the United States and the Prime Minister of the United Kingdom will broadcast to their respective nations later today, At 5 pm EST, 10 pm GMT."

*

Al Jazeera had the statement first, and then CNN.

"The Republic of Yemen and the State of Eritrea jointly announce that their territorial waters are closed with immediate effect to naval vessels of the United States, the United Kingdom and other NATO countries, Australia, New Zealand and the State of Israel. Areas adjacent to Bab el Mandeb (the Gate of Tears) (see attached annexe) currently used by international shipping do not fall within the international conventions relating to the right of free passage and free transit of vessels as they are within the exclusive economic zones and territorial waters of both countries. Neither the Republic of Yemen nor the State of Eritrea has signed or ratified such agreements established by other countries, and assert the right to control their own territorial waters. This closure also applies to non-naval vessels which are engaged in non-oil mineral extraction enterprises in the Red Sea."

This was quickly followed by a statement from the People's Republic of China, supporting these assertions, and mentioning its own interests in the Spratley Islands in the South China Sea in connection with free passage, though without making any prohibitions.

There was considerable concern in Washington and London, not least because of the effect in Tel Aviv. The right of Israel to navigate the Bab el Mandeb had been enshrined in a 1975 "Memorandum of Agreement between the Government of Israel and the United States – United States-Israeli Assurances," which the US underwrote diplomatically. Whether there was a secret codicil with a military guarantee was speculated upon. This added a new dimension to the complex scenario developing. Since their neutralizing of the Iranian nuclear threat, the Israelis had hardened their military stance and would be difficult to 'keep in their box' with this new development. They were still well in credit with the US for their successful Iranian adventure.

The European Union was urging 'caution and restraint', talking from a liberal diplomatic textbook like a toothless old woman past her prime, full of wisdom but with little acknowledgement of how the world had moved on since she had been a young virgin.

France, as a founder of the EU, was in a difficult position. Its influence with Djibouti was still considerable, and its historical and current involvement was very intimate. It pressed Djibouti to remain neutral, but issued a statement condemning attempts by several countries to destabilise the region and interrupt world trade, at the same time supporting the efforts of the EU. The contradiction was even starker, as France was a member of NATO having rejoined in 2009 after a gap of forty three years, and putatively an active partner in the Free Seas task force.

The Djiboutian Government correctly adjudged itself to be in a powerful position both geographically and diplomatically, and its government could see strong economic benefits if it sold its neutrality cleverly. China had become an increasingly important ally, and though Djibouti was a small, relatively insignificant country, it was overt in its support for the re-unification of China. The United States had a military base in Djibouti – its only base in North Africa. And what about its neighbours? Of course Yemen and Eritrea wanted Djiboutian support, but no support was better than joining the other camp. So, wisely, Djibouti elected to sit on the fence.

On the markets, oil prices had taken fright and were climbing rapidly. It was not about the physical closure of the Bab el Mandeb, but about the prospect of conflict.

Gold prices too were climbing, as investors fled to security.

*

"Hello George! To what do I owe this unexpected call?" said Tobin lugubriously.

"It's not a social call Charles. Close that fucking Red Sea platform down today" said the Prime Minister. "If you don't do it, then I'll do it for you."

Tobin chose his words carefully, though he had known for months what he was going to say. He had expected such a development, indeed, planned it.

"It's unlike you to use such language George, hardly Prime Ministerial. I'm not going to do that - it's a bit late now for small gestures like closing down *Universal Harvester*. And what about the tax revenues? You know very well that this situation is not about a production platform. It's about the Chinese flexing their muscles. They want to see the size of your balls. How big are they George?"

"Close that platform, Charles, I'm giving you 24 hours." Oliphant slammed the phone down.

Tobin sat back in the rear seat of his Bentley and smiled. They were on the M27 road approaching the airfield at Southampton and his Gulfstream was ready to roll. He had one call to make before they took off.

*

The makeup of a COBRA meeting is variable, and depends on the nature of the particular crisis in hand. If the crisis is a national rail strike, then one would not expect to see the Chief of SIS or the Chief of the Defence Staff in attendance, though the Commissioner of the Metropolitan Police and the Minister of Transport would certainly be present. Neither is the meeting necessarily held in Downing Street, but it would usually be held in a Cabinet Office Briefing Room (hence the acronym COBR) in Whitehall, unless of course the Government had been moved to a secure location.

On this particular morning, the meeting was being held 10 Downing Street, with the Prime Minister in the chair and indeed, the attendees did include the Chief of SIS, Chief of the Defence Staff (as it happened a Naval man on this rotation) and the Foreign Secretary. The Lord Chancellor was also in attendance – most COBRA activities had a legal aspect, be it domestic or international. The importance of the Lord Chancellor's input had been publicly clarified in stark detail following the questionable decision to invade Iraq, almost twenty years before.

The Prime Minister opened the meeting with the briefest of formalities.

"Good morning all. This is a meeting of the COBRA committee dealing with the Scarlet Horizon crisis, and the joint UK/US naval operation, Free Seas. Let's get started.

I spoke to the President overnight, and he outlined the thinking in the State Department and the latest intel they have. One of their nuclear submarines has been positioned up the Red Sea – she came through the Bab el Mandeb yesterday – sorry to steal your thunder Admiral – so we have some power in place. The Saudis are not keen to have any US combat airplanes on their soil at the moment, though the US does have some UAVs there – sorry, Predator equivalents for those of you who don't speak acronym. We'll be talking again later today before the joint statement.

If you'll forgive me Chancellor, I'm going to leave the Treasury perspective to the end, as I want to address the diplomatic, military and legal priorities first. We'll start with the Foreign Secretary. Anne, if you please."

The Foreign Secretary, the Rt. Hon. Anne Cruickshank, summarised the diplomatic activity and the statements that had been issued by the various countries, followed by a detailed update on the activity at the UN. She covered the Saudi position, which was basically motivated by a desire to keep oil flowing, and prevent any instability in the region. The US and Chinese stances were covered in greater detail, and an analysis paper was tabled. The paper contained an assessment of the probable playout of the crisis from a diplomatic perspective, and recommended courses of action depending on the moves made by other countries. She finished of her briefing with a note of concern:

"Prime Minister, as you know, the Lord Chancellor is working with the FO to clarify the legal position with regard to the specific conventions governing navigation in the Bab el Mandeb. However, there is a Memorandum of Understanding between the US and Israel, in which the US underwrites Israel's right of navigation through the Strait. The view of the FO is that the US President is having great difficulty in ensuring Israel takes no unilateral action. Certainly, the Israeli Ambassador is banging on my door very heavily."

George Oliphant responded. "Yes, thank you, Anne. The Israeli Prime Minister has been in touch with me over the weekend. Certainly, they have a lot of credit in Washington, having dug the US out of the political mire of Iran. Sir John, please proceed."

Admiral Sir John Arbuthnot GCB, OBE, Chief of the Defence Staff, began his briefing. UK and US Naval, air and military activity, disposition, states of readiness, NATO liaison, and contingency plans were covered. He summarised the intelligence about opposing forces, and expressed concern about the threat posed by Chinese forces and the capabilities of their weapons in theatre. Picking up on the Foreign Secretary's final point, he mentioned that two Israeli frigates had left Eilat and were proceeding south down the Red Sea. They were at cruising speed of about 20 knots, just less that 2 days from the Bab el Mandeb. There was more detail about the command structure of the new Task Force, Operation Free Seas and its immediate organisation. At this time, the CDS made no recommendations, his purpose being to advise and serve his political masters. Until there was a clear set of political objectives, advice would be general and unfocused, and limited to what was, and was not, possible. He highlighted the areas in which he required direction, as a matter of urgency, relating principally to Operation Free Seas in the context of the almost total closure of the Bab el Mandeb and US pressure for action, and looked forward to the Lord Chancellor's views.

"Thank you, Sir John. Now Sir William, what's the intelligence update?"

The Chief of SIS, Sir William Gore, covered the latest intelligence and highlighted the data about the Dong Feng ballistic missiles which had brought Scarlet Horizon into existence and led to further escalation.

"We continue to receive data from our sources and just so that there is absolutely no doubt on this, please look at the screen now for pictures of these missiles in an underground bunker in the Yemen. We have shared them with the Pentagon, and they confirmed our assessment, which led of course to the formal statement about Operation Free Seas." Sir William inserted an orange coloured memory stick into a socket on the table in front of him and the wallscreens showed a series of slides. The pictures had been edited so as not to suggest the camera height and eliminate any other likely clues about their source. It was always possible that the UK and US would choose to broadcast these pictures, to convince a sceptical world.

"Those are pretty big missile launch units. How did the Chinese get them there?"

"We believe that they were landed from a supply vessel, the *Weishanhu*, which visited the Chinese naval base two weeks ago. We had no useful intel link in place then, Prime Minster, and they obviously evaded the satellite overflights. More concerning is the fact that we have intelligence that TE-6 rocket propelled mines have been loaded onto a Chinese Sheng class nuclear attack submarine. Though I have no pictures, I attach a confidence of better than 90% to this intel. Even if the Chinese respond to our demands and withdraw the Dong Feng missiles, then these mines alone are capable, I believe, of keeping the Bab el Mandeb closed." He nodded across to the CDS.

The admiral responded "We don't believe their Shang class submarines are capable of laying these mines, but it's always possible they've developed a way. Mine laying submarines are special beasts, and these mines – if the intel is correct – are special beasts in themselves. We have fast reaction towed underwater detection systems such as SLAT, and countermeasures, on our carriers but whether they would be effective against the latest generation rocket mines, well, we just don't know. The only consolation is that the submarine would probably not get through the

Strait without being detected, so they could only lay mines on the Gulf of Aden side."

"That makes me so much happier Sir John. Tell me, could the submarine have got through last week?"

"Possibly, Prime Minister. We'd certainly know if she went through on the surface – and she didn't. The Pentagon would certainly have told us if she'd gone through submerged, that is, if they'd known. They may have some data on that, though the latest Sheng class vessels are very slippery. The western channel is very deep and there's plenty of shipping noise to screen a sub. Certainly we have no intel to suggest that the Chinese have located her there. However, the possibility remains, but they would be bottling a major asset in there, not a good move."

In fact, the Sheng Class submarine had got through the Strait undetected, and she had seeded mines north of the Gate of Tears. She had then moved up to the north of the Red Sea and laid mines at the entrance to the Gulf of Aquaba and the Suez Canal. She was now sitting at a depth of 1500 metres in the Shaban Deep, halfway between the Suez Canal and the Kebrit Deep. At that depth, she was well below what the US and UK believed was possible for a Chinese submarine. On passage, she had passed five hundred metres below the two Israeli frigates which were moving down the Red Sea. She was now stationary in the saline pool – a dense layer of highly salty water in the Shaban Deep – after laying a pattern of three rocket mines a mile apart, and which surrounded her. The highly saline water meant that she was hidden from any sonar probing – the difference in water density between the regular seawater and the saline pool would bend the sound waves from a sonar transducer outside the pool – they would just reflect away. These were tactics that submarines had used for many years to evade detection. The crew of the submarine were unaware that two years earlier the US navy had, under cover of a research project run out of the Woods Hole Oceanographic Institution in Massachusetts, seeded the saline pools of the Red Sea with passive sonar devices linked by cable to a shore station in Saudi Arabia. In the same Shaban Deep saline pool as the Shang Class submarine, less than half a mile away, was such a transducer.

"So, Admiral, we don't know then do we? Do we have any idea where she is?

"No, Prime Minister."

"Well that's clearly something we need to know urgently – let's leave that with you – we don't have much time before this afternoon's statement and I don't want us to get bogged down in too much detail. Please continue Sir William." The focus reverted to the Chief of SIS.

"Thank you Prime Minister. Our humint in the Yemen is not functioning at present. Our comms are now secure following two major attacks, which I have already briefed both you and the Foreign Secretary on, Prime Minister, and is best left outside this meeting. All we have coming in is what the regular embassy staff can provide the FO. We have other systems in place, but they are very local and specific.

On the other side of Bab el Mandeb, we have some resources. There has been a Chinese agent in action and the French have been working with us on this. It's a distraction though, nothing more.

Our resources in Eritrea and the Sudan are poor, and Cairo is relatively inactive, other than regular embassy traffic which the Foreign Secretary has already covered.

There's one more item which we are digging into. It seems that Charles Tobin has been talking to the Chinese. Specifically MOFCOM – their Ministry of Commerce. The Aussies have been providing background – ASIS and ASIO (equivalent to my lot and 'Five') – are working together on this – you know that they are paranoid about Chinese expansion on their patch. They think Tobin's cooking something up, met the Chinese Ambassador and screwed a Chinese commercial attaché while he was there earlier this year. The Aussies hate his guts because he took UK citizenship."

"That bloody man. What's he up to now – he's caused enough problems already?"

"We're still digging Prime Minister. I share your lack of enthusiasm for the man. His security is good though, very tight, run by an ex Special Branch chap. We have to assume though that his scheming is related to gold, in some way. My intuition though is that the Chinese are leading him by the nose.We've been looking at world gold mining operations, and a strange pattern is emerging, that of the deaths of key personnel in mining companies worldwide over the last ten years. There's no common feature to the deaths – accidents, robberies gone wrong, natural causes and so on, except that when we examine them statistically, the deaths are skewed and correlate loosely to later company mergers and takeovers. None are related to Tobin, I have to say, but Chinese involvement in these company acquisitions is there, in the background in many of the cases."

"That's concerning, Sir William. I'm sure you have a reasonable confidence in these conclusions if you raise them here."

"I do, Prime Minister."

"I'm sure you are turning the stones over exhaustively on this Sir William. Thank you."

"Now, Lord Chancellor, if you please."

"Thank you Prime Minster. I don't propose covering the issue of Tobin's platform – that has been analysed ad nauseam and is almost a thousand miles away from the Bab el Mandeb." There were enthusiastic nods of agreement from around the table.

"As we currently read the conventions about navigation in the Gate of Tears, there are thirty eight such Straits which are identified as connecting areas of high seas, exclusive economic zones or territorial waters. By Convention, these Straits are to open to free passage during times of peace or war. Innocent passage or transit, it doesn't matter. No state of war exists between any of the parties, and we are not belligerents.

The US has disputed a Djibouti requirement that all vessels with nuclear materials aboard should give prior notification before passing through their territorial waters – that is, the Strait. The US ignores the requirement. It will probably have no bearing on the current situation.

However, just as we faced problems of definition and inconsistency in the UNCLOS agreements, which Tobin Resources exploited to their advantage and our embarrassment, we face another set of inconsistencies in these conventions. Israel had spotted this problem and had the foresight to tie the US into that Memorandum of Understanding in 1975.

We are still working on the detailed legal arguments, and obviously discussions are underway with the relevant international bodies, principally the UN, to convince them that the closure of the strait is *ultra vires* for these states.

My current view though, is that Eritrea, the Republic of Yemen, and the Sudan are perfectly at liberty to do what they have done. We are still digging through precedent and the judgements made in such disputes in the past, but as I see it at the moment, it's basically a gunboat issue. They can deny access to military forces."

The collective intake of breath around the table was clearly audible.

"Further, we are examining the charts of the area in detail, so as to be able to advise the CDS exactly what geographical limits apply. Some of the international boundaries have been subject to dispute and I hope that we can make use of any lack of clear definition to give us more freedom of movement. Maps are disputed, islands are disputed and there's the Laval-Mussolini Accord which muddies the water further. Sorry – pun unintended. It dates back to when Djibouti was French and the Italians were running Eritrea or Abyssinia as it then was at least in part. The land maps govern the territorial waters - that's the problem. It's clear though that although the Strait is partially in Djiboutian waters, Eritrea and Yemen control the Strait, to all intents and purposes."

"Yes Admiral?"

"If I may just add to that, our hydrographic chaps think that there may be a way through, within Djibouti waters and outside both Yemeni and Eritrean waters - but it's tight, very tight. I'm arranging a detailed paper which I'll copy to the Lord Chancellor this afternoon. Of course, if the maps are in dispute, then it does complicate matters."

"Lord Chancellor, what's the US view on these navigational conventions?"

"Pretty much the same as ours, though as they tend to talk with a gun in their hands, they are a bit more gung ho, Prime Minister."

"Hmmm, we've been there, and I'm sure we don't want to go there again."

"Thank you. Finally, the Treasury view. Colin, what is the economic impact of this situation? We'll have to take the military cost for granted now. I'm more concerned about the commercial aspect and what the CBI will be chasing me about."

The Chancellor of the Exchequer, outlined his view that the effect on Britain's trade would be minimal. The Lord Chancellor had confirmed that commercial shipping was still free to navigate the Bab el Mandeb. The largest container ships (up to 160,000 tons) use the Suez Canal, and they serviced the bulk of Britain's Far East trade. The very largest oil tankers coming out of the Red Sea used the Bab el Mandeb, but the impact would not be severe as smaller tankers up to 160,000 tons use the Suez Canal. Freight rates would go up, and this would contribute to inflation.

"However, Prime Minister, I am concerned about the cost to the Exchequer of the naval operations. We don't know what we are getting in to here...." The PM raised his hand "Thank you Colin, we'll discuss the military impact outside COBRA. The commercial scenario is bad enough, and we'll have the DG of the CBI chasing us endlessly on this. The media love him." Oliphant grimaced as if there was a bad taste in his mouth and brought the meeting to a close with a summary and actions.

"Right, let's have your views about how we think that this may play out. Foreign Secretary, what do your people foresee?"

There followed a twenty minute discussion when the various possible plays were speculated upon, and then Oliphant brought the discussion to an end, with his 'statesman' summary.

"We are doing this as a matter of principle, that's why it's called Operation Free Seas. This should go down well in the media, as this is not only about British Commerce, it's about a principle too. Isn't that why we have the UN, to resolve issues of principle? This perspective will form the basis of our strategy. Operation Free Seas is all about freedom of the seas worldwide, and that China must be persuaded to see that we will not relinquish our rights to free and innocent passage, and that we too have the right to protect our trading routes. The seas made Britain great, we are a great seafaring and freedom loving nation."

There were nods of agreement around the table, though not all were enthusiastic or credible. Oliphant was no orator – his delivery was stilted with no imagination in his language and structure, and the very basis of his approach was doubted by some. The Prime Minister turned to Gerald Crosthwaite, the Downing Street media chief. "Gerry, we'll pick this up later, but get to work on our key media messages based around UN footdragging, Britain's seafaring heritage, Chinese global power. And play up the commercial aspect for all it's worth. It will help swing the media behind us. Commerce equals jobs equals paying media subscribers."

And votes too, thought a few around the table.

"Foreign Secretary – we need to be much closer to the Saudis. What are they thinking, other than about oil revenues. Coordinate with Gerry so that our diplomatic and media stances are consonant. Let me know when we look close to having that draft UN resolution agreed.

Sir John – find out where that Chinese submarine is.

Lord Chancellor – push harder, I need a legally robust position defined today – liaise with Sir John on the territorial waters issue.

Sir William – Get your people closer to Tobin. We need to know what the Chinese are up to, and whether it has any bearing on Operation Free Seas. I'm smelling something unpleasant here.

Now, as you all know, I'm due to broadcast late this afternoon, and I'll be talking to the President before that, to align our speeches. Alan will be on hand in the Crisis Control Centre to channel any critical updates to me, so please work through him as he will know where I am at all times.

One more thing – if any of you have lunches planned with Tobin, then cancel them. Stay well away from the bastard.

Next meeting, tomorrow, same place and time. We'll be looking closely at developments following this afternoon's speeches – Gerry, I'll want a full media analysis report.

We are aiming to define an agreed 'final outcome' that will satisfy the UK and US – political, economic, and military. We want that defined by midday EST tomorrow, Tuesday. Once we know what we're looking for, then we will plan how we achieve it. To support that, I want from each of you a set of objectives that we will need to achieve in each of your areas before we can consider this crisis to be, firstly, under control, and secondly, resolved. Both best case and worst case. I want your first draft objectives on my desk by 5 pm today."

The Prime Minister stood and left the meeting, accompanied by Gerry Crosthwaite and his Chief of Staff, Alan Coombes.

*

The flight to Melbourne was straightforward, though despite the private plane and fast-track access, Tobin was slowed down by a particularly obnoxious immigration officer, seeming deliberately to delay him. Shi Xue met him and the limousine took them straight to his suite in the Windsor. They spent the next couple of days in the suite, finalising the text of the announcement and the contractual details. The evenings were spent with Tobin exploring the Chinese approach to the arts of lovemaking and occasional food via room service. He also discovered a taste for Maotai spirit.

Tobin was using TRI's London commercial law firm for the legal work, and Xue was working online with Beijing. All Tobin's and Xue's communications were being automatically copied to Vauxhall Cross, courtesy of the Australian Secret Intelligence Service, ASIS, sourced from ASIO (under protest). The Chinese communications were impenetrable, but Thompson's were being prised open and read with increasing concern in London.

Tobin planned to be in Beijing for the announcement and formal signing of the joint venture agreement, with Shi Xue close by. His pilot had filed the flight plan and was awaiting clearance.

The ASIO and Sir William Gore's team in Vauxhall Cross were in discussion overnight to agree a plan, though there were inevitable delays whilst the frosty interface between ASIO and ASIS was agreed, following direct intervention by the Australian Prime Minister. Early the following morning – late afternoon Melbourne time, the clearance was given for the flight. During the pre-flight checks, the pilot discovered a fresh oil leak from a brake hose coupling, and a further delay ensued. Strangely, there were no spares available in Australia, and a replacement part was being flown in from the nearest Gulfstream service centre in Dallas, Texas.

*

At Camp Lemmonier, it was early afternoon, and Steve was very restless. He'd spent some time in the gym, eaten a good lunch and spoken to London. Booth was telling him to sit tight, wait for instructions and be ready to move within the hour. OK fair enough, but I'll just go over and check Adèle he thought. The situation in the Gulf of Aden was tense and the atmosphere on the base was palpable. He managed to wangle a ride to the dock with George Neilsen.

"I'll only be a half hour George."

"That's Ok Steve, I'm only here to serve – I'll hang out here for a half hour, see if I can't find a beer."

"Come over with me, and see Adèle?"

"No thanks Steve, boats ain't my thing, I'll go find a beer."

Steve walked down the jetty to where his rubber dinghy was cooking in the sun. He was glad he had trousers on and not shorts – the rubber was red hot and the dinghy looked fit to go pop with the internal pressure way up in the searing sun. His oars were still in the dinghy – he was lucky they hadn't been 'borrowed' by a local and cursed himself for having taken the chance.

As he paddled across he could see that the hatch over the head was open a couple of inches. Despite the heat, he was usually careful to close them. I guess I had other things on my mind that day he surmised. He came alongside and noticed that the main hatch lock had been forced. Swearing loudly, he climbed aboard and tied the dinghy. He stepped down into the cockpit and could hear noise down below – it sounded like groaning. He pulled out the emergency knife in its sheath from the corner of the cockpit, and listened at the hatch. Yes, definitely groaning. He gently pushed at the hatch until he could peer in through a crack of about half an inch.

Jesus, it was that Marie woman, lying down on one of the berths - her eyes were closed and she was groaning. He could see a pistol on the chart table behind her head – her head with a bandage around it. Where were his guns? Yes – there was a SIG in his bag at the base – but the other was in the waste oil container. Shit. He moved away from the hatch and stopped to think. She hadn't heard him come aboard, and appeared to be delirious. It would take him 1 to open the hatch, say 2 to climb in and reach the chart table – 3 seconds in total. Could she revive and stop him in that time? He reckoned the odds were on his side.

*

Steve slid the hatch back very slowly and quietly removed one of the washboards from its slot, all the while watching Marie groaning on the berth, ready to jump if necessary, but she was clearly out of it. He grabbed a hank of thin line and eased himself quietly through the hatchway and down the three steps into the cabin. He removed the gun from the chart table and put it up in the cockpit. Gently he slipped a loop of the line over one of her wrists and led it through a handrail and back to an ankle, across to the other ankle. She was still delirious. He tied off the other wrist. Then, he checked her pulse. Weak and irregular, she was sweating heavily. He got some water from the galley and splashed it over her. She blinked and looked at him, shut her eyes and tried to shake her head, opened her eyes again and tried move for her gun, or where she thought her gun was. Then she started shouting and he started shouting and slapped her face. Hard. He grabbed her by the throat.

The dream was about Kosovo, confusion, shooting, blood, stabbing, bodies, more shooting, flames, her mother, her father, her oldest brother Vaclav, a filthy Muslim taking a piss, pain, fear, delirium, more blood and then cold cold water, somebody slapping her, where was she? A man leaning over her shouting, slapping her again – that bastard – she knew him – who was he – the pain, the throbbing in her head, so hot, she was so hot I need more water. Then, the fading away of Serbia, her childhood and now her eyes trying to focus, that man again, who was he? I need to kill him, where's my gun? Trying to get up to scrabble for her gun, but so so weak, so much pain in her head, across her eyes, like and iron band being tightened. Someone slapping her face, swearing at her.

"You are done for, Marie or whatever your fucking name is. If you want to live you had better slow down and take some water. If you don't want to live, then I'm happy to put you over the side." She nodded at the cup of water in his free hand, and he let her sip some.

Steve checked her bindings and went up on deck. He took out his phone and called London.

"I've got the Pavkovic woman tied up on my boat. She needs medical attention, serious infection I think. What do you want me to do with her – Yanks, local police or the French, or shall I just finish her here and put her over the side? I've got Blue Bayou here with me and transport back to Lemonnier - I'd just have to get her ashore, but frankly I'd prefer to finish her now."

In London, Booth came on to the phone, weighing up the political fallout there would be whichever course of action he preferred.

"It'll have to be the locals ultimately, we need the credit with them. The French are on the fence as usual. There's serious politics involved. You know that Yemen and Eritrea have closed the strait to our naval vessels? Sit tight and let me organise it, we need to keep you out of the picture somehow."

"Yes, I heard the news. Let me know pronto or the decision will be made for us, she's pretty bad."

"What does Blue Bayou know?"

"Nothing so far, he's ashore – he gave me lift here from Lemonnier."

"Ok, keep him out of it if you can. I'll call you back in a couple of minutes."

Steve checked on Marie's condition. She was drifting in and out of consciousness, and had been struggling against her bindings. He found some plastic cable ties in his spares box and used them to cuff her wrists. Then Booth called back.

"OK, the Yanks are going to help us. Get her to the base and then once she's under treatment we'll call the locals in. That'll give us time to put a story together. Blue Bayou should be getting his orders now. They'll get the credit but the political weight will swing our way."

"Fine, I'll sort it. I'm going to get Blue Bayou now, and set it up."

Steve rowed ashore as George was on his phone.

"OK, Steve, I've got the picture. Nice catch."

"She's in a bad way. We can't bring her ashore here on the dock. Get your Humvee over to the south there – on the beach. I'll bring her across in the dinghy."

Back at Adèle, Marie tried to struggle as he dragged her out through the hatch, holding her by the plastic cable ties. He half dropped/half lowered her into the dinghy, but she had little strength and her wrists were bleeding. She was barely conscious as Steve rowed across the anchorage. The locals were out fishing, and her delirium was unobserved. At the beach, the Humvee was down at the water's edge by the time Steve got there. Once they had manhandled her into the rear, George set off for the base, promising to come back in a couple of hours to collect Steve. Back aboard, Steve cleaned up. He found some interesting stuff in Marie's carryall. The HK MP7 was a nice weapon, and worth hanging on to. He found an old towel, poured some oil over it and wrapped the gun up, bagging it in a plastic bag and stowing it temporarily in the engine compartment. Too big for his waste oil container. He taped her pistol under the deckhead, where one of his SIGs usually lived. The iPhone in her bag looked ordinary enough, but you never knew - London might find that interesting, but he couldn't do much with it, so he put it in his pocket, along with the French passport he found in the lining of the bag. His phone bleeped. It was London wanting an update.

"Don't say anything to Blue Bayou about her phone or passport, keep that to yourself for now. We want that phone. What's the name and number of the passport? We'll speak later."

He took a quick look round on deck and fixed the hatch as best he could. He didn't know when he'd be aboard again - the Red Sea was no longer an option for him now, at least not in the very near future.

*

By the time he got ashore the sun was well on its way down, a red disk. Still no rain in the air, he thought. At Dolphin Services he spoke to André, gave him some cash for his guardiennage, a key for Adèle, and asked him to fix the hatch. Then they chatted whilst he waited for George. The shootings were the main topic of conversation in Djibouti. A burned out milk truck had been found just down the road, with a body in it, incinerated beyond recognition. The discovery had been made before breakfast by an early morning fisherman, and the police were still there. Steve didn't say anything, but he could make a good guess at what had happened.

It was almost dark by the time George got to the dock, and they headed back to Lemonnier.

"They've got her in the ITU. She's got a bad infection, but she'll live they figure. May have damaged her kidneys. She's lost her ear too."

"She's fucking lucky to be alive, I nearly strangled her back there. At least I got her ear. She's a regular killing machine and there may be one more to add to her score." Steve explained about the milk truck.

"And this is the woman who wanted your children?" said George, shaking his head. "You were real lucky. I wouldn't have wanted my dick in the mouth of a woman like that. And you took her ear off. Boy, she will be seriously pissed with you. It's been a real bitch of a day – how about a couple of beers? Celebrate her capture?"

"But you're in uniform George."

"That's not a problem, believe me. My chain of command is 'not regular' shall we say?" I already guessed that, thought Steve. They found a bar and enjoyed a couple of beers, whilst George did his job and probed Steve for information. Steve showed him Pavkovic's bag – there was little left in it now, and Steve was economical with the truth.

"So, she left no papers, weapons nothing?"

"Nothing George – just the usual women's crap, some money and some bloody bandages – I obviously didn't bring those with me."

Back at the camp, there was a lot of anticipation and speculation about what the President's address would contain, but it would be after 2 a.m. in Djibouti when it was aired. Steve was not planning to watch the speech – he could catch up in the morning – and after yet another steak and fries with George, he turned in.

*

He was roused at just after 3 a.m., by George. "There's someone at the gatehouse to see you. Asked for Blue Bayou and then he asked me for you, so I guess he's in the loop."

"OK, let me get some clothes on and I'll be with you."

Steve checked his phone there was a 'call mother urgently' text. His mother was dead. Then he realised that it was London. George waited outside whilst he pulled on his fatigues and then quickly called London. He was still groggy and it took him a couple of attempts to remember the number, then got through to a desk officer.

"A courier - let's call him Sam - will call for that item that we discussed earlier. Give it to him. His maternal grandmother's Christian name should be the same as yours – check it before you pass him the item."

"OK, I think he's here now."

Steve checked his pockets – Maruška's phone was still there. At the gatehouse, George loitered nearby while Steve met the courier. He looked Egyptian or Sudanese, about eighteen years of age, dressed in baggy black trousers and tee shirt with hooded sports top. He had two days of adolescent beard, a pierced eyebrow and carried a black rucksack. His dark brown eyes, though, were searching, moving, seeking, checking, and Steve noticed that he held himself well, ready to act, like a coiled spring. They shook hands firmly, and Steve asked "Good to see you. How's grandma?"

"Violet was fine when I saw her, a couple of months back. I've got a new phone for you." He handed Steve a jiffy bag and Steve passed him a plastic bag with Marie's phone and passport in exchange.

"Thanks Sam."

"See you around." Without another word, Sam left for the taxi that was waiting outside the gatehouse.

George was shaking his head. "Gee Steve, he looked a bit young for our work. Are you guys taking them in diapers these days?"

"I reckon he's pretty smart, and handy in a corner. Terrorists are in their teens these days – you know we can't penetrate them with old guys like you and me."

"Yeh, the world is changing for sure. We're taking them in diapers as well."

"I don't think I'll get back to sleep now George – I'm going to the mess hall for a coffee and to find out what your President had to say. You look washed out - are you coming for coffee or getting some shuteye?"

"Coffee sounds great, and I can't miss the presidential address."

Whilst George was getting the coffees, Steve checked the Jiffy bag – a couple of pebbles which he dumped in the trash can. Six hours later Maruška's phone would be in the British Embassy in Cairo.

George returned with the coffee.

"How's Pavkovic?"

"Last time I checked the doc said she was through the worst."

"We need to give her to the locals."

"Yeh, I know, we'll arrange it later today, as soon as the doc says she's ok."

Steve didn't know that George hadn't been to sleep, but had been interrogating Marie. The problem was that hardly anything she said made sense – she was still delirious and speaking in Serbian, which he didn't recognise – but it was all being recorded and fed to Langley. George felt no urgency to hand her over to the locals – they would get what they could from her first. London and Langley had discussed the DNA linkage back to Serbia, but nothing more was known, except that there was a gap of about fifteen years.

*

On the wallscreen, the CNN analysts were in full swing debating the President's speech. The style was different to Oliphant's simultaneous broadcast in the UK, whose sentiments were a little less 'motherhood and apple pie', but the content was essentially the same.

The President had opened with a statement about the Chinese ballistic missiles in the Yemen, listing the basic facts. These Dong Feng missiles

235

were on mobile launchers, and could carry nuclear warheads a distance of three thousand kilometres, threatening Israel, Turkey and Greece. They were highly accurate and could hit a moving aircraft carrier. The evidence was incontrovertible – the US and UK had pictures of the weapons in their parking spaces. Further, the US and UK believed that the Chinese had other anti-ship weapons, and perhaps even a submarine in operation in the Red Sea.

The US, UK and many other maritime countries were seeking an emergency UN motion condemning the Chinese actions and demanding a complete and immediate withdrawal of the weapons.

There was a brief outline of the various international conventions and agreements guaranteeing freedom of navigation in the Bab el Mandeb and the President warned of dire consequences if the Eritreans and Yemenis tried to enforce their illegal ban on the free navigation of naval ships.

Rounding off with the standard phrases about Britain and the US standing resolutely shoulder to shoulder, the President confirmed that surface elements of the Operation Free Seas task force would be moving into the Red Sea to enforce a complete blockade of Yemeni waters. Passage through this Strait is a right of all nations, and the US and UK expected to do navigate there without any interference from other countries. Should they be attacked, then they are under orders to defend themselves vigorously. No mention was made of a sub-surface element of the Free Seas fleet - the US Virginia Class SSN attack submarine sitting at over 1000m depth in the Red Sea.

The analysts' consensus view was that if Operation Free Seas did not position either British or US forces in the Red Sea, then Israel would fill the vacuum, and that was not the best way to contain the situation.

The CNN Moscow correspondent was of the view that Russia was very concerned about Chinese naval expansionism, and was expected to support the UN motion, though no Russian government sources were available for confirm this.

They had an early breakfast and after the analysts starting repeating themselves, Steve decided to catch up on some sleep, whilst George 'went to check on the Pavkovic woman.'

*

Thompson's Troubles Triple

The drizzle was just starting to fall as Richard Thompson came out of the station entrance. He could see his Audi in the 20 minute waiting area, and walked across. The train had been on time, the new fast link had finally been completed and the service was far more reliable and speedy these days. He opened the car's rear door and threw his leather overnight bag on the rear site and held onto his attaché case as he climbed into the front passenger seat.

"Hi darling," he said, smiling as he kissed her on the cheek. He put his seatbelt on as she reversed out. "Bloody rain again" he complained as he squeezed her left thigh, more out of habit than anything else. She pulled out into the traffic leaving the station, heading for his nearby constituency home in Chester.

His Blackberry rang. It was the PM's private secretary in his car.

"Richard, the PM needs a meeting with you tomorrow at 7.30 am, Downing St."

"But listen Alistair, I've just got back to my constituency for the weekend, did he say what the subject is."

"The PM gave me no details, he says face to face only, no excuses. Please make arrangements to be there."

"OK, very well," Thompson sighed, knowing this was unavoidable short of *force majeure.*

"What is it this time Richard?" said Constance as she signalled for a right turn.

"Listen, I'm really sorry, I know you've been looking forward to a long weekend, even if it's only in the bloody constituency, but I've got to see the PM at 7.30 tomorrow, no excuses" said Thompson resignedly.

"Bloody right" she exploded, "what kind of marriage is this? I married an investment banker not a cabinet minister. The children never see you, I never see you, you see more of the PM and his cronies. Are you screwing him or someone else again? I get strange calls at home from Russian women, it's too much Richard, it's gone too far." A car coming the other way blasted its horn as she tested the tyres on the right turn across the oncoming traffic.

"Jesus, Constance, be careful, it's raining, what's got into you?"

"Be careful, be careful! What's the fucking point, we're not going anywhere anyway." She U-turned wobbling on the now greasy road amid cars hooting and sped back through the junction and into the station car park.

"Get out, get out you bastard, I've had enough, I'm sick of it."

"But Connie, for Christ's sake I've only just got here, can't we have supper at least. What's got into you?"

"No, Richard, get on your bloody train back to bloody London now, I'm through, it's all over!"

Climbing shakily out of the car he barely retrieved his overnight bag from the back seat as she accelerated away. He walked shakily into the station – there were a few interested onlookers who might have recognised him - and looked for the timetable. There was a Virgin train from Manchester Piccadilly in half an hour so he headed off to the bar for a large whisky.

He replayed the conversation. Constance had texted him that very afternoon saying that a Valentina from the Russian Embassy had been trying to reach him on their home phone number, so what? Then, the penny dropped and he realised that Vala was the affectionate dimunitive for Valentina. Shit! Vala didn't work in the Russian Embassy, it was just a smokescreen.

He had not immediately connected the two events, but in retrospect it was clearly Tobin putting pressure on. He was vacillating between rage at Tobin and worry about a potential scandal and the damage it would do to his image. The relationship with Constance was secondary. Affairs were the norm in Westminster and Connie was no fool. The important thing was not to shit on your own doorstep. His brain was crowding with options, actions and possible consequences, and aching.

He was on the train which was just approaching Birmingham New Street, and well into his fourth whisky when his Blackberry rang. It was James Warboys, his private secretary.

"Richard, I've just had a call from Julian Rogers on the scandal desk at the Telegraph. He's asked for your private number and I've said no. He's asked you to call him urgently. Something about you rushing back to London tonight, apparently some sort of domestic crisis."

Thompson looked around – fortunately the first class carriage was almost empty; he took a deep breath and collected himself, then launched into a defence. "Look, James, I've no idea what this is about – Connie's in Chester, so it's not my domestic arrangements. I've just been summoned to a meeting with the PM early tomorrow as you know but I'm not aware of any new national domestic issues or pressures. Would I be rushing back to London if there was a domestic crisis at home? I simply got on the next train so I'd get a chance for an early night and ready for the PM. Text me Rogers's number and if I get a moment I'll call him and find out what this is all about."

"OK, it's on its way. I'm on the train to Norfolk now, let me know if there's any damage limitation to be organised." Warboys's own constituency was in Norfolk.

"Shit, Thursday night, most MPs are heading home and I'm going back down to town" thought Thompson wearily, then:

"Look James, there's no crisis and no damage, so no limitation is necessary, have a good weekend."

"Ok, I hear you, you have a good weekend too, and if there's anything coming out of your meeting with the PM tomorrow that needs seeing to, then call me."

"Thanks James, good night."

As he pocketed his Blackberry, James Warboys shook his head wryly, thinking "he doth protest too much," and wondered what was going on.

Thompson finished his whisky and dialled Rogers.

"Rogers here, Rumours Blog."

"Hi Julian, you old bastard, I heard you'd been trying to reach me" he said smoothly, laying on the bonhomie. "What's a gossip like you want to speak to me for?"

"Ah ah yes Richard, thanks for calling me back," pretending not to recognise the voice immediately and score a point. "Thing is, I'm about to post a story on the Blog and I wondered whether you would like to comment on a little snippet I'm running about the pressures of parliamentary life for minsters. You know, since they changed the working hours for MPs to a more civilised structure, it hasn't made much difference for ministers has it? For instance, I heard that your own marriage is under pressure. Someone told me about a scene on Chester railway station this evening; I'm trying to get a comment from your wife as well."

Thompson replied oilily "Look here, Julian, there's nothing new here – everyone has ups and downs in their marriage, or whatever." This last word was a thinly disguised barb at Rogers who was gay and living on the edge, only just keeping own name out of the red tops, not having formally 'come out'. That was the trouble – the hacks closed ranks when one of them was involved, politicians' marriages or peccadilloes were always open-season.

"There's no need to drag Constance into this nonsense. I guess the rumour mill is quiet tonight and you're really scratching around."

"Sorry Richard, lots happening, maybe you know of someone else with similar problems?"

"Similar problems to what Julian?" he replied, avoiding the trap.

"Ah Richard, I've got to ring off – just been handed a note - your wife is on the other line for me."

Thompson opened his mouth to speak, as Rogers rang off. Furious, he rang back a couple of times, but the line was busy.

The train was by now through Birmingham and up to 180 mph, Euston was only about 40 minutes away; Thompson couldn't wait for the drinks trolley and headed off to the buffet car for a couple of top ups, carrying his bags with him.

After the battle at the buffet bar – the queue was long and tired, he worked his way back to his seat swaying more from the whisky than from the train itself – the new fast line was very smooth. He settled in his seat and then his Blackberry rang again. It was the Chief Whip. That could mean trouble. He ignored it.

When he got back to his flat in Southwark it was nearly midnight and he was well under the influence of half a bottle of scotch. He'd ignored a couple more calls from the Chief Whip, but now he had his story ready he called her up.

Stephanie Carswell was known as 'The Stiletto' at Westminster, and not for her shoe style. Tough, uncompromising and utterly merciless, Carswell had served the Party as Chief Whip for three years (the name had been changed some years back, but the original soubriquet persisted, and never had it been more apposite). Speculative jokes about her sexuality and possible bedroom preferences abounded, but she remained unsullied by them, and took pleasure in the new variations she heard every day. They were good for business.

"Hi Steph, sorry it's late but I've been on the train and you know what mobile signals are like, I've just got back to my flat."

"Richard, there have been 100% mobile signals on all trains for the last five years. We live in a connected society, or are you not reading the PM's speeches? Do you think I'm a fucking idiot? What the fuck is going on? What's this in the Telegraph's Rogers' Rumours Blog and in the early editions? Your marriage breaking up, trial separation blah, blah. Seems he's interviewed your wife."

Thompson winced – he'd meant to log on to the first edition on the way back from the station, but had been too pissed and forgotten to check it on the eReader in the back of the limo.

"You bloody well know that "Manage the News" is the first rule of politics, why wasn't I warned. Why is the PM's office getting calls asking for comment and whether you still have his confidence?"

Thompson took a deep breath and launched into his prepared and completely false defence.

"Listen Steph, there's obviously been some sort of cock-up. I was called back to London for an urgent meeting with the PM tomorrow morning. I managed to speak to my PPS before catching the train back, and he's obviously failed to get through. Thing is, Connie's under a bit of strain – she's always suffered from PMT and now the change is coming on, I don't know what she's going to do next, she's been hitting the gin."

"Well Richard, her interview with Rogers seemed to be lucid enough, and I really am the wrong person for you to try that pathetic 'hormone' excuse on. What's going on, is there anything more behind it, you'd better tell me, we'll need to handle it?"

"Absolutely nothing Steph, nothing other than the usual for Westminster marriages, no affairs, nothing."

"That's just it Richard, 'the usual' for Westminster marriages *is* affairs. If I find you're lying, you won't know what's hit you, you may find there's some truth in those rumours about my violence. You will be finished. Dead meat. End. Call me tomorrow after your meeting with the PM."

"Yes OK, Steph, goodnight." The phone was slammed down at the other end, if you can say that about a mobile handset, and Thompson winced.

He called his PPS, who was asleep and not best pleased, outlined the problem and asked for cover; Warboys agreed reluctantly and pointedly said to Thompson – "You owe me Richard, goodnight."

"That will come back to haunt me" Thompson thought as he filled his glass with his best Speyside malt and settled down to work through Rogers' Rumours in the Telegraph. There it was, online, 60" across on his viewing panel on the wall. It was grim reading – Constance had given quite a long interview and opened up about their difficulties. "She's always been a bit highly strung," he thought. "I certainly didn't marry an ice maiden, never wanted to either, she'll calm down."

The email icon blinked on the bottom of the screen – only his most private mail came through on that address – sender Charles Tobin. He clicked and read:

Good story in Rogers Rumours Blog. Remember that meeting when you see the PM. Further revelations awaited! C

"Bastard," Thompson thought.

He set the alarm for 5.30 and went to bed, drinking plenty of water with a few alcohol antagonists thrown in as a precaution. He had difficulty sleeping, turning events over in his mind. He didn't like the fact that Tobin was dragging Connie in to the shenanigans.

*

The shower didn't help much to bring him round, but as the events of the previous few days came back into focus he groaned inwardly and his brain clicked into overdrive. He didn't know what the PM wanted – the meeting had been set up before the fracas with Constance at the railway station, so that was OK, or was it? Tobin's email was nagging him. How did he know about the meeting with the PM? Then the possibilities started to fit together into a very unpleasant scenario.

He stepped into the car past his driver, without any acknowledgement at all, completely lost in the possibilities of the next couple of hours. By the time they reached Downing Street, he had checked the Telegraph on the eReader display – no updates on Rogers' Rumours Blog, but the others bloggers and commentators were in full flow; he had however come up with a couple of plan options, depending on what the PM wanted with him. He started to relax, as he realised he could, very possibly, turn adversity into opportunity. Things would not pan out quite as he had hoped all those years ago, but on the other hand, things may turn out better too…

*

After a few minutes wait, Thompson was shown into the PM's study by Alan Coombes, the PM's personal secretary, and was offered a seat. There were no pleasantries, no words of welcome - the PM was clearly in a bad mood. Once Coombes had gone out and closed the door the PM started:

"Right, Richard, will you tell me why the hell I've got that arrogant sod Charles Tobin telling me that I really need to have a meeting with him, and that I should ask you the reason? What's in your closet? Is it anything to do with Rogers' Rumours in the Telegraph and your wife? The whole thing stinks to high Heaven. You've got five minutes to explain, before I leave."

Thompson was taken aback – he had not expected this attack, but realised that it needn't affect his plan and so he launched smoothly into his prepared response.

"The thing is Prime Minister, Tobin is developing a strategic business which would be of great benefit to the UK and the Exchequer. He needs some high profile political help to pull it off, at an international level. I don't know much about it, but it is vast in scale and breathtaking in concept," Thompson lied. "You know about the goldmine that we've already bent over backwards to help him with – it's cost us some political capital but also a stack of grant aid – well, that has gone down terrifically well in what used to be one of our strongholds back in the 50's and 60's," said Thompson knowing that he was re-shaping history quite a bit. "We don't have many seats in Wales any more, but this could be a way back, consolidating those few gains we have made in the last couple of elections. Anyway, from the little I know, this Welsh goldmine is just the start. His view is that you are a man of great vision as he is, and few are capable of understanding and helping in this time of change and economic shakiness."

"Richard, the man's a megalomaniac, can't you see that? I want nothing to do with him," said the PM not disabusing Thompson of the notion that he was himself a man of vision.

Thompson's stomach fluttered. This was pretty much what he had expected, but he stayed on the tight-rope.

"Prime Minister, Tobin claims that this project of his could transform the British economy – he put it on a par with North Sea Oil – though that was well before our time. It may be at least worth a few minutes in your diary. I don't know any more than I've told you, but everything he touches turns to gold - his commercial nous is second to none. I believe the man. If there's half of what he promises in this then it must be worth finding out more. Tobin will only deal with the organ grinder, never the monkey. He will not meet with any of our minsters, Trade, Enterprise, not even the Chancellor."

"Arrogant sod. Nobody makes that much money without a few skeletons in the cupboard, Richard."

"And nobody who becomes Prime Minister has an empty cupboard either, George." Thompson knew he was very precarious ground here with this familiarity and barefaced cheek.

"Touché" said the PM, and Thompson knew he'd won out. "I'll see if I can find a few minutes to see him. Now, what's this about Constance?"

Thompson kept to the line he'd used with the Stiletto the previous night, knowing that the PM would have had the story already.

"Are you very sure that there's nothing else Richard?"

"On that specific front, I'm sure. But I do want to spend more time with Constance. As the PM stood up, Coombes entered to show Thompson out. Five minutes it was.

When he was in the car on the way back to his flat, he had a text come through from Tobin:

"Looking forward to positive news C"

"Looks good R" he replied.

He called Connie from the flat. She was very distant, perhaps regretting involving the Press, he wondered. They agreed to spend the weekend apart. She would come down to town on the following Wednesday and they would discuss the situation then. He casually mentioned that he was thinking of resigning as a minister, and left that idea with her to gestate, and expecting it to calm her down.

*

On the following Monday, Tobin was called by the PM's diary coordinator and told that there had been a cancellation in the diary, so the PM was offering a 15 minute meeting in a hotel near Carlisle on the Wednesday morning, at 9 am. The precise location would be provided 3 hours before the meeting. Other than that there were no gaps in his diary for at least 6 weeks. Tobin agreed to the meeting without hesitation. The number of his private mobile was requested, and given.

A plethora of hotel bookings were made in advance of a Prime Ministerial visit, but many would never be used. The precise hotels to be used were selected randomly from the bookings only 3 days before the visit. Cancellations were held back until the day of the visit.

An advance security team swept the hotel for electronics and explosive traces, the sniffer dogs had their wander round and the all-clear was declared on the Monday morning, following which a team member would be ensconced in the hotel until the PM left on the Wednesday morning. The guest list had been checked, the staff vetted and the bookings list frozen for the 48 hours spanning the visit. There would be another check on the Tuesday morning, by a different team of specialists.

On this occasion, the Crown and Mitre Hotel was selected for the stopover. A solid Edwardian-style pile in the centre of the city, close by the cathedral it was probably a predictable stop for a Prime Minister on a regional visit. The fact that it had been selected at random was coincidental.

Tobin was in his Bell 429 helicopter en route from Winchester to Carlisle when the call came through. The weather was good and his pilot expected them to land in Carlisle airport at 06.45, allowing sufficient time for the limo to get him to The Crown and Mitre by 08.30 for security clearance. He had been told that he would not be allowed to take anything into the meeting with him, not even a pen and paper or wristwatch. Security at Presidential level these days was severe. Threats were hi-tech and difficult to protect against after recent assassinations demonstrated the technologies that some governments and their terrorist affiliates had access to. They had moved on since the days of exploding cigars and the use of ricin-tipped umbrellas. Nowadays they were up-close and very personal.

Suicide bombers had carried explosives internally and killed two members of the Saudi Royal Family. A Pakistani President had been killed with a nerve toxin delivered via handshake at a tribal clan gathering. One prominent and promising presidential-material politician in the US had been deliberately infected with a strain of HIV engineered to bypass the highly effective treatments and antagonists by that time available. He had developed full blown AIDS within three months and was dead within six. Sex had been a tool for spying since man first walked, but now it was a hi-tech channel for death too. Though Tobin was a well known figure, the rules would be enforced stringently, not that sex with the Prime Minister was an option anyway.

He had had his eyesight corrected by laser surgery some years before. Before entering the meeting he handed over his wristwatch and was asked for his spectacles. He refused. The guard shrugged and pointed "As you wish, sir. We understand that your eyesight is perfect. If that is not correct then we can provide you with a suitable temporary pair for the meeting. Otherwise we are instructed to cancel the meeting."

He handed over his spectacles. Removal of one's shoes was *de rigeur* in these times of shoe bombers. Absolutely no chances were taken. He changed into the disposable slip-ons that were provided and was shown into the meeting room by Alan Coombes, the PM's personal secretary.

"Hello Charles, take a seat" said the PM, "Alan will take notes. I have to follow the protocols that my security team lays down. The days of pressing the flesh in an election campaign are over when we are away from Downing Street.

Anyway, you've got your meeting – fifteen minutes is all I can spare. Richard Thompson convinced me that you have a proposal worth listening to, I hope he's right. Over to you."

"I'd prefer it if this meeting was one to one George."

"Can't do Charles. Let's not waste our time talking about protocol, I've got better things to do."

"Very well George, if you want notes taken about the impending redtop press story concerning one of your senior ministers, then so be it."

The PM started forward, looked across to Alan Coombes and nodded. Coombes rose and left the room.

"Get on with it Charles, I'm running out of time and patience, and don't try to threaten me!"

Tobin continued smoothly: "I always believe that more is achieved working together than against one another, George. The bare facts are that I have developed a way of refining molybdenum, manganese and other metals from low grade ore which is available in vast quantities in certain parts of the sea bed. This will lead literally, to a bonanza for my companies. It could also lead to a bonanza for the UK Exchequer if the situation is handled with vision and ability. Ultimately, it could be on a scale to surpass North Sea Oil. I am here to enlist your – that is, the UK's - political backing.

I expect that the Foreign Office will react robustly against my plans. The fact though, is that my plans will come to fruition one way or the other. I would prefer to work in harness with your government than with any other. And, yes, there are other governments who are keen to provide political sponsorship for this enterprise.

Nothing I am proposing is in clear breach of International Law or any relevant conventions. However, there are certain countries which are bound to react strongly, in an area of the world which could be described as sensitive. In the longer term, this sensitivity will be circumvented as the technology is developed further."

At this point, Tobin began to stretch the truth somewhat as he built the fiction.

"For your - my - government's sponsorship I expect to pay appropriate levels of taxation, possibly amounting to hundreds of million pounds per annum when the technology is fully developed, perhaps even billions.

Time is of the essence now as I am moving into pre-production – I have a production rig en route from India."

"That's very interesting Charles. A couple of points though. As I understand it, you are Australian and not British. Secondly, if something sounds too good to be true, then it probably is. And that is especially apposite in politics. There are numerous instances of governments – UK governments even – being drawn into grandiose schemes and ending up with egg on their faces. De Lorean Cars for instance, many years ago – textbook fraud. I just don't believe in such bluebirds, and I'm not suggesting that your plans are anything less than genuine, at least in your own mind."

"Well George, I didn't expect you to believe such a story – it does sound incredible I know. But, you know my track record, and you know that in every generation there are a few individuals who can turn build massive businesses through sheer vision and determination. The list is endless – Edison, Gates, Murdoch, Jobs, Assange, Zuckerberg for example. And yes there are a few who are charlatans and are not found out until it is too late. You mentioned de Lorean, but I clearly belong in the first group – I've proved that repeatedly. I'm sure that your intelligence people have been following my activities for years. Certainly, I am an Australian by birth, and a proud one too – some of my family died fighting wars for England – but I now hold British nationality. My companies though, for the moment at least, are registered in the UK and pay a lot of tax to your – our - Government.

And, yes, I've sailed close to the wind on occasion, I don't deny that – what successful man hasn't?" raising an eyebrow to the PM "but you'll know that there are no dirty secrets in my closet – my scandals are well publicised and a part of my public image - perhaps unlike those of some of your ministers."

"Such as? Is there something I should be told about Charles?"

"Perhaps, Prime Minister, but I really do want us to agree how we might move this forward, how we might get the Foreign Office behind the enterprise, and begin to benefit Tobin Resources and the UK Exchequer. I'm very happy for your senior people to audit my plans if that is what is necessary, though naturally there are certain commercial secrets that I will not allow access to. At this stage we must be absolutely leakproof in order to maintain our technical advantage. That's why I'm here. I know you can be trusted."

The PM smiled and took in the flattery. "Before the FO you will have to convince me, Charles. What area of the world are we talking about?"

"Middle East, the Red Sea to be specific."

"You must be joking Charles, or a fool. You really cannot be serious about this?"

"Never more serious, George. And that's just a start. The potential is limitless in practical terms as there is vast potential in other areas of the world, though none have the political sensitivity of the Red Sea. We need to prove the technology first and then develop it further for the deep oceans. And, believe me, there are other governments keen to be involved and provide patronage. The implications are enormous. Eventually – maybe in ten years time – I hope to be able to use the technique for the extraction of gold, but at the moment I am focusing on the low hanging fruit."

The PM breathed out heavily and shook his head. "So, you are dangling golden offerings in front of me. Very well, Charles, I'll discuss this – in outline – with my senior people, and revert to you in a few days. We'll find a way at least properly to appraise your proposal."

"I am not asking for more at this time, but commerce is commerce and there's no stopping it. Thank you for your time George, and for listening to my proposal. I do hope that we can do business. It would be a shame to have to involve anyone else. Oh, and by the way, you might ask Richard Thompson if he has seen any Chekhov recently."

"Thompson, Checkhov what's this about?"

"I believe that The Cherry Orchard is currently playing at the Old Vic. An interesting cast - the actress playing Varya is quite exquisite. Richard will be able to tell you a whole lot more I'm sure."

Tobin smiled to himself as he was shown out, pleased with his performance and pleased with the outcome, thus far. The bluff was live.

In the meeting room, George Oliphant took out a folder from his red box. It was entitled 'Tobin Resources International'. 'Most Secret' was stamped on the front cover. He opened it up and annotated a page inside, "£1 billion + tax revenue!" smiling to himself and saying "the cunning bastard" as Alan Coombes entered. Later, a transcript of the meeting recording would be inserted, and the recording destroyed. Much secret material was still held in paper form – the WikiLeaks scandals in 2010/2011 had seriously frightened and embarrassed governments in equal measure, though how much of it was deliberate misinformation was hard to tell. Dematerialised information was much too easy to copy, lose, steal or make public. The best secrets were still kept in the head, or on sheets of paper. That's where this one would stay for the moment.

*

Gold – First Harvest

The pipeline delivering the putative gold ore slurry from the mine at Dolacothi was now operational. The Government had provided grants towards building the pipeline, eager to be sent to be helping the local economy, but, secretly and known by only a few in the Cabinet, the lure of gold and underpinning the Pound Sterling was at the heart of it.

The Welsh Assembly – the devolved government of Wales – had bridled at the suggestion of providing grant aid to a billionaire, but opposition had crumbled after a deal had been done with UK Central Government, which offset the grants and provided further additional funding to Wales; there were political concessions made too, about local tax raising powers.

Between 1999 and 2002, the then Chancellor of the Exchequer, Gordon Brown, had sold off 395 tonnes of Britain's gold in a series of 17 auctions. These are said to have driven down gold prices and to have lost the UK £5 billion. The world banking collapse in 2008 had led in 2011 to half-hearted suggestions about re-introducing the gold standard. Although these suggestions eventually came to nothing, the UK government saw sense in increasing gold reserves. After all, the strongest Asian economies were enthusiastic hoarders of gold.

So, Tobin's goldmine in West Wales had become a strategic issue for the Government, though a tight lid was kept on that at both the Treasury and the Bank of England. The eighty mile long pipeline was built, but only Tobin knew that it was window dressing.

*

The production platform *Universal Harvester* had been modified, having high capacity pumps capable of quickly emptying Tobin's tankers, pumping the bacteria-rich feedwater 2,000 metres down to the seabed. 36 remote inlet heads on the seabed in a circle of radius 3 miles surrounding the platform would recover the water back to the platform from where it would be pumped back down again. So, the enriched seawater was re-circulated continuously and its precious metal content was concentrated over what would be a 6 week cycle (according to projections) before it was of a grade suitable for the final extraction. Then, either the *Trader* or the *Enterprise* would be waiting at the nearby deepwater mooring to take on the cargo for shipping back to the TRI refinery in the UK for further refining before being sent to specialist gold smelters. And then the next ship would provide more feedstock. And so, a virtuous circle would be established, with eight tanker loads expected in the first year.

*

The first unload went broadly to plan. David Wallis, the master of the *Trader* had plenty of experience with offshore oil loading from SPMs – single point moorings - which have a supply connection to a source of oil ashore. These enable VLCCs (Very Large Crude Carriers) to take on cargoes of oil offshore where there was insufficient depth for them inshore and the construction of a deep harbour was uneconomic or inappropriate – environmental pressure groups were making themselves felt in this respect. So, the SPM was the mechanism being used for the unloading of the initial feedstock and then the re-loading of the enriched seawater six or so weeks later. Once the cycle was fully established then the initial feedstock would not need to be replaced.

After the first unload the *Trader* waited at the mooring whilst the initial cycle was established. It took eight weeks for the first batch to reach the required level of enrichment. The world average for yield from land based mining is about 5-6 grams per tonne of ore. Mines in Alaska might have 16-17 grams per tonne. Yields from Tobin's bio-harvesting would be less than that – less than one gram per ton of sea water, but it was much cheaper to extract and reserves were practically limitless. Whether they were politically accessible was the moot point.

The political problems were still being ironed out – Saudi Arabia was more receptive than Yemen, Egypt more so than Sudan; Israel was starting to take an interest. The issue about economic control of the deep sea bed which was not continental shelf had created a lot of discussion. The International Seabed Authority had called a conference in Geneva with the purpose of resolving the legal issues. Tobin had weighed up the political consequences, and likely stances of the littoral states in the Red Sea. Though he was as sure of his legal position as could be, there were still considerations which his discussions with the Foreign Office had worked through. Consequently, the *Universal Harvester* was positioned marginally on the Saudi side of the Red Sea median line through the Kebrit Deep – a mile or two further east and optimal positioning with regard to the black smokers would not be possible, and harvest yields would suffer.

There had been a mad international scramble to identify other areas where similar legal lacunae in UNCLOS might exist. Perhaps fortunately, the Persian Gulf was not such a region – this was the inverse to the Red Sea – the plates in the Gulf were actually colliding. Tobin, though had done his homework, and none were as valuable or sheltered as the Red Sea.

Commerce, though, continued through all the legal shenanigans, and after 5 weeks the *Trader* left the single point mooring and moved down to Yanbu in Saudi Arabia to take on 40,000 tons of Arabian light crude oil.

Yanbu, a major oil refinery and terminal is at the end of several pipelines which feed oil and gas from the interior and a major strategic pipeline from the east coast of Saudi Arabia.

The cargo of light crude would be unloaded at the TRI UK refinery and sold on as spot market prices allowed.

*

During the first six months, Appleton was based on the production rig. He monitored the density of the bacteria, their multiplication rates and their gold content. The sulphur content of the sea water was important too – this derived from the fumaroles along with the metal 'concentrate' and fed the *Thiovulum Aureus*. Bottom currents were constantly measured and plotted, and pumping rates were varied around the matrix of 36 intakes – they only wanted to recycle enriched water. So, at any given time, about half the intakes were abstracting enriched seawater where the current flowed outwards, and half were pumping it back where the current was flowing inwards on the opposite of the circle of intakes/outlets.

In this way they could maintain constant production. In fact, at the depths of the abstraction, currents were fairly constant and slow to change – the variable winds on the surface had little effect at these depths, and constant sustained winds were relatively rare.

At first, enrichment levels were slow to increase, but as the team gained experience then the software which controlled the inlet/outlet pumps was tuned and yields rapidly improved. Assay of the bacterial efficiency was now automated using improved biosensors and production costs were falling sharply.

Other than Appleton, none of the rig's crew knew to true purpose of the exercise – molybdenum and manganese recovery was the putative commercial process under way.

*

Tobin was himself at the refinery when the *Trader* arrived to unload the first cargo. He had flown over her in his helicopter as she entered Milford Haven through the western channel, passed St Anne's Head and the Mid Channel Rocks where the Sea Empress had come to grief in 1996 and spilled 73,000 tons of North Sea crude. Accompanied by the mandatory tugs (although the cargo was 80% non-hazardous), she made her way in near to Chapel Rocks and turned to starboard up the Haven at Thorn Island and then passed the gas terminal on her port side as she approached her berth. *Auric Adventurer* was anchored a short distance away, west of Stack Rock. After landing he took the *Adventurer's* launch the mile or so to the terminal. It was late in the winter's afternoon and what had been a fine day was darkening rapidly as the marbled grey clouds lowered and spat, the incoming front promising a wet and windy night. The Haven was starting to cut up as the strengthening westerly wind set itself against the ebb. Tobin stepped ashore to board the *Trader* to welcome David Wallis and his ship. He was met by the Customs and Immigration Officials who tried to keep him off the ship until they had finished their business, but he blustered his way aboard - "I'm the bloody owner, this is a historic moment for the UK."

Unloading would begin later that evening, but before that there was the question of the cargo manifest to deal with.

Tobin had argued that (apart from the Arabian Light Crude) the cargo should be declared as 'None'. It was after all, sea water and ships carried seawater in their tanks as ballast. His marine lawyers had advised against such a statement, and counselled that 'metal enriched seawater' should be listed. Of course, manganese and molybdenum was what the lawyers thought was in the water. In fact, the Light Crude was not to be unloaded as Richard Thompson had that very day agreed to fulfil a contract for delivery in 7 days time to a French refinery near St Nazaire on the west coast of France.

The Customs officers were amused to read 'Enriched Seawater' on the manifest. Tobin explained to them that the Exchequer and Customs and Revenue Department had recently agreed a clarification of the rules given the new developments in metal and mineral refining which he himself had pioneered. The moment was lightened when he pointed out that this was a historic moment and that a Sky News and a BBC news crew would like to film the moment. The Excise men declined to be filmed in uniform, but there was a lot of laughter and the Scotch was passed around. The film interviews with Tobin took place once the ship had been formally 'cleared in' and the Excise men had left.

*

The first 200,000 tons of enriched seawater were pumped ashore into holding tanks at the refinery. As planned, the *thiovulum aureus* bacteria had died off during the passage from the Red Sea. The dead, gold-carrying bio mass sank in the *Trader's* tanks and agitation and tank washing was necessary to clean out the most valuable layer of biomass next to the tank plating.

Four days later the *Trader* left Milford Haven for St Nazaire, into the gathering teeth of a southwesterly gale to unload her cargo of 40,000 tons of light crude at Donges on the Loire river. Fully laden, drawing fifteen metres, she would not have been able to enter the port, but with only 15% of her capacity it was possible.

By this time, Tobin was back in Winchester, and the *Auric Adventurer* was waiting for a break in the weather before heading down to Gibraltar and from there through the Mediterranean and the Red Sea via the Suez Canal.

The initial refining process proceeded well – there had been some trials, bit it was a relatively low-technology process. Appleton had flown back from *Universal Harvester* production platform to supervise the refining of the first batch. First the biomass was finely macerated and then centrifuged. The resultant higher density extract was cleansed to remove the last traces of *Thiovulum Aureus* cellular material and what was left was not quite pure gold – unexpectedly there was some mercury and platinum contamination. These metals were next to gold on the Periodic Table of elements, and platinum was itself a rare and valuable metal, with a higher price than gold.

Tobin was initially excited when Appleton called him to discuss the purity issue, but some quick research and calculations demonstrated that concentrations in this load were more a nuisance than a bonus.

Tobin, steeped in the family business of gold mining, knew what had to be done. Removing the 'contaminants' was straightforward, but had not been planned for. Miners had regularly used mercury in the extraction of gold – a miner would stand waist-deep in a polluted pond, and dump a capful of mercury into a bucket of ore, then mix it in with his bare hands. The liquid metal chemically wraps itself around the gold to form a silvery pellet – they have a strong affinity and the interaction of wood and gold has been likened to that of water and bone-dry wood. The open use of mercury in gold mining is illegal in most countries because it is toxic to both human health and the environment, but industrial refining processes would use cyanide compounds and calcium to break the bonds and separate the metals, though there were other, newer chemical processes being developed.

Appleton caught the full brunt of Tobin's displeasure at the unforeseen problem, and within four hours his helicopter was landing him onsite at the refinery.

"Why the fuck didn't you foresee this John? This is supposed to be bio-extraction process, not a bloody chemical factory" Tobin ranted in the meeting.

"Charles, the levels of bacteria we were testing during development showed no sign of this metal contamination. My thinking is that on the massive bacteria farming scale we are working on, some bacteria have mutated to concentrate the mercury, which has the closest atomic weight to gold in that group of elements. I've got some tests under way to investigate this mutation. The fact that there is also platinum – a trace only, suggests that it is a genetics consequence, as platinum is an extremely inert element and very rare."

"This will cost a fucking fortune to sort – I'll have to build additional refining stages, and it's a dirty process. There could be all sorts of complications, even political. It's costing a million dollars a week, let alone any additional capital required. What about the fact that we are breeding these buggers in Kebrit Deep? I'm not too worried about the platinum contamination, but if we're actually concentrating mercury there, then that will be a big problem if word gets out. And it certainly will get out when mercury starts deforming fish and the fishermen start catching them. We'll have all sorts of nosy environmental bastards crawling all over us.

Unless we can sort this quickly, there will be at least a six month delay whilst process plant is designed and built to deal with this contamination. The planning issues would be massive.

You are my Chief Scientific Officer on this project, and you've screwed up badly on this, John."

"Charles, I'm not a bloody gold miner, I'm a geneticist" Appleton shouted back.

"Ok, ok. YOU have to deal with this. Finish your tests and let me know your results straight away, then we'll discuss the conclusions. Then I want you back in the development lab working out how YOU stop this mutation effect screwing up MY investment."

There was a lot more to Tobin's plan than even Appleton, Thompson or Tobin's private investors knew. It was a setback, certainly, but not a major problem on the overall scale of things.

*

The Coup – Foundation

The announcement by TRI caused a diplomatic panic in the UK. Tobin was, as usual, making the running. This time he had finessed the British Government.

He had called Richard Thompson.

"Richard, Charles here. I'm bringing the press release forward by one week – I need to get this moving – HMG seem to be dragging their heels over it and I'm burning a million dollars a week. The press release goes out in twelve hours time."

"Charles, that's impossible – we're doing all we can to help, you know that. Diplomacy takes time and patience."

"I have neither of those Richard. How's Vala by the way?"

"For Christ's sake Charles, not on the phone!"

"I didn't bring her in to it – you made all the running there. Great performance too. I'm sure that my guests on *Auric Adventurer* next week will be hugely entertained by the clip. Anyway, maybe you should think very hard about that change of career I suggested. Get out of politics and back into business. You know that the offer I made you is unbeatable and still stands. You would be far better off as an operator running my commodities funds than as a second tier government minister. No worries about the press and other politicians. You'd just have to worry about me!" he laughed. "And, you might save yourself considerable embarrassment, even your marriage. Anyway, 7 am tomorrow, I'm issuing the press release."

Before Thompson could say anything else, Tobin had rung off, having had the last word, as always.

*

The Press Release was brief:

Dateline: October 15, 2015
Tobin Resource International, London

Tobin Resources International announces today that it has been awarded a licence by the UK Government for the extraction of 500 million barrels per annum of deep seawater in the region of the Kebrit Deep in the Red Sea. This licence complies with all relevant international treaties. The seawater will be refined for copper, molybdenum, manganese and other industrial metals at the Tobin Resources International Refinery in the UK using patented bio-refinement processes. The areas covered by the licence are identified in appendices to this announcement. Further information is available on the company's website www.TobinResources.com or from Corporate Communications corpcom@tobinresources.com .

END

Massive press speculation ensued, as industry experts could not understand how this could possibly be economic. Of course, they only had half the equation, as they were unaware of the seeding, recycling and harvesting process which would dramatically multiply the yield. Nevertheless, Tobin himself knew that the model was not economic based only on the extraction of industrial metals, unless market prices soared or other production and reserves problems occurred. It did serve, though, as a useful screen. Better still would be extraction of Niobium and Tantalum which were in massive demand for electronics – even causing a war in The Congo. Appleton was working hard on this, but it did not look as if concentrations were high enough even in the chimney ejecta for economic bio-recovery.

Following Tobin's meeting with the British Prime Minister in early 2014, the British Government had for several months been preparing the way diplomatically, and with some considerable difficulty. The United Nations Convention on the Law of the Sea (UNCLOS) had been tightened further since the Russian claim on the Lomonosov Ridge on the Arctic seabed in 2007 had led to a major fracas between Russia, The US and Canada, with sideswipes from Denmark. However, it was clear that whilst claims to economic zones could extend to 200 miles offshore, the provisions then covered only continental shelf areas.

The British Government issued a hastily prepared statement in support of the Licence granted to Tobin Resources International (TRI). This laid out the precise legal grounds on which the Licence had been granted and the case for it under UNCLOS and other relevant treaties including Exploitation of the Sea Bed. It noted objections from the International Seabed Authority. It stated that the UK was working closely with States in the region and was confident that any remaining issues would be resolved in the very near future.

At the time of the announcement, a Dutch tug was passing through the Bab el Mandeb, nearing the end of the long slow tow of a former oil production platform across the Indian Ocean to the Kebrit Deep in the Red Sea. TRI had acquired the platform and refitted it in India for sea water extraction. Tobin had named it *Universal Harvester*.

In response, the States of Djibouti, Eritrea, Sudan, Egypt, Saudi Arabia and the Yemen issued statements which ranged in tone from supportive (Djibouti) to extremely hostile (Republic of Yemen). By that time, the tug and the *Universal Harvester* were moving away from Yemeni waters and on the way northwest towards the Kebrit Deep.

Simultaneously, two platform tenders were emerging from the Suez Canal into the Red Sea, ready to begin the task of laying the deep moorings for the production platform. Normally, platform tenders would work out of Yanbu or one of the other Saudi harbours on the Red Sea, but Tobin was taking no chance over diplomatic outcomes.

He was sure that this was just too big an opportunity for the UK to ignore in its present parlous state.

*

The Prime Minister, as leader of the party, and the 'Chief Whip' met from occasionally as parliamentary business required – for example when a close vote was anticipated, or when delicate matters could not be discussed by text or phone. During one such meeting which fell, fortuitously, the day after his meeting with Tobin in Carlisle , Oliphant asked Steph Carswell to make very discreet enquiries about a Russian actress by the name of Valentina Oleynik currently in an Old Vic production, and whether she had met any MPs.

Carswell was no fool, with highly tuned political antennae coupled to almost infallible intuition. "Anyone in particular, PM?" she probed.

"No, no names mentioned. I just heard that she had been putting herself about a bit. If we find something on the Opposition then we can use it, but if it's one of ours then we'll need to close it down. Probably the former – the lefties always love a Russian. I could ask the boys on the South Bank in case she's linked to the Russian FSR or some other agency, but it is too early for that."

"I'll see what I can turn up and let you know" she said.

*

The following day, Carswell said that her initial digging had not turned up anything of interest – yes the actress had met MPs as part of the usual social milieu that most MPs enjoyed, but there was no salacious gossip in circulation, nothing that could possibly set a news reporter off on a mission.

"MPs no, actors yes, plenty of juice there."

"Fine, Steph, focus on the Department for Business and Trade, near the top, I think that's where there might be a problem."

"Ok, but there are still five ministers in that department, now that you've trimmed them back. Still, I'll keep digging" she told him.

Oliphant was still concerned – he was sure that Tobin would not bluff on this, though he knew that effective bluffing was as much a part of Tobin's armoury as it was for a Prime Minister. He could not afford to have another scandal to deal with at this point in the parliament. Certainly scandals were part and parcel of political life, but with the international flak that was about to fly because of this Red Sea expedition of Tobin's, then he wanted it bottomed out now.

He had a meeting set up with Thompson that afternoon to discuss Tobin's proposal. Following that meeting he would move forward and involve the Foreign Office and Exchequer. There was still a question mark over Richard Thompson. Tobin's proposals revolved more around the Foreign Office and the Exchequer than it did about Trade – Thompson's brief – but he'd like to find out exactly how much Thompson knew, there might be more. And Chekhov, yes, he'd see how that went down with Thompson. Maybe he'd wrong-foot him to start with….

*

The morning was fresh - a bright March day promised, with the plane trees starting to bud. The streets were damp from the overnight rain which had now cleared as Thompson passed through the security gates of Downing Street. The meeting was supposedly a routine meeting about Trade matters, but Thompson was still edgy about his situation. The whole panoply of his worries went through his mind as he walked towards Number 10.

Events were now running out of his control. Constance was a loose cannon and demonstrating a nature which was significantly at variance with her name, and with his own knowledge of her. After 14 years of marriage they had settled into the Westminster mould – she held the fort in the constituency whilst he pushed forward in Westminster. That solid foundation was now looking very shaky. Their night together in London the previous week had not been a success, and his weekend at their home had been stressed by constituency pressures and her mood. Hot and cold, frosty one minute and ranting the next.

The pressures of his responsibilities were pre-occupying him. The US economy was struggling as a result of the continued growth of the Chinese manufacturing behemoth and this was hitting the UK hard. Obama had failed to win a second term. The problems with Iranian and North Korean nuclear weapons had driven the US voters back into the arms of the Republicans. Obama's presidency was being seen in retrospect as largely a disappointment and a failure, with no major policy achievements to look back on, and an underclass left with no champion. The latest Republican government was struggling to keep the lid on its more extreme elements - there were strong moves afoot for the erection of trade barriers.

There was a real threat that the US would end up as had the UK by the 1990's, losing the bulk of its manufacturing base to overseas competitors specifically China. Brazil, now with a population of over 200 million and enormous, largely unexploited, natural resources was a real threat, and India now owned much of British industry. The European Union was by now completely impotent and a political sham, having been born out of the dreams of post-war European social democrats and de Gaulle's drive for control of Europe. Unsustainable levels of public spending and centralised control following the communist model had done for it. A fundamentally flawed model, yes, but the credit crunch of 2008 and the following years of unrest and the domino collapse of its component economies had finished it. His department had been trying to develop a coherent (and credible) trade policy which would move the UK forward and retain a special gap in any US protectionist barriers, but it was proving difficult, trying to square a circle.

Together with the problems with Constance at home, and Tobin with his carrot and stick, he felt increasingly strongly that his life was moving towards an inevitable crisis, and that he had no control over the flow of events.

Up the steps, in through the glossy black door and he was shown to the PM's office. The PM was behind his desk, not standing.

"Have a seat, Richard."

"Good morning Prime Minister."

Then as Thompson was sitting down, the PM continued "What's your view of the Cherry Orchard at the Old Vic – is it worth seeing?" taking him completely off guard.

"Jesus" thought Thompson, "what's this all about, what does he know?"

Oliphant watched Thompson's body stop briefly as he was lowering himself into the chair and saw the startled look in his eyes, like a young boy being caught doing something he shouldn't, he recovered quickly and smoothly. Oliphant observed keenly as Thompson swallowed, and could see him gathering his thoughts and assembling his reply, probably wondering how much to say and playing the hand out in his mind.

"The Cherry Orchard? The Old Vic? I thought we were here to talk about Charles Tobin's scheme" Thompson said, giving himself more time.

"We are Richard, we are" said the PM, "but my wife has been nagging me to take her and I've been trying to find an opportunity to see it." The PM sat tight and said nothing, as Thompson tried to mask his body language.

"Well, I did see it a couple of months ago. A slick production, though I'm not really one for classical works which are so far out of their original setting. Umm.. a novel idea, setting it on a Russian space station, but it didn't really work for me, too far out so to speak." He chuckled nervously at his attempted wit.

"I heard that you'd been to see it. One of the cast is quite exquisite I hear. What's her name – Vala something?"

"Valentina Oleynik I think her name is" Thompson replied, "Her role as Varya is rather overplayed."

"Have you met her, Richard?."

"No, I haven't, though I would certainly like to have the chance" parried Thompson.

"Are you sure Richard?" probed the PM, holding Thompson's gaze firmly.

"I don't think I would forget if I had, why on earth do you ask?" replied Thompson, instantly regretting the follow on question.

"Well, Richard, there have been some rumours"

"Rumours, what rumours, who has been spreading this about, not Rogers bloody Rumours again. The man's a – well, you know…"

"If there's no substance then I'm sure the rumours will die away, but if there's anything that the press can get hold of then you need to tell me now, right now. I'm giving you every opportunity. You know how bad it would look if there was a story about a Secretary of State and a Russian actress."

"Prime Minister, I assure you that there is no substance to this ridiculous slander." Thompson was sounding pompous now.

Irked, with his voice rising, the PM continued "Richard, frankly, I'm very disappointed in you. I know what's been going on. There is no *evidence* of you being compromised in any way – at least as far as I know - but it does not look good." The Prime Minister waved a red folder in front of Thompson. Thompson started in his seat. Oliphant replaced the folder under another on his desk. "I don't believe that this will come out in the press, though if they dig hard enough then you never know."

"Your handling of the Tobin licensing in the Red Sea has left us looking like a bunch of amateurs and now this Cherry Orchard caper to follow. That's just too much at once. And that's on top of the pipeline grant. What does Tobin have on you?"

Thompson's denials had ceased. Oliphant made up his mind – his judgement of people was acute and finely honed, and very rarely let him down.

Oliphant's voice quietened and then he was very controlled, as he said:

"I want your resignation in writing by 5 pm today. I don't give a monkey's fuck what reason you give, as long as it is not the truth."

Thompson's face was ashen and his mouth agape at the PM. He stuttered "There isn't, you can't…."

"There is, I can, and I just did. Don't lie any more to me Richard."

Thompson gathered himself, and said "Very well Prime Minister."

Coombes entered and showed him out of Number 10.

The PM sat in his chair and reflected. Thompson's replacement would have to grapple with the fallout from the Tobin licensing announcement, but at least it would seem that Thompson was carrying the can for that. The alternative of a press digging for the dirt about a government minister and a Russian actress was much less palatable and controllable, and the press would make a lot of it up anyway. His own judgement was astute, but the Opposition would appear to have claimed a ministerial scalp over the Red Sea Licence issue. He shook his head and smiled wryly as he thought of oft the quoted words of Harold Macmillan more than half a century before – "Events dear boy, events." The important thing was to be sure that you yourself controlled them…

*

As he walked, somewhat shakily, out of Number 10 and down towards his government car, Thompson's mind was tumbling, sorting, trying to make sense of it. He knew that the information about Vala could only have come from one person. But what about the red folder – maybe Vala was being watched – perhaps she was a security risk? He shivered as the implications sunk in. Perhaps there were people other than Tobin who knew.

*

After leaving Number 10, Thompson called his diary secretary and instructed cancellation of all his appointments, citing the flu.

"Warboys can wait" he thought "I'm not giving that vulture any carrion, he can find out with all the rest of them."

At that moment, the Prime Minister was taking a thinly coded call from Steph Carswell.

"Prime Minister, it seems that a person at the top of that group you mentioned took a break from his Italian holiday earlier this year, and went on a helicopter trip. He was away a couple of days. I'm waiting for confirmation, but it looks as though the helicopter was chartered to a mining conglomerate run by an Australian swashbuckler with a party of guests, including the actress you mentioned, aboard his yacht off Sardinia. There are some paparazzi photographs in the gossip magazines, but no pictures of any of our people, thank goodness."

"Thanks Steph, no more enquiries, however discreet. The matter has been resolved, and a career decision has been made by that person."

The PM put the phone down and wondered 'How did she find that out, she's better than Five?' remembering the empty red folder buried on his desk.

At the other end of the phone, Carswell was smiling and shaking her head "The cunning bastard knew already. How? I'm supposed to know this stuff before him!"

Oliphant made a note to let MI5 know that there was a potential security issue to be checked on.

*

Back at his riverside flat, Thompson put through a video call to Tobin, who was not available. He then called Constance.

"Constance, it's Richard."

"Don't you think that after fourteen years I know your voice and recognise your face?" she snapped. He always forgot that there was a video feed and hated using them.

It was downhill from there.

He told her that he was determined to make their marriage work, and that he had decided to resign his ministerial post so that they could see more of each other. He could see her face set like ice.

"For the moment I'll sit on the back benches, then bow out at the next election. I'll probably look for something to do in the City – I'm always getting approaches. Maybe we can sell the house in Chester and you can move back down – all your friends are here in London and I know you find it boring up there. I like it here near the river, but maybe we could find a place in Belgravia. What do you think?"

"Well, that is a surprise. It's a big step, and a big shock Richard, but it is typical that you made this decision without us discussing it first – it's just indicative of the gulf between us. Stay on the bloody river. It's too late for us. I've made my own plans."

Ice maiden - no emotion in her at all he thought, "At least give it some thought, Connie. The announcement will be on the news this evening." She closed the video call.

Then the call from Tobin came through. He was his usual lugubrious self, having just come out of an interview with CNN.

"I thought I'd let you know Charles that I've decided to spend more time with the family, so I've handed my resignation in to the PM this afternoon. I'm going to take a few months to relax and plan my next venture."

"Good decision Richard, when can you start?"

"Charles, your offer is most interesting, but you know the policy on ex ministers taking up posts after standing down, any proposed job has to be vetted by a committee. In any case, I might decide to take up another offer, or set up something on my own account."

"Yes Richard, I know the policy and how many have ignored it. Quote 'The Ministerial Code of Conduct is based on a single, overarching principle: "Ministers are expected to behave in a way that upholds the highest standards of propriety." '

I've got a great clip of Vala holding up your end of propriety"

"For Christ's sake Charles, let it go!"

"Ok, ok, but at least let's have lunch. Soon, very soon."

Tobin closed the link. A few minutes later, a call came through from Tobin's PA and lunch was arranged for the following day, at Tobin's estate near Winchester. Thompson knew that he was bowing to the inevitable, but at least it would be rewarding. And, looking at the positive side of not being married to Constance, there could be consolations. Divorce though, would be expensive. It was just as well that she didn't know about his fund in the Cayman Islands. He poured himself a whisky, and began to write his letter of resignation.

*

As Thompson wrote his letter to the Prime Minister, he reflected that Tobin was a master craftsman at whatever he turned his hand to, even blackmail. Thompson knew that he had been set up by Tobin, and knew that his secret was safe, whatever Tobin suggested about party viewings. Once any word got out, then Tobin would have no hold over him, so it was in both their interests to keep it quiet. That party on *Auric Adventurer* in the Med had been memorable though. Maybe there could be more fun with Vala to come?

It was fundamental to Thompson's nature that he turn very setback into an opportunity, so he mentally listed the advantages of no longer being married to Connie. He was forty seven years of age, with superb political and business connections, plenty of money to live comfortably (even after a forthcoming divorce) and some quite fascinating business offers, though even now he knew that he would be unable to resist the challenge of running a commodities business for Tobin. This gold farming business was more than ground-breaking – it had the potential to change so many things, and the political angle would make it very interesting – there might even be an opportunity to put one over on Oliphant. That would be worth doing.

Drafting the letter was mechanical – he had seen plenty of them in his time in politics and when he had printed it and signed it with a flourish, he felt pretty good. 'Now I will create the next chapter in my memoirs' he thought, what will it be, how would I like it to read in twenty years time when I write it?

He called for a courier and the letter was despatched to Downing Street at 4.30 pm.

The call from Warboys came through at 5.30 pm as Thompson was watching the news on the wallscreen. It hadn't been the top story – even ranking number nine in the Cabinet didn't warrant the story topping the latest US Presidential scandal in the UK news hierarchy.

"All this time as your PPS, Richard, and you couldn't call me in advance. I'm now out of a job too you know. So much for loyalty. Still, the reshuffle may well give me a promotion."

"Yes James, it's been such a hell of a day as you can imagine. There isn't really anymore to be said."

"I wouldn't bet on that Richard, Wikileaks might have something to say on that, maybe even Roger's Rumours."

Thompson winced as he disconnected. His wallscreen blinked a videocall notifier from Julian Rogers. He decided to take it and opted for sound only – he didn't want to look at Rogers's inevitably sweaty and gloating face as he ran through the latest gossip.

"Have you got any comment on this Wikinews story that the Prime Minister sacked you for mishandling the Red Sea Licence for Tobin Resources, Minister – sorry Richard" was Rogers's opening. Straight in, Thompson thought, trying to rile me.

"You know I don't comment on the nonsense that hacks like you dream up, Julian. My letter of resignation has been published and is a matter of record. Obviously this gossip started somewhere and it's a bit too creative to have been dreamed up by you, so tell me, who's behind it?"

"You know I wouldn't tell you that, and I'll ignore the other uninspired insult. Tell you what, though, your resignation letter does confirm my story a couple of weeks ago, about your marriage being in difficulties."

"Julian, you, of all people, know bugger all about marriage to a woman. Good to talk to you, as always. Goodnight."

He cut the link.

'Coombes or Warboys, which was it?' he thought. 'At least I shan't have to work with the slimy bastards any more.'

*

Tobin had sent a limousine for him – one of the newest Bentleys, energy cell powered, though the difference was hard to detect. Before he became a minister, Thompson drove a Bentley of his own – a classic petrol Mulsanne Turbo which had been just as smooth – well, until the turbo kicked in anyway, the thought. He had to stop for a moment and wonder where the car was – not in Cheshire for sure. It must be in the garage under the flat – he hadn't been in there in ages. Must make a note to check.

This was his first day without the ministerial limo – how rapid was the change he thought – though he did not particularly miss the limo or the driver. The red box though, he might miss that. Yes, that was a badge he definitely would miss. At his rank within the Cabinet, he had not been assigned a personal security guard, but had been advised on basic security. As they came onto the M3, he was smiling to himself at Tobin's scheming. 'What good is security if you can get caught on video as he had been? At least I performed well, I can be proud of that' he thought.

Lunch was excellent and straightforward, though he thought haunch of venison (from Tobin's estate), a little heavy for lunch. Food, wine and negotiation, that's what it was about. Tobin loved to show off.

"So, Richard, when can you start?" asked Tobin.

"As I said, Charles, I want time to plan my next move. I intend to remain a serving MP until the next election in two years time. I cannot take up a post for twelve months after my term as a Minister, anyway."

"Bollocks. They may have tightened the rules, but that can be worked around, I'm sure" said Tobin, "given modern communications. You know it's one big gravy train."

"Let me tell you how it is Richard. We – that is, you and I - are starting up a trading house, specialising in gold, minerals and oil, although as you know, gold is my major interest. You will be managing director, with a brief, and a fund, to trade those commodities. You are wealthy now, but working for *us* you will become *very* rich. You could work from home, or we could set up a 'front' front office for you" laughed Tobin at his poor wit. "Given your circumstances, our arrangement need not be formal at this moment – I'm sure that we can trust each other can't we?" said Tobin, with just a hint of steel.

*

One month after his departure from Cabinet, news about Thompson's forthcoming divorce became public. Journalists worked hard to fill their blogs with speculation about the reasons, but the episode on Tobin's motor yacht remained unexposed. Carswell had kept her knowledge guarded at Oliphant's instruction, and the information appeared to be secure at Tobin's end.

Three months after his departure from Cabinet, the announcement was made that Thompson was setting up a boutique trading firm, specialising in gold, silver and valuable industrial metals.

*

In the November of that year, six months after he had left the Cabinet, Thompson was seated in a meeting room near Finsbury Circus in London, back in the heart of the City where he had made his first fortune. He had driven in from his flat in Southwark. It was 5.00 pm on a Sunday afternoon, the quietest time of the week, before the Far East markets opened for another week. It was a 24 x 7 operation, Christmas Day included - commerce never stopped, though his team did not – officially - work Saturdays. With the largest firms operating off-market with programmed trading on private exchanges when the public exchanges were closed, it was challenging for the smaller firms to compete, but ways had been found.

It was his weekly meeting with his team leaders and traders. Face to face. Not video – you couldn't read their body language properly on video. Not that he wanted to see them squirm – they were the best, but sometimes even the best would hide things until it was too late. There was no danger or suspicion of that at the moment.

It was a small group – two leading traders and four other traders, but with plenty of experience, significant capital backing and a rapidly growing list of clients.

Experience was still important. Programmed trading (the automatic trading of equities, bonds and other so-called 'asset classes' by computers) had been heavily circumscribed internationally because it had caused several near catastrophes in recent years, but with private exchanges, the larger firms had found ways around this. It was an arms race, with investment banks and large trading firms building faster and faster network infrastructures to shave microseconds off the time it took to transmit data from one country to another. Beyond this, the Major players had been investing heavily in software development for automatic trend analysis and faster execution of trades. 'Network latency' was a critical factor – satellite links were too slow with a quarter of a second latency. Thousands of miles of optical fibre cables had been laid under the sea, and microwave links built across continents to render the fastest possible communications – more than ten times faster than satellite links. Microseconds shaved were billions saved – or, rather, profited.

The average profit on an individual trade had decreased from a 'scalp' to a 'haircut' to a 'shave' and even smaller – 'electrolysis' would be next. Costs though had been driven down faster, as software churned the trades in microseconds and high volume, at levels that even highly-bonused human beings could not achieve. The human trader was more like a ship's helmsman these days – he checked the course and adjusted the direction from time to time through the helm, but the momentum of the ship was beyond anything anyone of them could manage without that helm itself. In the case of the trader, that helm was the parameter control of the system, but even these were now being automated, and therein lay a loophole to be exploited. Tobin had identified this loophole and Thompson was ready to turn it to the firm's advantage.

Capital was being recycled many times a day. Economists had pondered the sense of such trading – yes, it made profits for many, but wasn't it a zero sum game across the world economy? The debate continued, but governments acted to control programmed trading, first with controls on the exchanges to force automatic business suspension on exchanges and prevent program-driven crashes. Now, wider controls were in prospect.

Following the crash of 2008, exchange trading of derivatives had also come under scrutiny. OTC ('over the counter') and exotic (custom tailored) derivatives had also been crawled over by financial regulators in the major financial centres, but these 'instruments' had proved resilient to interference. There was usually a good commercial case for the financial director of a large company to want to execute an in 'interest rate swap', for example. Increasingly however, instruments were being designed to exploit technical loopholes in trading systems and not to serve any justifiable commercial purpose, save the profits of the issuer. The derivatives party continued unabated.

The control of programmed trading had meant that there was still a place for smaller trading companies, though the 'arms race' had forced a high degree of consolidation amongst them.

The investments firm, Livengood Futures, named after the Alaska area where Tobin had made his first fortune, backed by Tobin and run by Thompson, was tasked to specialise in gold and precious metals. There was also one oil specialist in the group.

Thompson's name was well known in London trading circles, which brought clients to the door in a steady stream, but he picked his clients carefully, following a profile that Tobin had specified. Tobin in his turn, was being given privileged information about who some of those clients might be. They tended to be high wealth individuals with a lot of cash to invest. The cash was legitimately accounted for, much of it having come through foreign currency shops, black hotels, pizza outlets, massage parlours, bookmakers and a whole raft of other – mainly cash – businesses. Whether it was the result of genuine trading by these businesses was doubtful, and not questioned.

Thompson had an outstanding Commercial Director (i.e. salesman) – Simon d'Abbeville - on his team whose job it was to entice these particular individuals to spread their investments into gold; Thompson's name was in itself a powerful sales aid and was used to open the doors. There were less than thirty targets on Tobin's list, worldwide, and the job of enticing them aboard took many months, a lot of patience and much corporate hospitality.

They were by their nature, very suspicious and careful, even elusive. D'Abbeville spent most of his time split between London, Paris, the French Riviera and the Caribbean, depending on the time of year. After a prolonged courtship Thompson was wheeled in to close the deal - in most cases the combination of his name, backed by Tobin's investment in the firm was a key influence on the clients. After the first six months, the funds under management (i.e. the gambling stakes) were approaching eight hundred million dollars, with another (estimated) two billion in the pipeline for the next 12 months.

Tobin had targeted Thompson with five billion dollars under management after two years. Of course, there were other 'targets' than just those on Tobin's specific list – these were more 'regular' individuals whose wealth was more transparent, mostly based these days on software, social networking and web infrastructure companies. Some were even Chinese. So, there were plenty of targets to aim for, but there was a great deal of competition for their funds.

The sales pitch that was being used by Livengood Futures was that the fund was heavily engaged in looking for small gold mining operations with falling yields and finance problems, and putting new capital and management in. Tobin had vast experience of Alaskan and Australian gold mining, but for this fund was more interested in Russia and South America, where there was vast potential. Although China was a significant gold producer, it was still closed to any serious foreign investor which wanted control of its own mining operations. Thompson held out Tobin's unidentified (and completely fictional) Chinese connections as opening an investment route that the fund would take in the near future. The fund was to be closed once the target had been reached – it was exclusive – so anyone in doubt should invest before the door was closed.

Projected returns were quoted as well in excess of twenty percent per annum, and a few investors had questioned whether this was a Ponzi scheme – new investors providing the cash to pay high returns to existing investors – in other words, a scam. Anyone who asked this question was given special treatment by Thompson, occasionally even bringing in Tobin himself to allay fears. Generally though, targets who raised such questions were quietly sidelined.

For the first year, some genuine and profitable investments in gold mining operations were made, but even then some creative accounting was necessary to keep the early investors satisfied. As had so often been the case in the past, everyone was happy as long as the dividend cheques kept rolling in.

After 2010, when Tobin's grand plan began to crystallize, gold prices had started to lose some momentum, and from an average annual rate of increase of $125 and ounce, the price was now climbing at about $110 an ounce a year, and the rate of change was itself falling slowly. The 'secomd derivative' of the gold price – that is, the 'rate of change of the rate of change' was still steady, and that was underpinning confidence in gold analysts' offices, despite the rate of change having fallen back from $125 an ounce per annum. As always happens after a collapse in business confidence, there are those with cash to invest who start to cherry pick cheap assets when the markets are down, and eventually the recovery gains momentum on the back of their investments. Then, gold starts to become less attractive as investors switch out, with better profits to be made elsewhere. However, the more than 25 year rise in gold prices since the end of the '90s, which had made Tobin his fortune, showed no signs of abating.

Recent conflicts such as the Israeli/Iranian and Korean/US conflicts kept investors nervous, and that was a good thing for gold.

Thompson opened the meeting:

"Ok lady and gentlemen, let's get started. This is our twenty sixth weekly meeting. I want to congratulate you all. Six months hard work has paid off. Each member of the trading team has achieved his, and her – Clara not excluded – profit and volume target. Simon (and I) have brought the clients on board at the target rate, and our pipeline is healthy. Our team has remained intact – that in itself is remarkable and I hope that it will stay that way.

Today's meeting will not be about the nitty gritty of last week, nor about what our analysts are anticipating this week. I will keep the meeting short with just two announcements.

I am delighted to announce that we now have seven hundred and fifty million dollars under management. We are gaining momentum, but I have some news which you might find challenging. I am sure that you will all accept it for what it is, take it head on and deal with it professionally.

The firm is increasing its targets for profitability and volume by 25 percent, with immediate effect. That applies to each and every one of you. Simon and I have our targets increased similarly."

There was stunned silence as Thompson looked around the table. There was no way that even the shrewdest, most conniving, most adrenaline driven, most mathematically able of them could see how this could be achieved. They simply had no more time in the day, and this first six months had been tougher than any of them had experienced in their careers to date. Two of them were close to burn-out, and another was in the process of moving home due to a failed relationship, two others had already moved home. None had taken holidays in the six months.

"I do however have some good news. The firm has developed a new analytical system for short term gold price forecasting – and I mean very short term. We expect it to negate any latency and arbitrage advantages that the biggest players enjoy and actually give us an edge. I cannot divulge to you how it works, but believe me this is a key development. As you know, one of our principals is a renowned poker player. The new forecasting model is his concept and exploits a systems weakness which I myself identified. We have developed the system over the last few months. What I can say is that it is based on gaming strategy and opponent analysis. Back-testing on data stretching back to the introduction of programmed trading has been illuminating, and has given me great confidence in the approach and the new system will be piloted over the next two weeks. It's an aggressive plan, but we have to move fast. Toby – you will be the first to use the system, and we will be running comparatives against the rest of the team. You will be based in another location as from tomorrow, so that we have no 'crosstalk effects' – and I mean that in the technical sense. We will run the pilot for a fortnight and after some final tuning, we expect it to go live in twenty days time, in line with Far East markets opening on that Monday morning. So, keep that weekend clear. Any questions?"

The atmosphere relaxed slightly. No-one broke the silence, and after Thompson had met the eyes of each of them in turn, he said "Very well. I have one more announcement to make. You each have compensation packages well above the norm for your individual levels of experience, and you are better incentivised than any equivalent team of traders in the world - though there is not another team of your quality anywhere. We have increased your targets significantly, and believe that the new system we are introducing will help you achieve – even exceed them. As a reflection of our commitment to you, and in expectation of your continued commitment and loyalty to Livengood Futures, your bonus rates for the next six months will be increased by twenty five percent. Your annual bonuses, prorated for the first six months will be doubled. Thank you for all your hard work, now we will, as usual, adjourn for drinks."

*

Better Harvests

It was now a year since the Universal Harvester had gone into full production, and in that year, the TRI production crew had turned around eleven tanker loads. Yields had been good after only 35 days recycling – the fact was that as the bacteria extracted the gold they effectively sank lower and stratified in the bottom water. This both made extraction easier and decreased the time required to attain the required level of yield before return shipment to the UK.

The eleven tanker loads had yielded 3.2 tonnes of gold. This gold, as far as the mining industry was concerned, came from the Dolaucothi mine, though the mining industry found the story hard to digest. In fact the West Wales mine had produced very little – a few ounces only. However, as TRI was not a public company, it was not obliged to issue any statements about production levels, problems or anything else – the shareholdings were private and there was no public share price to manipulate. The miners were well paid and well-paid jobs in that part of Wales were hard to find; they kept their mouths shut.

There were regular visits to both Dolaucothi and to the refinery by Matt Hardacre, Tobin Resources's Head of Security, and there were permanent security presences on each site – not just regular gate security, but proactive quiet and tough-looking individuals who kept an eye on visitors, tradesmen and kept their ears to the ground in the local pubs and clubs. In a commercial sense they were almost like the political officers in a communist army – make sure everyone is 'on message' and loyal, that there are no gainsayers or spies and that any suspicions are reported back to them by the troops. Whilst Tobin's security team couldn't have a suspect tried and shot, there was the occasional 'punch-up' - *pour encourager les autres* – as the French used to say when the British Admiralty hung an Admiral for failing to win a battle. And, unlike their counterparts in some mining operations in other countries, Hardacre and his team did not have to carry out intimate body searches for smuggled gold nuggets.

Peter Reed, one of the Dolaucothi security team, had picked up on some local gossip about a couple of German visitors who had been seen with 'that poor surveyor, killed by a train' when D'or Mining owned the site, before Tobin's takeover of the company. There was little to go on, but that had been at the time of the van crash and loss of two flasks of an early strain of *Thiovulum Aureus*. Hardacre's enquiries into the loss of the flasks had led nowhere (he made sure of that), and the liberal amounts of cash made available to the local police had not elicited any useful information. The police had put the loss down either to a van driver who was on the fiddle, or bad record keeping at the laboratory. Hardacre was far from convinced, but this latest information had fanned his suspicions further.

It was now well over a year since the takeover, but fading memories had been sparked again when Hill's death had been reported. Someone had made the connection between a low key death notice in a sleepy Surrey dormitory town and the geologist's visit to the area - how had that come about?

Reed dug further into the background, with best bitter and whisky helping the locals at the pub remember how they found out about Hill's death. It seems that Bryan Allinson, one of Hill's original team, had come back to the area with his girlfriend for a week's working holiday. She was a photographer and they had spent the time in the area compiling a portfolio for her. Innocent enough, but during their pub evenings the tragic news of Hill's death had come out. That was how the locals knew.

Reed was tasked by Hardacre to find Allinson and interview him. That was straightforward enough, and led on to the other survey team member, Peter Duerr, who confirmed the basic details of the survey provided by Allinson.

Hardacre read Reed's email report with deepening unease – the conflict with Hill about the mine's potential, Hill's change in demeanour. There was also a vague passing reference to a couple of German hikers they had met in the pub during the week of the survey. Reed was getting too close. It might prove necessary for Hardacre to 'discover' the security leak himself, then the situation could be controlled. Whether Tobin's reaction to such news could be controlled, was another matter.

*

Press announcements were merely a way of telling the world what they were doing. Tobin had no need to become a Stock Exchange listed company and so use the capital markets to raise funding. He had access to private investors with practically unlimited funds via Livengood Futures. This minimised disclosure requirements and company governance issues – the ability to operate without swathes of interfering non-executive directors was critically important.

The price achieved for the gold had been at an average of $3,245 per ounce. The amount released to the market – 3.2 tonnes - was miniscule in relation to annual world gold production of over two thousand tonnes, and had little effect on pricing. $330 million dollars gross. Costs were running at about $60,000 dollars a day for the tankers and platform, the refinery was self financing, just.

So for the first year of operation, figures were good – roughly break even overall, with yields climbing steeply as TRI became more efficient at operations and the virtuous circle of recycling improved. The second platform was due to come online half way into year 2 and would be moored 30 miles further north, still in the Kebrit Deep.

Improvements in the operation of the tankers was continuous, and Tobin planned that later generations of *thiovulum aureus* would be hardier and even more productive. Appleton was now permanently back at the research base as the production platform and cycle was well established and Tobin was pushing Appleton relentlessly on improvements to the golden geese. More productive bacteria meant lower cycle times and therefore more tanker loads. Seeding of the seabed 'goldfields' was no longer necessary – there was continuous cycling and abstraction, and because of this, tanker costs could be halved – Tobin could charter tankers for the one way trip from the production fields to the refinery. The *Trader* and the *Enterprise* were being used for intermediate storage at the deep water moorings. The danger of 'over harvesting' was being monitored – it was difficult to split out accurately the effect of the harvesting, as the potency of the bacteria was increasing month by month, but after one year Appleton was confident that any effect due to 'over harvesting' was less than 2 percent. The ideal would be to achieve a steady state abstraction of gold which was suitably economic, and replicate the production operation with more platforms.

Tobin's commitments to his private investors were apparently generous. They had been promised zero first year return, ten percent the second year and twenty five percent thereafter on their initial investment of $100 million dollars each. These 'investments' were being managed through his private fund, Livengood Futures, run by Thompson.

The environmental problems with the mercury contamination had turned out to be minimal. More inlet/outlet lines had been installed for recycling and enriching the Thiovulum-laden seawater, and there was little in the way of escape of the waters seabed goldfield – some for sure, but more than 80 per cent of the *Thiovulum Aureus* was being recovered by the production platform, and the level of mercury contamination was very low in any case.

Tobin and Appleton had concluded that any concentration of mercury was effectively trapped at 2,000 metres depth. As Tobin saw it, any contamination at all would take many years to work its way through the food chain and into the near surface fisheries, and the concentrations would be barely detectable. However, the concentrations would be cumulative. Anyway, he didn't really care – he'd be long gone before any problem was discovered.

The degree of contamination, if any, would be nothing like that experienced in Minamata in Japan, the town after which Minamata Disease was named. Large scale mercury poisoning of the local population had first been recognised there in 1956, where a chemical factory had for many years been discharging methyl mercury waste (and other toxic chemicals), directly into the sea. The more immediate problem for Tobin had been the removal of the mercury from the gold, the issue of environmental pollution he perceived as insignificant.

The initial batches had been held in tanks at the refinery in the UK, and in tankers on short term charter. Whilst additional process plant had been built and installed at the refinery to deal with the mercury removal, the gold/mercury/bacterial sludge was cleaned and purified, and stored awaiting the mercury removal. This had delayed the final refining, but as Tobin saw it, the gold was essentially in the bank. All it would need was final smelting into fine bullion.

Appleton's solution to the mercury contamination was both inventive and elegant. He had identified the particular mutation of *Thiovulum Aureus* which had resulted in the mercury contamination, and suggested that they isolate and breed it, then use it to decontaminate the gold/mercury sludge. Tobin named it *Thiovulum Mercurius*. After nine months, there were sufficient quantities in the vats for the cleaning process to begin, and Appleton received a substantial bonus.

The benefits of the bacterium could be substantial, as the principle could be used in other parts of Tobin's mining empire. For several months Tobin pondered whether to patent the *Thiovulum Aureus* and *Thiovulum Mercurius* bacteria. To do so would provide protection, but also let the big secret out to other mining conglomerates.

For months he struggled to find a way to fit this into his overall plan; then external pressures meant that he had to concentrate on the main thrust of his strategy.

*

His early, formative mining years in Alaska, which had set him on the trail of the 'black smokers' when at the Red Bear zinc and lead mine, came back to him one morning. Though his main interest was in gold, and the havoc he planned for the world's financial markets, the potential to gain a monopoly in low cost bacterial farming of mercury, zinc, lead, copper and other minerals was of interest too.

However, the ideas were not lost on others – there were some sharp minds in the MOFCOM in Beijing, who were already focusing on this, and the instabilities it could cause. Of course, if the Chinese had the monopoly on the technology, then that would be useful. Unfortunately, China had no seafloor spreading zones to be exploited anywhere near her territorial waters. Japan was nearby, but the earthquakes there were generated by a subduction zone, where one tectonic plate was sinking under another. The nearest spreading zones were in the Mid and South Pacific, and the southern Indian Ocean. There were no territorial claims there, but the climate was hostile in the Roaring Forties. The nearest practical region was the Mid Pacific. Easter Island, governed by Chile, sat on the Mid Pacific Ridge, where the Nazca tectonic plate was moving away from the Pacific plate at seven centimetres a year.

The Chinese plan long term, and a team was set up by MOFCOM to look at the long term engineering issues and examine the potential economic scenarios with a view to exploiting the Pacific spreading zones, and even those in the Atlantic...

*

Unfortunately for Tobin, the politics of the situation were moving beyond his control. The Chinese intelligence service, the Guanobu, knew a considerable amount about his operations, and MOFCOM were taking a much longer term view. At this time, though, only Tobin knew the detail of the final coup which he would execute using Livengood Futures, and secrecy was his strong suit.

*

The Coup – Takeoff

2020 was only a few years away, and it had been nearly ten years since the Credit Crunch. The world had been recovering from that financial disaster, half hearted attempts had been made at banking reform, and the IMF had toyed with the reintroduction of the Gold Standard.

Nicolai Kondratieff in "The Long Wave Cycle" suggests an investment strategy: "We know that commodity prices reach their lowest level at the end of the downward wave of the long cycle. This means that at such a time, gold attains its highest purchasing power and the production of gold becomes the most profitable. On the other hand, at the end of the rising wave of a long cycle, commodity prices reach a maximum. Consequently, the purchasing power of gold is at its lowest, and the profits to be gained from gold production are minimal."

His advice during the downward wave is to invest in the production of gold, in other words gold mining stocks.

Economists had argued for decades about whether there is a 'long cycle' in commodity prices. Certainly, cycles are evident in historical economic data, but they are irregular in frequency. Many observers also point to the low correlation between gold prices and other commodity prices.

The question that Tobin had been struggling with, and was gambling on, was when the current cycle would end, for a cycle in gold there certainly was. The cycles are unpredictable, otherwise they would be 'managed away', or at least anticipated and hedged against (i.e. the 'bets' would be 'laid off'). The timing had to be right for him as he intended to make his own cycle, but any help would be welcome.

Since 2008 the world economy had been 'bumbling along' in a trough. The Chinese economy had been the exception, with double digit growth up to 2013 and near double digit growth for years after that, with their government hard pressed to keep the lid on. Unsustainable, that's what the pundits had said. Inflation had followed, fuelled further by world food price inflation which had led to riots in many developed countries. The expectations of the almost 2 billion Chinese had been raised, and their government had realised that the only way to take the pressure off was to allow private enterprise to flourish internally, and to give the population an outward looking perspective, instead of inward, as had been the Chinese way for centuries.

This outward looking stance had led to the growth of its naval forces and its investment in productive agricultural land overseas. It had invested heavily in Africa and other subtropical regions where there was a low level of agricultural development. There simply was no other way to feed its population. And so, the vicious cycle was set in place. China was fuelling the worldwide commodity price inflation, and gold prices were being dragged along in the wake of oil, wheat, iron ore and all the other raw materials that an advanced industrial economy thrives on.

Thompson, under Tobin's direction, had being 'going long' on gold for two years since Livengood Futures started operating, buying into mining companies. Gold prices had indeed proved to be resilient and returns for Livengood Futures investors, though not at the projected 20 percent level, were certainly a lot better than could be obtained legitimately elsewhere.

Livengood Futures had over-achieved its investment targets, and Thompson's net worth – which he assiduously tracked – had tripled since he and Tobin had started up Livengood Futures. Simon d'Abbeville too, had been well looked after. Tobin had always been generous with his profits, even when he was in Geelong Grammar School. He wanted the best, and he bought them. If he couldn't buy them, he coerced them.

Tobin's new gold pricing model had been very successful for Livengood Futures. By backward analysis of trades executed on the markets, he and Thompson had been able to deduce the trading strategies which the big players had designed into their programmed trading systems. These strategies changed from time to time in response to changing circumstances and market conditions. Thompson's master stroke had been to produce an adaptive system which read these changes and predicted the behaviour of the large program traders. With this understanding, Livengood's traders – there were now almost twice as many traders as when they had started - were able to stimulate predictable buy/sell patterns from the major investors who traded tens of billions of dollars worth futures on a daily basis, and profit from them. This enabled Livengood to produce outstanding investment performance. Gold futures trading volumes climbed, and profits made by the biggest speculators were on a slow downward trend - except those of Livengood futures.

Both Thompson and Tobin had discussed applying this to the Equities as well as the Gold markets, but Tobin was resistant, and on more than one occasion, during heated meetings he had said to Thompson:

"I was brought up on gold, I live and breathe gold. We will stick to what we know."

What Thompson didn't know though, was that Tobin was already well advanced in these preparations.

*

"Richard, this is what you are going to do. Starting on Monday week, you are to unwind all our gold holdings. I want you to liquidate the fund. I'm allowing eight weeks for the complete liquidation."

Thompson was speechless. They were eating dinner in Tobin's Edwardian mansion on his estate outside Winchester. It was a Friday night in mid January 2016, and venison was on the menu, again. He inevitably found Tobin's schemes and menus bad for his digestion.

"Let me get this clear, Charles. You want Livengood Futures to liquidate five billion dollars of gold over eight weeks, starting in one week's time. These are leveraged on an average 3% percent margin across all our contracts – a special margin which I've been able to engineer across all gold-related asset classes - spot gold, futures, bullion, mining equities, exchange traded funds, OTCs and exotics. That's almost one hundred and seventy billion dollars of outstandingly successful contract performance and holdings by our traders, to be put on to the market, dumped. We will no longer be credible."

"Yes, that's right, more or less. That's what I want. I know it will cost us money, maybe two or three billion – even seven or eight - but that's peanuts for now. Overall, the fund is small relative to world gold holdings. 'Dumping' is a rather emotive term, too emotional for my liking. I'm sure that most of the 'realignment' – yes, let's just call it realignment - it can be dealt with off-exchange and by judicious auctioning. Well within your team's capabilities. And don't worry about credibility – it's mine that's at stake, and I'm happy about that. For now. Anyway, we have a great precedent – Gordon Brown when he was Chancellor."

"That was before my time Charles, and was proven to be a particularly stupid move. I wouldn't want to do the same. Christ, Charles, it's a big move, massive. If word of this got out then the market would get seriously spooked and go into meltdown."

"Don't be dramatic Richard. As I said, it's small potatoes compared to the world's officially declared holdings of 40,000 tons – that's almost 4,000 trillion dollars worth."

"But what about all the gold stock you've got at the refinery in Milford?"

"Very few people know about that, and they are well paid to keep their mouths shut. I'm prepared to take a hit on that too, but if you handle your end properly, then gold prices shouldn't move by more than a few percent. Trust me Richard. Have I ever got it wrong?"

Thompson looked at Tobin and shook his head. "No Charles, you've always been right on the big decisions, I know. But there's always a first time, and this could be the last, too."

"Well, just get your plan together – you've got a week. Don't tell your team anything until next weekend. We'll keep it close, and bonus them well for the unwind. Subject closed, unless I haven't made myself very clear."

"Yes, very clear Charles. Frighteningly clear, in fact."

"Good. Don't worry Richard. I know what I'm doing. How's the cheese – it was flown in today for me? Enjoy it, and the port. And then, I've got some special entertainment lined up for us, to go with the brandy and cigars."

*

So, as directed, Thompson's team began to unwind their contracts. Tobin was visiting Australia, and out of Thompson's hair whilst the sell-off began. There were some rumours in the market about some large investors selling off their holdings, but on the whole it was well managed. It was done within eight weeks. The proceeds of the liquidated gold contracts were spread across government bonds – returns were still good as sovereign debt was in general still much riskier following the Credit Crunch, and some Eurozone countries were paying as much as 7% for their borrowings - across commodities contracts and other short term liquid assets.

*

In MOFCOM in Beijing, the sell off came as a surprise. They knew that it was Livengood – they had been tracking Tobin for years; they had software and one agent in place within Livengood Futures, but they were initially puzzled as to Tobin's reasons. The traders had been told to unwind the holdings, and not why. Further analysis led MOFCOM to a conclusion which they wanted to verify. They prepared to bring forward their plans by a year, and approached Tobin whilst the sell-off was underway.

Tobin was in Victoria, visiting Tobin Minerals (Pty) headquarters in Bendigo. It had been merged into Tobin Resources International for more than eight years now, since he took it over. His aunt Suzanne, and his mother were long dead, so there was no family aspect to the visit. He had made a visit to Geelong Grammar School to endow a new sports complex in his name and was back in Melbourne when the approach came. It was a telephone call on his personal mobile, one evening whilst he was having dinner at a restaurant on the Yarra River. It was a personal call from the Chinese Ambassador.

*

The meeting took place in Tobin's suite in the Hotel Windsor, on Spring Street at the 'Paris' end of the city, one hot, late summer morning in February. The Commercial Attaché, a petite and delightful Chinese lady in a western business suit introduced herself as Shi Xue, and then introduced His Excellency, Ambassador Chan Jianguo. A third Chinese, a man, was not introduced and waited outside the suite.

"It is quite simple, Mr Tobin. We have been watching your company's developments with great interest, and we are especially interested in your bio-technology for extracting gold, and in extending it for other valuable metals."

I'm not calling this guy Excellency, thought Tobin, whoever he is. "Excuse me Ambassador, gold extraction you say – what's that about? I know nothing about that – it sounds fascinating, but I'm extracting manganese and molybdenum. Gold is not technically possible. You are mistaken."

"Let us not fence, Mr Tobin. As I said we in China have taken a great interest in your operations – for many years – even your barren mine in Wales. We are a patient nation and take a long term view. We particularly like the designation *thiovulum aureus*. Your own idea I believe, and we did find the samples very interesting. Of course, you have made them more effective since we obtained the early samples. It was sad to hear about the death of the geologist who surveyed the Welsh goldmine before you bought it. And, your positioning of the *Universal Harvester* in the Red Sea was a farsighted and clever strategy – a stroke of genius."

Tobin absorbed the shock and the implications without any outward sign. "I don't know what you mean Mr Ambassador. Let's not waste any more time on things I know nothing about. What do you want?"

"It's very simple. We want to enter into a joint venture with you, to develop your technology further. In China we have no suitable spreading zones, but we could exploit the Mid-Pacific Rise. You are a clever and successful entrepreneur Mr Tobin. We can help you develop the deep ocean productions platforms and build them. Our resources are vast. I'm sure that you can see the advantages that would accrue to you."

"Mr Ambassador, your proposal is very interesting, though I think it is based on fantasy. I don't have such bio-technology. Perhaps I should ask you if China has it? It's a fantastic idea, and even if I did have it, you would just steal it anyway."

"Very well, Mr Tobin, as you wish. But please give it some consideration. We have time - as I said we are patient nation, and you are several years ahead of us with your genetic engineering of the extraction bacteria. Nevertheless, if you are not interested in a joint venture, we will be able to complete the project ourselves, though it may take longer; we have time and we are patient, as I said. Why, though, 're-invent the wheel' as you would say, although of course it is well known that the wheel was invented in China?" His smile was pleasant and appeared to be genuine – he was enjoying the play.

This guy would make a hell of a poker player thought Tobin.

"Mr Ambassador, I'm sure you would not want me to make a decision without giving it proper thought. I will give your proposals serious consideration."

"I'm glad to hear that Mr Tobin. Whilst you are in Australia, please feel free to discuss matters with Shi Xue, who works directly for our Ministry of Commerce in Beijing, and will be staying on in Melbourne for a few days, should you require a further meeting or information."

"Thank you Mr Ambassador."

"One more item, if you please Mr Tobin, before I leave. The People's Republic holds a large quantity of the US dollars – almost five trillion that we admit to publicly. We also hold some small quantities of gold. We are interested as to why you are liquidating your gold holdings, when gold is your business. Perhaps you would be kind enough to enlighten me as to your thinking." This was said with the stereotypical inscrutability expected of the Chinese, and a very slight hint of a smile – if those two aspects could in any way be seen to be consistent.

Tobin felt his stomach contract and worked to control his body language. He was a very capable poker player, but in poker you knew, up to a point, the limits to the cards that the other person could be holding. He was taking one hit after another. This was not poker – it was a whole new game. He held his nerve in the face of this exposé and his answer was smoothly delivered. It was not a bluff – it was after all, the truth and therefore easier to deliver with assurance.

"An interesting question Mr Ambassador, which I am happy to answer, though I am sure that it should be obvious to people as far sighted as you and Shi Xue appear to be. I believe that the bull-run in gold prices, which we have seen now for over fifteen years, is coming to an end. Are you familiar with the term 'bull-run'?"

"Yes, an interesting expression – I have heard it before. Thank you for your candour Mr Tobin. No doubt you anticipate that the bears will be very much in evidence."

"I don't know about the bears Mr Ambassador, but I believe that the bulls have had a good run, and that is coming to an end, at least for now."

And so the ground was laid. Tobin enjoyed a series of very pleasant evenings laying more ground with Shi Xue in Melbourne. In Chinese, Xue means White Snow. Shi Xue was neither cold nor pure, and she did not lie on the ground.

*

On his return to London, Tobin was refreshed and excited. He liked to think that he made his own luck, but this Chinese approach had been a real surprise in more ways than one. Clearly, they had penetrated Tobin

Resources, and had samples of the crown jewels. At least he now knew where those stolen flasks had gone. Any smaller, short-sighted nation – even the US – would have milked this long ago, but the Chinese – well, he was impressed. At least he had an explanation now for those missing flasks of *thiovulum aureus*, all those years ago. And they knew that the Dolaucothi mine was barren. Jesus, these guys were patient and thorough. No point in trying to bluff them any more. Let's see their hand.

Over the next couple of months, the negotiations progressed, with Tobin wanting access to Chinese goldfields, plus a cash premium of twenty billion dollars for access to the bio-technology. He though that he held the best cards and dug his heals in, sticking with opening bid.

*

The Coup – Execution

Late in April, Tobin called Thompson to a Friday night supper in Winchester. "Richard, you've done a great job on the liquidation so far, though I have heard rumours and know that at least one sovereign fund has rumbled us."

"Who is that Charles, and what you do mean 'rumbled *us*'? This whole scheme was your idea."

"According to Matt Hardacre, we've been penetrated. I'll say no more. It doesn't matter now anyway. We're going short on gold, starting next week."

Thompson groaned. "Jesus, Charles, do you never stop? Just eight weeks and you are turning everything upside down. Why on earth do that? What's your thinking?"

"I'm not going all-in on gold. 50/25/25 gold short, bonds and equities long."

Thompson looked at Tobin, open-mouthed, his forkload of estate venison halfway to his mouth. He put the fork back down on the plate, digesting the information and not the meat, which he disliked anyway as too rich for his stomach. Tobin could see Thompson's mind working, analysing, projecting, and then the smile forming on his face.

"That's stupendous Charles. But will the markets take it?"

"You tell me – you are supposed to be the expert. What do I pay you for? Surely they will. It's a two way bet, can't lose. I announce that we have perfected the technology to harvest gold from the sea, with a capacity of, say five hundred tons a year within three years, and stocks in hand already. That's about 20% of annual gold production. Gold prices plummet, the investors flee into bonds and equities and I cash in on the short gold positions, closing them at the lower prices. You, of all, know how it works. Play with the figures – you'll come out with a different number to me, but it will still be big, very big. Mind you we'll need to keep clear of those bonds of countries with large gold holdings."

Two and a half billion dollars to play with on gold futures, on a margin of maybe 2% if he played it right. That meant that they could control one hundred and twenty five billion dollars worth of gold futures contracts. Then, the upside on bonds and equities to be milked. It was a breathtaking prospect.

"Charles, the size of this coup could cause clearing house problems."

"What does that mean?"

"If too many people lose too much money in a meltdown and default on their contracts, then the clearing houses, which guarantee the settlement of contracts, may well be compromised themselves – they could become insolvent."

"Will this really be a problem – we're not threatening the world economy here?"

"Well, the impact could be very large. Your contracts could be defaulted on, big time, and you wouldn't get all your money. Shit Charles, the political ramifications could be massive as well. And there could be issues about market manipulation."

"Well, I'm not doing anything wrong, just telling the truth, as long as I keep the production forecasts reasonable and defensible. TRI is not a public corporation."

"I need to think about this carefully Charles. We need to cautious on both the practical and legal stroke political fronts. TRI might not be a public company but you are still subject to stricter governance and reporting controls than the local corner shop, private company or not. The regulators are very fussy."

"Well, on the technical front, I employ you to manage these risks for me, don't I? And on the political front I may just have found a friend to help us, a very clever, very farsighted, very powerful friend. You are getting to be too cautious in your old age, Richard."

*

The report from the Chinese Ambassador to Australia was analysed in MOFCOM, and Shi Xue was tasked with finding out more about Tobin's intentions.

In Beijing, the Chinese Treasury had identified the risk of clearing house default, and deemed it low, and the sell off of gold reserves began. Of course, the Chinese didn't sell the gold, they merely sold contracts for future delivery - there was no intention or expectation that the physical gold would leave China. China was one of less than ten countries worldwide which held more than 1,000 tonnes of gold, about 2% of total worldwide officially declared reserves. The move was done in stages over a couple of months, with a mixture of over-the-counter and standard contracts on the principal gold futures exchanges across the world, in New York, Chicago, Dubai, Singapore, Tokyo and Mumbai.

They didn't however commit all their gold reserves, just 500 tonnes – about half their holdings. Each tonne with thirty two thousand one hundred and fifty troy ounces, and each troy ounce of gold worth, at that day's spot price, over three thousand dollars. In round numbers, one hundred million dollars a ton.

*

A few days later, on the Tuesday, Tobin and Thompson met in the Dorchester Hotel in London.

"Charles, this plan of yours. I've had some thoughts. Let's start with the legal position and the politics. There is definitely an issue about me at Livengood Futures knowing what your intentions are. We need to manage that. Let's start to dribble stories out to the financial press, based on doubts about gold prices. Just some table talk, unattributable, to the FT, Wall Street Journal, The Street, Huffington Post, WikiLeaks, people like that, so that we start to colour market sentiment. I've got a pal who holds a chair in economics – I may be able to get him to make a few comments to his contacts. Let's just get the market to start to dither. After all, how long can this price climb go on? People have been calling the top for five years now, and still the rise is inexorable. If the market starts moving your way before you make the announcement, then that will be in your favour. Even the recent fall when we unloaded barely caused a blip in the charts. It will take a lot to change the sentiment."

"That sounds good Richard, obvious really, but I doubt that we can have much effect. What about the numbers?"

"Well, on reflection, I don't think that the total amount trading involved will endanger the clearing houses. If they see things going bad, then they have risk management systems which should pick it up. They could increase their margin requirements."

"Surely they can't do that with existing contracts?"

"If things look bad, then the clearing houses and exchanges will find political support to do anything. We're probably looking at a 15% fall in the spot price – that's my gut feel. However, if the panic sets in and investors see this as the end of a twenty year bull run, then who knows where it will end? We'll taper the contract sell-offs and close half at 15%, and then the rest tapered over further 5% drops. We may have to change this if the margin requirements change."

"That's a bit conservative Richard."

"I don't think that a thousand percent return in a couple of months on two and a half billion dollars is to be sneered at, Charles."

"Well, I knew you'd come up with lower numbers than me."

"That's just on the gold side. I suggest we look at the other two and a half billion in equities and bonds as the cream, with an even more conservative approach. There's a big problem though, Charles – we don't have any in-depth equities or bonds experience in our team. To build a team, even recruit a few good people would take months - at least six – the best are, well, like gold dust. The timing is not good. With more notice I could have got it organised."

"Can we instruct a specialist equities investment house to handle it for us?"

"In a week? That would be tough to set up, even without everything else that's going on. We could just buy futures in ETFs – that's exchange traded funds, but we'd have to spread it across a few funds – no one fund could digest this in a week. But what sectors would we get the right balance? I don't have the knowledge, neither does my team. Going for a general fund would be safest, but that might not be optimal for us."

"That sounds a bit too far from the action for me. I'll call someone I was in school with. He's been trying to get some business from me for years. He runs Quarryville – a specialist banking operation in Sydney."

"Charles, you have to be careful with this. You are holding this money on behalf of other people, there are agreements in place about risk management and governance, there are trust deeds. It's not your money to lay on the poker table. You can't do it, shouldn't do it. We could wipe out any gain on the gold side."

"Richard, you know yourself that the agreements are weak. A lot of the cash we manage has a poor provenance and the investors are as greedy as hell. Some of them you don't know – I do, I brought them in. They are serious people with serious estates in Italy and New Jersey. They trust me, me and my track record, they've got the returns they were expecting – more or less – so let's stop worrying about that governance crap. I've got – shall we say, insurance, on many of them. Remember Vala?"

Thompson winced as he remembered Vala, the end of his marriage and his political career. Insurance - he'd have some of his own this time. Christ though, what sort of people was Tobin talking about? Thompson blanched visibly. Tobin snapped him out of his reverie.

"I'm not worrying about it – I pay you a fortune to see that I'm protected. And you do a bit on the side yourself too, I'm sure. And, don't forget that underpinning it all I have *Thiovulum Aureus*, eating gold out of seawater. Now, if that's all, I'm going to call my mate in Quarryville Bank, to solve another fucking problem that you should have had covered."

"I'm not a bloody mindreader Charles! I strongly advise you to wait and take more advice, be sure of your legal position."

Thompson closed his briefcase carefully and walked out of Tobin's suite without saying another word, as Tobin was dialling Doug Dawson at Quarryville. Bloody megalomaniac mega-entrepreneurs. Still, it should be a nice little earner, he thought, and I have the bastard on camera, just in case. It's my turn to have insurance. Just who were these mysterious investors of Tobin's?

*

In the media, stories about gold prices being unsustainable were beginning to circulate. Underlying the stories was the view that previously uneconomic mines were being re-opened and improved bio-technology methods were improving yields, and there was therefore expected to be a growth in supply which would exceed demand growth. Although the retail demand for gold was still strong in India and Asia, and the Chinese retail market was growing exponentially, the prognosis for gold prices was turning bearish. It was rumoured that several large investors were moving out of gold and precious metals, and that funds were downgrading their internal advice to their traders. It was summertime and the summer weather in London was proving to be good. Sunshine always made people positive. Dire warnings about gold prices had the opposite effect. Still, money could be made whichever way the market went, for those with enough knowledge and ability, and the capital to put about.

On the following Friday, Thompson called Tobin with bad news.

"Charles, there are some big sellers in the market – the price has been going down all week. You mentioned a powerful friend - well, whoever they are they may not be friendly. There's a lot of supply coming onto the market – maybe several hundred tons."

"What impact will that have on us?"

"It depends on the sentiment – is this the end of the bull run, or is it just a state or states making a strategic unload? Strategic selling by one country – yes the market will absorb that, but if the bears win out then we don't know where it will end."

"And your view, Richard?"

"I wouldn't want to call it, Charles."

"It's your fucking job to call it, Richard!"

"Nothing of this scale has been attempted before, and if we've been penetrated as you said, then we're wide open. Look Charles, spot gold is down eight percent as we speak, on a ten year low, and my advice is to sit tight and see what develops before we move. You are the poker player, not me."

"I know what the spot price is Richard – gold is my business. If you remember, we set out to try to influence the sentiment. Matt Hardacre has told me that our IT security cleaned everything last weekend – new hardware, re-installed the software, swept the offices. Why the fuck am I telling you this – you know it already, you were there all weekend. At least, I hope you were."

"And what about our people – suppose it's one of them?"

"You hand picked them, yourself, Richard, so you tell me."

"OK, OK, they're good."

"No, they are bloody well not! Richard, your team was leaking. I engaged Control Risks two weeks ago to handle this. They have already tracked down the culprit and action has been taken – Darren Hapgood's desk will be empty on Monday. He has gone on a very long holiday and will not be back. Hardacre has been sacked this afternoon, and warned within one inch of his life. His holiday companion is ex-SAS, and not by Hardacre's choice."

There was long silence as Thompson digested the news.

"Hapgood? But why? Hardacre too – he wasn't my choice."

"Forget Hapgood, he's history and that was down to you. Hardacre had his price too, it seems. You need to concentrate on the sell-off. You and your team move office on Monday for this exercise. I trust no-one. You will use your team on a need to know basis."

"Jesus, Charles. Thanks for the notice."

"Need to know, need to know. This is a big one to play and it's got to be done right. Now, if a state was making a strategic unload, wouldn't they just set up a series of public auctions and sell their bullion?"

"That's the usual process, yes, an auction, releasing a few tons at a time, announced well in advance."

"Fine, so if there are no auctions in the pipeline, then it's not a sovereign state. So, then, who is it? It has to be speculators doesn't it?"

Tobin's logic was frustratingly precise for Thompson. "I guess so."

"You guess so! You fucking guess so! This is schoolboy stuff. You are supposed to be the expert. Get a fucking grip and do the business or get off the pot. I'll see you in Winchester tonight for our Friday night roundup, and we'll wait up for the close of business on the West Coast. We're going ahead."

Tobin slammed the new secure phone down and smiled. Thompson was shitting himself – he was a brilliant technician and market analyst, but no poker player. And right now he needed a poker up his arse to stiffen his spine.

It was many years since gold prices had fallen by eight percent in a week. Tobin expected more action, and some further instability. Were the Chinese involved? Could be, they liked to gamble, but at this level?

*

In Beijing, the specially constituted gold management project team, comprising representatives from MOFCOM and the Treasury were assisted by a small team from the Guoanbu who were once again connected into the supposedly 'cleaned' Livengood Futures trading systems. The Chinese were not as aggressive about their investment objectives, and they had already completed more than half their sell off. They were sitting on contracts to supply three hundred tons of gold in three months time, with a spot value of just under thirty trillion dollars, and which they certainly had no intention of delivering. By the end of this second week they would have about half a trillion dollars worth of futures in play, on a margin of 1%. A five hundred percent return on that half a trillion would be good enough for the Treasury, and for China. Their current currency holdings in US dollars was a shade under five trillion, and an ongoing sore point with the US as China stolidly refused to let its currency float against the dollar, despite its massive inflation and growth rates. In the context, half a trillion dollars for margin requirements for a short period was acceptable, though this financial project had to be approved outside MOFCOM, at the highest levels of the Chinese Communist Party, and the President ensured that this was not his decision alone. The plan was to buy strongly as the price fell to close their short positions well before Tobin. The gold price shouldn't be allowed to fall too far. That would not be good for the world economy, nor for the capitalist clearing houses.

*

The following Monday, the gold price fix had spot gold opening eight percent down on the previous week's open. Livengood Futures started selling gold short, to the tune of two and a half billion dollars on a margin of three percent. It was a bright April day in London, but the traders had already been up all night, selling on the Tokyo and Singapore metal exchanges. The market had started to dip the previous week with rumours rife about a major seller in the market and there was a general belief that a Far Eastern sovereign fund or funds were selling and trying to cover their traces. Thompson' team was having difficulties – there were not enough buyers and their unmatched sell orders were piling up.

As the week progressed, a large number of sell orders were still being placed and the price continued to fall. There were not many buyers in the market, and progress was slow. The week ended with spot gold down eleven percent, and Thompson's team were frustrated, though there were signs that the number of sell orders worldwide was falling off.

Over at Quarryville's trading room, the equities and bonds teams were having more success handling the mandate that Thompson had set up following Tobin's call to 'Darling' Doug Dawson, the Head of Trading Operations. The uncertainty in gold was pushing up equities and bonds, and their futures.

*

The Friday night session in Winchester did not take place at the end of the second week. Tobin met Thompson up in London at the Livengood Futures offices. They reviewed the week's progress, and Tobin proclaimed himself satisfied. The number of new sell orders had been falling off and there were signs that buyers were coming back into the market. It took another three weeks for Thompson's team to get all their short-sell orders matched.

Once the Chinese had placed all their short-sell orders, when the market was down eleven percent, they started to buy back in, and this new demand helped Thompson's team get their orders matched. It took a few more weeks for the Chinese to close out their positions completely, by they bettered their five percent target.

In the press though, there were questions about this ripple – more a wave – in the gold market, and further disturbances were expected. Investors were very twitchy.

Meanwhile, Tobin's consultants had finalised the documentation, and on the Friday afternoon the patent documentation for *Thiovulum Aureus,* and *Thiovulum Mercurius* was filed at the Intellectual Property Office in London.

*

Since the fracas over locating the *Universal Harvester* production platform a couple of years previously, Tobin had been loosely under watch by MI5. The international argument had still not been resolved completely, with endless commissions, UN conferences and all the usual bureaucracy that fills the working days of hundreds of thousands of people worldwide. They worked at high salaries with comfortable pensions, but when something really important such as Rwanda, the Balkans, Sudan, the Middle East or Libya needed resolution, then they wrung their hands and people died.

With the activity in the gold market having caused ripples in the UK economy, and talk about speculators threatening economic stability, MI5 had tightened up its monitoring of Tobin's activities. There was a view circulating at high level that he was bad for UK Plc in general. There had been a turf war between MI5 and the SIS over the matter, and once Chinese involvement had been identified then the SIS took control.

They had no bugs in place with Tobin – those that they had tried to install had been uncovered – Hardacre, Tobin's Head of Security was good. Unfortunately, his equipment, whilst it could find and neutralize the SIS listeners, was no match for the latest Chinese gear.

At 7am on the Monday morning, Charles Tobin, Chairman of Tobin Resources International, released a statement to the media, and then undertook a frenetic round of interviews on the BBC, CNN, Al Jazeera and WikiNews, and on the Indian satellite news channels.

Press Release

London, 14 June, 2017
TOBIN RESOURCES INTERNATIONAL
"After many years of research and development, Tobin Resources is delighted to announce that it has achieved production-scale extraction of gold from seawater using a new, patented bio extrcation process. Production costs are currently at the levels achievable with lowest cost terrestrial production methods for low quality placer deposits. The technique is an extension of its existing manganese and molybdenum bio-technology extraction process.

The *Universal Harvester* production platform in the Red Sea has now switched to full production of gold, which is further refined at the TRI facility in Wales, UK, from where it is shipped for final smelting into bullion.

Current forecasts are for production levels increasing to about five hundred tons per annum within three years, as additional production platforms and refinery facilities come on line.

This is a major first for British genetic engineering technology and environmentally clean metals recovery from the deep sea. TRI is talking to a number of parties about technology licensing and joint venture opportunities."

END

The London Stock Exchange suspended trading of gold mining equities for 2 hours from 8 am, until after the 9.30 am London gold price fix. The London Price Fix, moved gold down by 2.5% relative to the Friday afternoon fix of the previous week. The Exchanges trading gold funds and trusts likewise suspended trading.

Trading resumed and gold equities and funds fell 8% within an hour before the Exchanges again suspended trading.

Equities and bonds showed strong gains, as did the dollar, yen and Chinese Yuan. Oil was up, and climbing steadily.

Traders' nerves were fraught, the Treasury and Downing St were in panic, and the wine bars were empty. The US Treasury, the IMF and a host of other governments were in confusion. The People's Republic of China was silent on the matter, and its silence was not noticed in the general mêlée. In fact, the Chinese Treasury was quietly buying gold and taking some of the sting out of the fall in prices – after all it well knew what the next twenty years would hold for gold – it had planned them. Or so they thought. Oil prices would result in £10/gallon petrol prices in the UK, for the first time ever, and the British Cabinet could see major problems at the polls.

If the first day was panic, the second and third were no better. By the fourth day, gold prices were down fifteen percent and had not fallen by this much since 2008, and certainly not so precipitously even then. The pundits were saying 'told you so', as they had done for ten years, as if that made them perfect. The Globex exchange alone was trading over two million contracts (each contract representing 100 ounces of gold) a day.

On the Friday morning, Livengood Futures began closing its short positions – that is, committing to the purchase of gold at the new lower price. These 'long contracts' offset the short contracts, and the difference in price was profit. There were thousands of contracts to close out, and they were only aiming to close fifty percent of their gold futures investment at this time. The gold price fall slowed over the next week – China was still in the market, and the 'buyers' were demonstrating that gold was 'good value' at the new prices levels. Buy orders were coming in a flood from Livengood futures, and there were enough sellers desperate to get out of gold before they lost any more money.

*

In Downing Street, the Home Secretary and the Director General of MI5 sat uncomfortably in front of Oliphant, who was raging.

"I've just had the Chancellor on the line asking if I know what's behind this. You sit there and tell me that this gold price fall is being driven from London? It's your job to detect and monitor internal threats to Britain's security. Why did we not know about this?"

The Home Secretary, Stephanie Carswell, promoted in the recent reshuffle, responded with a hospital pass. "I think that's a question for the Director General," looking across at an uncomfortable Benjamin Broughton, wondering how he would play this in-swinger. She ignored the question as to whether the fall in the price of gold was really a threat to the UK economy.

"Prime Minister, London is the principal gold market in the world. Many companies and countries trade here. We have received no information that any of them has been unusually active up until now. As you know Tobin Resources has caused problems in the past and we have a watching brief on them, and specifically Charles Tobin. His security team is very capable, and we have had no success in penetration, though he has changed some key security personnel recently. We do know, though, that the trading activity of the team at Livengood Futures, his trading firm, has been intense over the last few months – that's easily trackable through exchange data. We can see that now in retrospect - but it's not something we ordinarily monitor – we are not auditors."

Oliphant was clearly exasperated and dismissive, at the defensive answer of a bureaucrat. "Very well. Thank you, Director General. My Chief of Staff will see you out."

Once they were alone, Oliphant turned to Carswell. "Give him a knighthood and retire him, Steph. I'm not impressed. Just as well you've only just taken on the brief - frankly, you need to sort them out. With the General Election approaching next year, we can't afford any fiascos. The oil price is a major issue. Keep me posted. I'm going to call Tobin."

*

Tobin's PA was instructed to decline calls from Downing Street staff; he would take only direct calls from the Prime Minister. A little after 2 pm, he took the call.

"Hello George, to what do I owe the pleasure?"

"You know damned well Tobin, cut the crap. What are you up to?"

"Up to, George? I should think that the statement from TRI is perfectly clear, or is there some aspect you don't understand? Gold from seawater – marvellous isn't it? What a dream. Now everyone can aspire to owning gold as it has become so, inexpensive, shall we say."

"The markets are in disarray, and oil prices are going through the roof."

"I'd hardly use the word disarray George, but they are certainly active. And oil – well that's always up and down – don't we use our armed forces to control the oil price – or have we stopped that now? All those traders making money, massive volumes. Equities, bonds, the dollar – well even sterling is climbing. Lots of churn means lots of profit for the dealers in London, and taxes for the Treasury, so I don't know what you are complaining about. I promised you a big tax revenue from my metals extraction."

"Oh, we'll tax you all right Charles, be sure about that."

"Punitive taxation, George? That's hardly British is it? Anyway, it's been good talking, but I've got some paperwork to clear. I hope we speak again soon."

Tobin smiled as he cut the call. Oliphant sat at his desk and raged, stood up, paced the room and raged more. Turmoil in the markets – that was the theme of the news feeds that were running across the wallscreen in his office. With an election less than a year away, this was not good news – unless it could be turned around. After all, strong equities were a sign of success. The British public loved a strong pound – it meant cheaper holidays, though imports would be more expensive; not so good for industry though. And, a British company blazing the way forward in deep sea minerals recovery. Yes, perhaps this could be worked to their advantage. Oil prices though – they were a problem. He picked up the phone and called Gerry Crosthwaite in – they'd start shaping something to run past Chalvers. The Chancellor of the Exchequer had called him several times that morning, and would be coming across for a meeting at 3 pm.

*

The Coup – Aftermath

At the end of July, one balmy Friday evening in Winchester, with the all the mixed smells typical at this time of year on the edges of Salisbury plain – freshly cut straw from the wheat and barley tinged with the smell of burning as some farmers began to clear their stubble, the stale scent of tired trees after a hot summer on the chalk uplands with little rain, and just a mix of the free range pig farms. You either loved it or you hated it. Tobin loved it – it was rural England and so different in texture to the lands of his childhood in Victoria and Perth.

Thompson was coming down from London, as usual. They were going to carry out a full review of the previous six months, and decide how they would play out the rest of the year. Historically, August had always been a quite time on the markets, but for the last ten years there was little in the way of seasonality in the markets (apart that is from the obvious, such as wheat). Trading was pretty even all year, prey only to economic news, new technology and natural disasters.

Livengood Futures had made a killing, and the reverberations were considerable. There had been smaller aftershocks in the gold market over several weeks following Tobin's coup. Oil, the dollar, equities and bonds all continued to show strong gains, and by the end of the third week after the 'gold from seawater' announcement (as it had become known), Livengood Futures was starting to go long on gold again as Tobin 'called the bottom' on gold prices. Livengood had cleared close to twelve billion dollars, and they had to invest it somewhere. Tobin was measuring up some of the other, larger 'miners' for takeover - the gold market fall had damaged their balance sheets and some were now vulnerable.

They had reached the brandy, reviewed the figures, and Thompson was anticipating the entertainment. Tobin, as was his wont for these evenings, had four lovelies come down from London for the Friday evening and Saturday. They were well known to both men (and each other), fairly regular (though not exclusive) visitors, and were presently elsewhere in the sprawling old building, preparing for the night ahead.

"Charles, we've multiplied the fund almost six-fold in six months. Over nine hundred percent return on the gold project, and two hundred percent on the equities and bonds. We need to pause and spread the risk. It's not a time for a reverse takeover of a company like Billiton or Xstrata. They are more than ten times the size of TRI."

"Richard, commodities are the basis of everything – what we shit, drive, build, fly. You can't get away from it. Widening TRI's base into metals and minerals on a larger scale makes sense. We would have the resources to tackle zinc and copper on a truly global scale – don't forget that these metals are also fodder for the right strain of *thiovulum*. Appleton is already working on these down at the lab."

"The problem is that if you are highly leveraged on one of these takeovers, then when international trade hits a slump, you get stuffed. Just a two or three percent fall and you are lost. It's not a time for big risk. Economies are still trying to recover from the last fiasco in 2008. Look for smaller targets. Livengood Futures was a small player last year – just five billion under management. Now we're up to almost twenty billion – people are watching us, particularly after our market coup. A lot of people lost a lot of money to you. They will not forget it, and neither will the politicians – they are out for you Charles. I couldn't support this kind of plan."

"I'm not looking for your support. Just good technical advice, and efficient execution of instructions. There are ways around the leverage problems."

Thompson sighed – he had fought hard. The trouble was that with his track record of success, Tobin believed that he was all-seeing and invincible; the bites got bigger with each deal, and one day Tobin would choke. He knew Tobin very well and believed that the inevitability of his business ideas – inevitable reality, inevitable success – couldn't work forever. Life just wasn't like that.

*

In the autumn, the markets slowly settled down, with gold trading at about nine percent below it all-time high of that spring. The Chinese were 'below water' on their gold adventure, having closed their short positions a little too early. The sums were miniscule in the overall scheme of the Chinese economy, but enough to have drawn attention to the failure of the plan.

The MOFCOM gold management team was disbanded and the senior level managers in the work unit were redeployed to pensions management and food supply planning in the western provinces – one even to Tibet, well away from Beijing. The ascendancy of MOFCOM was being quietly questioned in the higher levels of the CCP, and the senior cadres in the People's Liberation Army smelled an opportunity. The line being put about by those with the old communist agenda was that the bourgeois financial orchestrations of MOFCOM had weakened China (though only a few elevated cadres discussed this). The conservative masters of the PLAN saw that there was an opportunity to stretch their wings, exercise their new blue water naval forces and make some political gains along the way. The new naval base in the Yemen could prove to be very useful.

*

In the November of that year, Tobin was back in Melbourne, again in his suite in the Hotel Windsor. It was Thursday lunchtime, and the first southerly buster of the season was rolling in from the Tasman Sea with its violent front and thunderstorms, hitting Sydney. Melbourne was only catching the tail, but it was still unpleasant, with very cold air and heavy rain.

Tobin was meeting the Chinese Ambassador, along with Shi Xue. Tobin's relationship with Shi Xue had cooled – for Tobin it had never been more than fun and he was keeping her at a continental distance, reserved only for entertainment when he was in Australia. Since Matt Hardacre's discovery of the security breach earlier that year, Tobin had become paranoid about his personal security and electronic interception.

He was now using illegal encryption software for his emails, but he had not yet found anyone to fill the vacancy left by Matt Hardacre. Peter Reed was still on the payroll, now in charge of Physical Security, and TRI was using a specialist IT security firm for communications and IT.

The discovery of the leakage at Livengood had come just in time for Tobin to manage the Gold Futures Coup safely. He suspected the Chinese, suspected Shi Xue and suspected his Livengood Futures team. Thompson he had to trust, but to a point only – he suspected that Thompson still harboured resentment over the end of his political career.

In the event, the outcome of the meeting was a complete surprise to him.

He and the Ambassador bowed and shook hands, then Tobin smiled and shook Xue's hand gently, with a smile; her handshake though brief and unresponsive, and her face was without emotion and inscrutable and Tobin wondered what the reason might be.

"Mr Tobin, it is good to see you again, though I wish that the circumstances were more pleasant."

"It is good to see you Mr Ambassador, though the weather is a disappointment I agree."

"It is not the weather to which I refer, Mr Tobin."

Just at that point the waiter entered Tobin's suite with a tray, and there was some small talk as the waiter poured the drinks, and then withdrew.

"The matter in hand Mr Tobin, is the original plan to jointly develop your technology for use in the mid-Pacific."

"Of course, Mr Ambassador. Can I take it that the People's Republic has come to a decision then concerning the final terms of the joint venture? The latest commercial heads of agreement were, I think, very fair to both sides."

"Yes Mr Tobin, there is a decision, but I am afraid that it is not one you will like. The People's Republic of China has decided to withdraw from the proposed joint venture."

Tobin's external reaction was totally calm, smiling and apparently, entirely without surprise. His internal reaction was the opposite, though he was much too experienced a poker player to let it show through. The Ambassador's eyes watched him steadily as he responded, buying time.

"Ah, so it was not the weather you were referring to earlier then, Mr Ambassador?"

"No, not the weather Mr Tobin. The final decision."

Tobin's mind looked at his hand, calculated the odds. The bastards want to pay less – that was the ploy – they came to me first. Get me on the hook then play me. I'm not having that, I'm calling him.

"Actually, Mr Ambassador, that simplifies matters considerably as there are alternative options I am pursuing. Of course, I would have preferred to work with the PRC, but there are equally interesting opportunities for this wonderful technology."

Tobin sipped his Scotch and waited.

"Excellent whisky, as always, Mr Tobin, but I am afraid I have to leave now." The Chinese Ambassador put his empty tumbler on the table and stood up, followed by Shi Xue. He offered his hand to Tobin.

"It is a pity we cannot work together Mr Tobin. You should understand that this is not a negotiating ploy. This is a final decision. Do not waste your time submitting enhanced proposals."

The Ambassador and Shi Xue left, and Tobin paced his suite wondering what had gone wrong. He had a $20 billion hole in his cash flow projections to fill, platforms to build, and hungry investors to feed.

*

Platform Problems

The Free Seas Fleet had been split into two flotillas, with *HMS Queen Elizabeth* at the heart of the Red Sea flotilla. At 6.30 am - dawn - in the Bab el Mandeb, the Operation Free Seas Red Sea flotilla was moving north-north-west in the Strait. There had been some showers from the west overnight, but the dawn was bright and clear. They were technically within Yemeni waters and in the Traffic Separation Scheme.

The US and UK had elected not to complicate matters with the Djiboutian government, so the nuclear powered supercarrier *Gerald R Ford* stayed on station in the Gulf of Aden in international waters. The Red Sea flotilla making its way north west at 20 knots comprised the USS *Jason L. Dunham* – an Arleigh Burke class missile destroyer (US Fifth Fleet, Manama, Bahrein) at point, *HMS Queen Elizabeth*, the 65,000 ton electric-driven flagship of the UK Royal Navy with its complement of 36 F35-C Lightning II stealth fighter bombers, flanked by *HMS St Albans* – a Type 23 ASW frigate and her newer sister ship *HMS Ardent,* the French stealth frigate *Guépratte* – a La Fayette class ASW frigate and much younger sister ship of the *Surcouf* (that morning still docked at Djiboutii) further astern.

HMS Queen Elizabeth had had a difficult birth, her operational availability having been delayed to 2020 by the UK's Strategic Defence Review of 2010. The associated hurried decommissioning of *HMS Ark Royal* in early 2011 had proved to be a grave mistake, the UK having been 'caught with her knickers down' by the North African crisis and the revolutionary fire which had ignited in Tunisia and spread across the Arab world, into Libya, Bahrein, even Syria, and given the Saudi Arabian Royal Family serious cause for concern. Osama Bin Laden carried the popular blame for these first steps on the (under construction) road to a workwide Islamic Caliphate. Though his demise (sheltering behind a woman it was said) in 2011 was finally confirmed following a firefight with US Forces in Abbottabad in Pakistan, there were enough madmen, on both sides, to keep the idea alive. In 2011, a very public row had erupted at the highest levels of the armed forces, when the Libya theatre was consuming military resources at an unsustainable rate. The UK's glaring lack of carrier availability had been hurriedly compressed and the *Queen Elizabeth* programme had been accelerated again, bringing forward her availability to 2017, at vastly increased cost.

The flotilla passed through the wide gap in the 'Bridge of Horns'. This was the bridge being built to join Africa and Asia across the Bab el Mandeb. The construction conglomerate behind the bridge was founded by, and still carried the name of, Osama Bin Laden's family. The construction had been delayed by events in the Middle East in the years after the fires first started in Tunisia.

The aircraft carrier *Queen Elizabeth* was also accompanied by *HMS Duncan* – a Daring Class air defence destroyer (also electric powered) and finally the *USS Vicksburg* - a Ticonderoga class missile cruiser (US Fifth Fleet, Manama, Bahrain and now on her final cruise before decommissioning) bringing up the afterguard, astern of a fleet supply ship and fleet oiler.

Over the Gulf of Aden there was a US AWACS plane on radar picket, delivering the air picture for the fleet, an E2-D Hawkeye AWACS fifty miles ahead of the fleet for localised fighter control, and two ASW helicopters nearer the fleet dipping their sonars in rotation and listening to their passive sonobuoys, with one following the afterguard. The entire air, surface and sub-surface picture was consolidated in the Joint Tactical Information Distribution System (JTIDS) and sent onward by secure data-link to air and surface units alike. The carrier had her SLAT system fully deployed, with the towed passive sonar array and processors ready to detect underwater threats and provide optimum manoeuvring recommendations and trigger the hedgehog depth charge launches and active torpedo counter-measures. Whether this latest SLAT technology would be effective against the Chinese rocket-propelled mines was, as yet, unknown. The design team at the manufacturers in France had been called in over the weekend to review their test data against the limited knowledge of the threat, and service upgrades of the processor units were en route.

At any given time, there was at least one low orbit satellite looking down on the Red Sea, re-tasked overnight by the controllers in Fort Belvoir, Virginia. The maximum depth capabilities of Shang Class Chinese submarines were unknown. Russian submarines could reportedly exceed one thousand metres, and the Shang Class was thought to be an evolution of those designs. One sitting quietly at five hundred metres depth would be undetectable, but the areas of the Red Sea where there was more than even 300 metres were relatively limited, and these could be searched by remote active vehicles – low cost, low power, and expendable, but effective in the deeps. The analysts in the Pentagon had put the probability of the Chinese submarine being in the Red Sea at less than 30% - it would be an unnecessary move. The war gaming had predicted that the bulk of what could be perceived to be Chinese strategic objectives could be achieved without such a move. That assumed the status quo in the Chinese command structure - there had been no 'Monte Carlo' scenarios played with senior Chinese commanders in rogue roles.

The flotilla progressed in the internationally defined traffic lane and as it approached the northern limits of Djiboutian territorial waters and the island of Dumeira, it maintained course and crossed the median line between Eritrea and the Yemen and back into Yemeni territorial waters (depending on which chart you relied on). There was no secrecy – all commercial shipping was continuously warned of the flotilla via the GMDSS (global maritime distress system which covered both radio and satellite navigational safety information broadcasting), though the naval vessels had their Automatic Identification Systems turned off. Shipping was requested to give the flotilla a wide berth of five miles, with warnings of dire consequences for any shipping that approached nearer than two miles. This was not easy, as the sea room for deep draught tankers was very limited. However, there had been adequate notice and commercial shipping had slowed its approach to the Strait, waiting to the north, where there was more searoom, until the naval force had cleared the Bab el Mandeb.

The GMDSS also warned that GPS positioning systems were unreliable or non-existent in the Red Sea area and should not be relied upon. GPS signals were, of course, being jammed.

The ships were at high readiness, with live weapons on the planes. At 07.00, the US AWACS reported two flights each of three planes taking off from the Chinese carrier Shi Lang in the Gulf of Aden. They were headed northwest over Yemeni airspace at Mach 1.5, broadly parallel to the Free Seas flotilla, with a projected closest point of approach of about fifty miles. The *Gerald R Ford* was also monitoring a Chinese KJ-2000 AWACS which had taken off from a military base near Sana'a, and was circling in Yemeni airspace. The theatre controllers on the carrier were being piped satellite data which indicated another Chinese AWACS flying in from the airbase at Kunming in Western China.

*

The carrier air wing on *Queen Elizabeth* had been on various states of readiness all night, and there were already six F35-C Lightnings in two formations of four aircraft running fighter sweeps fifty miles ahead, as Eritrean and Yemeni airspace was closed to them. They had comprehensive real-time situational awareness via the JTIDS link, backed up by voice control from 'Freddy', the callsign of the fighter controller on the carrier. The pilots checked and re-checked their air to air weapons systems continually, and the formation leaders optimised the patrols to deal with any emerging threats. Their Rules of Engagement ("ROE") required that they remained 'weapons tight' – missiles unarmed – unless a 'hostile act' was experienced when they were authorised to release weapons in self defence. Nerves were taut as 'Freddy' called and they turned to fly south eastwards along the edge of Yemeni air space. As they changed heading, the Chinese flights turned west, and then north west again, slowing down to Mach 0.9, just below the speed of sound. The British and Chinese wings passed each other at about two miles distance, each being one mile away from the Yemeni border, and on opposite sides.

The air games continued all day, and the planes were rotated on both sides as the flotilla moved north to its planned patrol area north of the Hanish Islands. The intention was to interchange a couple of ships between the flotillas each day, to continually exercise the right of free passage through the Strait. This would coincide with the flotillas each being nearest the Gate of Tears simultaneously – the Red Sea element being at the south of its patrol, and the Gulf of Aden element being at the westward end of its patrol box.

*

Steve woke just before 11 am – a text from Mother. He called in – getting better at remembering the number now – and spoke to Booth.

"We've got another assignment for you. Have you seen the news about the Free Seas Task Force?"

"No, I saw Uncle Sam's speech, but since then I've been asleep."

"Well, we sent some ships through Bab el Mandeb this morning. There were no problems apart from the littoral states protesting about illegal entry into their territorial waters, and some dick-waving by planes from the Chinese carrier. We need you back at sea. You'll be flown from Lemonnier to one of our ships, and be briefed there. The flight is scheduled for 13.00 hours your time."

"OK, anything else I need to know, like this will not be another shit job for Queen and Country, relying on my great patriotic streak?"

"No, nothing for now – you'll get fully briefed aboard – you've met the chap already. Your cynicism does you no credit."

"I don't need credit. Has Tom turned up yet?"

"No, we're assuming he's out of the picture, probably permanently. How's Pavkovic?"

"Haven't seen her, though I'd like to ask her a few questions about Tom."

"Blue Bayou is doing that already, no luck. The locals will have her before long, now that there's so special rendition any more and she's done nothing against the US, as far as we (or they) know. We've already told Djibouti that we have her, so the US can't hide her – not that that would stop them anyway. The locals will not be too fussy about human rights."

"Well, it looks as though there's another notch on her gun. Tell them about a burnt out milk truck. It may be more than it seems. Right, I'd better get some grub before my flight."

"Good luck Mandrel."

"I'll certainly need it in spades if it's anything as hare-brained as the last trip."

*

The plane was an Osprey V-22. Its propellers – rotors really - swivelled and it was capable of both vertical take off and landing as well as conventional flight. It had been in use by the US Marine Corps for over ten years. Its fixed wing flight capability meant that it had a greater range than a helicopter, and greater speed. Steve had never flown on one, and on this occasion the take off was normal but the landing on HMS Queen Elizabeth two hours later would be an almost vertical one. He was accompanied by a dozen crates, each about a couple of feet cubed, and the Osprey crew said that it wouldn't be good to have a heavy landing with those crates aboard. They had been flow in overnight from France.

As they approached the new carrier, Steve could see the fleet in formation. The ships had formed a patrol pattern about a hundred miles to the north-north-west of the Bab el Mandeb, where the Red Sea was about a hundred miles wide. On the starboard side he could see the Yemeni island chain known as The Hanish Islands - the Osprey was keeping strictly to international airspace and curved around the western edge of the chain as it started to lose height for the landing approach. He watched as the rotors tilted and the Osprey changed from being an economic, almost conventional aeroplane, to a helicopter, and angled in towards the port quarter of the British carrier to land.

Once they were down and secured to the deck, the Osprey was unloaded whilst Steve waited near the flight control island. Within ten minutes he was airborne again, headed back to the Osprey's mothership, the carrier *USS Gerald R Ford*, out in the Gulf of Aden. Steve was led to a Lynx Wildcat helicopter, and lifted across to the *Ardent*. Don Williams was waiting for him. They shook hands warmly and headed down to the briefing room.

"What have you got for me this time, Major?"

"Cut the Major crap. You know I'm Don, and I've got a beauty for you today. Codename 'Bradawl'."

"Sounds like a drill, not boring I hope. And how much notice do I get this time?"

"Alright, I know, it was a bitch last week. This time isn't much better either, but a lot simpler and less risky. Look at this."

Steve settled in his chair with a mug of best British breakfast tea, while Don fired up the wallscreen. It showed a schematic of what looked like an oil production platform.

"This is *Universal Harvester*. One way or another she's at the root of our current problems, though God knows why. We have orders to put her out of action. Not sink, just disable her production capability. And, it has to be deniable – which is why we've called on you, and not our regulars. It's not life threatening to anyone, unless you're fish."

"OK, deniable I understand, but I'm going in from a British frigate. That's just a bit obvious isn't it? What exactly can you deny? Why not just tell them to shut down operations? And life threatening – what about me then?"

"Don't ask me why, maybe it's been tried. She's anchored in two thousand metres of water, in the Kebrit Deep, about seven hundred miles north of here and inside Saudi waters – not territorial, their exclusive economic zone they say, just twenty two miles off their coast. There's been a big row about it over the last couple of years.

Anyway, she's moored with four anchors and as you can see here, there are four twenty-four inch pipes from the platform down to the bottom. There's what is called a manifold there, where the pipes all connect to an array of other pipes coming in from collectors a mile or so away – there's a ring of them."

"Yes Don, I still remember that from my training – remember we learned what a production platform was, how to defend them and how to attack them if they had been 'hijacked' – if that's the word for something that can't go anywhere. Basic anti-terrorist stuff."

"Sure Steve, but this one pumps seawater, not oil."

"Seawater? Why?"

"Where the hell have you been this summer?"

"The Indian Ocean, sailing. Slowly."

"Ah, yes, of course. Well you missed the turmoil then. They extract gold from the seawater. Some kind of bio-refining process."

"Did I hear that right? Gold from seawater?"

"That's what they say. They announced it back in July or August, seems it caused a right ruckus in the finance world. A British 'first'. There was a big legal row about it originally – they said it was refining metals and minerals. The Saudis were OK about it. Now that they say it's gold – well you can imagine, though the Saudis are still quiet it seems. Some times you wonder if the politicians have got their heads screwed on at all – it's not like this area wasn't a hotspot to start with. Anyway, ours not to question why, so let's get on with it shall we?

We just need to blow the pipes. There's no pollution risk or anything like that - it's just seawater. Blowing the manifold would be best, but we can't go in there with a ROV – remotely operated vehicle – or deep diver, too obvious. So, all you've got to do is stick a few limpet mines on the pipes and presto, we're done. Keep it simple."

"OK, that sounds fine – I suppose the mines are hi-tech?"

"Not really, but I'll give you a refresher, of course, without the bangs."

"Best way" Steve said with a straight face.

"There's often a tanker on a single point mooring a mile from the platform. They use tankers to transport the seawater to a refinery in the UK. Don't ask me why, sounds daft to me. There's no tanker on the mooring at present – one left this afternoon - the *Universal Trader* – she's on her way down the Red Sea now, too big for the Suez Canal.

Anyway, let's cover the ins and outs. We'll use a Merlin helo for insertion and extraction. It's too far for the SWP in the darkness we'll have, and *Ardent* has to stay close to the task force – we've got our flagship in here and she needs all the protection we've got. It's at twice the nominal range of the Merlin, so we'll have to refuel in flight."

"How much loiter time will the helo have?"

"I'm allowing one hour maximum. It's over four and a half hours flight each way, seven hundred miles at a hundred and fifty knots, plus inflight refuelling time. Only the Merlin can do it. The Wildcats are on ASW duty."

"Can't we work out of Saudi – we're only twenty miles off the coast?"

"No, they are very, very twitchy about the situation. No go there."

"Ok, then we refuel a second time."

"No go, the tanker plane is fully tasked, one refuelling slot is all we've got. I tried for that already."

"It's not possible Don, another suicide trip. Stealthy or not, that Merlin's not going nearer than a quarter mile to the rig in the dark – talking of which, there'll be fifty percent moon. Swim in, plant, swim back – that's got to be an hour."

"But you do get a tow. We'll give you a DPD so it should be a joyride really."

"DPD?"

"Diver propulsion device – ok, a scooter, I was talking American."

"Great - that will make things much easier."

"Should do, our version has an integral gear locker, even some spare air. A couple of hours endurance at two and a half knots."

"Sounds plenty. Fuck all use if the helo's gone though isn't it? How deep are these limpets going? There's no time for a decompression."

"Ten metres should be enough."

"Ok that's good, the no-decompression limit is 40 minutes for a 20 metre dive – that should be fine.

About blowing the manifold - I'm wondering whether we could wrap a light chain around a couple of the pipes and just let the mines slide down on the chains – might even get to damage the manifold that way if the chains slide all the way down."

"That sounds like it could work. Four pipes - two with chain and two with the limpets on the pipes? That's a great idea. Twenty four inch diameter pipes means we'll need two-metre long chains, at least. Let's say three metres to give us some slack for an easy slide."

"Three metres sounds good."

"I'll sort it." Don made a note on his palmpad and continued. "The met are forecasting light westerly wind, less than ten knots, maybe some light broken cloud, so we are going to get moonlight after midnight. There shouldn't be any sea to worry about. Finally, there will be no comms at all. We're too far away from *Ardent* and the helo will be stealthy. Any questions?"

Steve shook his head. "You've covered it all as far as I can tell."

"Right, let's look at the gear and get you organised. The Merlin arrives from the carrier at 20:00 hrs, so we've got about three hours to prep you."

The Major ran through the equipment – the DPD was a simple cylinder with handles at one end and a caged propeller at the other. It was about six feet long, with a central locker - a military version of the Seadoo, used by sports divers the world over. The controls were simple – on/off and speed, and there was a tether, with a magnetic anchor.

The mines were simple discs about three inches thick with a basic clockwork timer, up to three hours.

"You've used these before, right?"

"Yes, trained with them, not in anger though. Arming pin, simple twist timer. Straighforward. Why the Chinese writing, Don?"

"Search me, Steve. I guess the MOD buys the cheapest it can get."

"Yes, I remember a pair of desert boots which let me down badly. Did my ankle in. That's why I left the Service."

*

The diplomatic deal had been done in a hurry and cleared the way. US Naval Command provided the data to the Israeli Defence Force within six hours of its being received. The two Saar 5 Eilat Class Israeli frigates on their way down the Red Sea to join Operation Free Seas turned around and went to full power. One of the new Israeli 'Son of Sa'ar' frigates left Eilat to join them in the northern Red Sea. Anti-submarine helicopter crews were scrambled.

Aboard the Chinese Shang Class submarine lying dormant in the Shaban Deep, the sonar operators were detecting increased activity at the surface. They had floated a string of small passive sonar buoys up just above the 84 metre thick saline layer which shielded the submarine. The active pings they received suggested that ASW sonar buoys were being deployed – probably from a helicopter. The crew aboard the Shang class submarine had been scrupulous in their observance of silence protocols, and felt secure inside their pressure hull, with almost three metres of rubber between that and the outside hydrodynamic hull helping to preserve that silence.

Though their own passive sonar buoys were good, the Chinese buoys had reflected the noise of some passing ships, barely above the level of the background. This reflected sound had been picked up by the 'Woods Hole' buoys which the Americans had in place, linked to a shore station in Saudi Arabia by cable. Automatic signal analysis showed a fixed reflection pattern and triggered an alarm. The US knew that there was something there, and called Tel Aviv.

*

Steve didn't bother trying to sleep, he was charged up and there was plenty to watch up on deck. The carrier was launching and landing her planes a mile away and the ASW helicopters were active. He'd heard a lot of jet aircraft over on the starboard side towards the Yemen as they headed north. Don had mentioned that there had been Chinese SU33's patrolling inside Yemeni airspace, and 'our boys' had shadowed them, but there hadn't, as far as he knew, been any provocation yet.

The flotilla was on a 100 x 10 mile box patrol, anticlockwise, from the Hanish Islands in the south, to the isolated island of Jazirat at Ta'Ir in the north. They were over halfway along their north-north-westerly leg and in the dusk he could just see a light on the archipelago to starboard, about fifteen miles away, on Centre Peak Island. The flotilla was now way north of the formally defined traffic separation scheme and they were being passed by commercial shipping on both sides. Steve could make out the distinctive profiles of the largest container ships – at more than 170,000 tons almost twice the displacement of even the latest US Gerald Ford class supercarriers – moving at twenty five knots, maintaining a clockwork-like service between Europe and the Far East, providing dollars increasingly for China and decreasingy for Japan.

*

At 20:00, Steve and the Major were strapped in and airborne, as the flotilla was nearing the end of its second northern run of the day. With him he had minimal gear and the scooter with four 5 kg limpet mines with low tech clockwork fuses, some light chain and snap shackles, and a pair of pliers. The only weapon he carried was a diver's knife – apart, that is, from the limpet mines. This was a straightforward jaunt on the face of it. Ignorance is bliss, he thought, as he settled in and tried to sleep during the long trip to the target.

They were flying at two hundred feet – enough to give them clearance over any shipping, and in stealth mode at one hundred and fifty knots. He had to admit that the blade design of the helicopters was much quieter than in his training days, and with active noise reduction in his helmet it was relatively peaceful. Even the airframes were better, with much less vibration. In fact, he actually managed sleep – or so he realised when Don roused him with some coffee, an hour before his drop.

The Major helped him suit up – just a very light membrane two piece for protection from stings and abrasions. Sea temperature was still 27 degrees centigrade at this time of the year. They checked and rechecked the BCD – buoyancy control device - and closed circuit rebreather gear. The scooter charge level was full and good enough for 2 hours. They synchronised watches at 00:25 hrs and Steve set his countdown timer. Then it was five minutes to drop - he got his fins on and moved past a black RIB, strapped down in the cargo bay. The Merlin slowed to hover. No spotlights were being used, just a laser ranger as the helo eased gently down to fifteen metres above the sea. It was a relatively quiet sea – apart from the driving spray of the Merlin's downdraught. The pilot reported that the wind was westerly as forecast, though through his IR all Steve could see was a swirling maelstrom. He checked his GPS, marking the waypoint where he'd be retrieved, five hundred yard due west from the rig, then rechecked his ccuba and BCD, and switched on his acoustic shark repeller. The Merlin rotated slowly until the side door faced the brightly lit *Universal Harvester* to orientate Steve. To the north of the rig, he could see a winking yellow light marking the single point mooring which the tankers used. In the cargo bay, all interior lights were on IR and the Merlin helicopter was invisible from the rig as the Loadmaster got the launch release green light from the pilot and gave the thumbs up. The Major pushed out the scooter on its long tether and then clipped it to Steve's belt. The loadmaster gave the ok to the pilot and the Merlin moved twenty yards or so away from the scooter. Steve put the collar around himself, stepped out of the door of the Merlin and dropped down the winchline forty five feet into the swirling wet blackness of the warm Red Sea.

*

It was a straightforward, almost pleasant ride, once he had reeled in the DPD. With no real waves to contend with, and the scooter towing him, it took less than ten minutes; it was hard work though, hanging on to the streamlined Seadoo at two and a half knots. He knew that the Merlin was nearing the end of its fuel load and was now undergoing its in-flight refuelling cycle with a tanker, and that he didn't have a second to lose.

As he approached the rig he surfaced briefly to check his bearings and he could see that she floated on four sponsons – hulls – one at each corner, with a three metre or so clearance underneath the central platform, from which the pipes went down into the sea. He'd seen all that on the plans, but not the floodlights. The whole area under the platform was brightly illuminated. He would have to go deeper. He angled the scooter down and got into the fish, which were being attracted by the lights. No sharks that he could see. He knew that fishing was one of the pastimes of the guys who worked on rigs, twelve hours on, twelve hours off, four weeks on four weeks off. He hoped that there were not too many big hooks dangling ahead.

When the depth gauge on his dive computer showed twenty metres, he moved in under the rig. In the bright area under the floodlights he could see the four pipes quite clearly, and hear the machinery noise from the platform, even feel the vibrations through the water. They can probably see me as well, he thought. Here goes...

Check time 00:50 hrs – forty minutes left. Magnetic anchor to tether the scooter to one of the pipes. Done. Out with first limpet, up to ten metres, clamp mine. Done. Next limpet, up to ten metres, clamp. Done. Set timers on both limpets for one hour, arm them. Back down to the scooter. Get first chain from locker – pass round pipe. Shit. My arms are not long enough to reach round. Use magnetic anchor – yes ok – clip chain ends together and attach steel mesh bag with limpet inside, fuse for 58 minutes, remove arming pin. Let it slide. Yes, great down it goes. Next one, this is easy fuse for 57 minutes, arm it, release it, down it slides. Job done. Get out of here. Detach magnetic anchor. Switch on scooter motor. No power. Christ! Try again, fiddle with switch. Check time – 25 minutes to retrieval. Check dive computer – still within no decompression limit. OK. Try scooter motor again. No Power. No time. Get out of here. Now.

*

"Major, we've received a coded abort message as follows:

'Abort Bradawl. Return immediately repeat immediately to base.'"

The discussion over the Merlin's intercom was fraught.
"But I've got a man down there."
"I know that Major, but there may be other operational reasons for the order, even a threat to the flotilla. We're at bingo fuel now – we've got to go or we'll be ditching ourselves. We were a hundred litres light from the tanker refuelling as it was."

"How much fuel will we save if we jettison the RIB in the cargo bay – two outboard engines as well – got to be half a ton of weight saved."

"Maybe ten minutes extra, but I've got orders to abort immediately."

"Bloody hell, give him a chance man."

"A bit of a giveaway isn't it – a British Navy RIB. I thought this was a stealth operation."

"It's not British – seems it's Chinese through and through. Flown in to *Ardent* today, I heard" said the Loadmaster over the intercom.

"Why are we carrying it then?"

"Search me. I was ordered to load it and secure it. No reason given."

"And I thought it was the Major's" said the pilot. "Blimey. OK, this is what we'll do. We drop the RIB near the recovery waypoint. We'll have no time or fuel to loiter. One pass only. He'll have to take it from there. And we're not going down below two hundred feet. Loadmaster, rig the RIB with a chute."

"Not necessary" said the Loadmaster. "There's a Chinese chute pack attached and ready to go." The Major collected up some packs of sandwiches and chocolate biscuits they had aboard, a flask of tea, wrapped them in a jacket and put them in the RIB. The loadmaster added a survival rations pack, a survival suit and some bottles of water.

It was then that the Major realised what had been set up, how he and Baldwin had been set up, and he swore. That's why the RIB was aboard. Though he didn't know it, the abort order had come from London, and had been conceived as a fundamental part of Operation Bradawl. Deniable, expendable. Baldwin was both, and always had been. He hoped that the Chinese built good gear. The Major was just piggy in the middle.

*

Baldwin's Bother

Steve swam due west, sixty strokes a minute for nine minutes, then triggered his GPS locator, and inflated his BCD, there was no point is using energy treading water, and the water was comfortably warm. His watch said 00:30 hrs as he felt the countdown timer vibrate. Twenty minutes before the limpet mines would detonate. The moon was rising and there was still no sign of the helicopter, though he didn't expect to spot it until it was more or less over him. Another five minutes waiting. Nothing. Shit, what's plan B? How much time? Less than twenty minutes. Options? No time to go back and try again with the scooter. So, keep clear of the rig. A twenty two mile swim to Saudi – no way. The tanker mooring – just a huge steel buoy with valves? That sounded like a desperate option. He decided to wait another fifteen minutes and think. If he could find a ship, then he would never be spotted, even in the day – he wasn't meant to be, after all, he was meant to be stealthy. Even his recovery flare was encoded electronic infrared. Unbelievable, he thought. Usual story – the plan never survives first contact with the enemy.

He checked his GPS – there was obviously some current here - and swum fifty metres north until he felt the GPS vibrate and he was back at the waypoint, or at least, within a ten metre circle of it. Then he thought he heard a low beating sound, but it faded again. Then he heard it, stronger, approaching, five carefully designed rotor blades minimising the noise.

"Bradawl RIB Parachute West"

He heard the words, loud, from the Merlin's loud hailer. Safe enough a quarter of a mile from a noisy production rig at almost 1 am in the morning, and he struggled to understand the words. Then he heard it again.

"Bradawl RIB Parachute West"

He lay in the water trying to make sense of it. Then in the moonlight he scanned the sky to the west and saw the three black chutes briefly, vaguely in the moonlight. He wouldn't have seen them at all if the moon was any higher, but its oblique illumination was enough. Then a splash about two hundred yards away to the west, away from the rig. He could hear the sound of the Merlin, just like the racing thud of his heart, but the helo's noise was fading. He swore, deflated his BCD, and started swimming, due west.

*

As Steve approached the RIB he felt the four detonations in very quick succession. He was now about half a mile away from the rig, but the pressure waves were still palpable, with an intensity which shook him. Then he could hear the sound of sirens from the platform.

The night shift - two men only - in the control room of the platform had been playing cards, and hadn't noticed the limpet mines which had slid down the welded pipes and on to the manifold. All production platforms now had CCTV installed so that any problems with the manifold could be detected and viewed early, before small leaks grew into big leaks and catastrophic failure. The failure of the BP rig 'Standard Horizon' in the Gulf of Mexico in 2010 had almost brought down that huge company. Although *Universal Harvester* was only pumping seawater, cameras were mandatory and good business sense. They had a good view afterwards though, with the images captured on hard disc right up to the time of the detonations. One of the mines was clearly visible, and when enlarged the picture would clearly show the Chinese instructions. The four explosions shook the rig, as the great gout of tons of water from the two charges ten metres down erupted from the surface and hit the underside of the platform, making it shudder. All four pipes were sheared, top and bottom, and the two kilometres of pipe, four times over, crumpled slowly to the sea bottom, and onto the smashed manifold.

Following a brief inspection, the Rig Manager decided not to issue a mayday – there were no bilgewater alarms from the sponsons, though there was some slow leakage from the drive units in each, and all other systems were working as normal, with the exception of the goldwater pumps. The rig captain then put in a satellite call to Tobin's UK operations headquarters, which of course was unmanned at nine o'clock in the evening London time. The call was diverted to the duty engineering manager's home in Staines outside London. He very quickly escalated it to the Director of Engineering who would have the unpleasant task of breaking the news to Tobin. Charles Tobin would not be a happy man. Over 300 million dollars a year of production was now on stop.

*

When he reached the RIB, Steve had to cut away the chutes which were draped over it, before he could climb aboard over the stern. He was trained to bury the evidence if he couldn't carry it – chutes and shit alike. He stuffed them into one of the watertight lockers built in to the floor of the RIB. He looked found a torch in a locker and looked at the controls of the RIB – they were all in Chinese. That wasn't a problem – he had driven enough RIBs, but why in Chinese?

Then, his brain assembled all the pieces of the jigsaw into a picture that made sense – a picture that brought a bitter taste to his mouth and a rage to his brain. His options were only slightly better than in the water. He easily got the engines started, and headed south-south-east, working out how far the *Universal Trader* would have travelled. He knew that, typically, supertankers had service speeds of between fifteen and eighteen knots. Don had said that she left in the afternoon – so, say ten hours at eighteen knots. One hundred and eighty miles – or anything from, say, a hundred and fifty to two hundred miles. As far as he could tell from figuring out what each pair of gauges was, the fuel gauges on the twin tanks showed, full. The RIB had twin outboards with one red twenty litre tank each on the cockpit floor. Maybe he had a couple of hours range, tops. The figures did not look good. He had little chance of catching the *Trader*, and if he did they would probably think it was a piracy sting and he'd have no chance of getting picked up. Ships these days were very careful about who they 'rescued'. He stopped the RIB, dug out the torch again and checked the engines. He looked closely at the engines – maybe not 100 horsepower each - maybe 75.

Military engines showed no numbers or brands. There was fuel pipework that hinted there might be tanks in the hull as well, though he had no idea of their capacity. He checked his watch, checked the fuel gauges and brought the rib up to twenty eight knots – some gauges at least had numbers he could read – where the rev counters were at about two thirds power. He ran over the smooth sea under a high half moon for fifteen minutes, stopped and checked the gauges – there had been barely a movement in the needles. Certainly the RIB felt heavy, maybe there was a decent fuel load in the hull. He decided to push on at two thirds power until the gauges were down to half full.

He had to find a ship soon, that was for sure. Find a ship, and then figure out how to get aboard. He scanned the console again - there was an electronic chart display in Chinese. He eventually got it started - the chart was readable to a sailor – at least he could see where he was and where the dangers were, even if he couldn't read Chinese. He altered course so as to bring him more out towards where he thought the shipping would be, aiming to run between the north- and south-bound lanes. In other conditions it might have been pleasant, but he was getting cold now in a steady twenty eight knots of wind, and put on the survival suit. Every half hour, he stopped to check the gauges. Then at 03:00 hrs he decided to shut down one engine – the RIB would maintain a shade under twenty knots with on engine at three quarter revs. The steering was harder, but the fuel would last longer.

Shipping at sea comes in pulses – a bit like buses. A small boat sailor can cross a notionally busy shipping lane one day and not see a ship. On another day, you may see fifteen, even twenty ships at one time, but for Steve, this was turning out to be a quiet night. There was no radar on the RIB, so he didn't know whether any shipping was passing beyond his horizon – he would expect to see the lights of larger vessels at probably ten miles range on such a clear night, but he hadn't spotted any. Ship owners were rarely covered for 'war risks' by their insurers, and Steve guessed that many ships were either being re-routed or anchoring until the conflict was resolved.

Finally, at 04.00 hours, he stopped the engine. Whilst eating some sandwiches and drinking his tea - somebody had been thinking of him - he pondered the fuel situation. The gauge for the port-side engine which he'd been using was down to just below three quarters full, and he'd been running for three hours, so he reckoned he could probably count on twelve hours more, with safety. The starboard-side gauge hadn't moved since he'd closed the engine down, so the tanks were not interconnected. That was good. He checked the chart and could see that the big Saudi port of Yanbu was about eighty miles away on his port bow. He wasn't sure what kind of reception he'd get from them, and wasn't going to chance it. There would surely be shipping movements in the offshore approach to the harbour. The chart showed clearly marked traffic lanes in the approaches, which shipping had to use - the Saudis controlled their territorial waters rigidly. Also though, he could see that the coast was fringed with reefs, and it made good sense to control the traffic, particularly when every second ship carried hundreds of thousands of tons of oil.

With his dive alarm set for half an hour, and a clear horizon, he lay down on the floor of the RIB, warm at last in the survival suit. He was calculating that at twenty five knots, the largest container vessel would travel ten miles in twenty four minutes – then he fell asleep.

*

He woke from a dreamless sleep just before vibration of his alarm started. His brain was refreshed and he had a plan. There was still no shipping in sight as he started the starboard engine and headed south-south-east at twenty knots. He was well offshore and there was no wind – if he'd been closer in, he would have picked up a strong land breeze as the cold desert air was drawn out over the warm air rising from the sea, and a choppy sea would have slowed him down. He planned to maintain course for three hours, but which time he hoped to be seeing shipping from Yanbu shaping up for the six hundred mile passage to Bab el Mandeb.

At that moment, eighty miles away, the *Universal Trader* was dropping off her pilot, having taken on three thousand tons of bunker fuel and forty thousand tons of Arabian Light Crude at Yanbu. A South African engineer had also joined the ship, with generator spares to be fitted en route to Cape Town, where he would be landed, to return home. The *Trader* was now heading southwest, away from Yanbu and into the central Red Sea. Her master, David Wallis, planned to follow the traffic lanes for forty six miles and then turn on to a south-south-easterly course for Bab el Mandeb. Two hours before, at about 10 pm London time, he had spoken directly to Charles Tobin.

Tobin had been fulminating about an attack on the *Universal Harvester*, apparently using mines, and ordered Wallis to make best speed for the Strait. Tobin had been dismissive of the naval manoeuvres, and told Wallis that they were just posturing. Wallis, though, was no fool. They had satellite TV and broadband aboard the *Trader*, and he was cautious. Tobin was a risk-taker, whilst Wallis was a careful professional mariner. Each had their place and at the current spot price, the *Trader* was carrying over twenty million dollars worth of gold in tanks, for which Wallis was responsible. An attack on Tobin's rig using mines was something that bore thinking about.

*

At 07:00 hrs, the sun had been up for about half an hour when Steve stopped the engine to level the boat and check his fuel – it was down to a quarter on the port-side engine, with an almost full tank on the starboard side. He checked the VHF radio – although the controls were in Chinese, they were all basically the same. He could use it to put out a Pan-Pan call to all ships. It wouldn't be a Mayday call, as neither the boat nor himself were in immediate danger, but a bit of help would not go amiss - even if it was only more fuel for the engines or better still a tow down to Djibouti. He switched the radio on and there was not even a hint of life in it. He found the fuse holder and twisted it open. No fuse. Pulling the wires apart, he twisted them together, but still couldn't get any power to the set.

He had been puzzling about the night's work, trying to understand why Don hadn't picked him up. He knew that the fuel situation would be tight on the Merlin. But then dropping a Chinese RIB — what was that all about? A bust radio too? Was it sabotage? Why give him a rib and fuel, with a useless radio? It just didn't make sense, but he couldn't sit there all day and cook in the sun. A ship would turn up for sure, but when?

As he re-started the engine, he spotted the tanker approaching from his port side, on a converging course. He reckoned that the ship was about eight or ten miles away, though its speed was hard to judge – maybe just a little slower than he was travelling. The starboard engine started straight away, and he accelerated up to about 30 knots. He adjusted his heading until the compass bearing of the ship was steady and they were therefore going to meet at the same place and time – that is, the intercept course.

It was a fair bet that if the crew on the sip's bridge picked him up on radar then they would assume he was a pirate vessel and prepare themselves. He couldn't call them in advance on the radio, so it would be a challenge to get picked up. A rummage in the lockers hadn't turned up anything of use, such as flares. He puzzled about his best plan of action – there was no point in trying a stealthy approach from astern as that would surely be misunderstood. He had to be obvious, and there was one internationally recognised distress signals that he could use – he still had two arms he could raise and lower slowly.

At thirty knots it would take about twenty minutes to reach the intercept. The anti-piracy tactics and equipment on ships was quite sophisticated, and during his last months in the Royal Marines, training courses had covered the measures used then. After all, if a ship was captured by pirates, then the pirates themselves could turn those very defences against any potential rescuers. High pressure hoses, conventional weapons (bad news on oil tankers) and even electric fences around the hull had been deployed.

The tactics could even involve the use of the ship itself as a weapon, to run down a potential pirate vessel, though it would be virtually useless against a nimble RIB.

*

"Skipper, we need you on the bridge – there's a potential piracy situation developing – it ticks a few boxes on the risk sheet."

David Wallis, Master of the *Universal Trader* had waited until the ship had cleared the Yanbu approach channel, before handing over to his First Officer, and had only been off watch for an hour when the intercom buzzed him awake. The news about the explosion at the *Harvester* production platform had come through on the TRI intranet a couple of hours previously and had been received with shock. The *Trader* was now on a heightened state of alert. Piracy might be less likely than a terrorist attack.

"We've been monitoring a very weak radar target overtaking from our starboard quarter at about 30 knots. It appears to be on an intercept course. I've adjusted our speed and course twice, and on each occasion the target has adjusted back to an intercept. We've got it on visual now, with a time to intercept of about twelve minutes. I don't rate his behaviour as normal. No other suspicious targets within forty miles. Just a couple of ships but they have their AIS on – regular commercial traffic. Also, GPS is down, and we're back to the old ways with our navigation. I guess it's the naval operations down at the Bab el Mandeb. GMDSS has issued a nav warning."

"Very well Tony, I'm on my way. Initiate the AP Plan. Given last night's fracas at the *Harvester* and the naval posturing in the Strait we need to be on our toes. It's probably a false alarm but the exercise will do us good."

*

At sea, the courses of ships intersect thousands of times a day worldwide. These intersections are governed by the International Regulations for Preventing Collisions at Sea – known as the 'Colregs', and apply to all vessels. They are a fundamental part of any seaman's training, amateur or professional. In a given situation, one vessel will be the 'stand-on vessel' – this means that it should hold its course and speed (at least until a risk of collision develops). The other will be the 'give-way vessel' – that is, the vessel which has the onus of altering course and/or speed to avoid a collision situation developing. In open waters a 'give-way' ship will generally make a course adjustment at two miles separation, though this can be more depending on the size and manoeuvrability of the ship, and whether there is a piracy or other risk. A small vessel moving at 30 knots in this part of the Red Sea was not normal behaviour, not even for a fishing boat. It might hold a team of armed and determined pirates, with nothing to lose and a few million dollars to gain, though taking a ship hostage was not as easy here as in Somalia.

*

By the time Wallis reached the bridge the off-watch was being roused and the First Officer, Tony Mowbray, was running through the Anti-Piracy plan. A message had been sent off to Tobin Resources operations HQ in London, advising that the AP Plan was being initiated.

"We've got him on visual skipper – looks like a RIB with maybe one man aboard."

The skipper and first officer walked out on to the starboard bridge wing using their binoculars to look at Baldwin's RIB, now about two miles away.

"Only one man aboard, though there could be six lying down inside. A RIB makes a pretty poor pirate vessel. We'll hold course and speed. Put out a VHF call to it."

*

The VHF call was futile. At about two miles range, Steve shaped his course to become parallel to that of the ship and slowed to match speeds, planning to make it as clear as possible that he was not a threat. He gradually converged to within a mile of the ship and could just make out her name on the bow. *Shit, it's the Universal Trader. I've just blown up their production system. What the hell's my story?*

For the last couple of hours, Steve had been wondering what his tale should be if and when he found a ship that would take him aboard. He hadn't expected to meet the *Trader*. "Well, I was dropped off by helicopter, blew up a rig, and the bastards left me to it with a RIB." That story would

316

do him no favours. It was certainly a tough one to explain. He checked around the RIB and slid his BCD/rebreather gear over the side away from the ship.

He held the RIB on a steadyish course with his knees bracing the wheel, whilst he slowly raised and lowered his arms together – an internationally recognised distress signal. Then he brought the RIB in to within half a mile and did the same again. He swung the RIB around in a complete circle, hoping that the watch officers on the bridge would be able to see that there were no other occupants. The, he came to within a quarter of a mile and repeated the exercise, finally matching course and speed and making the distress signal again, and awaited a signal.

*

"Right Tony, I want you down on deck with a pistol, and our sharpshooter on the bridge with a rifle. I want a radio dropped to him first, before we get him aboard. The RIB may look empty but he could have explosives in the bilge lockers – could be a suicide job, though it's unlikely. Get two firehoses ready and aimed to fill the RIB. Any problems and we'll put some bullets in his airtubes, and a couple of tons of water over him? Any questions?"

"No, that's ok Skipper. I'll give you the thumbs up when I'm ready on deck." Tony Mowbray gave the orders to their nominated sharpshooter waiting in the bridge. Wallis and Mowbray unlocked one of the small arms lockers in the chartroom, and passed the rifle to the worried-looking seaman. Mowbray left the bridge with a Browning pistol and portable radio. He headed down the five flights of steps to deck level, just forward of the bridge.

Since the level of piracy worldwide had started to increase, all major ships had anti-piracy plans, defences and protocols, and many ships were carrying arms, with crew trained in their use. Fortunately, they were rarely used in anger – few crew wanted to be trained in the use of weapons as it marked them out.

*

Steve heard the ship's load hailer over the smooth sound of his engine and the slow thudding that was the ship's engine.

"Black RIB starboard side. This is *Universal Trader*. If you can you hear me raise your right arm for Yes."

Steve complied.

"If you behave suspiciously, you will be fired upon. Do you understand? Raise your left arm if you do."

Steve complied again, thinking 'OK, so they know I've got two arms and can understand English – that's a start.'

"Move in to one hundred metres range, onto the edge of our bow wave, and just forward of the bridge."

Steve swung the wheel over and moved closer as instructed. He could see a crewman on the bridge wing with a rifle, a bit too obvious and unprofessional.

On the edge of the bow wave of the ship the RIB was rolling heavily. The ship's crew could clearly see inside the RIB, and the aim of any armed pirates would be badly off mark.

*

"Do you require assistance? Raise both arms if you do." At least they don't want me to bloody dance, he thought as he slowly raised his arms.

"OK, we are going to drop a portable radio for you. We are not going to slow down. I remind you that any suspicious behaviour will result in us sinking your vessel. Hold your station." Steve raised his right arm, struggling to hold his course straight as the RIB corkscrewed in the ship's bow wave – he expected a lot of caution. At least they were following the universal seaman's law, being bound to investigate a distress signal and offer assistance, though in these days commercial pressures and 'economic refugees' could make it an expensive, complicated and sometimes ignored convention.

Steve could see a seaman on the stern throw a small holdall over.

"Black RIB, collect the radio. Do not come within a hundred metres."

Swinging the RIB round in an arc to starboard, Steve picked up the floating holdall from the ship's wake and accelerated to catch up with the ship, taking station about a hundred metres off its starboard side. The radio was a standard handheld portable VHF set and Steve initiated the radio call.

"Universal Trader, Universal Trader, this is Black RIB, Black RIB, over.'

"Black Rib, Universal Trader, Channel 9."

"Channel 9."

"Universal Trader, Black RIB. Good morning. May I speak with the Master?"

"This is the master speaking. What is the problem?"

"My name is Steve Baldwin, a British National. I am a sailor, currently based at Djibouti. For reasons I cannot explain on open radio, I am effectively marooned out here, I have limited fuel and no papers, so cannot land in Saudi Arabia. I would appreciate a tow down to within range of Djibouti – you appear to be going that way." Steve knew that this was stretching it – Saudi was a possibility but the complications would be endless. Asking *Trader* to contact HMS Ardent was not a possibility either.

"Is there anyone who can vouch for you?"

"Yes, but I cannot give names over an open radio channel."

"Very well. This is what we will do. We will take you aboard and tow the RIB. It's almost two days to Djibouti. I expect you to be vouched for within 12 hours or we drop you off near the next port. Is that clear?"

"Trader, Black RIB, that's understood."

"Fine, then let's get you aboard. We'll drop a ladder and take you aboard through the pilot's door under the bridge wing. We will drop you a towline. Make it secure – if you lose the RIB we don't go back. We will not be slowing down."

"Trader, Black RIB, understood. I'll await your tow rope and ladder and then close in. Black RIB listening, out."

Wallis spoke to his first officer on his deck radio, who went down to the pilot's boarding door with two other seamen.

It would be a tricky exercise – even though the sea was quiet, there was plenty of motion from the ship's wake. Hoisting the RIB aboard was not an option – if it had a bomb aboard then the ship could be held to ransom; Steve recognised that a tow was very reasonable in the circumstances – it would have been easy for them to ignore him.

*

Once the Merlin had landed back on *Ardent* shortly after 05:00, Don Williams had contacted his senior officer to report, and had ranted about leaving a man down in the water. The response had been unequivocal. The Major had listened in disbelief to his Lieutenant-Colonel dressing him down for dropping the Chinese RIB, and then being told that the mission didn't take place at all, and to forget Steve Baldwin.

"Major, your orders are clear. You are to forget that the incident took place. I will say no more."

"Then why did we take the RIB if it wasn't to be dropped?"

"Orders, Major, those were our orders, and they did not include dropping the RIB, so don't push it - the matter is closed. Get some sleep. And, off the record - well done – the mission was a success and the rig's production is closed down."

The Lieutenant-Colonel did raise the issues with his senior officer, but the matter stalled. If Baldwin had been a regular marine, then this just would not have happened.

Deniability was essential, and very useful, but Major Don Williams did not know why.

*

319

As soon as the tow line was secure, Steve waited for the right moment and stepped across onto the ladder, timing his move carefully. As he got to the top of the ladder he recognised the pistol as a Browning, aimed at him.

"Welcome aboard the *Trader*, Mr Baldwin. I am Tony Mowbray, First Officer. I have been trained in the use of this weapon and will use it if I have to. We have to take some security precautions - you will be searched and confined to a cabin until we have checked you out."

"I understand," though Steve could see that the training did not extend to close-quarters prisoner handling – he could have disarmed him in less than a second.

Once he had been searched – competently though not covering all possible hiding places - Steve was led up to the crew accommodation area. In the small cabin he was joined by the Master, still under the aim of Tony Mowbray's Browning.

"Before I answer any questions – which I am very happy to do, can you confirm that this is a British ship, and that you are both British nationals?"

"That's correct, though I ask the questions here," said Wallis. "What's the story – this is a strange set of circumstances – not the usual distress situation we might expect in the Red Sea, and your diving gear is unusual. Yes, we saw you ditch that. You had better be convincing."

"Well, it's quite simple, though probably incredible. I have been engaged on a joint British/Saudi security exercise, ashore in Saudi Arabia. There was a snarl up in communications and here I am. I cannot give you any British contacts to vouch for me. That would breach my security. Even telling you this is exceeding my authority." It was a thin story, Steve knew, but these were not military people and it might just wash with them.

"Do you know anything about the attack on a British production platform north last night – about a hundred and fifty miles north of here?"

"No, I don't know anything about any attack on any platform, but I will say that our exercise was related to the protection of oil facilities, given the current tense political situation. That mustn't go outside this cabin though. What happened at that platform?" Wallis briefly outlined what he knew, even down to the fact that Chinese involvement was suspected. Just as well they didn't hoist the RIB aboard then, thought Steve. The Chinese lettering on the controls was a dead give-away.

"Now Mr Baldwin, I need someone to vouch for you. You have until 20:00 hours – that's about twelve hours. You will be confined in this cabin. Your vessel is not in distress, and if by that time you have not been confirmed as someone I can trust, then we will give you some food and fuel and let you go. We will be over two hundred miles southeast of here and about a hundred miles off both Saudi Arabia and Eritrea. If you are confirmed, then we will take you as far as Djibouti. Understood?"

"I'm grateful for your help, Mr. Wallis. Call Master Sergeant George Neilsen at the US Military Base Camp Lemonnier in Djibouti. He will vouch for me. Sorry, I don't have the number."

Wallis wrote down the details and confirmed them with Steve, then both he and Mowbray left. Steve heard the door being locked and lay down on the bunk, with a pait of ship's overalls to change into. A few minutes later, the door opened and some breakfast was delivered. Two seamen stood outside. After about an hour, the First Officer returned and asked Steve to re-confirm the contact details.

"We've spoken to Camp Lemonnier. They advised us that they were unable to give out names on the grounds of security, but did say that there was no Master Sergeant George Neilsen there, nor had there been recently. Full stop. That could just be their security, or bullshit from you. You'd better come up with something more convincing."

Steve lay back on his bunk, wondering why he was suddenly untouchable and unknown.

*

Trader's Trials

Tomaso Vestuti, a junior engineering officer, had died in his berth without waking up, dispatched by a silenced bullet. Ten days previously, during a night watch, as the *Universal Trader* was passing through the Bab el Mandeb on her way north to the *Harvester*, he had loosened an oil-feed union on the number two generator and disconnected the oil pressure and level warning lamps, induced by a payment of $10,000. The oil had slowly drained away and the bearings of the generator armature had seized when it was started for its twice weekly test run later that day.

Tomaso didn't know why he had been paid handsomely to sabotage a generator. It was not life threatening on the face of it – there was another main generator, backed up by an auxiliary. A replacement for the damaged half-ton armature was ordered from the manufacturers in China via the TRI London office and flown in to Yanbu for loading. It had been accompanied by a South African engineer brought aboard to oversee the specialised refit en route to the Cape of Good Hope, where he would disembark at Cape Town.

*

At noon on the third day out from Yanbu, the watch on the *Trader* had just changed, the day's run had been worked up, and the junior officers had practiced their sextant work. The South African generator engineer, Hansie Van der Waal, walked down to the stowage area below the aft deck. This area was serviced externally by a gantry and deck hatch aft of the superstructure, which enabled engine parts and stores to be brought aboard and moved down to the engineering space if necessary. Earlier that morning they had passed the Free Seas flotilla on its way north in the other lane, and they were by now a couple of hundred miles to the north.

Hansie dogged the watertight door shut, then located the generator spares cases, one of which was marked as containing a replacement generator armature manufactured in Shanghai, China. It was a large case, some 2 m high, 4 m long and 2 m wide. He broke open the rough wooden casing, and located the hatch in the fibreglass module inside.

The smell was strong. The three other members of the team had been confined in this module for 5 days in transit by plane and in the Saudi Arabian climate, with food, water, a chemical toilet and minimal ventilation. They were not in peak physical form, but training came to the fore. The prospect of immediate action and the consequent flow of adrenalin pushed the discomfort to the back of their minds. Hansie shook hands with Pieter, his second in command, nodding to Joost and Wim. Hansie confirmed that the plan of the ship which they had committed to memory 2 weeks ago was still accurate, and that there had been no internal layout changes in the accommodation area.

Finally, they quickly talked through the plan of action which had been prepared over the last 2 months and which they had memorised. Pieter passed Hansie an Uzi-Pro, a Czech pistol, a knife and ammunition. Then they checked their weapons and set to work.

The assault on the bridge was direct and quick. The Captain was off watch and asleep in his cabin. The first officer and an ordinary seaman were on watch in the bridge. Hansie entered first, and within thirty seconds the bridge was under new command, with the ship proceeding under autopilot on an unchanged course.

The first officer, having been quickly persuaded of their intent by witnessing the execution of a seaman, acted as guide whilst the other crew members were rounded up and confined. The Chief Engineer and two engineering crew were kept apart to maintain two six hourly engineering watches.

*

Two hundred miles to the south of the *Trader*, the airborne stand-off had been going on all morning and into the afternoon. It was now after 16.00 hours and the parade continued. The British and Chinese air formations passed each other on reciprocal headings, sometimes less than a mile apart, each side of the boundary of Yemeni airspace. There were no hostile acts, just routine fly-bys. The carrier group was now on a southeasterly leg, just approaching the isolated reef of Jazirat At'Ta'ir, about 30 miles off both the Yemen and Eritrea. The waters here were relatively restricted for big ships, with extensive reefs off both shorelines, and the fleet was preparing for its turn back to the north and more searoom.

This was the best moment of all, the one that Lieutenant Commnader Andy Rowson savoured. Strapped into his F35-C on Alert 5, that fluttering in the stomach, mentally preparing himself for the task ahead, digesting and rehearsing the flight briefing, he was combat leader of the four-ship formation, callsign 'Satan'. The air was rich with the smell of combusted jet fuel, the carrier was making 25 knots in still air so that the Lightnings would have enough airspeed to take off. The composite JTIDS picture before him was live, with the hard walls of friendly airspace clearly visible. The Chinese fighter tracks were clearly defined, labelled as 'bogeys', and would only be coloured red and relabelled 'bandits' by the battle staff commander in the event of a hostile act. Then, targets would be allocated.

Andy's second radio, for chat within the formation, came to life.

"Andy, Chas, black box, looks like we may be launched soon – there's a new group of six J20's in the picture."

Andy's formation comprised two pairs of two Lightnings, and Chas, as Satan 3, was his subordinate formation leader and led the other pair of Lightnings, providing mutual support.

After the writing-off of the UK's maritime strike capability with the paying-off of *HMS Ark Royal* and the scrapping of the Harriers in early 2011, a group of displaced Air Arm pilots, including Andy, had been sent to train with the US Navy flying the F18-E Super Hornet off US carriers. With conversion training, this group would be ready to fly the British carrier Lightnings when they were delivered. And so they were. And so they were here, now, potentially facing combat for the first time – man and plane alike.

"Start the Alert 5 Lightnings."

Andy's reverie ended as the plane captain with the brown 'surcoat' gave him the 'wind up' signal. He ran through the extensive checklist automatically, drilled into him during hundreds of hours of training on simulators and real flight time.

The green surcoats were holding up his weapons arming pins which they had withdrawn.

His flight were all wound up, anti-collison lights on and with a fist held aloft by the plane captain, they were ready for off. The ground crews were one part of the flight operation that outsiders overlooked. A capable leading-aircraftman could, at only nineteen years of age, be responsible for the air-readiness of two formations. They had vast responsibility, and each team member was essential.

More browncoats, holding the tie-down chains aloft, thumbs up confirmation. The plane captain pointed with both hands to a yellow coat. Andy chopped his hand in acknowledgement and he was taxied along the deck to the forward catapult shuttle. Another fist and brakes confirmed on. Final check, and the Flight Deck Officer takes control. Connection to the shuttle, blast deflector raised, and Andy's brain is on autopilot as all the myriad of tasks are completed with one end. Flyco lights go green. Wind up, brakes off, slam to full power, check gauges, through the gate with the throttle to light the afterburner, left hand on the restraint to prevent whiplash reducing the power, right hand on its handhold, plane straining against her restraints, nav lights on, like a dog baying for release after the prey.

At last, a green flag from Flight Deck Officer.

Away.

The catapult drags the F35 up to take-off speed in less than two hundred metres. 6G plus acceleration punches Andy back in his seat. Check engine, speed, alpha, climb, cancel afterburner. Not bad, less than five minutes from the start order. Satan 4 now off the waist catapult.

Now, the formation check. "Satan 1", "2", "3","4".

IFF Transponder OK, and Freddy cleared them to sweep northwest.

JTIDS showed a new group of six J20s designated Bogey Group One heading up over the Yemen from the Chinese carrier. The British F35's were still following a clockwise fighter sweep pattern, northwest up the middle of the Red Sea and then southeast along the edge of Yemeni airspace. *Queen Elizabeth* also had Cougar formation, led by Andy's boss aloft - there were two formations up at any given time, on opposite sides of the 'racetrack'.

The *Gerald R Ford*, out in the Gulf of Aden, was busy too – JTIDS showed four USN F35-Cs callsign 'Waverider' on combat air patrol.

"Satan, Freddy, Bogey Group One allocated Satan target, mission shadow."

Andy acknowledged and confirmed weapons safe, then with Chas set the plan to fall in behind the approaching Chinese planes, expecting to turn about fifty miles north of the carrier formation, away from their forward firing missiles.

"Satan, Freddy, hard wall north ten miles."

"Satan 1, Roger, Satan turnabout starboard go."

The Bogeys, though, did not turn as expected. This was different.

"Satan, Freddy, picture. Northern group Bogey Group One. New group just launched from their carrier, designation Bogey Group Two, tracking north."

"Satan copy, good link picture."

"Andy, Chas, no sign of a Bogey turn yet - shit, they've lit their burners."

As Satan turned they could see the J20s of Bogey Group One cross ahead about two mile away, accelerating rapidly, going supersonic within 3 seconds and continuing northwestwards. Their hot exhaust plumes were bright in their IR helmet-mounted sights.

"Freddy, Satan, Bogey Group One extending northwestwards, speed now super, request intentions."

"Standby."

Decisions, decisions – not Andy's, but the battle group staff. Seconds were ticking away and the Bogeys were extending their lead by a mile every four seconds.

Then, Freddy was back. Satan was cleared to breach the hard wall and shadow, Cougar was allocated Bogey Group Two. The chase was on, the prey forty miles ahead.

Following Andy's instruction, Chas fell into line ten miles behind as the pursuit began as they acclerated to Mach 1.5.

If the chase went on for very long then fuel would become an issue – the F35s were not capable of supercruise – that is, maintaining supersonic flight without afterburners lit up - and the F35-C, the carrier variant, heavier with its larger folding wings, strengthened airframe and carrier landing gear was no exception. The F35s were carrying 2 AIM-120 AMRAAMs in their internal weapons bays, together with 2 AIM-132 ASRAAMs (the ASRAAMs enabled attacks just beyond visual range without using active radar which would alert a target). The Chinese J20s however, were capable of supercruise and could outrun the F35s on duration. It was moot whether the Chinese Chengdu J20s could also outperform them in visual combat manoeuvering – the vectored thrust Kulbit manoeuvre was well within their flight envelopes at low speeds – so close quarters dogfights were preferably avoided – until either a Chinese or NATO pilot found out the hard way.

"Freddy, new picture. Bogey Gourp Two now allocated to Waverider. Cougar, snap northwestwards to support Satan."

This was a significant step, as the US fighters would have a dog leg flight path around the southwestern corner of the Yemen and the Gate of Tears, unless they opted to breach Yemeni airspace to pursue Bogey Group Two directly. The US Navy F35-C Lightnings chose the direct flight path over Yemeni airspace, and as they crossed the coast, another flight of Chinese J20's took off from their carrier, just 40 miles away from the *Gerald R Ford* in the Gulf of Aden. At the time, a US Navy S3 Viking tanker was taking off from Camp Lemonnier to refuel the USN Lightnings once they crossed out of Yemeni airspace into the Red Sea.

*

Back on the *Queen Elizabeth*, the battle management software was forecasting a bingo range for the J20s as being in eighteen minutes, and after that they would have to turn around and head back to their carrier or find somewhere to land – the Chinese had no known inflight refuelling capability in this region. Bingo fuel for the F35s was about the same, and the air controller instructed them to go subsonic to conserve fuel – supercruise was not an option for the F35. Another wing of F35s was launched from Alert 5 on *Queen Elizabeth* to set up a point defence combat air patrol while Satan and Cougar were dragged further from the carrier. The probability was very high that the Chinese would return to their carrier as there were few military airfields capable of handling them within their range – Egypt had suitable airfields, but was not diplomatically orientated towards the Chinese, and Saudi Arabia was no friend at all. Unfortunately, the battle management software was not programmed with the fact that the Chengdu ('Annihilator') J20s were equipped with long range fuel tanks that they had used and jettisoned over the Yemen on their way north.

The AWACS then detected a split in the Chinese flight, with three of the planes heading out into the middle of the Red Sea as they approached Saudi airspace, with the other three J20s going into a holding pattern at 20,000 feet. Andy saw the developments on JTIDS.

"Chas, Andy, what do you reckon?"

"Not sure, but do you see that smoke plume on the surface on the same bearing?"

"Yeh, could be they've hit something down there."

"Freddy, Satan, Bogey Group One may have hit a surface target – we see a plume."

"Satan, Freddy, AWACS reports the same. Marine AIS identified a British ship close to that position. Bogey Group One now designated hostile, repeat hostile bandits. Satan clear engage. Bandits now forming a single group strength five. Cougar cover Satan."

"Satan targeting Bandit Group One northwest forty miles. Satan, commit, switches live."

The Bogey target symbols on the JTIDS changed to Bandit designators, track colour red.

"Chas, Andy, standard wall attack, check gravy."

"Andy, Chas, playtime ten minutes only, that chase used up a lot of gas."

"Roger, too risky to close to Fox Two range. We'll take long range Fox Three then pump out southeast to outrun their PL11's. Cougar can de-louse any bandits in our six."

"Chas copy."

Fox Two and Three were the NATO brevity codes for the AIM-132 ASRAAM and AIM-120 AMRAAM air to air missiles.

Satan manoeuvred into 'wall' formation, line abreast with a mile between each aircraft, and the pilots refined their attack radar scan pattern for optimal accuracy. The adrenaline was flowing.

*

In the Shaban Deep, the Warfare Officer on the Shang Class submarine knew that they were exposed. They did not have their towed array of hydrophones deployed – their submarine was sitting on the bottom in the saline pool which shielded all sound from the outside world. Instead, the submarine had floated up a line of four small hydrophones, which sat just above the 84 metres deep highly saline layer, in normal sea water.

On the Israeli frigates, their sonar had not confirmed the anomalous reflections received by the 'Woods Hole' buoys which had triggered their search.

One of the frigates, *INS Lahav*, released a spread of sonar buoys into the saline layer. When they went active the submarine was painted by sonar probing from the buoys inside the layer, but the submarine's sound absorbing tiles worked efficiently.

The operators on the frigate turned up the sonar power on their spread of buoys and the sonar shadow of the submarine against the sea bottom sonar backscatter was clear. The submarine was apparent by its lack of reflection. The Chinese crew monitored the active sonar from the buoys. The Shang Class submarine could not quietly rise off the sea bottom – its buoyancy tanks had to be pumped partially clear of water for it to rise above the bottom - usually done by releasing compressed air into the water-filled tanks – 'blowing them'. Despite a host of engineering feature to make this process as quiet as possible, it still created noise, and would expose them, though they didn't know that they had already been exposed by the US passive sonar chain. One of the other frigates, *INS Hanit,* launched an unmanned remotely operated mini-sub – an ROV – to investigate.

Within two hours it was stationary in the water, next to the submarine, and the Chinese were sweating – they had detected its almost silent electric motors only during the last couple of minutes of its approach, as the Israelis had been using decoy whale-noise emitters scattered around the submarine to confuse the sonar picture.

For the captain of the submarine, the choices were stark: should they run, fight or surface? Or, just wait for the inevitable?

Then, the sound came clear through the hydrophones, repeatedly. It was a stark series of dots and dashes. In the command area of the submarine, the captain and first officer looked at each other as they heard the morse signal. It was being transmitted by the *Hanit* via the ROV. The Chinese officers checked their code books, International Code of Signals. The code grouping was UY4 ZL2, confirmed by their signals officer. It was in an Appendix entitled "USA/Russia Supplementary codes for Naval Vesels".

UL4 I am preparing to conduct/am conducting operations employing explosive charges

ZL2 Do you understand? Request acknowledgement.

The Chinese captain smiled ruefully. So, the Israelis have a sense of humour? His decision was made and he instructed the weapons officer.

*

"Move. Now. Two paces ahead. I will use this if I have to, no problem." Steve was wakened from his dozing as the door was unlocked and a man dressed in a blue boiler suit entered, prodding him with his Uzi-Pro. Gesturing with the gun, he motioned Steve to move out through the door –

the signals were not difficult to understand, assisted by broken English with a heavy Africaans accent.

Here we go again, thought Steve, twice in one day, though this one is much more capable than the First Officer was, with efficient weapons. Chinese, Serbian, South African – this has been a real international mission. What next?

Moving slowly with his hands in the open, Steve walked ahead of the hijacker and out of the accommodation section onto the side deck, and along the side deck to the stern where the other crew were assembled.

He stood quietly and assessed the situation – three well-armed and capable-looking men that he could see at this level, and one on the deck above overlooking them. All appeared to be professional and well-trained, working by the book, with the hard, knowing demeanour that separated special forces guys from regular grunts. David Wallis and Tony Mowbray were standing together, separated from the group – he met their eyes, shrugged slightly and shook his head almost imperceptibly.

The man on the upper deck addressed them.

"Captain, please tell your crew that they will follow my orders and those of my men, instantly and without question. If they do not then they will be subject to severe sanction. Pieter, if you please."

One of the men led the radio officer to the taffrail at the stern. The rest of the crew were grouped on the starboard side and gasped in unison as the radio officer was shot through the head with a pistol and his body neatly pushed over the rail as he collapsed. There would be little doubt now about the crew's compliance.

"I hope you understand that we are serious. Captain, please issue the orders." The man on the deck above spoke English well with a guttural Afrikaans delivery and a politeness that was menacing, almost with a measure of enjoyment. Steve could see that he was good at his work and really did enjoy the buzz of power and the adrenaline of action. He also appeared to be without any moral compass.

Wallis stepped forward, his face white and his voice trembling.

"There is no need for this barbarity. My crew will follow your orders."

"Good, thank you Captain Wallis. My name is Hansie. You will sail the ship on her planned course until we reach the traffic separation scheme at the Bab el Mandeb. In the meantime, please introduce me to your security officer. Now."

"Hansie, whoever you are, you surely know that the master of a vessel does not know who the security officer is. That is a basic precaution."

Hansie turned to one of his team.

"Pieter, again, if you please."

Pieter turned and dragged a deckhand to the taffrail, but before he could shoot him, the Second Officer stepped forward.

"I am the security officer."

"Thank you, please take me to the emergency transmitter panic button. I know you have one and need to know your protocols; also where your arms are stored. Wim, take him to the bridge, I will join you there. The rest of the crew may return to their watch. At the first sign of any problem at all, I will shoot the Captain. I trust that is clear. Captain, carry on please." Wallis and Mowbray were led away under guard to the bridge.

Steve started to walk away with the other deck crew, but was brought up short by the barrel of Joost's Uzi-Pro. Choosing not to meet the man's eyes and mark himself out even more, he was led back into the accommodation block and towards his confinement.

At that moment a roar shook the ship and startled them both. Steve took the opportunity quickly. His guard took Steve's left elbow to the throat with a crunching gurgle. The short burst from the Uzi ricocheted down the passageway past Steve's right side, before Steve wrenched the weapon from his hand and smashed his head against the steel bulkhead, crushing his communications headset between skull and steel. The noise of the burst might have been covered by the departing plane, but Steve was taking no chances. He grasped the guard's head in both hands and twisted it sharply, hearing the cartilage snap. He bundled the body into his cabin and shut the door. A pistol and a couple of grenades, plus a knife and the Uzi-Pro, with some spare clips. That would do for a start. He held the initiative now and intended to keep it. Three to one – the odds were not good against these guys.

Then, the stuttering sound of cannon fire hitting the ship followed by another roar as a plane went over. He heard the fire alarms go off and started running for the bridge.

*

The first Chinese J20 stealth fighter bomber had come in low and fast, and started banking to the right as it passed over the ship to confirm identity. Then it turned for a strafing run from ahead of the ship – a more difficult approach, but if done right it was much more satisfying to stitch a line of shells along the length of the chip and be almost certain of hitting the bridge; and so it was – perfectly executed. The chain of cannon shells rippled along the deck from the bow, up the front of the superstructure and found the bridge with four rounds dead centre. For the pilot, this was like training, and there was time for some target practice before using her bombs.

The mission plan was that each of the three planes should have one run, but the pilots stretched the definition of 'run' – this was a real mission, an undefended target and they intended to enjoy it to the full. The ultimate purpose of the mission was unknown to them, but their orders were clear. Sink the *Universal Trader*. They each had two 500 lb bombs in their underbelly weapons bays – well under half their full weapons payload, but they had carried external fuel tanks as far as the Saudi border.

*

When he got to the ship's bridge about two minutes later, the scene was chaotic. Steve ducked his head in through the doorway and saw Hansie picking himself up off the floor, one of the two Filipino bridge lookouts and helmsman shocked, and other bodies strewn over the floor. Wallis, the Master, was dazed, but working at the touchscreen controls and issuing orders, trying to bring his remaining crew back into focus. Mowbray was on the floor, lying still in several pints of blood, with half of his left shoulder missing. A loudspeaker was echoing the words "Crash Stop, Crash Stop, Fire, Fire, Fire."

Across the bridge he saw Wim raise his Uzi. One squeeze, six rounds, right to left drove him back against a radar console. Three shots had connected across his ribcage and Wim was dead before he reached the floor. Hansie had retrieved his Uzi and was bringing it to bear as Steve continued swinging his own weapon likewise, just as another burst of cannon shells came through the bridge, this time from the port side. One clipped Steve's upper right arm and exploded in the main engine control LCD touchscreen display, the other shells exploding across the steel floor of the bridge. The bridge shook again under the roar of the overflying J20. Hansie had dropped to the floor for cover and loosed off a burst as Steve ran out through the starboard side bridge access door and down the stairway.

Running down the starboard sidedeck towards the stern, every step jarred his right arm. He could see the RIB at the end of its towline. He had no time to get down through the decks to the pilot's boarding door, and it was a drop of about 40 feet into the water. Anyway, he thought better the jump than to be below decks when the vessel was being attacked by a fighter-bomber, forgetting that the tanker was filled mainly with seawater. By now the plane was half way through its turn and he could see the wingtip vortices as it banked hard. Just then, there were a couple of metallic clangs against the superstructure next to him followed by the sound of an Uzi – a stuttering purr, like a deathly sewing machine. He glimpsed Hansie pausing to loose off another burst. Although the range was at least 50 yards from the bridge door where Hansie had emerged, the detached professional in him thought it was pretty good shooting with an Uzi in the circumstances.

There were no options.

*

Steve threw himself over the side rail, drew breath as he fell and curled himself up pulling his limbs in tightly. He hit the water agonisingly on his back and surfaced about three seconds later. He rolled onto his side and struck out with his left arm, sidestroking as best he could to get some distance from the ship. Hansie was now about 50 yards away aiming over the side rail as the *Trader* was losing her momentum, with her massive single screw, thirty three feet in diameter, idling and not yet in reverse – reversing the screw meant stopping the engine, then restarting it in the opposite rotation, as there is no gearbox on most supertankers. A crash stop would take a mile at least, and she was still travelling at over fourteen knots. Steve realised the difficulty of his situation – holding on, let alone getting aboard the RIB, would be next to impossible at that speed.

Hansie was aiming very carefully. And then, a deafening roar as the fighter-bomber went over from the port side at less than 100 feet high. Steve, lying half on his back as he sidetroked, had a clear view of the plane's underbelly and felt the percussion of the explosion through the water. He saw the starboard side of the tanker bulge and split as the compression wave of the explosion found relief, driving a huge gout of biological soup out, followed by Hansie arcing outwards through the air over the side of the tanker, launched by the explosive bulging of the deck beneath his feet.

The second J20 was now about a mile away and starting to turn. The 500lb bomb had penetrated the port side through both hull skins and exploded in the number 7 tank, in the midst of 10,000 tons of gold enriched seawater. The deck above had stretched, rippled and split as the compression wave ran along and across the ship, and launched Hansie overboard atop a crest of water.

Steve could hear the structure of the tanker groaning as its deck beams and longitudinal bulkhcads struggled to cope with stresses for which they had not been designed, as the rents on the starboard and port sides of the tanks spread to meet with the splits in the deck. The *Trader* continued on its way, the stern passing him as he struck out for the towline of the RIB, still thirty yards away and many feet above him as it curved down from the *Trader's* stern. Steve was now directly behind the ship and in line with the course of the towed RIB. He and could feel the dragging turbulence of the ship's stopped propeller jostling him and a hard prodding in his lower back as he swam. Then he realised that it was Joost's knife digging into him. He still had the Uzi on its shoulder strap and with his good left arm held it aloft as the RIB approached, and the towline came within reach. He kicked and bobbed above the surface, just managing to hook the Uzi's handgrip/magazine over the towrope, the sling still around his shoulders. Hanging on by his left arm as he slid the last ten or twelve yards along the towrope, he reached down with his weakened right arm, pulled out the knife from his waistband and started sawing.

The crunch of the RIB as it hit him at more than twelve knots was sickening, and the sling of the Uzi finally broke from its snaphook just before he had finished severing the towline. He broke surface just as the stern of the RIB passed him, snatching at the end of its part-cut towline in the slight sea, still attached to the *Trader*.

Steve lay on his back in the water, recovering from his crunch with the RIB, wondering what he would do next. He checked his right arm – there was no major blood loss, but it would need stitching. Still, there would be enough blood to attract sharks. That would be a quick ending - or maybe not - but what a shitty way to go.

Then, he heard the roar of a jet and watched the second Chengdu 'Annihilator' J20 come in for another run. He actually saw the bomb release from the J20 weapons bay about a quarter of a mile away from the ship. The pilot pushed his nose down slightly and banked to starboard, his bomb already on a line to the *Trader's* stern. Then the pilot realised, too late, that he was too low and clipped one of the short wave aerials projecting above the tanker's superstructure, just as the bomb drilled into crew quarters above the engine room, and exploded.

The detached section of aerial was only 3 inches long, and of relatively soft GRP with a copper core. Nevertheless, turbine blades spinning at 15,000 rpm could not digest this and one blade twisted slightly, bent, fractured and set off a chain reaction which started stripping the other blades in the compressor stages on the port engine. The armour around the compressor blades did its work and kept the detritus within its confines, allowing them to move backwards through the engine and combustion chamber to emerge at the rear end, together with some additional engine materials collected along the way. By this time the pilot's brain was struggling to grapple with loss of thrust, and a general melee of audible and visible warnings. The plane had been continuing its banking, slightly diving turn to the right and the roll continued as the pilot prepared to eject. But, at 100 feet altitude, with one smashed engine and a bad attitude, there was no time for recovery, even to upthrust the second engine. The plane hit the water at 400 knots, upside down, almost skipped once, went nose up and then plane and pilot disintegrated.

*

He knew that the chances of seeing a ship were close to zero, and the chances of him being seen by one were less than that. After ten minutes, Steve looked around the horizon again, kicking and bobbing up to give himself a greater range of view. The *Trader* was barely visible – she was a couple of miles away and from the sea surface Steve could only see the top of her superstructure and a cloud of smoke. That was a swimmable distance, though she would probably go down soon given the damage he had seen her sustain. But, any port in a storm, he thought. Then, he kicked and bobbed up again and smiled when saw the RIB a couple of hundred yards away – her towrope must have parted. He struck out slowly for her.

*

When he was about twenty yards from the boat, Steve noticed another swimmer in the water, moving towards the RIB. He saw Steve and accelerated his stroke for the RIB, getting there just ahead of Steve. He struggled to climb in over the side a couple of times, falling back on each occasion. It was Hansie - the bastard had survived being blown into the water. Fucking amateur, thought Steve. Hansie obviously didn't know that the best way to board a RIB was over the stern.

As Steve reached the stern, Hansie was still struggling alongside to get aboard, but then he saw Steve at the stern and swam around, pulling at Steve's legs. They fell back into the water in a clinch and surfaced, struggling to get a purchase. Fighting in water is quite different to fighting ashore. Legs and arms move more slowly with the drag of water on them, taking the some of the weight out of blows and kicks. Heads move quickly above the water, and on the next surfacing Steve's butt broke Hansie's nose immediately, as he felt Hansie's knee connect with his groin, with little force in it as Steve twisted his body instinctively.

Then, they were under again. Hansie scrabbled to get a strangle hold around Steve's neck, whilst Steve clawed to get his hands on Hansie's shoulders and so use his weight to push Hansie under, managing to get some air as they re-surfaced and went under yet again. Hansie went for Steve's eyes. Pushing his knees against Hansie's torso, Steve fell back a couple of feet and Hansie came for him, prone on top of him, his smashed nose streaming blood into the sea. Steve rolled, starting to black out as Hansie's fingers closed again around his throat and held on immovably. The breathe reflex was in control, his mouth filled with water but his airway was blocked.

Steve reached for the knife in his waistband and just as he pulled it out he felt something brush hard against him and knock the knife out of his hand. He struggled and kicked hard, but Hansie's fingers were like iron, his thumbs pressing into Steve's windpipe. He tried to kick away, to butt, to twist, but Hansie held him tight at arms length. Steve had little power in his right arm as he tried to pull Hansie's hands free. Strangulation was not a good option for fighting under water, as the strangler would usually have to release his hold before the other person would die. Steve knew this – he only had to outlast Hansie - but the instinct to fight for survival was overwhelming.

They were down to three or four metres below the surface, both desperate for air, when Steve's rapidly blacking vision barely saw the vague shape approaching from behind Hansie. There was a violent jostling and he felt the vice-like grip around his neck relax as Hansie screamed silently underwater, his mouth trailing a long stream of bubbles as the seawater flooded his lungs and the Whitetip shark tore into him, its half ton momentum dragging him off, dying. Steve kicked and struck for the surface and the RIB before any more Whitetips joined the feast. They were renowned for their feeding frenzies, particularly of shipwreck and plane-crash survivors. He knew that he had been very, very lucky as he pulled himself over the transom and collapsed into the bottom of the RIB, and the waters around him frothed red.

*

Aerial Aggravation

The AWACS E2D-Hawkeye had tracked the first J20 flight through an attack cycle on a surface ship two hundred miles north west of the flotilla. Though a stealth plane, the Chinese J20 Annihilator stealth technology was not as good as that of the F35 Lightning, and the radar of the Hawkeye could be effective if the plane was very close to the same height as the target. There is a 'chine' between the underbelly and topside of most stealth aircraft providing a slightly stronger radar return than on the rest of the fuselage; JTIDS feedback from the F35s on the Chinese position and height helped the radar tuning on the Hawkeye. Based on Automatic Ship Identification data, the ship under attack was the *Universal Trader*. The AIS information indicated a cargo of seawater and crude oil, that the ship's heading was 134 degrees True, speed 16 knots and destination Milford Haven, UK. Then, the AIS transmission had ceased, and on the AWACS radar the ship had slowed to a stop. On secure voice comms, the hostile act was reported to the Battle Staff and relayed immediately to PJIIQ in Northwood, London, where British Naval operations were controlled. The ROE were relaxed and JTIDS now showed the Chinese tracks as red.

The attack had started with three Chinese planes, now there were only two returning, to join up with the loitering three planes before heading back across the Yemen to their carrier. They were climbing.

At that moment, the US F35-Cs – 'Waverider' formation - were crossing the Yemeni coast just south of the Saudi border as Andy Rowson's wing was pressing home its attack. Cougar formation was forty miles away and accelerating towards the action.

"Satan 1, countdown engagement in 30 seconds, Bandit Group strength five."

"Freddy Roger, Cougar 40 miles trail"

"Andy, sorted two leftmost targets."

"2 sort", "3 sort", "4 sort".

Each pilot used his tactical display to designate his allocated target. Andy would fire one AMRAAM each at the two targets on the left of the formation and his wingmen would individually target the others with a single AMRAAM each. On the JTIDS display, Andy checked that all targets would be engaged. The countdown timer in the helmet mounted sight showed 15 seconds to first engagement opportunity and the J20s flew straight at them. Their closure speed was 1 mile every 3 seconds. 5 seconds to go, Andy raised the late-arm guard on the trigger. In range. Squeeze, Squeeze. Two AMRAAMs were ejected from the weapons bay, the rocket motors fired and they accelerated to Mach 3, climbing as they went to get into the thinner air.

"Satan 1, Fox Three double, cranking right"

"Satan 2 Fox Three", "3 Fox Three", "4 Fox 3".

Five missiles were now en-route to their individual targets. Andy turned his formation through 60 degrees to keep his radar illuminating the target whilst also minimising the engagement envelope of the J20s. They knew that AMRAAM could outgun the Chinese PL11 missiles, particularly if they turned their F35s away from the target in mid engagement.

"Satan, pumping southeast, Cougar, monitor."

"Cougar, Roger. Good radar picture"

The AMRAAM was an autonomous radar guided missile, and in the final stages of the attack, needed no support from the firing aircraft, so when Andy was sure that the missiles had entered terminal guidance phase, he turned his formation away from the Chinese fighters and let the missiles do their work. Having turned their backs to the targets, Andy was now effectively blind, so Cougar formation to fill in the blanks with their own radar and provide a JTIDS link picture. The time to intercept (TTI) counted down to zero.

"Satan, time out. Cougar report status"

"Cougar shows Bandit Group now strength two"

"Satan, time out kill three bandits, pumping south east. Remaining bandits chasing us down. Request de-louse"

"Cougar, Roger. Wait. Heads up new group strength 4 fast, your six o'clock, closing. Andy, you've got four missiles inbound. Shit, they're Mach 4 and not slowing."

"Satan 1 has them on link, don't worry they'll never have the legs to intercept."

Andy knew that the PL11 heat seeking missile didn't have the range to intercept them now that they were running away. The solid fuel rocket motor would only burn for about 7 seconds, and after that was burned out, the missile became a glider, decelerated quickly and eventually lost flying speed and aerodynamic lift from its body shape. He was concerned however, that his passive radar detector had been silent throughout the engagement. A PL 11 either needed the host fighter radar to lock the target so that it could home in on the reflected radar returns, or if it was an active variant, it would lock the target using its own radar. But nothing. What was happening? What if they were not PL11's?

"Andy, Chas, missile approach warning active. Six missiles inbound six o clock. Less than 30 seconds. Six not four."

"Yeh, I've got the same indications, Shit, they should have fallen out of the sky by now. Definitely six."

"Satan 1, Cougar 1, we can delouse you in two minutes."

"Cougar 1, Satan 1, that's copied but these babies will have timed out by then. We may have to take them on ourselves."

"Satans, deploy active decoys, widen, climb angels 30 and reduce to 250 knots. We'll have to go for a Kulbit kill Fox Two. Cougar, keep the picture coming."

Andy Rowson knew that this was on the edge of their envelope as pilots. Manoeuvring an agile fifth generation fighter beyond the normal stall envelope could generate massive rotation rates and surpass their tolerable G levels, but right now they were running out of ideas, and it was their only chance. Andy encouraged the Squadron pilots to fully explore the F35's flight envelope during Air Combat Training and he had learned huge lessons from his days as a Harrier pilot when he had been taught to fully exploit the Harriers' vectored thrust in combat by seasoned Royal Navy Sea Harrier veterans of the Falklands war, when the verb 'viffing' had been coined – vectoring in-flight. It was the same now, but with far superior aircraft agility. They had all practiced the Kulbit manoeuvre during routine training. The manoeuvre relied on 'supermanoeuvrability' – the ability for a fifth generation fighter to continue to turn in the desired direction despite being in a stalled condition. Normal maximum rates of turn were about 35 degrees per second in conventional flight, however, if a maximum performance turn was entered at a certain speed, the F35's natural instability in pitch would jack-knife the aircraft into the turn, and a 180 degree turn could be completed in as little as two or three seconds. The speed would wash off rapidly so the amount of Gs sustained by the pilot would remain manageable (at a bone crunching 9G), but the challenge was always to keep the engine going. At 90 degrees angle of attack (or more), the engine needed to suck a huge amount of air through the intakes and require it to turn a sharp corner – no wonder that the engine often momentarily stalled during a Kulbit. So, the manoeuvre worked, all of Andy's pilots could fly it, but it had never been used in anger and Andy had also never heard of a Fox Two kill against another air to air missile. Would the ASRAAM even launch properly under such extreme conditions? There was only one way to find out.

*

The Chinese pilots knew that their opponents were flying F35-Cs from the *Queen Elizabeth*. That was a good start. The target definition and approximate position was downloaded into their PR10-J air-to-air missiles, and they launched a spread of six at a range of thirty miles astern of their targets.

The F35-C has a radar cross section of about $1/10^{th}$ of a square metre, compared to several tens of square metres for a jetliner (the design of which, of course, does not attempt to minimise radar cross section for stealth purposes – jet liners *want* to be seen). However, even with a stealth aircraft, high power radars can obtain useful reflections, and the radar 'visibility' is not constant – some angles offer better visibility to radar (sharp edges such as chines, and exhausts, in particular).

During the immediate post launch phase, the Chinese missiles fanned out, and their radars were electronically linked to offer a synthetic aperture – effectively a much bigger 'radar aerial'. The target definition meant that the missiles 'knew' the flight envelope of the F35s, and could therefore predict the limits of their position given inputs about target speed and attitude. The plane's flight envelope was relatively predictable, governed by what a human pilot could withstand in given circumstances, what could be gleaned at airshows, and what could be predicted from analysis of the aircraft design, even from YouTube videos.

Planes could be stealthy, could use flares to confuse heat seeker missiles, and electronic counter measures (ECM) to jam radars on missiles. They used specialised chaff, too, to confuse missile radars, which in their turn used anti-chaff filters in their radar signal processors. However, the human eye knew a flare when it saw one, and knew a plane when it saw one, and the eye could usually see chaff. So, during the final approach of the Chinese missile to its target, it slowed and took a visual look-to-kill feed directly from a missile jockey on the Chinese AWACS fifty miles away, via a real-time camera link. Slowing down required variable engine power provided by a ramjet engine, not a solid fuel motor, and air brakes. Slowing down offered the big advantage of allowing missile controllers to acquire and track the target and agree target priorities. Once the software in the missile had the visual lock confirmed by its jockey, its own autonomous image processing software took over in the final attack phase when additional aerodynamic surfaces were deployed as the missile's 'body lift' was lost during slower flight. Its launch plane and pilot were free to deal with other targets. In the final kill phase, when within visual range, the missiles would co-operate and agree targets then de-link from one another.

'Pugachev Cobras' (where the plane presents a very high angle of attack to the air flow – its nose pointing at almost 90° to its flight path – and slows dramatically), a Kulbit (where the Cobra continues into a backward somersault), and all the other aerobatics of which modern vectored thrust fighters were capable, could not out-manoeuvre the human eye and a more manoeuverable missile which had slowed to almost matched-speed on its final close approach. There were few defences – principally cloud and burner jetwash, but even these were hit and miss, literally. There were rumours of spoofing lasers, but these were, apparently, still the product of novelists' fertile imaginations and defence journalists' thirst for sexy copy.

The Chinese missiles took all inputs – radar, thermal, and visual, then the fuzzy logic of their command computers made the final decision and piped the coordinates to the guidance computer which guided the missile for optimum kill probability when its warhead fragmented. Data was updated two hundred times a second and the kill rate was very high unless the missiles could be intercepted - at least in theory, as these missiles had never been fired in anger. With a missile speed of Mach 4 and a flight time of barely 30 seconds from 30 miles, there was little that could be done unless a laser capability was present. The *USS Gerald R Ford* had an ultra-secret 50 megawatt free electron laser, but was hundreds of miles too far away, and out of line of sight of the targets.

*

"Satan 1, what the fuck, they are slowing. TTI is going up, but they are not falling" Seven seconds became eight seconds to impact.

"Freddy, Satan. These are not PL11s, repeat not PL11s."

"Satan, Freddy. Not PL11s copy."

The Chinese missiles were reducing ramjet power as they entered the kill phase at six miles range, closing at Mach 1.2 – just supersonic. The Royal Navy F35-Cs were at 30,000 feet, slowing to 400 knots as they bled energy and began levelling.

"The bastards are stalking us. How can they do that?" They all thought it, but there was not ime to voice it.

"Satans, flip and fire, GO!"

The British F35s AIM-132 ASRAAMs were the latest Block III variant. With lock-on after launch, and either JTIDS, radar or Helmet Mounted Cueing System (look-to-lock), these missiles were at the peak of technical development.

Cougar formation was continuing to provide ultra accurate JTIDS pictures from radars, and each pilot designated two JTIDS missile tracks for ASRAAM cueing.

As the F35s started the flip into their Kulbits, their weapons bay inner doors swung open. The ASRAAMs were mounted on the inside of the doors themselves, and were deployed into launch position as the doors locked open. As the Lightnings reached the vertical, each pilot increased power to push more of the thin air through the engine and keep it alive. Then, as they inverted, their missiles launched, already cued to JTIDS missile tracks. The Safe/Arm fusing required five seconds at 20G acceleration for the missiles to arm – effectively about 1.5 miles minimum range. There was no time or possibility of look-to-lock-on – the pilots would have been unable to spot the Chinese missiles head-on with their low-smoke ramjet exhausts and their heads moving with the maybe 9G force and rotation of the Kulbit. The six ASRAAMSs had autonomy-on and acquired their targets automatically and easily – the Chinese missiles were only slightly 'off-boresight', though their ramjet exhausts were not as hot in IR as rocket motor plumes would have been, and as they slowed their control fins cooled, reducing the IR signature even further. The rocket motor of one AIM-132 misfired and fell harmlessly into the sea. Three destroyed their targets. One exploded in the fireball of another. One missed and self-destructed automatically.

One Chinese missile got through. Proximity fuses, which detected a plane's magnetic field and triggered the warhead, were no longer used. Modern fighter planes were built mainly from exotic non-magnetic materials and used shielded electric cabling. This missile was triggered solely by the position prediction software in its command navigation computer confirmed by its image processing software. Its 10 kilogramme annular fragmentation warhead exploded within fifteen metres of Satan 1, sending a spray of white hot shrapnel in an expanding ring of lethal capability, peppering the cockpit and port canard of the F35-C.

Despite ceramic honeycomb armouring in the cockpit, Andy Rowson was wounded by a sliver which ricocheted into an artery in his shoulder. As his punctured G-suit was losing pressure, he just managed to pull his ejection handle whilst his plane dropped like a shattered stone out of its Kulbit backflip. The ejection seat software 'knew' that an inverted ejection was safe at this altitude, speed and rotation, and banged Andy out safely without need to use the rocket motor for altitude. Then, his chute opened as he lost consciousness, bleeding profusely, strapped in his ejector seat, before it splashed into the sea a few minutes later.

"Satan, Freddy. RTB, RTB. Weapons now tight. Hold fire, acknowledge."

"Freddy, Satan 1's down, saw ejection and chute open, Satan 3 has the lead. Weapons tight. Satan flight of three RTB."

The Merlin recovery helo from *HMS Queen Elizabeth* was tasked immediately for the signal from Andy Rowson's recovery beacon. Cougar formation was fifteen miles away from engaging the remaining two J20's when the weapons tight order was given and they were recalled. In the confusion the Chinese J20 airplanes released another spread of the PR10-J ramjet air-to-air missiles, unaware that their target group was now the US 'Waverider' formation – a data-link problem had developed with their own Chinese AWACS circling over the Yemen, and their missile jockeys were confused and not in their saddles.

*

The RIB was now running on one engine at about 20 knots, occasionally airborne in the wave pattern, and generally behaving itself. The occasional bouncing made Steve once again aware of his arm. With no autopilot on the RIB he was going to have to stop to attend to his injury. The wind chill at 20 knots on a tired, injured and wet body would soon tell, even with an air temperature of nearly thirty degrees. At least it had dried him out. It was now late afternoon, about an hour before sunset when it would cool down rapidly.

Steve heard the confrontation six miles above him.

In the lowering sun angle he could see the planes engaging as 'Waverider' wing faced up to the Chinese, and he saw burning wreckage falling into the sea.

He was headed south west, to get as far away as possible from Yemeni waters, with the Hanish Islands ahead.

He heard the rippling whine of a shell going overhead and saw it detonate about 200 yards ahead. Warning or ranging – does it matter he thought? He started a slow turn to starboard and then quickly to port, a series of irregular jinks. Turning in his seat, he could see a vague grey shape atop a white bow wave, and a puff of smoke in its wake, about 3 miles astern. "Yemeni patrol boat" he guessed, swearing to himself. And then another shell flying close by. Wrenching the wheel hard to starboard the shell exploded well off to port and astern. He thought he could probably outrun the gunboat in a straight line, but the jinking to avoid the shelling was effectively slowing him down – he reckoned that it would take about 30 minutes before he would be in range of the cannon. He would not be able to easily avoid that. And how long before the next bomber arrives, he wondered?

He was now approaching the south going shipping lane in the Traffic Separation Scheme, but with only a hundred or so ships a day, fifty in each direction, he would be lucky to find one suitably placed to give him a bit of cover and an opportunity for some straight line speed. It would obviously be easier after sunset, but with shells coming in every 15 seconds he doubted he could last that long. He guessed that they had maybe 100 shells maximum on the gunboat – certainly enough to keep him slowed long enough to catch up. One shell splinter was all it would take to stop him. He couldn't see any shipping ahead in either direction, although there was what appeared to be a fleet of fishing vessels a few miles away on his port beam.

If he turned to run through the fleet, then the gunboat would be able to intercept him more quickly – not an option then, he thought.

The chart plotter showed him that he was still about 5 miles inside Yemeni waters – seven or eight minutes at 40 knots if his fuel would last. At this speed he had about an hour's fuel left, as far as he could estimate. Djibouti territorial waters were about ten or so miles away. Would the Yemenis follow him into Djibouti waters? The Djiboutians were hardly a force to be contended with, he knew, but there were French warships in port. And of course, that was where Adèle was moored.

To cap all that, he realised that he had no papers – if he was challenged. Where were his papers? The last time he remembered having them was at Camp Lemonnier – he'd taken then off Adèle during his midnight swim. That would be a tough one to solve if everybody at Lemonnier denied his existence.

Then, another shell, close by; and suddenly, a ear-splitting roar as two jets flew over him, heading north. Royal Navy markings – though his aircraft recognition was not up to scratch and he didn't know they were F35s. He heard their cannon and looked around to see two lines of cannon fire hit the water on each side of the Yemeni gunboat. The planes climbed and turned, and the Yemeni gunboat swung sharply to port, altering course for Perim Island, realising that pursuit was not the best option.

*

Twenty five minutes after being tasked, the recovery man on the Merlin helicopter was lowered to the bobbing ejector seat. After a quick check he told the Merlin pilot that the Lightning pilot was dead. The mood was professional and sombre as they winched Andy's body aboard the helictopter and turned for the *Queen Elizabeth*.

*

The USN F35-C 'Waverider' flight which had engaged the Chinese lost one plane in the confrontation. The Chinese lost four planes over the Red Sea, and one in the chase over the Yemen just south of Sana'a. The effectiveness of the Chinese air-to-air missiles was rendered near to zero by the undisclosed technology on the USN F35s. The missiles' liquid argon-cooled thermal sensor heads and cameras were burned out in flight by the laser spoofers with which the US planes were equipped. The Chinese AWACS tried to support with two PR10-J missiles, but these were also spoofed. In return, the AWACS over the Yemen was sent two US AIM-120 AMRAAMs which were only partially effective – one was apparently foiled by the Chinese ECM and exploded harmlessly, but the other exploded ahead and above, with a lucky-strike piece of shrapnel ingested into one of the AWACS's engines. The Chinese AWACS landed safely at a Yemeni military airbase.

Another Chinese flight went airborne from the Chinese carrier and was engaged by 'Mako' wing from the *Gerald R Ford*. Two planes were lost on each side before the RTB orders came through after frantic radio traffic from Washington and Beijing. The fleets withdrew to lick their wounds, whilst the politicians talked. Again.

*

After the bombing attack, the *Universal Trader* was in poor condition, limping along towards Bab el Mandeb and Perim Island at 4 knots, in limbo between the two traffic separation schemes. Her steering gear was damaged, her anchor windlasses damaged and she was now in danger of running onto the island. Alexander Strait, between Perim and mainland Yemen was only 2 miles wide and barely deep enough for her. It was also prohibited for vessels of her size, and the traffic lane in the western channel was in the opposite direction – *Trader* was heading into the North bound shipping..

David Wallis, the master, had little choice. A tow had been ordered and there was a Dutch deep sea tug on the way south from Yanbu on a Lloyds Open Form Contract – the towing would be done, and the fee decided by an Arbitrator in London at a later date, though whether the insurers would pay was a matter for debate - Wallis's first responsibility was to his crew and ship. The money was Tobin's problem. However, the weather was worsening from the west and a severe sandstorm was forecast. It would take more than twenty four hours for the tug to arrive.

The Yemeni coast radio station had been in contact and ordered that *Trader* stayed outside their Yemeni territorial waters, as Perim Island was now under military control.

By now, at least half the cargo had drained away, and she was floating higher in the water – it was fortunate that no bombs had penetrated below the water line.

The call from Tobin was brief and typically aggressive.

"Wallis, get that ship back onto course and heading out of the Red Sea."

"Mr Tobin, that's just not possible. She's virtually out of control, the weather is worsening from the west and we have to turn north to keep away from Yemeni waters and get some sea room. We're under clear direction not to enter Yemeni Territorial waters, under threat of being sunk. Quote "your ship will cause a pollution problem, so we will sink it." Bollocks. I've ordered a Lloyds Open Form Tow, and I'll be lucky to turn her to meet the tug from Yanbu. She's in danger of breaking her back and we are a danger to shipping."

"Cancel the tow and get back on course. Find a way and just do it."

"Mr Tobin, I am Master of this ship, with her safety and the lives of my crew to consider, under a legal obligation and moral imperative that goes back centuries. Your view is of no interest to me right now. Fuck you!"

Wallis cut the call.

Tobin keyed his quick-dial code for the switchboard at Downing Street.

*

In London, the atmosphere at that morning's COBRA meeting was fraught. The complexities of the political and military events were proving impossible to disentangle, and policy differences were emerging with the US, who were now in 'cowboy' mode. The Prime Minister refused to let the British contingent of the Free Seas Red Sea Flotilla become embroiled in the rescue of the *Trader*, and *HMS Duncan,* already despatched by Admiral Callaghan aboard the *Queen Elizabeth* was brought quickly to heel when she was less than a hundred miles from the *Trader.*

The Armed Forces Chief of Staff pointed out the legal obligations of vessels to help other in distress, and that there were other ships in the area which were nearer. It was a neat piece of fence-sitting.

The Foreign Secretary gave a lengthy report of his meeting with the Yemeni Ambassador to discuss Britain's formal protest about the bombing, and was adamant that assistance should be provided, particularly as the *Trader* had been bombed by Chinese aircraft.

The Yemeni Ambassdor had told the Foreign Secretary that the *Trader* was a danger to shipping and the environment, and that must be evacuated as the Yemenis intended to bomb and sink her whilst she was still in deep water – he said that they had tried to do that already when she ignored warnings and entered Yemeni territorial waters. This was hotly disputed by the UK. The Yemeni Ambassador emphasised that the US and UK naval forces should stay outside Yemeni waters, and that the incursion of the UK and US airplanes over the Yemen was a matter of grave concern and was being raised in an emergency session of the UN Security Council, under the auspices of Yemen's ally, the Republic of China. Again, the Foreign Secretary had protested that UK planes had not entered Yemeni airspace.

In Sana'a, His Excellency Stewart Thwaites had been called in to the Yemeni Foreign Ministry. A furious disagreement had ensued when the Yemei Foreign Minister handed him a formal protest note.

The UN was still dithering.

After forty minutes of heated debate in the COBRA meeting, Coombes entered and handed a note to the Prime Minister. The PM's face was grave as he addressed the meeting.

"I've just been advised that two Israeli frigates have been sunk by rocket mines or torpedoes off the coast of Saudi Arabia, about two hours ago. They were believed to have been pursuing a Chinese nuclear submarine. A third Israeli frigate was in pursuit of the submarine but has lost contact. The

Chinese deny that they have authorised one of their submarines to enter the Red Sea."

The Armed Forces Chief of Staff stood up and asked to be excused the meeting.

"No, you may not leave, Chief, not until we agree what we do next."

"Very well, Prime Minister, if I may just speak to my Deputy then?"

"Certainly. You have five minutes. Coombes will take you to a comms cubicle."

The situation display at the far end of the room was switched on, showing a translation of an Israeli news feed, and a feed from Al Jazeera, as the news became public and the meeting watched the initial analysis. The PM privately wondered how many votes he was losing, and then after a couple of minutes the secure telephone in front of the PM started to blink. He answered, and the meeting listened to the London end of the call.

"Yes, I'll speak to the Israeli Prime Minster. Now."

"Hello Ben, I am in the middle of a COBRA meeting here, and we are discussing the situation. I've just had news about the sinkings. International waters you say? Definitely Chinese? The US have confirmed the sonar signature you say? We will speak again later – yes, when we have considered the situation and have more facts. Thank you, Ben. Please accept the condolences of UK for the loss of your seamen. Yes, yes, only one aircraft, thank God, and two crew on the tanker. Goodbye."

There was no mention of the other British person who was unaccounted for. The wallscreen was turned off, and the meeting returned to its deliberations.

*

Tobin's calls to Downing Street were obstructed, and eventually that afternoon, his number was blocked. He ordered his Gulfstream to City airport.

*

The BBC website had the story first, and the television news had the exclusive interview. Charles Tobin was making a statement at the small BBC news studio overlooking College Green, next to the Houses of Parliament. He was venting his anger in his own typically arrogant style, with a smattering of truth dressed up and twisted to suit his world view.

"I have come here today, to the seat of British government, to demand that the Prime Minister takes action to protect British Shipping in the Red Sea. The Free Seas flotilla is a sham. My production platform in the Red Sea has been attacked and blown up by Chinese Special Forces. I have a tanker which is in distress and sinking, after being bombed by Chinese airplanes, and is under further threat of attack. There are twenty three crew aboard who have been subjected to piracy and bombing, and several have already been murdered.

Where is our government? Where is our response? Do I have to go there myself and sort it out?"

The diatribe continued for several minutes with the interviewer's questions being ignored, and Tobin's raging arrogance finally ceasing to be entertaining. The BBC program director returned the feed to the main news studio and a more analytical than emotional follow-on to the Israeli frigate sinkings by their Defence correspondent.

After leaving the BBC's parliamentary studio, Tobin's car took him slowly along the Embankment in the late afternoon rush, and just after six p.m. he left for Djibouti from City airport.

*

David Wallis failed to bring the *Trader* around head to wind. There were two ships standing by, and the deep sea tug was making good speed but still a good twenty hours away. The weather was thickening and the ship was currently heading downwind towards Yemeni territorial waters.

Then, Wallis was called by the Yemeni coast radio station and ordered to abandon ship. He was given two hours notice of her being sunk by planes of the Yemeni airforce. He acknowledged the message and said he would comply. He called up one of the nearby ships, the *Baltic Transporter*, and asked that they standby whilst he and his crew left by lifeboat. The wind was strengthening steadily, and visibility was poor to the west.

The crew mustered at the aft lifeboat station, where the fireproof orange motor-lifeboat was waiting.. They climbed aboard and strapped in for the forty-foot slide down the launching rails into the Red Sea. Wallis gave the launch order as the sandstorm hit. The wind went up to an average of over forty knots, with gusts of sixty, led by a sharp squall line driving sand and spray before it as the lifeboat slid downward. With *Trader's* stern to the wind and sea, the launch could have been catastrophic but for the lee provided by the *Baltic Transporter* a quarter of a mile away.

It was another sixteen hours before the sandstorm cleared. The deep sea tug had heard the navigational warning on the GMDSS and stayed outside the ten mile exclusion zone whilst ageing Yemeni Mig fighter bombers delivered the final blows to the *Trader* and she sunk in 200 metres of water with five bodies in storage in her galley freezer room. By that time Wallis and his remaining crew were heading southeast on the *Baltic Transporter*, towards the Gate of Tears, and Djibouti.

*

James Marinero

Adèle at Last

Steve was back on Adèle at long last, wondering whether he had the appetite for the long leg up the Red Sea – he had seen enough of it to last him a lifetime, but it was the quickest through to Gibraltar. On the other hand, Adèle could catch the southwest monsoon and head across the Indian Ocean, maybe call in at the Spice Islands, and then through the East Indies and on up to Japan, then across to Vancouver, maybe stopping in the Aleutians. Although he had also wanted to visit Madagascar, it would mean a leg down past Somalia, and he'd had enough of pirates for a while.

He had finally landed on the north coast of Djibouti just as his fuel expired, about six miles south of the Eritrean border. How or why the Navy F35s had turned up he didn't know, and would probably never find out, but they had certainly saved him from the Yemeni patrol boat.

A friendly fisherman met him on the beach, and Steve offered him the RIB in return for a ride to Djibouti. The fisherman was more than happy with the deal, though it took some time for the lift to be arranged through his brother, after a welcome meal with the fisherman's family and attention to his arm. No explanations were sought, or given. It took the best part of the next day to travel back to the city – it was almost two hundred miles. Back at the dock in Djibouti, he had waited out of sight until the staff at Dolphin Services had left for the evening and the guard was snoring. His dinghy was still tied to the pontoon and he was glad to climb aboard Adéle at last. It had only been a few days, and his arm was still giving him trouble. He retrieved his key from the cockpit cooking gas locker and found a small holdall. With a coffee and a whisky in front of him he opened the bag. It held the shorts and tee shirt he'd left in Camp Lemonnier. Under his clothing was a plastic wallet containing his passport and ships papers, and the few dollars he'd been carrying. He checked his passport, and a slip of paper fell out. It said

"I put your piece out of sight. Good Luck, G."

Steve smiled to himself, thanking George – or whoever he really was – as he found the SIG wrapped in an oily cloth under some hanks of mooring line in the cockpit locker. With the SIG was a pint bottle of Jack Daniels.

The following day he got some provisions loaded and checked Adèle over thoroughly. She was ready to go, but the traces of Maruška's blood would take some time to scrub out of the upholstery. The day after that he paid off Dolphin Services and checked out with Immigration and Customs, then moved Adèle up the coast to the Mouillage Ambada - an anchorage near Black Rocks about eight miles to the west of Djibouti docks. It was much more peaceful and relatively secluded with some snorkelling in prospect, and only the local fishermen to bother him with offers of fish.

That first evening in the Mouillage, he was enjoying a sundowner in the cockpit, when the text came through. Call Mother. Steve called and Booth answered his call.

"Have you heard the news?"

"No, I've had enough news for a while. I should have turned the phone off. And I've had enough of you lot too. I got stitched up three different ways, and nobody is answering my questions."

"You know how it is, ours to do etcetera."

"It's OK for you sitting in London fucking up people. You're not doing, and you didn't get shafted. And, whatever happended to Tom? "

Booth trundled on "I thought that you should know that Pavkovic escaped from the Djibouti police this morning, on her way to court."

That was certainly enough to spoil the evening, though he didn't give Booth the impression of concern.

"Well, I'm not losing any sleep over it. I'm surprised they were bothering with the court. Anyway, I'm well out of it, down the coast. She can fuck off to Timbuctu as far as I'm concerned. And you can join her."

Booth continued, ignoring Steve's vitriol.

"They think she has, more or less. The police 4x4 she took has been found near the Somali border."

"I hope they bloody eat her. And, you can bet that the she didn't cross into Somalia. Too bloody obvious. Goodbye."

Steve's anger finally came out and as he was ranting he stood up and threw the mobile phone over the side. *Finis.*

There were so many unanswered questions, and he was wise enough to know that no-one knew the complete story or saw the whole picture, and that is the way it would stay unless you were religious. You could get Tobin, the Chinese, George Neilsen and Booth together and they would never agree on what had really happened, or on who had betrayed who; certainly though, the shit had percolated down to Steve. He wasn't religious, and didn't want to waste time pondering further as he realised that he had now made his decision to carry on with his original plan – the Mediterranean and Gibraltar awaited; before that, though, there was the long leg up the Red Sea. Again, yes, but he planned a more leisurely voyage this time.

*

Epilogue

The diplomatic efforts had been intense – such confrontations have a momentum of their own, like an unstoppable escalator – ever higher, the potential for a disastrous long drop growing continuously. When it was done, the main agreement between China and the West (NATO - effectively the US and UK) and underwritten by the UN was made public. There was a separate side agreement, which was not published, and would remain embargoed for a hundred years. Publicly, the basis of the agreement was essentially as follows:

Within 30 days, the People's Republic of China would withdraw its Dong Feng missiles from the Republic of Yemen to within Chinese territory.

The Republic of China (Taiwan) and The Philippines would withdraw all claims to sovereignty over any of the Spratly Islands in the South China Sea (this was particularly difficult clause to negotiate - heavy US pressure was applied to Taiwan, with, in turn, a secret agreement between the US and Taiwan for additional military support, including the future supply of a light aircraft carrier).

The exploitation of undersea mineral and metal resources in 'open ocean' ridge areas, such as the central Atlantic and Pacific oceans would be acceptable under existing conventions, outside of the exclusive economic zones of any countries. No countries would license deep sea production platforms for metals extraction in disputed areas such as the Red Sea Deeps until such time as the UN Convention of the Law of the Sea had been amended and ratified by all signatories to the most recent version. Any current licenses (such as for the *Universal Harvester*) would be revoked within 180 days.

The UN would guarantee the rights of free and innocent passage and transit in all Straits (currently 38) which were deemed to be 'open waters' for the world's shipping, notwithstanding the territorial claims of any nations within whose territorial waters or exclusive economic zones the Strait might be located, whether they were members of the UN or not.

Secretly, the parties agreed that:

> The People's Republic of China would decommission and remove the remaining TE-6 or equivalent anti-ship mines which it had seeded in both the Red Sea and Gulf of Aden approaches to the Gate of Tears (at the time of signature, and unknown to China, there were, in fact, only 16 to remove as the US had used a remotely controlled submersible to recover two; three had been used in the confrontation with the Israeli frigates).

A month after the agreement was signed, the People's Republic of China issued a brief statement:

January 21, 2018
Beijing

"The former Chief of the People's Liberation Army General Staff, General Jiang Bingde, has been tried by a special court of the Central Committee of the Communist Party of China. The charge was one of military adventurism contrary to the interests of the Communist Party of China. He was found guilty, and executed this morning."

End

*

Charles Tobin's flight to Djibouti had proved to be a waste of time. By the time he arrived there after two re-fuelling stops, the *Trader* was resting on the bottom of the Red Sea in three pieces, and leaking her cargo of oil. En route, he had kept up with events via radio and occasional broadband as his Gulfstream overflew Italy and then Cairo.

As his plane had flown down the Red Sea towards the Gate of Tears, he had weighed up his situation as he emptied a bottle of Jura malt whisky. It was dark at that time, and poor weather – there was a serious sandstorm raging over a large area – had prevented him seeing the *Universal Harvester* 29,000 feet below. The platform master was in the process of closing her down, in preparation for her tow. Tobin had yet to decide where to take her.

He had lost a ship – would the insurers pay? Was it an act of war? There was $300 million dollars a year of cash flow which had stopped in one day. There were specific investors he was concerned about – two in Italy and one in the US – who would still expect their dividends to be paid and would not be interested in excuses. Big players, big stakes. It would be very dangerous to disappoint them. In both poker and life he played for big stakes, but this time his life could be on the table with the chips.

On the positive side, he still owned *Thiovulum Aureus;* he had gold stocks in hand and the *Enterprise* had a full cargo on the way to the refinery in Milford Haven. His second production platform was due to leave the shipyard in Korea in two months time, and tanker capacity was easy to charter. All he needed now was a new site. Maybe a deal with the Saudis?

At Djibouti, without leaving his plane, he ordered his pilot to file a new flight plan for Melbourne. He had a small score to settle with Shi Xue, and a big one with George Oliphant.

*

Three months after the Israelis lost their frigates and seventy four sailors, a series of poor quality, long-range pictures arrived at the desk of the Chief Naval Analyst, at the Department of Defense in Washington, from a usually reliable Chinese source. They appeared to show a Shang Class submarine arriving at the Chinese naval port of Zhanjiang, headquarters of the South Sea Fleet. The vessel appeared to have some damage to her sail (conning tower).

*

Maruška received the forwarded text. Then the next, then the next again, over a space of a few days. Finally, a couple of weeks after the first, she took the Metro to Simplon. Since her return from the Middle East several months previously she hadn't been to the Rue Simplon apartment. Her escape via Ethiopia couldn't have been achieved without the help of Chuntao via the Chinese Embassy in Djibouti. The getaway from the police had been easy enough – they just didn't appreciate that a woman could better them hand-to-hand and with weapons. It was cultural, and that led to laxity on their part and opportunity for her.

Over just the few months she had been away, the Simplon area had become rougher, with more junkies and prostitutes in evidence – it was almost as if the area had lost faith in itself and was losing its self-esteem. You could always tell the quality of an area by the cars parked in the streets, and Rue Simplon was beginning to look like a scrapyard. The apartment hadn't been broken into, fortunately – though there was little worth stealing (at least anything that could be found without a thoroughly professional search).

Under the floorboard, her latest Chinese phone, palmpad computer, passports, euro and dollar reserves, pistol and ready-to-run bag were dusty, but just as she had left them. She took out the phone and called Chuntao.

"Chuntao, you called?"

"At last. I hope you are recovered. I have details of your next assignment for you. But first, how are you after your reconstruction?"

Two weeks and forty thousand dollars lighter, her left ear was now looking much better after reconstruction in Geneva, though reconstruction wasn't quite the right word.

Over a three month period, a new ear had been grown for her in a laboratory. The Vacanti ear as it was known, was a simple ear-shaped cartilage structure with her skin cells covering it. It looked good, and with her changed hairstyle she felt comfortable with it. There was still a score to settle with Baldwin for that, a big score.

The time in the clinic had given her time to think, and she hated thinking. More than ten years working for the Chinese and what had she achieved? She had made plenty of money for sure, and had some fun following the path she had chosen for herself. Compared to Carlos, the Jackal, she measured herself as far superior and much more successful; but she was not notorious. Who would ever know about her success? The Chinese, but what was that worth? The next assignment could be her last. She had been lucky this time, very lucky. Now approaching forty years of age, her reactions were slowing and her motivation – well, what was that? She realised that she was losing confidence and drive, and started to play with the idea of retiring.

Plenty of money, but no family. Maybe she should look for a woman she could settle with, buy a villa on Cap d'Agde, learn to paint, keep cats? She just couldn't see it.

"My ear is healing well, but I'm not ready for the next assignment. I am retiring."

"OK, there is no urgency for the assignment, but I don't think that retiring is a good idea. You have been a very great help to the Chinese people, and you know we Chinese are good at waiting. Are you feeling any pain?"

"Pain? No, I'm fine."

"How is your back, between your shoulders?"

"My back is fine, no problems, why are you asking?"

"I thought you might be feeling some pain there."

Maruška felt a searing stab of pain between her shoulder blades and as her legs weakened and trembled, she leaned against the wall and closed her eyes whilst the pain cleared. This was not the sort of pain she enjoyed.

"Well, I, er.. how did you know, it just started?"

"Just remember Maruška, we are not far away, ever. I will call again soon to talk about the new assignment. *Au revoir.*"

*

353

A month later, following a series of nagging texts and another attack of intense pain between her shoulders (which doctors had been unable to detect the source of), she went to Rue Simplon and called Chuntao. "Maruška, I hope you are well. Your next assignment is the chairman of a mining conglomerate called TRI – his name is Charles Tobin. His death is to be slow and painful, and you are to make sure that he understands it comes with the compliments of the People's Republic of China.

*

Lieutenant Commander Andy Rowson was posthumously gazetted for a Distinguished Flying Cross. The Kulbit Kill Fox Two became a new element in the Fleet Air Arm combat training program, and eventually in that of the RAF too. It saved the Treasury (in the all-important short term) the expense of having to fund a laser-spoofer retrofit in the UK's fleets of F35-C Lightnings, whilst the SIS's rapidly expanded Far East Desk initiated an operation to uncover the secrets of the Chinese PR-10J missile.

*

The obituary in The Times was fulsome, though electronic. No newspapers were printed in the UK anymore. Commuters on trains and the Underground with their Kindles and iPhones digested the summary of Booth's life and service to his country. A massive embolism had prematurely ended his stellar rise in the SIS. Three people in London knew the underlying cause of death, and they would keep the secret to the grave. Less than a dozen other people in London knew that Booth had worked for the Chinese, and that knowledge would also stay secret, on pain of their own deaths.

Why did he do it? Not money, not status, not idealogy – just the satisfaction of proving it could be done – one of the most complex of all life's possible challenges. It had happened many times before, and it would surely happen again. And in most cases, the results demonstrated, that no, it couldn't be done successfully, at least not for ever.

*

In a small house in a modest, private, gated development in Kingston upon Thames, a still grieving young family continued to believe – completely inaccurately - that their father had committed suicide in a toilet cubicle in his office somewhere in London. Eventually, the mother would meet another man, the children would have a new father and surname, and life would continue much as before.

References

Anonymous (1989) The bacteria that are creating gold fever in Canada, New Scientist, March 25 1989.

Baturin GN (1988) Gold in oceanic ores, Priroda, v. 3, p. 93, Moscow (Russian) Translation by Burk 1989.

Burk, Maksymilian (1989) Gold, Silver and Uranium from Seas and Oceans, ARDOR Publishing, Los Angeles, CA.

Chinese Submarines:
http://www.globalsecurity.org/military/world/china/type-93.htm
http://www.sinodefence.com/navy/sub/default.asp

Dworetzky T (1988) Gold bugs: a sulfur-munching bacterium has been recruited to help extract the precious yellow metal from the increasingly stingy Earth, Discover, March 1988, p. 32.

Fault based cryptographic attack:
http://www.eecs.umich.edu/~valeria/research/publications/DATE10RSA.pdf

F35 Lightning:
http://www.jsf.mil/
http://www.lockheedmartin.com/products/f35/

Glover JE, Groves DI, (1981) Gold Mineralization: Seward, TM, Modern hydrothermal systems in New Zealand and their relation to gold mineralization processes, Published by Geol. Dept. & Extension Service, Univ. West. Aust., 3.

Gold from Seawater
http://news.nationalgeographic.com/news/2001/08/0830_goldbug.html

Guoanbu:
http://intellibriefs.blogspot.com/2008/03/chinese-secret-service-from-mao-to.html

Herzig PM, et al, (1988) The distribution of gold and associated trace elements in modern submarine gossans from the TAG hydrothermal field, mid-Atlantic Ridge and in ancient ochers from Cyprus, Geological Society of America, v. 20, p. A240.

Keith ML (1989) Violent volcanism, stagnant oceans and some inferences regarding petroleum, strata-bound ores and mass extinctions, beochimica et Cosmochimica Acta, v. 46, p. 643-650.

Kondratieff, Nikolai, The Long Wave Cycle, 1926; tr. Guy Daniels 1983

Krauskopf KB (1956) Factors controlling the concentration of thirteen rare metals in seawater, Geochimica Cosmochimica Acta, v. 9, p. 1-32.

Lapidoth-Eschelbacher, Ruth, (1982) International Straits of the World, Volume 5, The Red Sea and Gulf of Aden.

Letnikov FA, Vilor NV, (1981) Gold in the Hydrothermal Process, Moscow: Nedra, English translation: Univ. of W. Australia, No. 19 (1990)

Lucas JM (1985) Gold, Chapter in Mineral Facts and Problems, Bureau of Mines Publication 675, US Department of the Interior, Washington DC.

MaClaren, JM (1908) Gold: Its Geological Occurrence and Geographical Distribution, The Mining Journal, London.

McNulty, Timothy (1994), Gold from the Sea, http://goldfever.com/gold_sea.htm#Articles

Mines (naval)
http://en.wikipedia.org/wiki/Te-1_rocket_propelled_mine

Missiles (anti-carrier)
http://tagseeworld.blogspot.com/2010/12/china-power-dong-feng-missiles-series.html
http://www.globalsecurity.org/wmd/world/china/df-31.htm

Pain S (1988) Crocks of gold at the bottom of the sea, New Scientist, June 2 1988.

Pashkova EA (1988), Colloidal and dissolved forms of gold and organic carbon in the waters of Bering Sea and northern part of the Pacific Ocean, Okeanologiya, Moscow, v. 28, p. 393-398.

Rennie J (1992) Bug in a gilded cage: all that glitters is sometimes bacterial, Scientific American, Sept. 1992.

Saline pool Kebrit deep, 84 m thick
http://www.ncbi.nlm.nih.gov/pmc/articles/PMC92984/

Seward, TM (1979) Hydrothermal transport and deposition of gold, Gold Mineralization, Glover JE & Groves DI, Published by Geol. Dept. & amp; Extension Service, Univ. West. Aust., 3.

Spencer RT (1991), Phanerozoic ocean cycles and sedimentary-rock-hosted gold ores, Geology, v. 19, p. 645-648, June 1991.

Ulberg ZR (1992), et al, Interaction of energized bacteria cells with particles of colloidal gold: peculiarities and kinetic model of the process, Biochimica et Biophysica Acta, v. 1134, p. 89-96.

Vacanti Mouse:
http://en.wikipedia.org/wiki/Vacanti_mouse

Watterson JR (1993) Reply: Preliminary evidence for the involvement of budding bacteria in the origin of Alaskan placer gold, Geology, March 1993, 280.

Wood ED (1971), Gold in Seawater, Discourse, University of Alaska, Fairbanks, Alaska.

The Sicilian Channel

Steve Baldwin is in action again in James Marinero's searing new novel, set in the Mediterranean Sea. Look out for it at your bookstore – online or, local bricks-and-mortar.

Follow James Marinero at
http://www.jamesmarinero.blogspot.com
Twitter @jamesmarinero
Facebook: www.facebook.com/james.marinero
www.jamesmarinero.com

Lightning Source UK Ltd.
Milton Keynes UK

176709UK00001B/12/P